"Just what do you think you're doing?" asked Tessa . . .

Cody smiled lazily at her. "I'm warming up before you send me out into the cold."

He reached out his hand and traced one long finger down the delicate length of her graceful jaw. Tessa drew back, trembling at the shivers of delight he aroused in her . . .

Cody's free hand reached for the book she still held. But Tessa clung tightly to it, feeling if she relinquished it to him she'd somehow lose her hold on reality. It was a threshold she did not want to cross. . . .

ONE GOLDEN HOUR

ONE GOLDEN HOUR

MAUREEN REYNOLDS

PAGEANT BOOKS

PAGEANT BOOKS
225 Park Avenue South
New York, New York 10003

Cover artwork by Charles Mole

Printed in the U.S.A.

First Pageant Books printing: August, 1988

10 9 8 7 6 5 4 3 2 1

For Josh, Brandon and Kyle

Chapter One

◆◆◆◆◆

1877

MISS TESSA AMESBURY clutched her broad-brimmed straw hat to her head as the wagon bounced and swayed over the deeply rutted trail road. Perched like a sparrow on the edge of the hard wagon seat, she peered anxiously toward the town stretched ahead of her. She couldn't see much from this distance, but what she glimpsed was nothing like she'd expected; she was almost tempted to ask the wagon driver to drive her straight back to the train depot.

As the wagon jolted over a particularly deep pothole, nearly spilling Miss Amesbury into the long, dry prairie grass, she clapped a hand to the crown of her head where her hat sat comically askew. Damn, but if it wasn't a chore trying to appear proper and respectable!

1

It would please her immensely to toss the wretched hat into the wind!

She glanced at the two male passengers in the back of the wagon; they rode on sacks of grain, their portmanteaus tucked between their legs. The older man looked past her toward town, but the other met her eyes and gave her an insolent half-smile. She bristled and purposely looked away. Then she felt a slight tug of guilt and swore inwardly again. Ladies *never* cursed. Well, she thought, no one would ever hear her swear *aloud*. But an instant later when the wagon careened dangerously to one side and her backside came inches off the seat, she quite nearly changed her mind. She hissed something between her small white teeth and was grateful for the old wagon driver's interruption.

"Well, there's Harper City, Miss Amesbury!" There was unmistakable pride in Hal Witherby's voice as he nodded toward town. Miss Amesbury followed his gaze.

"Yes, there it is," she echoed, trying to conceal her dismay.

Harper City, Kansas. Her haven; her refuge. Its advertisement in a Boston newspaper for a qualified schoolteacher had been her salvation. Just miles from the Colorado state line and from the nearest railroad depot, the town bragged of its progressiveness, of new settlers crowding in, of its promise. Well, thought Tessa Amesbury with a frank look at the false-fronted buildings that lined the wide main street, Harper City was not *quite* what one would call a city. It was nothing like Boston. But she'd left Boston behind. There was nothing for her in Boston anymore.

As the wagon jounced into town Tessa could see the shimmering, dusty haze that settled finely over the buildings, horses, and vehicles that passed in the street. She smothered a wave of disappointment as her eyes scrutinized the rough, unpainted structures: a general store, a restaurant, a hotel with an outside stairway, a saloon, a feed store, and other assorted businesses—and the crude board sidewalk rising up from the dusty road. The town was only months old; why there were still establishments going up! She could see men working, their bare backs browning under the hot mid-September sun, heard their hammers ringing and the shouts of their jovial voices.

Tessa pressed her clasped hands to her stomach, her knuckles digging into her belly, trying to quell the nervous fluttering she felt in there. So what if the town had sounded more promising than it looked! Give it a chance, she urged herself. After all, she hadn't much choice now.

She glanced down at the crumpled piece of paper she'd been gripping tightly in the palm of her sweat-damp hand since departing the depot. On it was written a single name: Cody Butler. Instructions from Widow Rawlins, with whom she would be living, had been left with the station agent at the depot that Cody Butler was the man Tessa should find as soon as she set foot in town. Cody Butler would escort her to the widow's home.

The wagon slowed and stopped a short distance from some more construction. Tessa nervously wiped her palms on her thighs and glanced down at her simple wine-colored dress. She hoped she looked proper enough. Looking proper was important to Tessa. But she didn't *feel* proper with the sweat trickling down between her breasts and dampening her wrists under her starched cuffs. She longed to remove her hat and fan her flushed face with it but instead she reached up and drew the brim of it low over her dark eyes. She didn't consider herself pretty, but there was something about her, she knew, that caused men to look at her twice, and she needed none of that now. Especially now.

She touched the nape of her neck, tucked up a few errant wisps of hair under her hat, and readied herself to alight from the wagon. Longing to ease the stiffness in her muscles, she found it hard put to remain seated until the driver came to assist her. Again her gaze scanned the cluster of men toiling not far down the road, and Tessa thought how the reverberating sound of their iron hammers and the scrape of their saws against wood sounded like a chorus in the hot, dry air.

One of the men, a tall, broad-shouldered, and deeply tanned man, worked so diligently he did not notice the wagon's arrival. His biceps muscles bunched and flexed as he unloaded a pile of lumber near the new structure; then he leaned one knee on the ground and reached for his hammer.

"Better put your shirt on, Cody," suggested Abbott Robbins, making himself heard over Cody's resolute banging.

The big, dark-haired man glanced over at old Ab. "Huh?" His hammer did not miss a beat.

Abbott nodded toward the halted wagon, nudging his hat off his creased forehead. "Looks like our new schoolmarm has just arrived."

Disinterested, Cody continued hammering, not turning from his work. But old Abbott watched Hal Witherby help the schoolteacher to the ground. Abbott spit into the dusty road. "Hell, she's no wider than that hitchin'-post rail over there," he commented, dismay mixed with scorn in his voice. "I can't see much of her face . . ." He peered closer, then straightened. "Oh, for crissake, she's no bigger than some of those kids she'll be teachin'! I could fit my hands twice around her waist!"

At last, his interest piqued, Cody glanced over one bare shoulder at the young woman standing by Hal Witherby. She was modestly dressed as expected, but that broad-brimmed straw hat gave her a saucy flair. She stood clutching her carpetbag while Hal unloaded her trunk from the wagon. Cody, too, peered closer, though he could not detect much about her from here except that she was as slight as a twelve-year-old kid.

"We'll be fortunate if she lasts a week," he

remarked, adding to Abbott's skepticism, and he turned back to his work.

"Why is she wearin' that hat, d'ya suppose, Cody?" interjected another man. "Maybe she aims to use scare tactics with the young 'uns! Ain't no one seen her face yet an' I bet she's hidin' it under that hat for a good reason!"

The men laughed and Cody laughed with them, his white teeth flashing against his sun-browned skin. Their sudden laughter caught Tessa's attention and her eyes stopped on a man who stood a head taller than most of them. He was shirtless and even from here she could make out the long, firm muscles in his broad back, the sinewy strength of his wide shoulders, and the fine film of sweat glistening on his swarthy skin.

She'd known far too few men in her twenty-three years, and just the sight of these rough-looking laborers made Tessa uneasy. And *that* thoroughly masculine man in the midst of the others was the most unnerving of them all. She was relieved to be on the opposite side of the road.

Both the male passengers had already gone their separate ways, yet Hal Witherby hesitated nearby. Tessa glanced at him. "Sir," she asked politely, once again adjusting that hat, "are you familiar with a Mr. Cody Butler? I was told to inquire for him upon my arrival in town."

Hal scratched his head. "Cody? Why, sure. I'm real familiar with Cody. Seems most folks are. But it's not Mister—"

Tessa nodded curtly, cutting him off efficiently. "Show me to him, please. He is to escort me to Widow Rawlins's home."

Hal pulled on one ear, wondering at the same time why the schoolteacher wore that damned straw hat so low over those dark eyes. Hell, from what he could tell, she weren't half bad-looking, so why in tarnation did she hide her face? Ach, women! Hal hefted her trunk upon one shoulder, nearly staggering under its weight. All he wanted to do right now was to visit Charlie's saloon and have himself a quick shot. Hell, it was hot as July today!

Tessa hid a smile as Hal weaved his way across the road, cursing all the while. She'd packed some of her favorite volumes in that trunk—maybe too many. Her smile faded when she suddenly realized where Hal was leading her. They headed straight for that group of working men. Oh, surely, Hal was mistaken! Cody Butler couldn't be one of this half-dressed lot! She had pictured the name to fit a suave elderly gentleman!

"Mr. Witherby!" She hustled up alongside the struggling man. "Are you certain you heard me correctly?" A buckboard rattled past them in a swirl of road dust and Tessa choked back a cough. "I said Cody Butler. Surely, this group of men . . ." Her words died when some of those men looked up from their work as she and Hal came upon them. She eyed them warily, then looked toward Hal again.

Hal Witherby, impatient now for a shot of

whiskey, waved off her anxious words. He was singling out a man from the group.

"Cody, seems this here new schoolteacher has an interest in you," Hal announced loudly.

The others hooted as the tall man stepped forward, grinning crookedly down at her while Tessa froze in place, blushing furiously and wishing that the earth would swallow her whole.

Cody Butler snatched his faded blue cotton shirt off the end of a sawhorse and he shrugged into it, yet left it unbuttoned, which offered her a display of broad, masculine chest, shadowed with black curly hair that glistened with sweat. His worn trousers fit snugly across his narrow hips, and he stood with his long legs braced slightly apart.

Never in all her life had Tessa confronted such an overpowering man, and she felt a strange, unsettling sensation rise within her. But then her uneasiness returned; she dared not look at his face yet.

"Yes 'm, at your service," he drawled, and the rich timbre of his voice swirled around her, and she found it as commanding as his looming form.

Cody stood not two feet from her, his booted feet squarely planted, both hands shoved into his back pockets, but it was still difficult for him to make out her features, her hat was so artfully positioned. He couldn't even guess her age. But Cody was intrigued by her mouth, which was wide and sensuously full—an exquisite, lush curve—he'd never seen a mouth so beautiful, or so tempting.

She hadn't yet lifted her face to his. Cody's long, brown fingers idly scratched his bare chest and Tessa's eyes strayed there. Flustered at this sight, she began to stammer. "I—I—that is—Mrs. Rawlins left your name with the station agent at the depot. You are Cody Butler, aren't you?"

"Sure, that's me. Cody." She felt his eyes watching her closely. "But how do I know you're really the new schoolteacher?"

At last her eyes flew up to meet his. Cody was taken aback. Because he was so tall, she'd tilted her face up to see him and he got a full view of large, almond-shaped eyes of the richest, deepest brown. With their black, spiky lashes and flecks of soft honey lights, her eyes were mysterious, yet alluring. Cody's eyes flickered over her wide cheekbones and slim, graceful nose, and down once more to her full and passionate mouth that bespoke anything but primness. Hell, he thought, she didn't look like any schoolteacher *he'd* ever known!

Tessa was equally startled by Cody's face. My goodness, he was ruggedly handsome! His thick black hair waved back from his wide, tanned forehead, and his straight nose was bold and proud over a hard, well-cut, beautiful male mouth. There was strength and a touch of arrogance in the hard line of his jaw and chin, in the straight dark brows above his eyes. But his most striking feature was his eyes: a dark green—so dark that she caught a tinge of deep blue in their depths. And they were gleaming with humor and a hint of teasing. Tessa suppressed a smile of her own, but she relaxed her narrow shoulders.

Finally she answered. "I am the town's new schoolteacher, rest assured." She spoke up in clipped Boston tones. "If you'd like proof, I have certificates here in my bag, signed by—"

"Hell, no. I trust you."

Flustered by his language and the penetrating look he gave her, she turned her attention to the workers and tried to make conversation.

"What are you building here?" she asked them.

"Saloon," one of them answered tersely.

"But I already see a saloon over there!" she exclaimed, amazed that a town this size would foster two saloons. One was trouble enough! she thought.

The men chuckled. "That's right," one said, "and there's two others off Union Avenue on the west side of town. Ain't never enough saloons, ma'am!"

"Ain't never enough wimmin either!" chimed another, and they all laughed again. But another, a fatherly looking man, scolded them all.

"Now fellas, there *is* a lady present!"

Cody, who had turned his attention toward drinking water from his canteen, wiped his mouth with the back of his hand, secretly watching Tessa's reaction to the men's bawdy talk. Her wide cheeks had colored deeply, a dusky rose blush against her skin. None of the others had seen her face up close like he had, none of them knew what she really looked like under that hat. He noted that her skin was not the creamy white of most women of the day, but held a warm, golden cast to it, a color that accentuated her dark eyes. She was not what one would call a conventional beauty, but Cody found her looks very appealing. As he looked closer, he discovered that she was older than he'd initially thought; she was at least twenty-three. He also saw that she was regarding the men frostily now, and they had become silent and solemn, some of them mumbling that they had more work to do.

Her eyes found his again.

"Ready?" Cody asked. "I'd offer you my arm, but I don't think you'd want to take it, seeing as how I've been working and all."

She glanced sidelong at that long, dark, hard-muscled forearm shaded by soft, black hair, and she thought, no, she didn't want to take it, but not for the reason he thought.

Effortlessly, he bent down to pick up her trunk, which Hal Witherby had long since abandoned, and they started off together, leaving the other laborers behind.

"Gee, that's hard work, Cody!" one of the men called after him teasingly.

Cody laughed good-naturedly and Tessa, embarrassed, nearly stumbled over a loose board in the walk, but Cody caught her elbow with his free hand. "Watch your step," he warned, his mouth surprisingly close to her ear. She ventured a peek up at him and saw that his eyes held that humorous glint in them; otherwise he was straight-faced.

They continued walking, she trying to match his long strides, nearly out of breath, until he noticed and slowed a little. Her heels clicked smartly on the wooden sidewalk in contrast to the solid thunk of his boot heels. Late-afternoon dust motes danced in the air and she peered into storefront windows, admiring the merchandise. They passed a dressmaker's shop, the general store, the bank. Men lounged in the doorway of the billiard hall and she was quick to drop her eyes as their bold stares lingered upon her.

"Howdy, Cody," one of them called out lazily, and Cody acknowledged him with a curt nod.

Others passed them on the boardwalk, most of them calling out a friendly hello to Cody, and he answered them amiably in turn. Not many seemed to be bothered by the heat, but Tessa's throat was parched from the dust and hot wind. She glanced down at her wine-colored dress, noting the dust on it, and feeling the damp stickiness beneath it. Cody wiped his forehead with his shirtsleeve, still balancing her trunk on one sturdy shoulder, carrying it effortlessly, as if it were no heavier than a single book. Tessa thought of the way

Hal had staggered beneath its weight and she silently marveled at this man's strength.

"I never caught your name," he said suddenly, in an easy, friendly tone. Tessa felt a little shy in this impressive man's presence, but she chose to ignore her jumbled emotions and answered him evenly, her chin elevating a notch.

"Miss Amesbury," she said with a certain amount of pride and dignity.

She missed the amused twitch of his handsome mouth. When she glanced up to his dark face, he looked perfectly serious—and alarmingly handsome. Her mind groped for small talk—any words that might soothe her nerves. "How do you know Widow Rawlins?"

Cody seemed to find her question amusing. This time she saw the corners of his mouth curl slightly. "Oh, the Rawlinses knew my folks from Kentucky. Old Jake died last year and the widow has been pretty lonely."

"I'm sure," Tessa murmured, wondering about the widow.

"And you're from New England?"

"That's correct," and her mouth tightened primly. A gentleman never asked a lady too many personal questions. And this man was delving a little too deep for her tastes.

"Why aren't you married yet?"

She missed a step, her back stiffening as straight as the planks he'd sawed not a half hour ago. "*That* is none of your business, Mr. Butler!" she hissed, watching a foolish grin spread across his unforgivably handsome features. Her anger seethed within her as he continued watching her with laughing eyes. He shrugged lightly.

"Can't blame a man for wanting to know," he said. "And I sure do wish you'd call me Cody. Everyone does."

As if to prove it, a tall, buxom blond woman wearing an aqua-colored dress glided up to them, stopping momentarily as she rested one hand upon Cody's forearm. Dropping her eyelashes seductively, she cooed, "Hello, Cody."

Cody grinned. "Hi, Angie." He lifted an amused brow at Tessa, who wore a look of immense disgust on her face. The blonde looked from the trunk Cody balanced on his shoulder to the plainly dressed woman beside him and drew her own conclusion. She pressed Cody's arm meaningfully, then moved on, without giving him a chance for introductions.

"See?" Cody said as they started up again.

"Yes, I see," Tessa said dryly, ignoring Cody's cockeyed grin. "But I don't feel we should address each other by our first names, sir. I met you not five minutes past."

"Hmm," he grunted. "I guess that means I have to continue calling you Miss Amesbury."

She hid her smile as he waited with cocked brow. "Yes."

He nodded shortly. "And you aim to teach thirty kids all by yourself."

"Why, of course! I've much experience with

children! What do you find so amusing, Mr. Butler?" His slightly secretive smile was beginning to annoy her.

"Well, there'll be some in that classroom one could hardly call children, *Miss* Amesbury. Some of the boys are bigger than you—easily. How do you aim to handle them?"

"I'll manage perfectly well, Mr. Butler. I hardly think that my size is a qualification for teaching and managing a classroom."

"Mmm. Even so, if you ever need help with the . . . er . . . more unruly ones, I'll be glad to lend a hand," he offered pleasantly.

Tessa glanced down to his broad, swarthy hands and thought those hands would no doubt silence a child—quickly. But she raised her nose slightly and said, "I do not approve of violence, Mr. Butler. And I certainly don't use it in my classroom."

"Well, I only use it when necessary," he said with a barely repressed note of mockery in his deep, smooth voice. He chuckled when she gave him a disdainful look. "In any case, you won't have to contend with the bigger boys until the weather turns cold. They'll be working on their families' claims till then."

"My goodness, you make it sound as if I'm to battle with them!"

He laughed. "Well, I don't mean to scare you off. I'm sure of one thing, and that's that they've never been taught by anyone nearly as pretty as you."

She felt her cheeks grow hot. "Well," she said briskly, daring a sidelong glance at him, "we've established that I'm a schoolteacher. And what is it you do for a living, Mr. Butler?"

"Anything that pays well, Miss Amesbury," he responded. Together they stepped off the wooden walk onto the hard dirt path tufted with prairie grass.

"Oh." Disdain weighed heavy in her voice as she thought, He erects saloons and no doubt spends a good deal of time in them.

"Do I detect scorn in that sweet voice of yours?"

"Not at all," she answered icily.

"No? Why, Miss Amesbury, I beg to differ. There was clearly disdain in your voice. You don't think the building of a town is important?"

She felt her skin prickle under her high snug collar. "Well, it's just that you and those men seem in such a hurry to put up that saloon, even though the town has three others. Why don't you all build an establishment that everyone can utilize—such as a library?"

"To tell you the truth, Miss Amesbury, I think a new saloon will get more use than a library. Two of those three *saloons* cater to a different clientele altogether." He gave her an almost comically suggestive look and Tessa realized that he meant they were brothels. Her face burned. This was the *last* kind of conversation she wished to have with this man—with *any* man—especially on her first day in town! But Cody didn't seem to notice her uneasiness. "After a day under the hot sun or a long day behind the counter even, a respectable man's more likely to head for the saloon than the library."

Her correct demeanor slipped for an instant and Tessa grinned. Cody felt a sudden tightening in his chest and he gripped the trunk, forcing his eyes away from her. Ah, he thought, there lurks humor beneath that cool facade.

They'd approached a tall, clapboard house with a long, freshly whitewashed porch surrounded by a white, spooled railing.

"Well, here we are," Cody said, nodding toward the yellow house. On the wide wooden swing perched a white-haired woman who looked up upon their arrival.

"Why, hello!" she called out to them and came to her feet as the two mounted the steps. As she stood, her apron full of—all things—dandelions fell in a yellow heap at her feet. "Oh! Oh, my . . ." She stared at the flowers, then, with a little shrug, stepped over them and approached Cody and Tessa.

"Hey, Mrs. Rawlins!" Cody greeted, making no move to put down the trunk. "Here's the new schoolteacher!" He glanced toward Tessa, who felt suddenly shy but managed to extend her slim hand in greeting. Mrs. Rawlins took it and pressed it between her green-stained, comforting palms. She was a funny little woman, Tessa thought, with plump pink cheeks, an even pinker nose, and wide, blinking blue eyes. There was something about her that looked slightly askew—maybe it was her white, windblown hair, or the way she'd buttoned her bodice—each button slipped into the buttonhole beneath the proper one, the top two left undone. And those dandelions! On the swing, there was a huge basket brimming with them, and of course those she'd dropped on the porch floor. What on earth would she want with all those weeds? Tessa sent a strange look to Cody, but he only grinned, amusement glowing in his eyes.

"How was your journey, dear?"

"A bit tiresome," Tessa admitted. "I'm just glad to be here at last."

"You both must be hot after that walk from town. Let me draw you some cool water."

"Sounds good," said Cody, "but first let me put this trunk inside. Feels like she packed lead."

Mrs. Rawlins laughed gaily and led Cody indoors as Tessa stood blushing to her hairline, trying her best to ignore Cody's teasing grin. Once they were inside, she leaned to put her carpetbag down, then removed her hat and pressed the back of her hand to her forehead to blot it dry. Tessa walked to the edge of the porch and leaned against the post. She drew in a long, easy breath and smelled the aroma of September flowers heavy on the wind. The dry prairie grasses seemed to whisper secrets. So peaceful here . . . She briefly thought of the life she left behind and shuddered slightly.

Cody walked up quietly behind Tessa, studying her for the first time. He glanced at her severe bun, taking in the honey-spun strands of hair weaving themselves through the light brown mass, and he felt an urge to free it all, to see how it would look falling about her shoulders.

"Here's your water," he said, and handed her a tall, cold glass. His fingers brushed hers and she felt a quick flick inside her.

She tore her eyes away from his and looked over at Mrs. Rawlins, who was walking toward the swing. "Thank you," she managed. "And thank you for sending Mr. Butler here to escort me to your home. It was a thoughtful gesture."

At the mention of Cody's name, the old woman started to say something, but she stopped herself as Cody winked at her over Tessa's head. She settled back against the swing, slightly befuddled.

Cody gulped down his water, then set the glass down on a nearby table. "Well, I guess I'll leave you two alone now. If you need me for anything, I'll be back in town," he offered amiably, and flicked his glance one more time Tessa's way before lithely bounding down the porch steps and starting off toward town. Tessa's eyes watched his broad-shouldered frame until it was nearly out of view, when Mrs. Rawlins's voice forced her out of her reverie.

"Such a dear boy," the old woman was saying. "I knew him when he was a baby, and he's nigh thirty-four now." Mrs. Rawlins shook her white head, chuckling softly to herself. "Dear me, listen to me go on! Come, dear, come inside. You've had such a long trip. I'm sure you'd like a nice bath and perhaps some rest. Let me show you your room—Tessa, is it?"

"Yes, that's it."

"It's a lovely name," Mrs. Rawlins said warmly, leading her to the kitchen, "and it fits you fine. You don't mind if I call you that, do you?"

"I'd be pleased."

The old woman's eyes twinkled merrily. "Come with me. I'll show you the rest of the house, then we'll have an early supper and perhaps you'd like to retire early."

Down the hallway they went, Mrs. Rawlins in the lead. "That's the parlor." She nodded her little head toward a room on her right and Tessa caught a glimpse of a flowered-chintz settee, but that was all, for Mrs. Rawlins did not stop her pace. "And here's the sitting room, where I do a little informal entertaining." They stepped inside the cheery room where a flowered carpet covered the floor and a rocking chair was positioned in one corner with a sewing basket beside it. There was a coal heater with isinglass windows in the center of the room and a few chairs gathered around, and a long, comfortable-looking sofa against one wall. Pretty china lamps were set on polished tables, and the waning sunlight slanting in through the curtained windows lent the room a cozy glow. Tessa pictured herself sitting in this room by the heater winter evenings, going over school lessons.

"I hope you don't mind an upstairs bedroom. These old legs haven't the energy to climb all those steps."

They climbed the stairs to a simple room, dominated by a large, four-poster bed covered with a blue-and-cream-colored patchwork quilt. A lace doily was spread on the oak dresser, which held a white china lamp, and the window seat had blue cushions, the white organdy curtains tied back at the window. Old-gold sunlight splashed through the window, warming the floorboards, and there, at the foot of her bed, stood her trunk. Mrs. Rawlins followed Tessa's gaze.

"I had Cody bring it into your room. You don't mind, do you?"

"No." But the tips of her ears burned as she thought of *him* in her bedroom. She glanced at Mrs. Rawlins's worried eyes and smiled at her. "It's a beautiful room. The entire house is lovely, and I'm sure I'll love living here."

The older woman's face brightened. "I'm so glad to hear you say that. Now, come, let's heat some water for your bath, and while you're in it, I'll finish snapping the heads off those dandelions. Put them in one of the crocks in the cellar, add a little water and sugar to them, let them sit a couple of weeks, and we'll have us some of the best medicine known to man—or woman!" she added with a mischievous twinkle in her eyes.

Tessa bit her lip to hide her smile. Wine!

The woman brewed her own dandelion wine! She must have dug the weeds from every scrap of land in town to have gathered the amount she'd had on the porch! Maybe that was why she had that pink nose—it was sunburned—or maybe she'd been sipping some of her own brew.

It was a relaxing night. After a leisurely, scented bath Tessa put on a clean muslin dress, casting aside her despised corsets for the evening. They were nothing but a constricting nuisance as far as she was concerned, and she was slight enough that Mrs. Rawlins would never know the difference.

The two women ate a chicken dinner with mashed potatoes and buttered carrots, and they had cake and tea for dessert.

"I swear, you'll get me fat!" Tessa protested when Mrs. Rawlins handed her a second piece of cake. "Really, I can't eat it!"

"It would do you good to put some flesh on that body of yours." Mrs. Rawlins smiled across the table. "Out here it's a hardy style of life."

"Mmm." Tessa daintily wiped her mouth with her linen napkin. "Maybe so, but do I have to put the flesh on all at once?"

Mrs. Rawlins laughed and they cleared the table together and washed the dishes, then Tessa went upstairs to unpack. Her fingers ran over the lid of the trunk, noting that Cody had untied the rope that had secured it, and now she thought of his long brown fingers, of his quick, flashing grin.

As she unlocked the padlocks and opened the lid, the fragrant scent of cedar rose up into her nostrils, and Tessa let the sweet scent fill her. The trunk had been a present from the orphanage that had been her home all her life, and where she had taught once she was old enough. The children, the nuns, the other teachers, the superintendent had all been her family. Tessa's fingers paused over her clothing, and for a brief instant she closed her eyes. Oh, Miss Crowell, she thought, please understand why I left the way that I did. . . .

Tessa's fingers clutched at the folds of a dress. She wouldn't think of all that now. She'd come west to Harper City to build a new life, a good life, and put the past behind her. Harper City was not *quite* what Tessa had expected, but she realized that it would be just as easy to lose herself here in this small, insignificant town as it was in a big city.

"There," she said to herself when all her dresses were hung and her shoes neatly put away, "that's done." Last she removed her beloved books, placing each one carefully in the bookshelf near the dresser. Her fingers caressed the gilded letters of titles. It was these that had made her trunk so heavy, these Cody had jokingly referred to as "lead," but Tessa could never have left her precious books behind.

Finally she changed into her nightgown and slipped into bed. The sheets were freshly starched, and the smell of the cool September night mingled with the clean scent. She burrowed beneath the quilt, sure she had never laid her body on a bed so big or so comfortable.

Her eyes drifted closed. Her body relaxed as sleep began to curl deliciously about her. But then, without warning, her body jerked and her eyes flew open in the darkness as William Forsythe's face flashed through her mind.

Forget it! Forget him! she told herself fiercely. He'd *never* find her, even if he bothered to try. This town was too remote.

Tessa tried to lull herself back to sleep, but her heart was pounding, and her eyes stared blankly at the ceiling. Forsythe's hawklike face seemed imprinted in her mind, and it scared her. What if he did try to find her? What would he do when he—

Stop! her mind shrieked. She pinched her eyes tight—tight, forcing his image from her mind, trying in vain to replace it with another. And into it came Cody Butler, startling her but somehow soothing her. She let herself picture that big strapping man with the broad shoulders and easy smile. And she carried that image into sleep with her.

Chapter Two

✦ ✦ ✦ ✦ ✦

THE ONLY THING on Tessa's mind the following morning was finding the schoolhouse. Although classes would not begin for a few days yet, she was anxious to see her school. Her school. She thought about it as she made her way down the dry road. The sun shone warmly on her back and shoulders, and the dark thoughts that had plagued her last night were temporarily forgotten as she strode briskly into town.

Walking down Main Street, Tessa passed the open stores and some of the merchants who had come out for a brief spell to look at the gold-drenched morning. Some of them nodded at her in a neighborly way and Tessa returned their greetings with a nod.

Men were working on the new saloon, and involuntarily her eyes searched for Cody Butler. He was nowhere in sight. Yet she flushed with guilt, remembering her thoughts of him last night.

She turned her attention back to the town as she crossed a vacant lot, following the wagon-wheel tracks again, and she looked up to see the schoolhouse. She stopped for a moment, studying it from where she stood, admiring its fresh white paint and the rows of gleaming windows. Her heart felt light for the first time in months. This charming little school seemed to promise a pleasant new life.

Tessa walked up the steps and tested the door. Finding it open, she walked inside. The schoolhouse was new and bright and shining. The sunlight seemed to dance through the windows. There were long rows of desks up each side of the room—one side for the boys and the other side for the girls. The teacher's desk stood on a platform and was long and polished. Behind the teacher's desk stretched a long blackboard, and Tessa's fingers itched to write on it with new white chalk.

She passed the central heating stove and sat at her desk, running a palm over the varnished desktop. Soon these desks would be crowded with children. Today was Saturday and on Monday school started. This would be a nine-month school, in session from now till June, closed only during inclement weather and holidays. There were some schools in the West, she'd heard, that stayed in session for only three months at a time!

Tessa gazed out one of the windows, and in the distance she could make out two claim shanties. She supposed the town was growing all the time, and she knew that, according to the law, men and their families had to live on their claim for six months of the year, even if their business was in town. If they did so, and planted crops on their acres for five years, then they would be granted title to the land. Still, Tessa thought, how lonely it must be out there on the prairie!

"So, how do you like it?"

Tessa nearly fell off her chair. Her heart thumped wildly against her chest.

"Goodness!" she cried when her eyes adjusted themselves to Cody Butler, who came striding into the classroom with that utterly overwhelming grin on his dark face. He was so tall and wide-shouldered that he seemed to fill up the room.

He stopped before her desk, his long legs apart. "I thought I might find you here." He chuckled, then laughed outright when her eyes narrowed suspiciously on him. But he was holding something shiny in his outstretched palm. Tessa glanced down at it. "Thought you'd need the key."

"What are you doing with it?" she asked stupidly, and realized just *how* stupid she sounded when he laughed again. "I—I mean why didn't someone on the school board bring it to me?" She felt the flush creeping up her cheeks, knowing that she sounded ruder by the moment.

But Cody's eyes showed a twinkle of light. "I *am* on the school board."

Tessa felt her mouth drop open and she quickly shut it. "But—but what do you care about the school in this town?" My goodness, couldn't she keep the blunt words from spilling out of her mouth? She could tell by the sudden tightening in Cody's hard jaw that her abrupt questions were beginning to annoy him.

"I care a great deal about the school in this

town," he answered evenly. "This town has many fine people in it and they deserve a decent school for their children just as people do anywhere else. I hope you don't bring your condescending attitude into the classroom with you, Miss Amesbury."

Tessa stiffened, stung by his words. Of course, she had sounded like an awful Eastern snob, but he had misread her words. Her own delicate jaw tightened belligerently, prepared to defend herself and her precious profession.

"I am not in the least condescending toward this town or these people, Mr. Butler. I feel honored to teach here." She arched a slim brow at him for emphasis, but shrank inside as a cool light flickered in his dark green eyes, which regarded her steadily. "How was I to guess that a man who"—she paused, letting her eyes rake patronizingly over him, though she couldn't find one displeasing thing about his appearance—"builds saloons would hold an interest in this school, never mind being a member of the school board?"

Why, she was deliberately taunting him! Torn between anger and amusement, Cody moved a step toward her, then stopped himself, wisely keeping the desk between them. The twitch of his lips could hardly be called a smile. "Yes, but I *am* a member of the school board and I can send you packing if I choose." Now it was his turn to let his eyes rake over her. Tessa nearly gulped. "Hasn't anyone ever taught you any manners? The ones you have are atrocious."

"My manners?" Tessa repeated blankly. For a moment she was at a loss, her mind still lingering on the possibility that he could send her packing. But she quickly regained her composure, and straightening in her chair, she eyed him coldly. "I don't see what *my* manners have to do with anything. I asked you a simple question and you interpreted it as you saw fit. Now, if you don't mind, you may drop the key on the desk and leave. I have work to do."

She was dismissing him as efficiently as she would a schoolboy. Cody would have laughed if he wasn't so annoyed. She was sitting there as tight as a trussed-up chicken, waiting. Her haughty expression seemed to challenge him. And Cody never could resist a challenge. He wasn't about to drop the key on her desk; he was going to make her take it from him.

He half sat on the corner of her desk, calmly regarding her with disinterest. She dropped her gaze and saw that he still held that key in his broad hand, extending it toward her. She wished he would just put it down. She didn't want to touch him. The longer he sat there, the more flustered she became. "The door was open," she murmured. "I didn't need a key to get in."

"I know," he said, thoroughly amused now at his own deliberate taunting, and by the look of distaste on her face as she tried to avoid looking at his hand. "I opened it this morning, figuring you might come this way today."

Tessa sighed inwardly, realizing he was not going to drop the key on the desk. She had no choice but to stretch out her own hand and hope that he might drop the key into it.

Amusement tugged at the corner of Cody's mouth. What the hell, he'd compromise. He took her hand gently but firmly and pressed the key into the most sensitive area of her palm. And then he closed her fingers over it and gave her fist a little squeeze. "Don't lose it," he teased.

He sat just an arm's length from her, and the soft wind wafting through the open door behind him carried upon it the scent of his shaving soap. That meant, Tessa thought, he must have shaved before coming here. She lifted her dark eyes to his face, moving them over his hard, tanned features, noting that, indeed, the whisker stubble that had darkened his cheeks yesterday was now missing. Her gaze dipped to the strong column of his throat where the soft gray shirt that he wore was opened, revealing a v of chest hair.

Her eyes quickly returned to his face and she saw that he was returning her scrutiny with humor, the tiny creases around his green eyes deepening as he cast her a mocking smile.

Horrified that she'd been caught staring, Tessa stood, attempting to gain control of the situation. "I said I have work to do!" she snapped.

His mocking smile had turned into an infuriating grin. "You did say that, didn't you?"

He glanced pointedly at her empty desk. "And I can see that you have," he drawled dryly. "Piles of it."

Tessa flushed, embarrassment and anger sweeping through her. She had absolutely no control over this man and was totally unable to deal with him. Any *gentleman* would have departed immediately after leaving her the key. It was simply not proper for him to be alone with her in this classroom. But Tessa was fast learning that Mr. Cody Butler was no gentleman.

In an effort to appear the cool-headed and poised schoolteacher—an image on which she prided herself—Tessa drew in a deep breath and confronted him directly. "If you are so dense that you cannot take a simple hint—" A sarcastic lift of his black eyebrow stopped her in midsentence.

"Hint?"

His taunts were insufferable! Why did he persist in antagonizing her?

"All right—so I lied!" she snapped, noticing to her dismay that Cody was enjoying every moment of her ill-concealed temper. The gleam of laughter in his eyes told her that!

"Do all schoolteachers lie so glibly where you come from?"

She gripped the edge of the desk, her knuckles white. If only he knew how closely he'd come to the truth. She was living a lie and hating the circumstances that had forced her to live it.

"And do all schoolteachers dress like that?"

His deliberate gaze roamed over her severe dark gray dress, which so ill-suited her. Once again his eyes dropped and passed over her slender curves. Tessa stiffened at being so thoroughly inspected.

"Is there something you don't like about my appearance, Mr. Butler?" she inquired in a miffed tone. He was wearing that *damned* secretive smile and a rakish glint entered his green eyes.

"Well, now that you mention it," he drawled, and let his eyes travel critically over her, masking his genuine appreciation of her slender body, "that dress. My God, it's awful."

Tessa's shoulders stiffened and she glared at him.

But Cody ignored her indignant scowl and he cocked his head, considering her closely. His gaze lifted to her hair, scraped back into that severe bun, and his lips twitched. "And you should loosen your hair some. It's pulling the skin of your face so tight you could bounce a nickel off it."

Tessa sucked in an outraged breath, but before she could speak, Cody reached up a strong brown hand as if to loosen her hair himself. Angrily Tessa slapped his wrist away.

Cody drew back in mock surprise. "And *this* from the woman who doesn't hit her children!"

As furious and affronted as she felt, Tessa had to bite her lip to keep from laughing at his ridiculous expression and the way he'd mimicked her. She was torn between wanting to swat him again and wanting to share his humor. However, she quickly recalled his insults and she schooled her features into a mask of cool aloofness. But Cody caught the sparkle of laughter in her dark eyes, appreciating it.

"All right, Mr. Butler, now that you've had your fun making sport of me, haven't you something better to do?"

Cody frowned. She might not look like any schoolmarm he'd ever known, but she sure as hell spoke like one! With prickling irritation, Codey realized she was once again dismissing him, waiting loftily with her arms crossed over her bosom. He made himself shrug lightly and he came to his feet in one fluid motion. "Now that you mention it, Miss Amesbury, yes, I have some important business of my own to tend to."

Tessa raised a slim eyebrow at him, as if doubting his statement. Cody's lips quirked with lurking amusement, but with a pleasant touch of his fingers to his wide, tanned forehead, he turned and sauntered off down the middle aisle.

Tessa watched him leave, her eyes running down his broad back and slim, straight hips, noting the snug fit of his black breeches. And then Tessa stiffened where she stood. My word, she thought, what was wrong with her, noticing such things about a man? And such a rude, annoying man at that? And yet, standing there, she need only glance out the window to find her eyes on him again as he strode off toward town in that graceful, assured walk of his.

How *could* she admire that man's looks after what he'd said about her dress, her hair—oh! Tessa squeezed her fists tight only to realize that she still held the key and it seemed to burn in the palm of her hand. She recalled the way he had squeezed her fist, and her fist now opened, letting the key drop with a clinking sound upon the desktop. Oh, she was being ridiculous! That man did something funny to her nerves, that was all, and she wasn't going to let him get the best of her.

Tessa snatched up the key and her straw hat, which she'd put aside, pressed the hat upon her head, and started down the aisle, sure she'd allowed Cody enough time to put a good distance between himself and the schoolhouse. She wished to avoid the man at all costs.

She stepped out to the warm, clear day and closed the door behind her, stopping to insert the key into the lock and turning it until it clicked to her satisfaction. Frowning, she glanced down at that key again, then without a second thought, she slipped a finger into the high neck of her dress and dropped the key down the front, feeling a forbidden thrill as the warm metal caressed her bare skin, and as it nestled there against her breasts she remembered the way it had rested in Cody's callused palm.

A rustling sound by the side of the schoolhouse caused Tessa to glance up. Seeing nothing, she moved quietly down the wooden steps and crept to peek around the corner. What she saw brought her up short. A child was standing on tiptoe, both hands cupped about his face as he peered into the window of the schoolhouse. Feeling Tessa's presence, the child whipped around to confront her. The child's brown face was streaked with dust as was his buckskin clothing. There was no telling his hair color because it was tucked under a fur cap.

Before Tessa could open her mouth, the child was off like a shot, scampering like a rabbit over the softly rolling prairie.

"Wait!" Tessa called, her voice falling flat against the wind. But the child had already vanished. Tessa frowned. "Strange," she murmured to herself. The wind whipped her skirts about her slender ankles and she held on to her hat as she stood there looking out on that level land. As her brown eyes scanned the prairie—that forever rippling grass under the vast, endless sky—Tessa felt a stirring, a restlessness within her. She longed to ride out far beyond the horizon, to let her hair down, to laugh out loud—yes! to ride astride, explore the land, and listen to it as she had when she was a girl. She'd been an awful tomboy when she was young; she could race and swim and climb as well as—sometimes better than—any of the boys, yet as she grew older her lively spirit had been curbed by the nuns and was now hidden behind a refined and correct demeanor. Still, sometimes, she had to work to restrain her inner spunkiness and, more importantly, her quick tongue.

Her gaze drifted to the high white clouds racing in the azure sky. The day was too beautiful to resist. If she couldn't ride out to explore the prairie, she could certainly walk and discover the town. She pressed her broad-brimmed hat to the crown of her head and started off toward South Street, then crossed over to White Avenue, avoiding Main Street altogether. She was amazed to find even more frame structures rising: another hotel, restaurants, and businesses. Perhaps she hadn't given this town enough credit! Oh, the buildings were crude and unattractive, but they seemed decent establishments. Why, even some scrawny cottonwood trees had been planted!

She turned left and found herself on Union Avenue, and she stopped a moment to catch her breath. There was little on this road she found appealing. A gun shop was just across the street and the livery stable was beside it. Down the street a short distance was another with a sign that spelled LILY'S DANCE HALL.

This was apparently the bad side of town, and she should not be strolling in this area. She drew herself up proudly, as if to show anyone who might be watching that *she* was not to be mistaken for one of those fallen women.

And just as she started up again, the door to

Lily's swung open and out strode Cody Butler, big and broad-shouldered, with a hard-
looking woman on his arm. Tessa froze,
drawing in a swift, audible breath. Unable to
stop herself, she watched with a hungry curiosity as the woman leaned close to Cody,
saying something that made him throw back
his dark head and laugh.

Tessa's eyes narrowed on the two of them.
So, this was the important business he had to
tend to! Well, it didn't surprise Tessa one bit.
She'd already guessed what kind of man he
was—unprincipled and indecent. It certainly
hadn't taken him long to get from the schoolhouse to this evil place!

Tessa's eyes widened as the woman slid her
hand up his sleeve and into his hair, tugging
his dark head down to meet her mouth in a
lingering kiss. Tessa's facial muscles tightened, and her mouth drew up tighter than a
bowstring. She'd seen quite enough! Spinning
sharply on her heel, she marched off, thoroughly disgusted with Cody Butler.

She headed out toward the west edge of
town, refusing to give him another thought,
finding solace in the peaceful outskirts of
town. More claim shanties dotted the land
and Tessa wondered how many of them shel-
tered her students. In the distance she could
see Mrs. Rawlins's house and she figured
she'd swung around in a half-circle, but she
wanted to see some of the other side of town.

She walked a good quarter mile farther and
just as her steps began to lag a building

caught her attention. It was long and low-pitched, its wood a weathered gray. Curiosity piqued, Tessa stepped closer. She glanced about, finding not a soul. Across the grassy road, she glimpsed a house, but there was no one to be seen. She cast a cursory glance over one shoulder, but there was only prairie out there.

Tessa took off her hat and fanned her flushed face with it. The gentle breeze cooled the nape of her neck. Her gaze lifted to the high, unopened window just above her. This was no ordinary building, and she just wanted a quick peek inside. She edged even closer, standing on tiptoe, peering in much like the child had peered into her classroom earlier. Tessa could see only the tops of mysterious-looking bottles lining high shelves. Curiosity now consumed her. Frustrated, she jumped a little, but to no avail.

"Darn!" she muttered, and then her long-lashed gaze fell to the padlocked door. It was not locked!

Daringly, Tessa moved in and lifted the latch. She pushed the door open, hesitating; if grizzly bears or gun-toting bandits were waiting in there to accost her, now was their chance. When nothing happened, Tessa stepped inside.

It was dim, and a strange, medicinal scent tickled her nostrils. As her eyes adjusted themselves to the fainter light, Tessa took in the high shelves against the walls lined with glass containers, porcelain jars, and thick leather-covered books. The sunlight fell in through the window, showing her rows of bottles and scientific-looking apparatus that cluttered tables pushed against the walls.

Why, this was a laboratory!

Tessa put her hat aside and walked to a low table, her eyes scanning the open crates upon it. She peeked into one and found glass carboys filled with colored liquids. Over there, in the center of the lab, stood a plain wooden table covered with all sorts of microscopic equipment. She wandered over to it and found an opened medical text written in Latin. How fascinating!

She leaned closer to peer into one of the microscopes.

"What in the bloody hell do you think you're doing?" an enraged male voice roared from behind, and Tessa nearly jumped a foot out of her skin. A mindless shriek emerged from her as she whirled, and in the process of doing so, her flying elbows collided with bottles and flasks and microscopes, swiping madly at everything until more than half of it ended up on the floor in a violent shattering of glass.

"Goddammit!" Cody barked, his towering form in the doorway a very real threat. Her heart slammed hard against her chest as Tessa bent to retrieve her mess, but her hip whacked the table behind her, upsetting it so that more bottles and tubes caromed off each other, skidded precariously over the tabletop, and crashed at her feet in a splintering of glass that was almost as loud as Cody's bellowing voice.

She started for it again, but his strong hand clamped over her arm in a death grip, causing her to gasp, and he hissed through his teeth, "Leave it!" He grabbed her by both arms now and hauled her back against the table, trapping her there with his hard body pressed tight to hers. "You little idiot! Look what you've done!"

Tessa had been momentarily stunned by his anger and startling attack, but her courage flooded back to her in an indignant rush. How dare he call her an idiot! "I didn't mean to!" she huffed.

"But you have and the whole room is a goddamned mess!" he said, glaring savagely at her.

"Well, if you hadn't startled me so, growling like a rabid dog and scaring the wits out of me, this wouldn't have happened!" She ignored the sudden tensing in his strong, muscular body leaning into hers and tried to ignore the fine white lines that had sprung up around his mouth. "Now if you let go of me, I can clean it up!"

Cody shook her. "The damage is irreparable! Don't you realize that? And don't you realize you're trespassing?"

"So are you!" Tessa shook free of him. "Let me go!" And to her mortification, her swinging arms batted the final batch of liquid-filled flasks off the table. In a wildly awkward gesture she reached to salvage them, but instead sloshed their wet contents all over the front of Cody's trousers. Tessa heard his quick, indrawn breath as the cold shock of it clung to his groin, and she held her own breath, torn between laughing at the comedy of it all and fleeing before he vented his wrath.

Cody ground his teeth and clenched his big fists at his sides. He closed his eyes in exaggerated patience, forcing himself to command his roiling temper. Watching him, Tessa bit her lip; her dark eyes lowered to his trousers where the wet fabric hugged him and her cheeks grew hot when she realized where she stared. When she raised her gaze, she found him scowling blackly at her. "You ought to be damned thankful it wasn't acid in those flasks!"

Tessa bit back the quip that *he* should be even more thankful! But Cody caught the laughter in her eyes. His jaw went tight.

"So you think it's funny, do you?" He took a threatening step toward her, but Tessa backed up. "You little menace, I ought to make you mop it all up with your hair!"

"I could use a rag," she admitted ruefully. Not wanting to test his anger any further, Tessa darted away from him in a graceful, doelike movement, and squatted down, her skirts billowing around her. She started picking up the shards of glass, the spilled liquid from them dripping off her fingers. She looked helplessly about for a rag. She'd made a terrible mess and was not only appalled at her clumsiness but sorry too.

"The doctor who owns this lab could have

you arrested for trespassing, you know."
Cody's voice loomed from above.

Knowing she was at a definite disadvantage
kneeling at his feet, Tessa arched her neck
anyway, tilting her head up to look at him.
"There were no signs, and no lock on this
door!"

He gave her a look of utter disbelief. "People have to warn you off their property—
lock you out of their homes to make sure you
don't invade their privacy? Christ! Remind me
to notify the unsuspecting citizens of this
town!"

Heat flooded Tessa's cheeks. "You're trespassing too!" she flashed back hotly. "What
are you doing here?" She sat back on her heels
and narrowed her eyes suspiciously at him.
"Were you following me?"

Cody snorted. "Don't flatter yourself!"
When she flinched, he frowned harshly. "I
work here—satisfied?" He glanced at a nearby
shelf, grabbed a cloth in disgust, and went
down on one knee to help her wipe up.
Having him so close to her made Tessa very
nervous. Her shaking fingers dropped a
jagged piece of glass. When she reached to
retrieve it, Cody impatiently brushed her
hand away. "Just get the hell out of here.
You're a walking calamity. Every time you
move I fear for my life."

She was somehow hurt. "I was just curious," she said defensively, and to her horror,
her voice quavered.

Cody looked up, holding her with his eyes.

"I can think of another word for you," he offered with suppressed tension in his drawling voice. "Nosy." He leaned back and cocked his head, draping an arm across his raised knee. "Or how about a snoop? And there's busybody, also jinxed, disastrous, dangerous as hell," and he continued listing words, his voice mounting with annoyance and disgust, ignoring Tessa's glaring eyes. "And," he finished, "I can think of names and words a lady like you probably would not know the meaning of, but I'll refrain."

"Why stop now!" she spat, her fists balled tight on her lap. Her ears and cheeks were burning, yet she could think of no insult to match the ones he'd flung at her. She gave up and huffed, "What are you getting so upset about? All we have to do is clean it! I'm sure the doctor will understand this was all an accident."

"I'm sure he won't. This"—Cody gestured with an outflung hand to the disaster spread at their feet—"happens to be a certain strain of bacteria the doctor was trying to identify. He'd been working on it a long time," he said through clenched teeth.

"I guess *you* would know all about that, seeing as how you're the caretaker of this place, huh?" she said sarcastically.

"And I guess you don't know how close I am to strangling you or you'd have been long gone by now."

"You don't frighten me." But he did. He was so big and so strong looking—probably strong enough to knock her flat with the mere sweep of his hand. Still, Tessa's chin lifted impudently. "And you can't tell me what to do." She was testing herself as well as him. "But I think you're quite afraid of this doctor. He must have a terrible temper. Or maybe you're just afraid he won't pay your wages."

His look would have cowed any woman. He stood up, and he caught her none too gently by the elbow, hauling her to her feet. It didn't please Tessa in the least that she had to look so far up to meet his dark green eyes. "Out," he ordered in a dangerously soft voice. He let go of her arm abruptly, as if he'd been touching vermin.

Tessa was no coward; however, she knew when she must admit silent defeat. Still, she lingered in the open doorway, the sun streaming in from behind her, and watched Cody picking up glass with his long fingers, swearing softly under his breath. She stared at his dark head, bent over the task, feeling quite responsible yet not knowing quite how to remedy it.

"Should I wait for the doctor to come so I can explain what happened?"

Cody looked up sharply, as if surprised to find her still here. His lips compressed in exasperation. "I'll tell him."

"But I should—"

Slowly Cody came to his feet, giving a long, disgusted sigh on his way up. In an exaggeratedly slow motion he shook down the wet, broken glass from his fingers to the table, wiped his hands on the seat of his pants, and placed them loosely on his straight hips. His eyes moved over her in a slow, deliberate study that made Tessa's skin tingle. A devilishly wicked light came into his eyes as he drawled, "If you insist on staying, Miss Amesbury, I'm sure I can find another use for you." And he took a threatening step forward.

"I was just leaving!" Tessa said, scampering out the door. Cody took another quick stride toward her, but she lithely danced away, looking like none of those names he had called her.

On Monday, the first day of school, a group of youngsters appraised their new schoolteacher. Seeing how slight Tessa was convinced them that she couldn't be much of a threat, even if she did choose to whip them for misconduct.

In their tightly fastened collars, with their heads bent over their books, the boys felt mighty uncomfortable and restless. The warm air, scented with grass and earth, beckoned to them through the open windows of the schoolhouse. Summer, they felt, was far from over, and school was the last place any of them wished to be.

When the class broke for noon recess, the boys plotted their escape.

"Let's go swimmin' down the creek," redheaded Josh Jordan suggested to his friends. He was ten years old and full of mischief.

"Yeah, I'm powerful hot," agreed his older brother Sam. "And that skinny schoolteacher ain't got the strength to lick us hard."

None of the boys were supposed to go home for lunch, but Tessa did not know that. When she glimpsed them heading away from the schoolhouse, she was certain they would return shortly.

"My pa'd tan my hide but good if he ever found out I played hooky." Will Mason hesitated, scuffing his tight shoes in the dirt.

"Aw, come on," Josh jeered. "He ain't gonna find out. Why, she ain't gonna bother you or your pa."

The boys' empty seats were conspicuous for most of the afternoon. The students tried to study but they were all wondering what this new teacher would do to punish the boys. A whipping was in order, and some of the children began to fidget just thinking about it.

At half past two, when the five damp-headed boys stole into the classroom, it was obvious where they'd been. With anticipation the class waited for the teacher to take action.

Before the boys could slide into their seats Tessa called them up to her desk. They paraded up the aisle and stood sheepishly before her.

"Where have you been, boys?"

Josh Jordan faced her boldly. "We got lost on the way back to the schoolhouse, it bein' our first day an' all."

Tessa almost smiled. "Oh, you did, did you?"

They nodded vigorously. Maybe it wouldn't be hard to fool this teacher, after all. It appeared she believed them. And there was no whipping switch in sight.

"And did you happen upon a creek as you tried to find your way back here?"

"Yes'm, we did!" It was Sam speaking now, and he looked so earnest Tessa bit the inside of her cheek. "And it was so hot, an' we'd been wanderin' about lost fer so long we just had to cool off. The time got away from us is all."

"Mmm. Enjoy yourselves, did you?"

The boys hesitated. They noticed that cagey smile hovering about the teacher's lips. Maybe she was hiding that switch under her desk. But she looked as if she wanted to hear more of their story, like she'd enjoyed it so far. So Sam and Josh glanced at each other and then nodded.

"Yes'm, it was cool as ever."

"But you found your way back here right after you'd had enough swimming?"

At last the boys had the grace to look guilty. Will Mason hung his head a little and the freckles on Josh Jordan's thin face seemed to stand out. Jake McGuire, the littlest of them all, went pale and rubbed his nose nervously.

Tessa knew they expected her to whip them. If she didn't, they'd all think her soft and would continue to misbehave. But Tessa

could still vividly recall her own schooldays—
the sick *thwack* of the ruler coming down on
her fingers—and she knew in her heart she
couldn't whip these boys.

Tessa looked each one square in the eye. "I
can think of a way that will help you to
remember where the schoolhouse is," she
said firmly. "Each of you will write a report on
a country of your choice. Included in that
report will be physical aspects of that country
and *all* bodies of water. You will draw a map
and explain how to use it. And each of you
will earn the grade of one hundred because I
will make sure your reports are letter-perfect."

The boys stifled a collective groan.

"You will stay every evening after school
until it's done to my liking," Tessa went on
relentlessly. "And I will send a note home to
your parents so they will expect you to be late.
Now sit down and open your spellers."

The boys filed down the aisle, muttering
amongst themselves. Their fingers would ache
anyway. A whipping was far preferable to
this! A whipping would have been over with
quick, but *this* torment would drag on for
days. Miss Amesbury was smart, all right.
And she had quickly won their respect.

But the following day Tessa had another
problem. One of her pupils was a thief. When
everyone was out of the classroom at lunch-
time, someone had snuck in and stolen
Hannah Brown's *McGuffey's Reader*. Unfairly,
Tessa suspected one of the five hooky players,

but she had the entire class empty their desks and the reader was nowhere to be found.

The next day after recess little Benjamin Worth woefully announced, "My slate's gone, Teacher."

Again Tessa hunted for the missing article to no avail. She waited for the thief to step forward and announce his guilt. But no one did.

On Thursday a slate pencil was stolen and Tessa lectured her class long and hard on the wickedness of stealing. The children sat solemnly listening yet no one came forward.

Frustrated and determined to put an end to the stealing, Tessa stayed indoors on Friday at noon. She felt *she* was being punished, for she enjoyed eating outdoors with the children in the warm sunshine.

She straightened up the room, then busied herself with writing spelling words on the blackboard. As she wrote she felt a movement behind her—just a whisper of a sound. Tessa glanced over her shoulder and saw no one. She returned to her chore. After writing one word she sensed that presence in the room with her again and spun around in time to catch a flash of brown as the child made off with Sam Jordan's arithmetic book.

The chalk fell from Tessa's fingers with a clatter. It was that wild-looking creature she'd seen peering into her classroom last Saturday! Tessa picked up her skirts and ran after the little culprit. She charged past a cluster of girls standing on the sidelines of the boys' baseball game.

"Rebecca!" Tessa called to the oldest girl. "Watch the children!"

The children stood, wide-eyed, watching their teacher race by them.

Chapter Three

✦✦✦✦

TESSA HADN'T RUN so fast since she was ten years old. The wild, buckskin-clad child scampered far ahead of her, but not too far away to catch. Tessa hiked her cumbersome skirts even higher, almost to her knees, as she flew through the tall, rough grass, her legs and her heart pumping hard.

"Get back here, you little scoundrel!" she yelled at the top of her lungs. But the child raced on in the wide-open country, darting and leaping over the tall prairie grass, staying in Tessa's range of vision, but as elusive as the wind.

Now each breath hurt her throat. The child ahead of her seemed to gain in speed while her own pace started to lag. She was flushed and sweating, furious that the little scamp had got the best of her. But Tessa knew if she stopped now she would lose him for sure.

Her legs seemed leaden as they carried her forward. The child raced on. Tessa's eyes seemed to blur, her heart thundered within her, and suddenly, without quite knowing how, she tripped and lay sprawled ignominiously on the ground. For a moment, her chest heaved, pulling in grand gasps of air, then she remembered the child and sprang to her feet. But the child was a mere dot in the distance now. They'd come almost a mile and he bounded lightly away before her eyes—like a rabbit—and Tessa shaded her eyes with her hand, watching him vanish. She caught her breath.

"Holy Saint Patrick! That kid can run!"

"Holy Saint Patrick, so can you," murmured a deep, amused voice from behind. Tessa jerked and clapped a hand to her thundering heart as she swung around. Unfortunately the heel of her shoe caught the edge of the prairie-dog hole that had tripped her in the first place, and she fell down again, completely at the mercy of Cody Butler's laughing eyes.

Sitting astride his huge black mount, he looked even larger than usual, especially from Tessa's lowly position. The cutoff sleeves of his black-and-white-plaid flannel shirt bared his shoulders, powerful and packed with sinewy muscle; the sun gleamed off his smooth, bronze skin, and a red neckerchief was knotted loosely around his neck, damp with sweat. With his thumb he nudged his black, flat-crowned hat off his forehead and squinted down at her.

"Every time I see you, Miss Amesbury, you're falling over something." Cody's lazy glance flicked over her and he drawled, "Next thing you know you'll be falling over me."

Tessa scrambled to her feet, her face so pink it looked sunburned. "It is unlikely I'd be that clumsy, Mr. Butler!"

Unperturbed, Cody unknotted the bandanna from around his sturdy neck, lifted his hat, and drew the bandanna across his forehead. "I'm willing to wait and see."

His softly uttered words made shivery tingles run over her skin. As he stuffed the bandanna into his back pocket she glanced to his hair, somehow irresistibly stirred by the imprint of his hat on those damp black locks.

As she watched his smiling eyes leisurely rove over her, what little amount of feminine vanity Tessa possessed suddenly surfaced. She was uncomfortably aware of her damp dress sticking to her skin, of her straggling hair clinging to her sweaty neck. But Cody kept on looking. Her tolerance and patience were evaporating fast.

"Do not look at me that way!" she bit off tightly.

Cody frowned. "What way?" His eyes flicked to her breasts, trying to see more of them beneath her simple brown bodice.

"That way!" Tessa spat.

Cody chuckled, liking her temper. "I can't help it, Miss Amesbury. You're the sweetest thing I've seen this side of the Mississippi."

Tessa stopped in the motion of plucking bits of grass from her straggling hair. She lifted her chin at him and there was pure censure written in her eyes. "Oh, I doubt that, Mr. Butler!"

"What the hell does that mean?"

Tessa reached for a hairpin dangling from her lopsided bun. "Oh, I think you know very well what it means." He waited, leaning one arm across the pommel of his saddle. "I saw you coming out of a—a brothel last Saturday with a woman on your arm. You seemed much taken with her."

Cody's lips quirked with humor. She must have meant Lily. He chuckled low. "Saw that, did you?"

"Yes. Don't try to deny it."

Cody lifted a brow at her. "Hell, why would I try to deny it? I like Lily."

"Yes." She smiled coldly. "I'm sure you do." She tucked her hair up into the bun but it was still a mess. "It doesn't surprise me that a man like you frequents houses of prostitution."

The flash of white teeth in his wind-burned face startled Tessa. "Perhaps I like a decent woman every now and then too," he drawled, and let his eyes wander suggestively over her. "Like a schoolmarm."

Tessa straightened abruptly, scandalized. Before she realized what she was saying, she responded. "I know of one schoolmarm who would rather wallow with pigs in mud than be subject to your depravity!"

A healthy laugh burst from him and the rich sound of it filled the air with such vibrant life that something grabbed Tessa's stomach muscles. "How do you know? You've had no source of comparison yet."

Tessa's heart jumped in her throat. Yet? But before she could force herself to move, Cody had swung down off his horse. He started toward her in a long, lazy stride, the firm muscles of his thighs pressing against his snug-fitting jeans. As he advanced a slow, provocative smile crept up one side of his mouth, and his compelling eyes told her of his intent. A tremor of alarm darted up Tessa's spine.

"I've got to get back," she muttered, and adroitly sidestepped. But just as she started to speed up Cody caught her by the shoulders and swung her around. He was laughing at her, but there was no mistaking the intensity in his green eyes. He lowered his head to kiss her, but Tessa turned her face sharply aside and he missed. She pushed at his broad chest, but because his shirt was unbuttoned almost to his abdomen, Tessa's palm pressed bare flesh, hard muscle, and crisp hair. To touch him so intimately was shocking, and Tessa momentarily froze. Cody used the fleeting moment to get a firmer grip on her slender upper arms. He hauled her up close, one broad hand releasing her arm to cup the back of her head, controlling her even as she continued pushing at his shoulders.

"No—" But his warm mouth snuffed the denial from her lips. Tessa made a small, surprised sound as Cody pushed his tongue insistently into her mouth, delving deep, filling its warmth and sweetness with lusty, compelling strokes. Tessa's stomach pitched, her senses reeled, and she was hardly aware that her hands ceased battling him; they now circled his wide, strapping shoulders, her fingertips absorbing his sweat.

Cody groaned and slid his hands up her back, pulling her up flush against his hard, warm body. The pressure of his hands on her shoulder blades crushed her breasts to his thundering chest, and lower down, Tessa could feel his hard want leaning into her. Cody made another gruff sound, his tongue dancing against hers in a hot, demanding rhythm. With each probing thrust of his tongue Tessa felt a queer flutter deep in her belly, and a liquid, sizzling heat seemed to simmer in the most intimate, feminine part of her. It was so *good*. She felt she was swimming in a sea of sensation. No one had ever kissed her this way. She hadn't enjoyed it in the least with William—

Wildly Tessa tore her lips from Cody's and jerked out of his arms. Panting, she lurched away from him, pressing her fingertips to her swollen, well-kissed mouth. She heard his muttered curse, his labored, ragged breathing. And she turned on him like a dervish, the

gold specks in her dark eyes flashing at him.
"Lecher!" she choked, wishing she could
spew the taste of his kiss from her mouth. He
stood there frowning, hands resting on his
hips. "You take anyone—anything—any*time*
you please—is that it, Mr. Butler?" Tessa
fought for control but her heart was beating
desperately fast.

One hand went up to rake through his hair.
"Call me Cody!" he snapped, his voice tight
with frustration.

"I'll call you anything I darn well please!"
Tessa snapped back. "Especially after that
little display!"

Cody stood there rubbing his jaw, considering her. "Hell, and I thought you liked it. I
could swear you kissed me back. That was *you*
kissing me back, wasn't it, Miss Amesbury?
You mad at me or yourself?"

She looked as if someone had slapped her.
Her mouth opened but no words came out of
it. Cody wanted to laugh but he didn't. His
eyes roved over her standing there in that
ripe grass and hot wind, fists clenched into
small balls on her slender hips, showing him
more spunk than he had ever witnessed in
any woman. There was a certain luster to her
golden skin, and the pink flush in her cheeks
matched the color of her generous mouth.
She was looking better and better to him all
the time. He rubbed his jaw, suddenly
grinning. "You looked much primmer and
much more proper that first day you set foot

in town, Miss Amesbury. Why's that, I wonder?"

Tessa's heart stood still. She hardly dared to draw breath, yet alarm and fear were coursing wildly through her. She *wanted* everyone to believe she was a prim schoolteacher—nothing else—but Cody Butler happened upon her at all the wrong, unfortunate moments. He'd caught her with her guard down too many times, and had easily provoked her temper. Suddenly it became very important to Tessa for him to believe she was prim too. She drew herself up, coolly smoothed her palms over her mussed hair, and dropped her eyes.

"Don't."

Her startled eyes jumped to his.

"You're much too lovely to pretend you're not."

Oh, God! Again her eyes skittered away from his.

"Why are you hiding those eyes?"

"I'm not."

"You are. And you shouldn't. You have the most arresting eyes I've ever seen in a woman. They could make a man forget everything."

She had known that already. Men had been telling her that since she was fourteen. One had told her that her eyes sent out an invitation. But Tessa didn't want that kind of power. She had been taught that a pretty woman caused trouble, was bad, and that a plain woman was somehow virtuous. And at twenty-three there was a part of her that still believed it.

Now, with Cody standing there looking like he might try to kiss her again, Tessa jerked as if seared by a branding iron.

"Lavish your compliments on Lily, Mr. Butler. I'm not interested in them—or in you." And with that she stalked off, his short laugh of disbelief ringing in her ears.

"Why, you little chit—" His steely arm caught her around her waist and hauled her back against his side. Helplessly she clung to his muscular forearms, her heels dragging in the grass as Cody strode with her toward his horse. Could the man possibly humiliate her more than *this?*

"Let me go!" Tessa wiggled uselessly. "What are you doing?"

He stopped by his horse and abruptly released her. It was all Tessa could do to keep herself from sprawling at his feet again. She clung to his plaid shirtfront and hung tight. His wide hand beneath her elbow steadied her, but he was smiling crookedly down at her. "I'd love to oblige you, Miss Amesbury, but your pupils are going to be wondering what happened to their teacher."

She leaped back as if he'd burned her.

"Get up there on the horse," he ordered.

"No." And she turned toward the schoolhouse once more. Again, his broad hands circled her waist and he lifted her easily. She struggled, trying to kick him, but his wide, masculine hands pushed her high, settling her onto the horse. Outraged, Tessa swatted at his head, missed, and knocked his hat off the pommel of his saddle where he'd left it. Cody swore at the nervous movement of the horse. He gentled the animal, then cast Tessa a warning glare before bending to retrieve his hat. He straightened, slapped it against his hard thigh, and eyed her coldly as he settled the hat on his head. Tessa tossed her own head.

"Don't move," Cody warned. She met his commanding green eyes in his deeply tanned face and knew he meant it.

He swung up behind her, the saddle creaking under his weight as he adjusted himself. She wanted to die, positioned this way between his hard thighs. She glanced to the reins trailing through Cody's lean brown fingers and wondered what he waited for.

"Well?" His low voice by her ear made her jump.

"Well, what?" she snapped, impatient now to return to the school. She missed the hint of laughter in Cody's eyes.

"Is it pigs or is it me?"

The utter absurdity of the question caught her off guard. When it hit her, Tessa nearly clapped her hand over her mouth to keep from laughing aloud. Her shoulders shook with silent laughter.

"Pigs it is, huh?" he muttered wryly, and Tessa let out an irrepressible giggle this time. Cody smiled and nudged the horse in the direction of the schoolhouse, and slipped his arm around her narrow waist, keeping her steady. Tessa stiffened and tried to hold herself carefully away from him, ignoring his knowing chuckle.

But after a few moments of riding with the breeze against her face, cooling her flesh, and the movement of the horse beneath her, Tessa relaxed in the saddle. It had been a long time since she'd ridden and she felt a freedom and unwinding inside her as they rode now.

The smell of horse, sweat, and man swirled around her, making her feel giddy. Her glance dropped to Cody's hands and she studied them silently. They were big, square, masculine hands, and the way his long thumb caressed the reins roused a queer, light feeling low in her belly. Her eyes moved to the horse's gently blowing black mane and she was reminded of Cody's equally black hair. The sleek muscles rippling beneath her brought to mind the same rippling of muscles she'd felt in Cody's broad, sweat-shiny shoulders as he'd kissed her. And his kiss . . . she was horrified to realize she *had* kissed him back, and was angrier with herself than with him.

It took great effort for her to keep from sliding into him, against his crotch. Heat stole up her cheeks as she accidentally nudged him there. And worse, she had to fight the impulse to lean her head back against his hard, smooth shoulder.

"You like to ride, Miss Amesbury?" His

deep voice once again startled her. But she couldn't hide her pleasure. "Yes, I do." She reached a hand to stroke the horse's flowing mane. "He's beautiful."

"That he is." And there was unmistakable pride in Cody's voice.

Tessa's teeth pulled at her bottom lip; her forced proximity to this man was making her jittery. "Did you ever get that lab mopped up?"

She felt him tense behind her. He was obviously still touchy about that!

"Was the doctor mad?" she ventured, not wanting to persist but still feeling somewhat responsible for it all.

"Yup," came his terse reply.

"I've been meaning to get up there and explain to the doctor what happened. I'd like to tell him I intend to pay for the damages I caused." Although, she thought with a sudden surge of anger, *he* should pay for half. He'd nearly scared her half to death that day with his shouting and blusterings! But she didn't want to start *that* again.

"I'll tell him."

Had she heard a trace of amusement under-lying his voice?

Tessa hesitated, knowing she had to ask. "Where's my hat?" But what she really wanted to know was why he hadn't returned it to her by now. Out of common courtesy he should have.

"What hat?"

Tessa pressed her lips tightly together. He knew what hat! "The hat I left in the lab that day."

"I don't know what you're talking about." But he did. He'd found it one night and picked it up, thinking of her beneath it. It distracted him so he'd flung it aside and forgotten about it.

"Well, it's there," she said stiffly. "And I'd like it back."

"Well, tell me what it looks like."

Exasperated, Tessa snapped at him. "How many women's hats could *be* in the lab, Mr. Butler!" His laughter annoyed her. "It's straw and has a broad brim—"

"Oh, *that* hat!" His mocking voice told her that he knew all along what she'd been talking about. "The hat that hides your face."

She blushed hotly.

"And you want me to return it to you?" he questioned, as if this was utterly impossible.

"Why not?"

"Because it hides your eyes, Miss Amesbury. And you know how I feel about that."

A quiver of excitement ran through her at his nearly caressing words. But she'd had enough of his teasing, and she did want her hat. "I want it back," she said tightly, and silently breathed relief when the back of the schoolhouse came into sight.

Tessa's eyes made a quick scan of the schoolyard and saw nothing amiss; the children were still playing ball, the older girls were still clustered in their little group and little Tommy Alcott was coming out of the privy hoisting his red suspenders over his thin shoulders. Tessa and Cody chuckled together.

She suddenly wondered what she would tell the children; she'd run off after the stolen book and come back with Cody Butler.

"Think they'll forgive their teacher for leaving them high and dry?" Cody murmured with a smile in his voice. "It's probably been the longest recess they'll ever have."

A slight frown pulled at Tessa's brow. "I don't know. I told Sam I'd get his book back." She got angry all over again when she thought of how much that little thief had taken from her classroom.

"Aha. So that's why you were tearing after little Smoke Eyes as if the demons of hell were on your tail." Cody laughed when she stiffened, irked at his choice of words.

"Little Smoke Eyes?" she repeated blankly.

Cody halted the horse alongside the schoolhouse, just in sight of the baseball game. None of the children seemed to notice them. He slid off the horse and reached up to assist Tessa down. His wide hands circling her narrow waist made her heart beat doubletime. He placed her before him, his hands lingering on her waist. "There's nothing to you, you know that?"

Tessa smacked his hands away. Cody just laughed and rested his hands on his hips, squinting against the sun glare to look down at her. Once again Tessa noticed those dark blue glints in his green eyes.

"Little Smoke Eyes," he explained, "lives with her Arapaho grandfather about two miles from here in a shanty."

"That child I was chasing was a girl?" Tessa could hardly believe it.

"That's right. Her mother and father died of typhoid fever two years ago. He was an Irishman from the East, she was Arapaho. Smoke Eyes, I understand, is interested in medicine. She'd like to practice it someday, but she's too stubborn to attend school. It's my guess she's trying to teach herself."

"With stolen materials."

"Well, her grandfather is too old to pay much attention to her wild ways. She's a bright girl, but she's nearly thirteen now and runs free too much."

"But none of this is excuse enough to take other children's materials," Tessa said sternly, as if *he* were excusing the child. "It's not right that three of my students are going without. Their fathers paid money for those materials. If she'd come to school I'd be glad to teach her."

Cody's eyes took in Tessa's tipped-up face. It was true what he'd said about those eyes of hers—they were drawing him in now, captivating him with their black, measureless depths. "She won't come into school. She knows what some kids say about Indians and she doesn't think it's worth the trouble. But if you want to talk to her about the stuff she took, I can ride you out there on Sunday afternoon."

Tessa dropped her eyes to his chest, considering. She really didn't want to ride anywhere with him again, but it might be her only chance to retrieve the materials—especially considering how fast the child could run. Besides, she had no idea where this Smoke Eyes lived. Above all, Tessa felt a sudden compulsion to teach this child.

Tessa raised her eyes to Cody's. "It depends," she said, a hint of sparkle in her cocoa eyes.

"On what?"

"On whether you bring my hat with you when you come by."

He laughed openly, those white teeth so startling in his dark, handsome face. The smile lingered in his eyes. "I guess it's a deal then. I'll come by around three o'clock." He swung up on his horse and wheeled it around, leaving Tessa standing in the dust wondering why on earth she had ever agreed to go anywhere with that man.

Hundreds of miles east in a train depot in Philadelphia a middle-aged man with gray side-whiskers pushed a photograph of a dark-eyed woman across the counter of the ticket window.

"Seen her?"

The ticket agent peered close, then shook

his balding head. The side-whiskered man pursed his lips and reached inside his waistcoat pocket, producing a bill. This, too, he slid across the counter. The ticket agent quickly swept it up.

"I still ain't seen her," he vowed.

The side-whiskered man was losing his patience. He leaned closer, his steely-gray eyes boring into the agent's wide blue ones, looking owlish behind his spectacles. "She would have been here maybe a month or so back. Think."

The ticket agent thought. He peered once again at the dark-eyed woman and shook his head. "No," he said slowly, cautiously. "I sure haven't seen her. But you might want to ask the conductor out there on the platform."

The other sighed, frustrated. He'd been looking for this woman since William Forsythe had hired him three weeks back. Once he thought he'd had her but it proved to be a false lead. She had no kin and more than likely had stayed in the East. Forsythe was paying him daily so he was in no rush, but Forsythe sure as hell was.

The investigator slid a card with his name and address printed on it to the ticket agent. "If you see her or hear about her, contact me, please."

The agent nodded and tucked the card inside his vest pocket along with the bill. He watched the investigator amble out to the conductor, watched the conductor shake his head. The agent frowned. What did the man think? That he studied every face that walked in here? Though he had to admit that the photograph of the wench had intrigued him. He might not forget a face like that after all.

The conductor hadn't seen her either. The side-whiskered man ran a hand through his curly gray hair and shook his head, staring down at the photograph that seemed imprinted on his mind. Maybe she'd gone west after all. But where in the West? There was California, Texas, all of the Midwest. It would be a tedious, nearly impossible task trying to locate her. But he'd never traveled west and he was being paid handsomely. It might be a welcome change after all.

The man glanced up at the conductor, who was watching him closely. "If you see her," the investigator told him, "you know where to contact me. Oh, and she will more than likely be using the name Miss Tessa Amesbury."

The first week was over, and on Saturday afternoon Tessa and Mrs. Rawlins walked to the general store to purchase a few items.

"Eb Taylor is a good friend of mine," Mrs. Rawlins explained as she held tight to Tessa's arm, urging her to slow a bit. Tessa did, hiding a smile as Mrs. Rawlins's cheeks colored. "Eb and his only son run the store. Eb's been a widower for thirty-three years. He raised his boy on his own."

"Is Eb one of those guests you sometimes informally entertain?" Tessa teased gently.

Mrs. Rawlins laughed lightly, but her color deepened. "Yes, he is. And sometimes," she confessed, "we go to the Saturday-night social together."

"Oh? And do you engage in such risqué activities as dancing?"

"Yes we do!" Mrs. Rawlins laughed again. "And sometimes," she confided, lowering her voice in a conspiratorial whisper, "we'll sneak a snifter of brandy before we arrive, since liquor is limited at the socials!"

"For shame, Mrs. Rawlins! I'm shocked!"

They were nearly falling on one another, laughing like schoolgirls, as Tessa pulled open the door to Eb's general store. A little bell tinkled above them and the two giggling women stepped over the threshold. As their eyes adjusted to the dimness, good, rich smells of freshly ground coffee and spices and tangy cheeses and new leather curled invitingly around them. The murmur of men's voices drifted over to them and Tessa glanced to them sitting by the unlit potbellied stove. A couple of them reached into the open cracker barrel, sat back, and munched on crisp crackers, resuming their conversation with full mouths.

Tessa's eyes flitted from them to the long counter at her right laden with dry goods such as hats and books, playing cards, music boxes.

The shelves behind the counter were crammed with hat boxes and toiletries, shoes and bolts of cloth, and more. The rear of the store held tools and hardware and the counter on Tessa's right was for groceries and kitchenware. The shelves behind that long counter were also stocked with goods—shiny cooking pots and pans, canned goods and spices. On the floor were kegs and barrels stocked with molasses and pickles and sugar, and the wooden pails on the counter were brimming with colorful candies.

"My goodness," Tessa breathed, astonished by the variety of merchandise Eb carried. And just then the old man standing behind the counter caught sight of Mrs. Rawlins.

"Hey there, Audrey!"

Mrs. Rawlins turned and blushed. "Hello, Eb. Here"—she drew Tessa forward by her elbow—"I'd like you to meet the new schoolteacher! Her name's Miss Tessa Amesbury."

"Well, how do!" Eb reached across the counter and held out a big, friendly hand. Tessa put hers lightly into it and smiled at him.

"Hello, Mr. Taylor."

"Aw, none of that now! Eb's my name."

"Well, then, you'll have to call me Tessa. You have a wonderful store here, Eb."

The white-haired man chuckled and gestured across the room to a tall, brown-haired man with a pleasant face. "Hear that, Mike? This here is my son, Mike."

Mike was every bit as friendly as his father. "It's a real pleasure to meet the schoolteacher in town!" he said, beaming. "You'll be teaching my own boy someday soon."

"I can't wait." Tessa smiled back at him. A few women hovered over bolts of cloth that Mike had spread on the counter for them. Upon hearing the introductions, they turned and insisted that Mrs. Rawlins introduce them too. In the midst of it all the door swung open and in strode Cody Butler.

All eyes turned to the tall, rugged man; his presence seemed to fill up the room. Tessa caught her breath, awash with guilt and embarrassment and a queer excitement upon seeing him. She desperately hoped he would not mention their last encounter to those present.

The townfolk greeted him and he grinned at them, walking up to the counter behind which Eb was standing, and asked for a pouch of tobacco. His eyes glanced about the room and stopped on Tessa. She stood still as a statue beside Mrs. Rawlins, and there was a faint look of pleading in her big eyes. Cody's mouth curled up at one corner and he acknowledged her with a slight nod of his dark head. Tessa offered him a tentative smile and one of the women noticed it.

"You've met Cody, haven't you, dear?" kind Mrs. Wilson asked.

Tessa watched Cody lean slightly forward, reach into his back pocket, and remove his money. "Yes," she murmured faintly as he watched her with an amused expression. Oh, we've met all right, she thought, and knew by his devilish look that he was thinking the same thing.

With his eyes still on her, Cody handed Eb the money. As he stood there with his hands on his hips, his bold stare made her feel intensely feminine and Tessa could feel her pulses thrumming with wild life. Surely, she must force herself to move, to pretend to browse through Eb's store, but Cody's intense stare held her mesmerized.

"Hey, Doc—" a bearded man called from the stove area, and at last Cody shifted his gaze. "How's that little Holmes baby you delivered yesterday? I heard tell he was a big critter."

"You heard right." Cody laughed, white teeth gleaming. "He was nine pounds."

A general exclamation swelled from the group around her as Tessa stood with obvious signs of confusion showing on her face. She couldn't possibly have heard right. Had that man just referred to Cody as "Doc"? And had Cody answered like he knew what he was talking about?

"How's Betty doing?" Mrs. Wilson asked Cody.

"Both mother and baby are healthy!" Cody grinned. His eyes flicked to Tessa, who looked like she wanted to scratch his eyes out.

"Oh, I'll have to bring some bread and goodies to her," Mrs. Wilson was saying, but Tessa barely heard past the thundering fury in her ears. *He* was the doctor whose laboratory she had nearly demolished? Oh, she wanted to die of mortification! Why had Cody hidden his identity from her? If it was to embarrass her, he had done a masterful job of it!

Tessa didn't trust herself to look at him. She touched Mrs. Rawlins's sleeve and told her she had to run an errand across the street. "I'll come back for you in fifteen minutes or so," Tessa promised, then, without looking back, marched out of the store and down the board sidewalk, past the barber shop, past Grady's Restaurant, past the dressmaking shop. She didn't know her destination, only knew she had to get out of that man's sight!

But already she could hear the clunk of boot heels behind her and knew, by the sound of that long-legged stride, that Cody was after her. What now? To humiliate her further? God, had the man no mercy?

She hastened her step, but it was all in vain, for he took one stride for every three of hers. And suddenly his wide hand slid under her elbow, slowing her but not stopping her.

"Hold on!" Cody had to struggle to keep the laughter out of his voice. "What the hell are you so upset about?"

Tessa's lips grew pinched. "I don't want to talk to you!" She jerked her arm free and kept walking, ignoring the curious glances of passersby.

"Hell, don't be angry because you made a fool of yourself when you were trespassing in the lab."

She took in a hissing breath. "Has anyone ever taught you to watch your language while in the presence of ladies? I am sick to death of hearing your filthy swear words and curses!"

"My swear words have got nothing to do with your being a lady. Nor are they the reason you're angry."

Brown eyes clashed with green. Tessa drew in a slow, deep breath, and her nostrils flared slightly. "All right, Dr. Butler," she said distinctly, "I'm angry because *you* made a fool out of me in the lab!"

Cody kept his face carefully sober, but his eyes were glinting with humor. He leaned close enough for her to smell his shaving soap. "Yes, but only you and I know that."

He looked so pleased with his little joke that Tessa wanted to take him down a notch or two. "Let me tell you something. I'm glad I ruined your little experiments and your certain *strain* of bacteria!" She remembered his words exactly. Childishly she continued, her voice rising in a most unladylike manner. "And I hope it takes you years to identify whatever it is you're trying to identify! And if I had a chance to ruin it again, I'd do it! Only this time—"

"Be quiet, you little minx!" Cody's voice shook with repressed laughter as he took a firm hold of her arm and steered her between two buildings, getting them both out of the town's view. He urged her back against the wall of the newspaper office building and kept her there, his palms flat on the wall on either side of Tessa's head. Their bodies were about a foot apart. His hard, tanned features leaned close and he chuckled, "My God, you're a tempest, you know that?"

Tessa's delicate jaw tightened. "Why didn't you tell me you were a doctor?"

"You didn't ask."

"But you had plenty of opportunities!" she insisted.

"But *you* were so all-fired bent on calling me Mr. Butler I didn't have the heart to correct you." There were warm, teasing lights in his green eyes but Tessa felt new heat flood her face. How preposterous she must have sounded!

Reading her flushed features, Cody said, "I told you to call me Cody."

Silently Tessa admitted that was true. But it just wasn't right to call him that. But she recalled everyone in that store today greeting him by his first name, except that one by the stove. "I haven't heard anyone call you Dr. Butler."

Cody shrugged. "Some do. But I'd rather be called Cody. I've known some of these folks for a long time—they come from Kentucky where I once lived."

Tessa stood quietly studying him. She supposed if she had been in town this week she might have heard a bit of news regarding Cody Butler. But as it was, she'd stayed late after school with the five truant boys, and the shortcut she took through Grady's back lot caused her to skirt the busiest area of town.

"Now that you know my full title," Cody was saying, "how about you giving me yours. I've got Miss and Amesbury. What's the rest?"

Tessa's eyes flashed up at him. "I'd eat a goat before I'd give you my first name!"

Laughter burst from him and his eyes moved warmly over her face. "Now is that the stance to take after you practically ravaged my laboratory?"

"It served you right!"

"Ah, but you promised to pay for damages."

Tessa's teeth caught her bottom lip; she was suddenly contrite. She dared a glance up into his crinkling green eyes. At the humor she saw there, her chin lifted mutinously. "But now that you've played this dirty trick on me, I've changed my mind."

Cody's body moved in closer, his elbows on either side of her head now. Their bodies were not quite touching. Tessa felt a tingling awareness prickling her skin. She saw his mouth go crooked. "I won't let you change your mind."

She felt a bit skittish. "You can't force me to pay."

His look told her to reconsider her words. Her heart beat wildly against her chest. He was too close! She could make out every tiny crease around his smiling green eyes, the firm fullness to his handsome mouth . . .

"Yesterday," she said suddenly, "when you came by in the field. You were returning from delivering a baby?" She still found it hard to believe. This man just didn't fit her image of a doctor.

Cody only grinned.

"You could've told me then," she pointed out.

"Could have. Would you have believed me?"

No, probably not.

"You have a terrible habit of jumping to conclusions," he scolded her as if she was a child. "For instance"—and he let his eyes flicker to her pretty mouth, which was parted slightly as if she couldn't quite draw in enough breath—"that day you saw me coming out of Lily's. I was there for a medical reason."

Her lifted brow expressed her doubt. "Oh, now what possible medical reason could you have for being in there?"

His mouth lifted at one corner. "Bawdy houses are often in need of regulating, Miss Amesbury."

Of course it made perfect sense. But Tessa couldn't have known that then. She remembered him outside the dance hall with Lily and her eyes narrowed accusingly at him. "But I saw her kiss you."

"Exactly. *She* kissed *me*. That's Lily's way of expressing gratitude."

Only an idiot would believe that one! "I didn't see you turn away," Tessa said with censure.

Cody's intensely suggestive look made her

flush from her scalp to her toes. "I never reject a lady's kiss. It's impolite."

"No, you wouldn't!" She wondered why on earth she was standing between two buildings discussing a man's personal habits with him. Yet, the question lingered, *how* does one become friends with a harlot?

Cody's black brows rose provocatively at her. "You better hope you don't get sick, Miss Amesbury. You'll be left entirely in my hands." His body just brushed hers.

His meaning did not escape her. A fresh wave of hot anger surged through her. "Respectable doctor or not! You have taken unforgivable liberties with me!"

"And I'm about to take more." His hard, callused palm cupped her under her chin and lifted her face gently as he leaned to capture her petal-soft mouth with his. Everything melted in Tessa as his warm tongue slipped into her mouth, seeking, coaxing, drawing her tongue into his hot mouth, then dancing it back to her own.

Sweet, hot longing washed through her as Tessa felt his fingers slide into her hair. Oh, no, she mustn't let him! Soft sounds of protest were muffled under Cody's urgent mouth. She pushed at his shoulders but Cody wouldn't have it. He plunged his tongue deeper, bold within her mouth as he deftly caught both her hands and swung them behind her back, where he locked them with his one hand. Forced into this undignified position, with her breasts jutting forward, Tessa made an outraged sound. She moved her shoulders, trying to shake free, but her breasts touched Cody's shirtfront, tantalizing him further. He groaned and caught her to him with one arm around her waist, pressing her up against his ferocious, tigerish heat.

She must stop him, she must! But his kiss was sweeping her into a hot, wild world where she seemed to have no will of her own. His masterful, stroking tongue seemed to pull her depths up and toward him, and she was trapped here between his hard body and the wall, her hands imprisoned; she felt she was drowning. . . .

Just as her little teeth caught the tip of his tongue Cody leaped back, his face as dark as a thundercloud. "You little viper! You were going to bite my tongue!"

"Darn right I was going to bite your tongue! How dare you sully my reputation right here on Main Street?" Tessa glared back at him, rubbing some life into her aching arms. She felt hot and weak all over, as if she could use a tonic.

"Maybe I am interested in you. Not your reputation," he said, his breath ragged.

Tessa pulled in a swift breath. "Oh!" What nerve! "Someone should should have bitten the end of your tongue off long ago, Mr. Butler. How dare you be so presumptuous!" She was so furious she didn't stop to think she'd once again called him *Mister* Butler. "You conceited, insufferable cur!" She went on bravely, ignoring his dark glower. "What on God's green earth makes you think I even like you? You're rude and loud and quite a bit of a bully and I—I don't like the way you kiss!" Oh, that sounded convincing all right, even though it was an outright lie. But she saw the tensing of his shoulders, the bunching of his fists at his sides. No woman had ever said that to him. And it rankled him to think that this plain little twit possessed the nerve to insult him!

Cody's eyes narrowed on her. Ah, God, but she wasn't plain! "Fine with me, Miss Amesbury. You're not much of a treat yourself."

She flinched. But she quickly regained her composure. "Does that mean you'll stay away from me?"

Cody looked like he wanted to strike something—or her, Tessa thought, and gulped. Instead he thrust his fist into his pocket. "Gladly! That is"—and he let his eyes move insultingly over her—"if you don't come tripping onto my property, or even into my arms."

"I never—" But she snapped her mouth shut at his icy stare. Perhaps she should have kept quiet about her not liking his kissing. The man had quite an ego!

Cody turned his broad back on her and headed for the dusty street. But they were both thinking about that wagon drive over to Smoke Eyes' place tomorrow.

Will he come by for me?

Does she want me to come by?

And when he was gone Tessa leaned back against the wall. She closed her eyes a moment and thought of his kiss. She thought of its power and of Cody's. And she thought of how right she had been to fight it, to repel Cody's advances. For she was a married woman. Yes, she had withheld her real title from him too—and from the citizens of Harper City. Her legal name was Mrs. William Forsythe, not Tessa Amesbury.

Chapter Four

✦ ✦ ✦ ✦

TESSA SAT ON the porch swing with an open book on her lap, not reading. The soles of her sensible black shoes gently pressed off the floor, idly nudging the swing back and forth. Its rhythmic movement coupled with the creak of the swing ropes seemed to hypnotize her; she stared unseeingly at the words on the page before her.

Her eyes drifted to the edge of the porch, noting the strip of late-afternoon sunlight waning there. It was after four o'clock now and obvious Cody was not coming by to drive her to Smoke Eyes' claim. Tessa had been sitting here since before three o'clock wondering if he'd come, wondering if she wanted him to come. But, after all, what could she expect after their confrontation yesterday?

She dropped her head back and stared up at the rafters, swinging idly. She was so tired; she hadn't slept well last night. Images of William had started to keep her awake too often. William Forsythe, her husband. It was hard to think of him as that; she'd lived with the man less than an entire night. And in that night their marriage had not been consummated. But other acts had been performed and Tessa shuddered now to think of them.

She didn't feel married; she still thought of herself as Miss Tessa Amesbury. But the fact remained, she *was* married, and if anyone in the town learned this, or if Cody learned this, they'd send her packing, just as Cody had once threatened to do. And Tessa's spirit recoiled at the thought. She could never go back to William. She'd fled to Harper City to be rid of William, and to start a new life of her own. That life would be the quiet and proper life of a schoolmarm; the life she'd lived at the orphanage before marrying William.

But those plans changed the instant she'd met Cody Butler.

Cody. Just thinking of him now made her stomach tighten and her skin prickle. She remembered the way he had looked out on the prairie last week, all sinew and sweat. She recalled the feel of his hard body pressed to the length of hers, the way he'd kissed her, those unwanted sensations he'd aroused in her. . . .

Tessa bolted upright, furious with herself. She had no business remembering any of those things! Remember how he insulted you, Tessa, if you are going to remember anything! she thought. He took great pleasure in criticizing her appearance, her demeanor, even her reputation! To him, she was just another conquest. And she could not afford to be anyone's conquest, even if she wanted to be.

Cody Butler was rude and overbearing and utterly annoying. But, oh, could he kiss! And how it angered Tessa that he could make her react to those practiced kisses!

She closed her eyes and massaged her throbbing temples. Why couldn't she get that man out of her mind? All day—in church, and later, after the noonday meal as she set her lessons in order for the week—his handsome image lurked at the back of her mind, and sometimes sprang right into it! It mingled with William's image until she had developed a mind-reading headache and had to retire to the porch while Mrs. Rawlins napped in her bedroom.

Just as Tessa shut her book with a sigh she thought she might go into the kitchen to prepare a light supper for herself and Mrs. Rawlins. But the nickering of a horse and the creaking of wagon springs made her look up, and sure enough, there was Cody Butler driving toward her. Tessa felt a sudden leap in her stomach; annoyed with herself for feeling it, she quickly opened her book and pretended to read it. She appeared unduly interested in its contents, acting as if she hadn't been waiting for him. But as she heard the wagon come closer Tessa's fingers gripped the book and her mind did not absorb one word of what she read.

He drew up alongside the porch and demanded, "Why don't you get your nose out of that book you're pretending to read and get down here so we can get a move on, Teacher."

Tessa stiffened, feeling the hot blood singe her face. Oh! He was so thoroughly annoying! She ground her teeth and warned herself, *Don't* let him get your blood boiling. Stay calm.

Coolly Tessa closed her book and placed it beside her on the swing, and lifting her chin, she leveled him an icy stare. That stare soon turned into a glower when she saw that he hadn't bothered to shave.

"What are you scowling about?" he snapped. "I'm here, aren't I?"

"You're more than an hour late," she pointed out acidly.

"Well, get in, woman!" he ordered, wearing a surly expression. "I haven't got all day!"

Silently she seethed. He wasn't even going to help her up! Well, that suited Tessa fine! She'd be glad not to have to touch him! She stood and smoothed her skirts. "It appears, Dr. Butler, that you are the one scowling." She edged closer to the wagon and caught his gaze raking over her; now he wore a look of pure disgust on his face.

"What are you dressed in *that* for?" He said "that" as if she wore a gunnysack.

Tessa glanced down at herself. She wondered what he could possibly find fault with in this dark dress she saved for Sundays. She rather liked the lace edging around the collar and cuffs. She looked up, meeting his frowning eyes. "This is my Sunday dress. I never change my dress after church."

Cody snorted his disgust. "That's the ugliest goddamn getup I've seen since my grandma's funeral! She was buried in a dress just like that." Then why in hell did she look so appealing to him? There was something of a sprite about her, even as she stood there with her pretty mouth pinched up that way and her eyes spitting fire at him as she tried to maintain her poise and dignity. A peachy glow flushed up from the surface of her golden skin and he caught the gold strands threaded through her honey hair. But it was the angry gold sparks in her dark eyes that grabbed his attention now.

"At least I don't dress like that harlot you see!" she spat.

"I told you I don't see—aw, what am I explaining to *you* for?" He glared ferociously at her.

Tessa smiled smugly at him. "Darned if I know, Dr. Butler."

"Well, get up here, dammit!"

Tessa gave a little flounce of her skirts and

lifted her nose. "I don't think I'll go with you after all, Dr. Butler. I'll find another means to get out to that claim, and it won't be with a surly, snarling, badmouthed lout!"

But before she completely turned her back on him, his icy voice stopped her. "Get in the wagon."

Tessa pressed her lips tight and braved a glance up at his rigid features. The uncompromising set to his hard jaw told her that he would climb down, pick her up bodily, and toss her in the wagon if he must.

"Now!"

And she jumped as if he'd uncoiled a biting bullwhip across her naked back.

Just as she grabbed hold of the wagon to hoist herself up, Tessa was delighted to catch sight of her straw hat there beside him on the seat. When she lifted her gaze to his face to thank him for it, Cody's scowl grew darker. She knew she had better not waste another moment. Daintily she picked her way up the side of the wagon while he sat stock still, not moving a muscle to assist her. Before Tessa even touched the seat, Cody impatiently flicked the reins, the horses jolted, and she nearly landed in his lap. As it was, she grasped his hard thigh for balance and her backside plunked flat on the center of her straw hat.

Cody's mouth lifted in sardonic amusement. As soon as she realized that she still gripped his muscular thigh, Tessa jerked her hand back as if she'd been bitten.

"You did that on purpose!" she hissed as Cody swerved the wagon out toward the open prairie and she gripped the edge of the seat now to steady herself. Once she'd straightened herself out, she yanked her squashed hat from under her.

Cody gave a mild shrug. "I can't help it if you trip over everything in sight."

"I'll have you know that I haven't fallen as many times in my life as I have this past week! And oddly enough, you're always in the vicinity when I do fall!"

Cody's eyes glanced sidelong at her. "Are you implying that my presence rattles you?"

"Hardly!"

The corner of his mouth curled up knowingly and he almost laughed at the way she was punching that hat back into shape. But he grimaced again as she smacked it onto her head.

"You do grab hold of me a lot," he said in his drawling voice. Tessa bit back the hot words that trembled on the tip of her tongue, refusing to rise to the bait. From the instant he'd driven up he had managed to set her temper aflame.

She drew in a deep breath and tried to calm herself. Cody must have sensed the wisdom in her silence for he tightened his lips too. Tessa let her gaze wander over the rippling grasses stretching away to where the sky seemed to touch the land. She felt dwarfed by the wide, vast country, a tiny figure in the slow, creaking wagon that jogged over the rough wagon track. Cody's knee bumped hers and he straightened to avoid touching her again. Tessa's eyes slid back to study him from under her long lashes. He sat hunched forward now, his wrists hanging slack between his knees, reins trailing through his lean, brown fingers. Sunlight glinted off the hairs shading his wrists and forearms, and as Tessa noted it, something stirred in her. Her gaze skipped up to his jet-black hair curling up thick over his pale blue collar. She forced her eyes to look away.

Still, she was keenly aware of him beside her on that seat. There was always a smell of worn leather about him, and that smell teased her nostrils now. Beneath his deceptively lax pose Tessa could sense the brimming energy in him and it struck her just how much energy this man possessed. It took formidable drive to do carpentry work, practice medicine in town and the surrounding countryside, and maintain a social life. Tessa frowned, disturbed that she'd found something to admire in Cody Butler.

They rode past a shanty where a child straightened from his play and waved to them. It was too far off to identify the child but both Tessa and Cody lifted a hand and waved back. Tessa wanted to ask Cody whose claim it was but she didn't open her mouth. It seemed every time she did he'd fling back a nasty retort.

Cody relaxed back again as they drove on, the long dry grass rustling against the wagon wheels. Tessa burned to ply him with questions—wanting to learn more of Smoke Eyes, of Cody's practice and what brought him to Harper City, of the older boys who would be coming to school in late autumn. But she kept silent.

Cody's eyes slid sidelong over her and a smile tugged at his mouth as his gaze passed over her slightly battered hat. She sat stiff as a corpse, her slender hands knotted into fists on her lap, exercising great control over her temper. He tried to hide his smile but she caught it. Their eyes connected, then each of them looked sharply away. Cody scowled again and Tessa pinched her mouth tight, and luckily the crude tar paper shack they'd come to visit was in sight.

The shack was tiny, its roof sloping to one side, but there were no signs of the squalor Tessa had expected from the looks of the child living there. Tessa's eyes searched for Smoke Eyes, but she was nowhere to be seen. An old man with plaited silver hair was bent over the vegetable garden at the side of the shanty.

Cody halted the wagon in front of the house and tied the reins around the brake handle. With a lazy grace that surprised Tessa, he swung down from the wagon and stood for a moment with his hands on his hips, squinting over at the old man. Not waiting for him to snub her with his lack of manners a second time, Tessa grabbed hold and boosted herself from the wagon, landing lightly on her feet. She caught his raised brow, as if he couldn't quite believe what he just saw, and Tessa gave him a lofty smile. Ha! She didn't trip *that* time!

It was then that they both focused on a brown flash tearing from the back of the house. Before Tessa could even open her mouth Cody was in hot pursuit. Tessa followed him around the side of the shack and stood not too far from the old Arapaho man who continued working as if all of this was nothing out of the ordinary.

Cody had already caught up with Smoke Eyes and scooped her up, hooking her over one muscular forearm. Carrying her this way, he crossed in long strides toward Tessa, his lips compressed as Smoke Eyes wriggled and kicked at him helplessly. Cody tightened his arm to subdue her, but his attempt earned him an even fiercer struggle and Smoke Eyes released a spate of words Tessa could not understand. Tessa was grateful now for Cody's company; she could never have handled this little spitfire by herself.

He set the girl down firmly before Tessa, but the moment Smoke Eyes' moccasined feet touched earth she was off like a shot, only to find herself running in air, snared once again by Cody's strong arm.

"Hey, you ornery little cuss! It's me, remember?" Cody shook her.

"Yeah, an' yer with her!" Smoke Eyes jerked her head at Tessa, who stood with her knuckles pressed to her half-open mouth, her wide eyes watching them with dismay.

"That's right, I'm with her. And we both know the reason for that, don't we?"

In rebellious response the girl wriggled again, but her efforts were futile and she dangled uselessly in midair. "Let me go!"

"The hell I will," Cody muttered, and Tessa bit her lip, resisting the urge to tell him to temper his tongue in the girl's presence. "And you better stay put when I set you down again," he warned, "or I won't let you come up to the lab anymore and watch me."

Miraculously the girl stilled.

"Been a while, hasn't it, Smoke Eyes?"

The girl hung her unkempt head.

Cody released her and stepped back. He stood with his hands on his hips, examining her dust-streaked face, her dirty matted hair, her torn buckskin clothing. He shook his head, exasperated all over again. "Damn you, Smoke Eyes, when are you ever gonna clean up yourself?"

Smoke Eyes stuck out her jaw at him and hitched up her leggings. "Soon as you clean up your mouth, Doc."

Tessa smothered her laughter behind her hands but Cody looked up with a warning glare, and Tessa quickly sobered, though her eyes were dancing at him.

"A man's got his hands full with the both of you," he muttered, and for some odd reason that Tessa couldn't fathom, a ribbon of warmth unfurled within her at his words.

Cody laid his hand on Smoke Eyes' shoulder and his eyes went to Tessa's again. "Miss Amesbury, this here's Smoke Eyes. Her pa named her Katherine but she might bite you if you call her that. Maybe"—and his mouth twisted wryly now—"you can teach her some respect." He nudged Smoke Eyes. "Say hello, Smoke Eyes."

The girl kept her head lowered; Tessa had yet to see her face. "Hullo."

Tessa found her mouth dry when she opened it to speak. "Hello . . ." She hesitated, her eyes glancing up to Cody's. "Smoke Eyes."

"I'm going to go talk to your grandfather," Cody was saying. "You're to stay here and listen to what the teacher says, understand?"

Sullenly Smoke Eyes nodded.

Cody glanced up and met Tessa's gaze. "She's all yours." And he left them both to go talk to the grandfather who had worked his way farther down the row. Tessa watched Cody walk off, then she returned her gaze to the child who stood with head bent, her moccasined toe drawing patterns in the dirt. It was hard to tell what color the girl's hair was, it was so dirty, but Tessa could make out the reddish glints and she recalled that Smoke Eyes' father had been Irish.

"Well . . ." She sighed and clasped her hands before her, suddenly at a loss for words. She glanced toward Cody, who was occupied talking with the old man. She forced her gaze back to the girl and smiled secretly at her stubbornness. "You could look at me at least, Smoke Eyes."

Slowly, hesitantly, the child lifted her gaze. Tessa nearly grimaced at the dirt on the girl's face, but she kept her features expressionless. Sure enough, in that dirty face were eyes huge and round and unblinking—gray as smoke.

"How old are you, Smoke Eyes?"

The girl's eyes glanced askance at Cody. "Thirteen," she answered shortly.

Why, she looked no more than eleven! Again, Tessa hid her reaction. "Certainly old enough to know how wrong it is to take someone's belongings and keep them for your own."

"Ya mean stealin'."

"That's right. Stealing."

Smoke Eyes' jaw tightened. "You accusin' me o' that? Stealin'?"

Tessa stared her down. "Why did you take them, Smoke Eyes?"

"Did I say I took 'em?"

"There're some boys in my class who want those things back desperately."

Smoke Eyes puffed up her chest. "Yeah, well, I can whup any of 'em boys! With one hand tied behind my back!"

"I'm sure you can. But we're not talking about whipping any boys, are we?"

"I am."

"Well, you shouldn't want to whip any boys. What would your mother say if she saw her daughter so wild and belligerent?"

Smoke Eyes doubled up her fists and moved in, snarling, "You leave my ma outta this! An' my pa too!"

Without thinking, Tessa jumped back. Dear God, she hadn't meant to bring them into this at all! "All right," she said calmly, "let's talk about those missing materials from my classroom."

"Ya mean the books and slate I took?"

Tessa blinked, wondering if she had heard correctly. Did the child just admit what she had been vehemently denying not a minute ago? "Yes," she said cautiously.

"Well, I got them in the house. I'll go get 'em."

Not trusting her, Tessa stopped her in midstride. "Ah, Smoke Eyes—"

The girl smirked. "Don't worry. I won't go anywhere with him"—and she jerked her head at Cody—"here. He'd tan my hide if I took off again." She dashed into the shanty and Tessa stood awkwardly, wondering why it had become so easy all of a sudden. She wanted to talk to the child, convince her to come to school. Despite herself, she felt sorry for the girl. How lonely she must feel out here with only an old man for company!

Without realizing it, her gaze had drifted to Cody, whose tall, muscular frame was etched in shadow by the lowering sun behind him. He, too, was studying her, almost absently, and Tessa sensed he'd been contemplating her for some time. He cast her a brief, lopsided grin, and flustered, Tessa turned her eyes away from him, glad to see Smoke Eyes coming out of the shanty.

The girl thrust the books and slate at Tessa.

"I think," Tessa said, "we both know why you took them, Smoke Eyes." She paused, her eyes going over the glowering young face. "I understand you'd like to practice medicine someday."

Her chin nudged upward. "So?"

"Well, how are you going to study it if you can't read?"

Smoke Eyes scowled darkly. "Who says I can't read?"

Tessa ignored that. "I can teach you."

"I don't wanna learn."

"I don't believe you. You wouldn't have stolen these books if you didn't want to learn. Are you afraid to come in?"

"Hah!"

And Tessa knew she was. "I won't let the children bother you."

Smoke Eyes' gaze raked insultingly over Tessa. "*You* can't stop nobody! Besides, I ain't afraid of nuthin' an' nobody!"

"I can see your language needs working on. Your use of double negatives is atrocious."

Smoke Eyes screwed up her dirty little face.

"Oh," Tessa said lightly, catching sight of Cody coming toward them, "if you change your mind, school opens at nine o'clock and you must come clean. I will not allow such an untidy student into my classroom."

"I ain't gonna change my mind! I ain't never gonna come into school!"

Tessa rolled her eyes, and Cody, now beside her, caught her expression. He leaned and chuckled low by her ear. "She won you over I can see."

Tessa gave him an exasperated look and Smoke Eyes jabbed a finger at him. "Thanks fer bringin' her, Doc! Yer a traitor, yer are!"

Cody rubbed his stubbled jaw and flicked his eyes from Smoke Eyes to Tessa. "I can see you were able to teach her some respect too," he muttered. He lowered his brows at Smoke Eyes. "Don't point that grimy finger at me, little one, or I'll blister your backside good."

Immediately Smoke Eyes retracted her finger. She scuffed her moccasined foot at him. "Aw, you don't scare me. I'm too old to spank."

Cody lifted a brow at her. "Don't press your luck, Smoke Eyes. Besides," he drawled for good measure, "a woman's never too old to spank." He heard Tessa's indignant indrawn breath, and when she turned to glare at him, his amused eyes bored meaningfully into hers. But he turned his attention back to Smoke Eyes. "I'll be back to visit you later this week. Take a bath or I won't bring you back to the lab." He hid his amusement when the girl stuck out her lower lip. "Now go on. Go help your grandfather."

The girl scampered off and Cody's eyes returned to Tessa's. "Ready?"

Tessa nodded, but called past him. "Remember, Smoke Eyes—nine o'clock."

"I ain't comin'!"

Cody laughed softly and Tessa let out a frustrated sigh. They started for the wagon, and when they'd come alongside of it, Cody offered her a hand up. She could see that he'd done it without thinking, that it had been a natural courtesy with him. And it surprised her indeed that someone had taught him some manners.

Long lavender shadows followed them home and the evening air began to cool. There was an almost companionable silence between Tessa and Cody now as the wagon jogged on and the wind crooned softly through the long tangle of grasses. They'd traveled almost a mile when Cody glanced sidelong at her profile, half in shadow under the brim of that straw hat. A corner of her mouth tipped up and Tessa cast him a curious glance of her own.

"You know," he said, cocking his head to one side, "that hat becomes you more than I give it credit for. There's something saucy about it, and"—his eyes flickered to her mouth, then met her dark eyes again—"about you."

Only the slight puckering of her brows gave him an indication that she'd heard him. She glanced out to the horizon again, biting the inside of her cheek. Cody frowned, surprised she hadn't snapped at him.

"What's the matter?" Surely something was

if her temper didn't flare after a comment like that.

Tessa glanced back at him. For a moment the blue flecks in his eyes mesmerized her, but she shook herself from her reverie. "Doesn't it disturb you that Smoke Eyes lives the way she does?"

Cody shrugged. He shifted his gaze to the horses ahead of him. "She's living with family."

"That's not what I meant and I think you know it." Tessa seemed to rearrange herself on the seat and her tone, when she spoke again, was earnest. "She's so dirty and unrestrained and she must be terribly lonely." Tessa paused, glancing down at the books and slate she held on her lap. She lifted them an inch or so, staring at the lettering on the *McGuffey's Reader*. "Do you know that she returned these materials willingly? She started off denying she'd taken them, and then—" Tessa shrugged, thinking of the child's smoky eyes looking out of that dust-streaked face.

Cody grinned wryly. "What else could she do? She was caught red-handed."

Tessa threw him an exasperated look. "I want to teach her."

"You heard her. She ain't comin' in." Cody mimicked Smoke Eyes' words. He glanced again at Tessa's face. "Besides, you have twenty-three other kids in that class to tend to and I guarantee Smoke Eyes is trouble."

Tessa jerked her chin up at him in much the same fashion as Smoke Eyes had earlier. "Just what is it about you, Dr. Butler, that can't believe I am perfectly capable of handling a classroom full of children?" Her eyes sparked with challenge. "The girl wants to learn no matter how adamantly she denies it. Somehow I'll get her into my classroom."

Cody cocked an eyebrow at her. "Should I warn her?"

Tessa scowled at him. "Stop teasing!" But she couldn't stop the glow of laughter in his eyes. "You know," she said slowly and let her frankly curious gaze rove over his sunbronzed face, "I find it strange you'd let Smoke Eyes into your lab."

"Oh, you do, do you?"

"Yes. You quite nearly had an attack that day you found me in there."

"That was different."

Tessa gave a miffed little toss of her shoulders. "I fail to see the difference."

"Smoke Eyes," Cody drawled with a sarcastic tinge to his tone, "was invited. *You* were not. Smoke Eyes doesn't fall over everything in sight, break my test tubes, or damage my equipment." He was getting hot under the collar just thinking about it. His eyes came back to hers, pinning her unmercifully to the seat. "Nor does she soak my pants with potentially harmful chemicals. That child has more caution in her little finger than you do in your whole body!"

"It was water," Tessa shot back, "not harmful chemicals!" But even her eyelids burned with embarrassment, and she felt truly chastised for the first time. Worse, he had compared her to Smoke Eyes and found her wanting.

They had pulled up alongside Mrs. Rawlins's porch now, and Tessa stood straight up in the wagon and glared at him. She was set to run into the house without saying another word to him, but her intentions were put to a halt as Mrs. Rawlins banged the door behind her.

"Cody," the sweet old woman exclaimed, "I was hoping I would catch you! How are you, dear?"

Cody's eyes flicked to Tessa before he answered, "Just fine, ma'am. And how are you?"

Mrs. Rawlins clasped her hands before her and beamed, all bright-eyed after her nap. "Oh, wonderful!" She was flushed and undone, wearing a funny little hat that balanced a concoction of birds and flowers. It was crushed as if it had been lying at the bottom of a trunk for some time. "Did you enjoy your ride out to the country?"

Again Cody looked with amusement at Tessa, who was still glaring at him as she helped herself down the other side of the wagon. "I sure did." He could have laughed out loud at the way Tessa was spearing him with her eyes.

"Wonderful! Would you like to join us for supper next Saturday evening? Eb is coming along and I know how you enjoy a home-cooked meal."

Tessa nearly spun and gagged the dear old woman. Her features froze and her eyes glared warningly at Cody. He rubbed his stubbled jaw and chin, as if considering the dinner invitation. She prayed fervently he would decline, but she knew all along what his answer would be. At last his face broke into the most engaging smile she had ever seen.

"Mrs. Rawlins, I accept. What time?"

Mrs. Rawlins clapped her hands once. "Six o'clock sharp."

"I'll be here." And he whistled to the horses and flicked the reins, silently laughing at Tessa's sour expression as she followed Mrs. Rawlins into the house.

Tessa took a second look when she spotted Mrs. Rawlins's hat. "Mrs. Rawlins, why are you wearing that hat?"

Mrs. Rawlins touched her hat and smiled vaguely. "Oh, I thought I might go to town for a spell."

But Tessa knew that was a ridiculous notion at this hour and wondered if Mrs. Rawlins had been sipping some of her "medicine."

"Won't it be nice to have company next week?" the old woman asked gaily over her shoulder.

Tessa closed the door behind her and murmured dutifully, "Yes, wonderful." But she secretly hoped Cody Butler had five babies to deliver next Saturday and would be too exhausted to join them.

* * *

Smoke Eyes did not show up in class on
Monday morning. But on Tuesday afternoon,
as Tessa stood on the step and rang the bell
after recess, she glanced up to see Smoke Eyes
standing on the prairie watching her and the
children. The girl was shading her eyes with
her hand, and when Tessa took notice of her,
she dashed off in her usual rabbitlike fashion.

Tessa pressed her lips together and murmured to herself, "I'll get her here yet."

That afternoon, after waving good-bye to
the last child, she went out to the back of the
schoolhouse with a ruler and began to form
letters with it in the dirt. First she wrote *A*,
and drew an apple beside it. Then *B*, coupled
with a butterfly, and finally *C* abreast of a cat.

Now, let's hope it doesn't rain tonight,
Tessa thought, dusting off her palms and
laying the ruler against the schoolhouse. She
crossed her fingers, hoping Smoke Eyes
would come around and study the letters,
perhaps even duplicate them.

Taking her satchel up, she started for home.
Already the light was beginning to fade from
the early autumn sky and the air was clear and
sharp as Tessa hurried across the vacant lot in
her customary shortcut. As she walked down
Main Street toward the dressmaking shop,
she noticed a blond woman talking with Cody
Butler. The same woman she had seen him
with her first day in town.

Tessa's stomach clenched tight; she looked quickly about for an escape route, and seeing none, she bolted for the cafe behind her and charged through its door. She stood in the entryway of the deserted cafe, suddenly feeling very silly and wondering why she had behaved so. She'd certainly have to get used to encountering Cody Butler every once in a while if the man lived in the same town!

Just the same, she wasn't in the mood for another confrontation with him now. Tessa stood there and breathed in the delicious food smells wafting in the warm air. Her glance skipped over the simple round tables in the room. In the corner sat two bearded men, enjoying their bowls of stew. From the rear, Tessa could hear the clinking of cups and dishes, the tinny clang of pots and pans.

Just then a tall young man wearing a white apron came from the kitchen. He was carrying two coffee cups for the customers in the corner, and his glance fell on Tessa standing by the door.

Tessa, feeling decidedly conspicuous, grabbed the chair closest to her and plopped down upon it. Unfortunately she'd chosen a window seat and had a perfect view of Cody Butler.

"May I help you?"

Tessa started and turned her eyes up to the tall young man. He was very nice-looking— blond and lanky with soft blue eyes. Tessa guessed him to be about her age, yet his skin had such a youthful glow that it appeared he needn't shave.

He suddenly smiled at her. "You're the new schoolteacher, aren't you?"

Tessa smiled back at him. "Yes, I am."

The man extended a long, thin hand. "Welcome to Harper City. I'm Ned Winston."

Hesitantly Tessa glanced to his hand. Nervously she placed her slender fingers against his, then quickly withdrew her hand but offered him a shy smile. "I'm Miss Amesbury."

"Pleased to meet you, Miss Amesbury. Now, what can I get you to eat?"

"Oh . . ." Tessa's fingers fluttered at her throat. Of course, she was sitting in a cafe, and she must act like she had come in here to eat! "Just a cup of tea, thank you, Mr. Winston. I really just stopped in to take a look at your place."

He smiled again, a gentle smile that lit up his blue eyes. "Oh, it's not my place. It's my father's. He named it after himself. Grady's. My mother works here too."

"Oh, how nice."

He nodded. "I'll get that tea now."

When he had gone, Tessa glanced about the room, wanting to look anywhere but out that window. She trained her eyes on the two in the corner until they grew uncomfortable under her direct scrutiny and stared back. Her eyes darted away and out the four-paned window where Cody stood, still talking with that young woman. Tessa remembered that

Cody had called the woman Angie that first day in town, and it appeared the two were more than casual acquaintances.

Cody stood with wide-spread legs, his thumbs hooked in the waistband of his pants, while Angie clung to his arm, looking up at him. She was, Tessa thought sourly, a very pretty woman with that strawberry-blond hair and those tilted blue eyes. And she was certainly more shapely than Tessa. But her behavior, brushing her breasts up against Cody like that, was positively indecent! Cody, of course, was no better, just letting her go on while he rocked back on his boot heels and smiled crookedly down at her. The expression he wore was one of amused tolerance, almost as if this sort of female attention was commonplace with him.

Annoyed with herself for watching them, Tessa looked sharply away, keeping her eyes lowered to the table. But her eyes crept stealthily back to them and she wondered in that moment, Does he kiss her the same way he kissed me? Is she his mistress? How many others does he have? And—oh! what did she care if he kept mistresses!

As Cody started for his horse, Angie followed him to the hitching post. Has the woman no shame? Tessa thought. Cody turned his back to her and started to mount the big black, but Angie stopped him with her hand on his arm. He looked questioningly down at her and Angie stood on tiptoe and brushed her lips against his.

"Here's your tea."

"Oh!" She almost jumped off her chair and knocked the teacup over, but she steadied her nerves and smiled up at Ned to cover her embarrassment. "Daydreaming," she murmured by way of explanation.

Ned smiled. "We all do that from time to time."

"Mmm. Yes. How much do I owe you?"

Ned held up his thin hands as if to push her question aside. "Oh, that's on the house. Seeing as it's your first time in here and all. My father told me to treat you right."

Wonderful, Tessa thought, because she had no money with her. But just at that exact moment, out of the corner of her eye, she caught the motion of Cody swinging up on his horse; knowing he had full view of her now, Tessa chose that instant to bestow upon Ned her most dazzling smile. "That's so kind of you, Mr. Winston," she murmured. "You certainly know how to make a newcomer feel welcome. And you can tell your father I said so too."

It was all Ned could do to stammer, "Y— yes, ma'am. I mean, my pleasure." And he stood gawking at those beautiful lips of hers and her shimmering dark eyes. But he was called away then and Tessa peeked surreptitiously out at Cody, who sat astride his horse, looking straight in at her. It was clear he had witnessed her little scene, and as he caught and held her gaze he smiled slowly, lazily at her. Tessa could feel the flush stealing up her neck as he just sat there and grinned knowingly at her. And before she had the chance to salvage her pride and look away first, Cody wheeled his horse around and headed for home. Tessa then noticed the bulging saddlebags thrown over the back of his saddle. She knew those saddlebags were filled with bottles of medicine, bandages, instruments, and other items a doctor would need, and she wondered how often he made his rounds. And then she scowled, cross with herself for thinking of Cody Butler at all.

Before she departed, Ned Winston came out with a plate of muffins covered with a towel. "Compliments of my mother," he said, handing them to Tessa. "She says to stop by another time when we're not getting ready for the supper crowd. She'd like to meet you."

"Thank you," said Tessa, "I will." And she left the restaurant with her plate of muffins and high spirits, feeling truly welcomed to Harper City.

On Wednesday morning, before any of the children had arrived at school, Tessa hurried out back, looking for signs of Smoke Eyes. She could make out the barest trace of a footprint by the letters, but nothing else. Frowning pensively, Tessa turned her gaze out to the prairie and moved her eyes over the waving brown prairie grass. Nothing. No one.

She sighed and turned back to the schoolhouse. After the close of school that day she would return to her crude dirt letters and recarve them. She was determined to lure that girl to this school!

She continued the process for the next few days and on Friday afternoon, as the last child wandered off, Tessa scooted out to take a peek. When that child could have sneaked up and written anything in the dirt under Tessa's hawk eye Tessa didn't know, but sure enough, there beside her own letters stood a wobbly *A*, *B*, and *C*. Tessa clapped her hands once and nearly jumped for joy.

"Smoke Eyes," she called to the softly rustling grasses, "before long you'll be sitting alongside the other children, at your own desk, reading your own books!" She didn't expect an answer, even doubted if Smoke Eyes was out there now.

Tessa took hold of her ruler and drew *D*, *E*, and *F*, hardly able to contain her excitement. She stopped then and straightened. "Darn!" she said aloud to herself. "Why does tomorrow have to be Saturday?" And then she gulped. Saturday! Oh, dear heavens, that was the night Cody Butler was joining them for dinner!

Chapter Five

✦✦✦✦✦

THE FOLLOWING EVENING, just as the sun was going down, Tessa hastily began to set the table for their dinner guests. She smoothed a snowy-white tablecloth over the kitchen table, then went to the cupboard for the dishes. Making her way back to the table with the stack of plates, she inhaled all the delicious food smells mingling in the warm kitchen—the yeasty smell of fresh-baked bread and sourdough biscuits, the pot roast simmering on the stove, and the slightly tart aroma of rhubarb Mrs. Rawlins had stewed for pie filling. Tessa's stomach fairly growled with hunger; it seemed she could barely wait another minute to eat.

She glanced out the open window to see the sky awash in pink and lilac streaks. The late-September day was unseasonably warm and Tessa cherished the last breath of mild weather. The evening breeze caressed her face and she closed her eyes briefly, savoring the tranquil moment.

Cody's sharp knock at the front door shattered her dreamy state and nearly sent the dishes she grasped crashing to the floor. Tessa opened her eyes and frowned. Leave it to him!

She set the dishes carefully on the table and moved a step toward the front door. Maybe it was Eb at the door. Maybe Cody had been detained, maybe he was miles out in the country attending to someone, maybe—

"Tessa," Mrs. Rawlins called in her sweet voice from the bedroom, "could you answer the door? I'm not quite dressed!"

Tessa found herself staring at her reflection in the little mirror that hung on the wall by the lean-to. She passed a hand over her honey-colored hair and wondered if she would surprise him. She had dressed differently tonight. The lawn dress she'd chosen was cream-colored and sprigged with pink rosebuds and tiny green leaves, buttoned down the tight-fitting waist with pearl buttons. She wore her hair differently too. Instead of winding it into its customary tight bun, Tessa had swept it back into a softly rolled chignon. A soft, feminine allure emanated from her; no trace of the stern, tight-faced schoolmarm remained. Would he notice? And what did she care if he did? She would have the last laugh anyway and the thought made the gold in her dark eyes sparkle.

Impatient now, his knock sounded again, spurring Tessa to action. Briskly she started down the hall, eager to get this evening over with as soon as possible. She passed through the front room and stopped cold at the sight of Cody Butler standing out on the front porch. The sight of him took her breath away. He was all shoulders in an impeccable suit of the deepest, darkest blue, like a midnight sky, and his deeply tanned face made a striking contrast to his high, stiff white collar. Tessa's astonished eyes ran down his beautiful silk brocade waistcoat and lingered a moment on the gold chain of his pocket watch. She felt slightly giddy.

Her breath seemed trapped in her throat as she dared to slowly raise her gaze to his again, but Cody was looking her over too. He subjected her to the same thorough scrutiny as she had him, only his lazy, appreciative gaze took much longer to travel her figure than she had taken to travel his. And when at last his intense green eyes found hers again, the burning light in them seemed to ignite a radiant fire within her.

Separated only by the doorframe, they stared at each other as if they were strangers. But Cody suddenly broke the spell by flashing a half-wry grin at her.

"I must have the wrong house," he teased. "I was looking for Miss Amesbury, the new schoolmarm in town, and I can't see her anywhere in sight." He glanced behind her and all around the porch as if searching for the prim teacher.

Tessa's smile froze. She'd almost forgotten whom she was dealing with here. He was still the same annoying man behind the spectacular suit. "Yes," she agreed coolly, lifting her chin at him, "you must have the wrong house. I was expecting the town doctor, who is no more than a boor at best, and here stands before me a man who appears every bit a gentleman."

Cody laughed, his open smile disarming

her. "A truce," he murmured, his warm green eyes making little pleasant shivers race up and down her spine.

Mrs. Rawlins came bustling out of her bedroom then, adjusting her clothing and glancing from Tessa to Cody. Spurred to action by her puzzled look, Tessa forced a smile to her lips and moved to the side, allowing Cody to step inside. He shifted his utterly charming grin from Tessa to Mrs. Rawlins.

"If I don't miss my guess, Mrs. Rawlins, that's pot roast and rhubarb pie I smell cooking, and I don't mind telling you that smell has been tormenting me from clear across town."

Cody leaned to place a kiss on Mrs. Rawlins's soft cheek. His devilish glance flicked to Tessa, who backed up a wary step, making it clear that he'd better keep his distance. Cody's eyes mocked her, then once again dipped to the small, plump woman before him.

Mrs. Rawlins, oblivious to the exchange, glanced to Tessa. "Why don't you take Cody into the sitting room until Eb comes, dear?"

"Oh . . ." Tessa's voice faltered as she caught the amused arch of Cody's black brow. "I'd like to finish setting the table, Mrs. Rawlins."

"Nonsense!" Mrs. Rawlins cheerily brushed aside that remark, nudging the two of them toward the sitting room while she breezed down the hall toward the kitchen, leaving Tessa alone with him.

The gathering dusk filled the sitting room

with lavender-blue shadows; Tessa moved to the table by the window and lit the lamp, keenly aware of the man standing behind her. She thought of him in that expertly tailored suit, and her fingers shook as she replaced the lamp chimney. The thump of her heart seemed to fill her ears. Nervously she turned to face him and she caught his crooked, slightly mocking grin. So, he thought this amusing, did he? No doubt he took perverse pleasure in having her act as hostess to him. Well, Tessa thought, drawing herself up, she would not grant him the satisfaction of gloating.

She gestured to the comfortable upholstered chair near the heater behind him. "Have a seat, Dr. Butler."

But Cody outmaneuvered her by gesturing with his own wide, brown hand. "Ladies first, Miss Amesbury."

Annoyed with him, she stiffly lowered her frame to the edge of the wing chair. She smoothed her hands over her lap as Cody sat across from her and settled back, knees spread, elbows resting on the arms of the chair, long fingers laced across his stomach. There was a touch of arrogance about him that thoroughly annoyed Tessa. He was wearing that damned secretive smile of his and he looked as comfortable in his stunning, expensive suit as he did in the more casual clothes he wore about town.

Tessa, on the other hand, felt like a fly

caught in a spider web; she sat with her knees tightly pressed together, palms flat on her thighs. Her insides were wound so tight it seemed she could spring from the chair and out of the room at just a mere sound from him.

Yet she looked straight into his amused gaze and stated crisply, "Entertaining you, as you must realize, Dr. Butler, is the last thing I feel like doing this evening."

"What *do* you feel like doing this evening, Miss Amesbury?" His lazy drawl and lazy eyes smiling into hers caused Tessa's stomach to flip-flop. Yet she glared at him.

"I'm sure you feel smugly satisfied that you've managed to wheedle a supper invitation out of Mrs. Rawlins."

Cody cocked his thick eyebrow at her. "Wheedle? I wouldn't call it that. She invited me."

"You could have declined."

"Ah." His eyes silently contemplated her. "I never refuse a dinner invitation, Miss Amesbury."

Tessa's soft mouth tightened. A spark of anger showed in her eyes. "I thought we decided to stay away from each other."

Cody flashed her a rather sarcastic smile. "We did. I'm here for Mrs. Rawlins's cooking—nothing else."

Tessa's face flamed scarlet. He'd made it sound as if she were hoping that he'd come to see her. The nerve of him! Tessa nudged her chin up a bit, but kept her voice even. "Nevertheless, I live here and you undoubtedly knew I would be here this evening."

"An added pleasure," he drawled softly, and Tessa's eyes jumped sharply to his, but they mocked her. "If you wanted to avoid seeing me tonight, you could've gone to the social."

"If I'd thought of it I would have, I assure you."

Cody chuckled. "But since you didn't, let's make the best of it. We'll suffer together—in silence."

Their eyes locked, and Tessa restrained herself from leaping to her feet and leaving him to entertain himself. If only Mrs. Rawlins would call to her for assistance in the kitchen, but from the sound of clinking dishes the older woman was managing just fine. Tessa intertwined her slender fingers on her lap and darted a glance out the window, looking for signs of Eb, but there were none. She glanced back to Cody, lounging indolently with an ankle now crossed over his knee.

The room, in its intimate twilit shadows, had grown much too quiet, and it was filled with an awkward tension. Tessa grew fidgety under Cody's steady gaze. Years of proper training, of proper manners, made her want to ease the tension and she groped for something to say.

"Have you finished building the saloon yet?" she ventured.

Cody lifted an amused black brow at her,

knowing she was totally uninterested in that saloon. "Yup." A rakish glint entered his eyes. "Maybe you'd like to join me there sometime for a drink." He laughed as Tessa sucked in an outraged breath.

"I am not in the habit of practicing lewd behavior, Dr. Butler," she bit off in clipped tones. "However, you are apparently so accustomed to fast women that you do not know how to act in the company of a lady." She started to rise but Cody's next words stopped her.

"Did you know, Miss Amesbury, that when you are angry your Boston accent becomes more pronounced? You sound prim and proper without even trying."

Tessa's heart shot to her throat. How did *he* know she was from Boston? She looked straight into his eyes, wondering if he could sense her panic, but he looked only amused, staring back at her. She seemed suddenly shy as she asked softly, "How did you know I'm from Boston?"

Cody quirked a brow. "Remember I *am* on the school board, and my memory's not that bad. Besides, anyone can detect a Boston accent. There's no other like it."

"But—"

They were interrupted by a knock at the door. Tessa jumped to her feet, ignoring the unsteadiness of her knees as she stood.

"That's Eb," she said unnecessarily as she started toward the door. But before she had taken a step, Mrs. Rawlins was greeting Eb.

She must have been watching for him, Tessa thought with some amusement as she sat down again, allowing the two older folks a moment of privacy. She made the mistake then of looking toward Cody, who was giving her a long, assessing look. A hot blush stained her cheeks. Cody grinned at her. "Do you always dress this way for dinner?"

"Always," Tessa flung back, and turned her attention on Eb and went to greet him as Cody's soft laughter followed her out of the room.

Outside the darkness was now complete but the kitchen was bathed in light from the lantern set on the table. As they ate the delicious meal, Eb kept them entertained with lively anecdotes. He glanced over at Cody, who ate steadily, hardly coming up for air.

"What's that, your fifth plate, Cody?" Eb teased, winking at Tessa.

Cody laughed good-naturedly. "Didn't know you were keeping track, Eb." He went on spreading the butter. "I'd sell my soul if I could eat biscuits like these every day, Mrs. Rawlins."

Mrs. Rawlins beamed at Tessa, who busied herself with another sip of wine. "Oh, I can't take credit for those. Tessa made them."

Tessa almost choked on her food as she sat up abruptly. Oh, she didn't want Cody to know her name! And by his expression she could tell he wasn't going to let her off easily. "Oh, *Tessa* did, did she?" Her name, coming from him, sounded too intimate. But Cody's glowing eyes were merciless as he watched her squirm on her chair. He was pleasantly surprised. He thought for sure her name must have been Temperance; her teaching certificate had simply said Miss T. Amesbury. Cody's mouth twitched with amusement as he thought of it. "Well," he drawled, "it's a real pleasure to learn that our schoolteacher can cook. She must have had a lot of practice."

Tessa gritted her teeth and said in a deceptively sweet voice, "If I were you, Dr. Butler, I'd save some room for Mrs. Rawlins's pie. That hollow leg of yours must nearly be filled by now."

"No fear of that," Cody said amiably. "Your biscuits are so light a man could float if he ate enough of them."

Mrs. Rawlins looked at Cody intently. "You must not get enough to eat, dear," she interjected warmly. "A boy works up a mighty appetite when he works the long, hard hours you do. What you need is a wife to look after you."

Both men laughed, but Tessa felt she couldn't endure this torture any longer. She sprang to her feet and went to the stove to pour them all coffee. Then she brought over the brown-crusted pies and set them on the table.

"Apple or rhubarb?" Tessa asked Eb first.

"Rhubarb for me." Eb smiled and Tessa sliced him a good-sized wedge, then one for Mrs. Rawlins. Cody asked for apple and Tessa cut him an enormous piece, hoping he would make a fool of himself and push half of it away. But when he was finished with his main course he happily dug into the pie, swallowing it down neatly.

They lingered at the table talking of the new school and of the winter to come and of how the town was growing. The breeze drifting through the open window was a touch cool now, but refreshing. It ruffled Cody's dark hair as he pushed his chair back from the table and stretched his long legs negligently before him, then laced his long, sun-browned fingers over his lean middle.

At last, Eb stood up and hooked his thumbs inside his red suspenders. "Well, Audrey," he said to Mrs. Rawlins, "that was the best meal I've had in a very long time. And I thank you kindly for inviting me." He offered his hand to Mrs. Rawlins. "It's such a perfect night, I'd hate to waste it by hurrying home. Why don't we sit on the porch for a while?"

Mrs. Rawlins's apple-cheeked face broke into a pleased smile. "Why, Eb, I'd love to!" She took his hand and came to her feet. "Let me get my shawl."

Tessa stood too, glad for the excuse to stretch her own stiff legs, and she started clearing the table. "I'll wash these dishes, Mrs. Rawlins, so you stay out and enjoy the fresh air."

"Oh, Tessa, leave them!" Mrs. Rawlins insisted. "I'll wash them when I come back in."

"Don't be silly," Tessa said, starting to stack

the plates. "It'll only take me a minute to clean them up."

"I'll help her with them," Cody volunteered, lazily coming to his feet. He smiled at Tessa's stricken face.

"Oh, Cody, thank you!" Mrs. Rawlins beamed and the two older people left without noticing Tessa's tightly pinched lips as she fetched the washbasin from the pantry shelf. Keeping her back to Cody, she dipped some hot water from the kettle simmering on the stove into the washbasin. When she turned to collect the dishes from the table, she found Cody removing his jacket; carelessly he tossed it over the back of a chair and Tessa saw the fabric of his vest pull taut across the wide spread of his shoulders. The deep blue color of the silk seemed to throw shadows into his jet hair, which curled up at his pristine white collar. Tessa felt a fleeting desire to touch those thick curls, to feel the texture of his hair between her fingers. But she quickly whisked around and slid the dishes into the basin.

"You may as well go," she said with her back to him. "I can handle these myself."

"And you may as well resign yourself to the fact that I'm going to stay and help you with them," Cody returned with a tinge of humor in his voice.

Tessa watched him roll up his sleeves over his dark, hard-muscled forearms. It appeared that she wasn't going to be rid of him easily, and a frown furrowed her brow. "I'll bet you don't even know how to do dishes!" she accused.

"And who do you think does *my* dishes?" he returned dryly.

Tessa let her eyes rove deprecatingly over him. "It wouldn't surprise me in the least to learn several, ah . . . women help you with more than just dishes."

Cody laughed. "What do you take me for? A libertine?"

"Yes," Tessa answered without a qualm, and she heard him laugh again. He gestured with a nod of his head to a chair. "Come sit over here with me while those dishes soak awhile. Let's finish off this wine."

Tessa's heart accelerated as she watched him drop his big body into the chair behind him, and he waited for her to join him. Tessa grabbed more dishes and plunked them into the basin.

"Come on, Tessa," he teased, using her given name, and laughed when she glared at him for it. "Come on," he urged again, "I don't bite . . . even though I know you do, Tessa."

She let out an exasperated sigh and stalked to the table. She pulled out a chair and sat down hard. "Yes, my name is Tessa," she hissed. "And I don't recall giving you permission to use it!"

"Oh, and do I need permission to use it?" He raised his black brows quizzically, almost comically.

Tessa bit her bottom lip, trying not to laugh.

"You're a nuisance and an unmerciful tease!"

"Mmm . . . that's what my sister always said."

"Sister?" Tessa was truly surprised. "You have a sister?" She privately envied him his sibling.

"Well, sure, is that so unusual?" He reached for the bottle of wine and filled his glass with the light amber liquid. Then he filled hers. He chuckled at her obvious surprise. "I have a brother too. What did you think—that I was a stray?"

Tessa dropped her eyes. He had no way of knowing, of course, about her background. But the word "stray" hurt just the same.

"Well, what about you?" he asked.

Tessa lifted her head. "Me?"

"Sure. Don't you have brothers or sisters?"

Tessa's eyes darted away from his. "No," she breathed. "And I prefer we don't discuss my family."

Cody's eyes narrowed slightly. His long fingers tapped idly at his glass. "Ah."

The silence grew heavy. Tessa wanted to rise and start the dishes but something held her back. She took a sip of wine and found herself staring at Cody's strong, swarthy hands. She shook herself out of her reverie. She mustn't let him get curious about her past! And she must steer the subject away from herself and back to him.

"Do your brother and sister live here in Harper City?"

"No, they live back in Kentucky with my

folks. My sister is married and my brother is, ah, undecided." Cody smiled.

"Are you the oldest?"

"No. I'm in the middle. My brother's two years older than me, my sister a year younger."

"What brought you out here?" Instantly her teeth clamped over her bottom lip. She could have kicked herself for asking such a personal question.

Cody lifted a brow at her. "Let's just say I was smitten with wanderlust—me and a few others. A man gets lots of satisfaction out of building a new town from virgin wilderness. And in a new town there's a need for doctoring."

"Didn't you have a practice in Kentucky?"

"Yes, but I have a friend with whom I worked very closely and he took on most of my patients." Cody leaned back with a smile in his green eyes. "Any more questions?"

She blushed. "Yes. One. But it has nothing to do with your family or profession." She paused. "Did Smoke Eyes come into your lab this week?"

Cody chuckled. "You don't want to spoil the evening by talking about that little she-devil, do you?"

"What's to spoil?" Tessa returned tartly. "Besides, Smoke Eyes is a child, not a she-devil. And I think you harbor a particular fondness for her, though you will not admit it."

"You think so?" Cody's amused eyes stayed

on her as he raised his wineglass to his lips and drained it. When he put it down he said, "Yes, she came in—clean too."

Tessa sat silently musing.

"What about you?" Cody asked, "have you been able to lure her into school yet?"

"No, but I will." She ignored his doubting look and raised her chin a little. "I'll have you know," she said coolly, "that I've been forming letters in the dirt behind the schoolhouse and just yesterday Smoke Eyes duplicated an *A, B,* and *C.*"

"That's a rather unorthodox method, wouldn't you say?" Cody commented dryly. "What happens when the ground freezes?"

Growing impatient with him, Tessa said testily, "By then I shall have her learning *inside* the schoolhouse. Don't raise that infernal eyebrow at me! The girl wants to learn and this week she's going to learn how to spell her name. Her *real* name!"

"Smoke Eyes is her real name."

"Her given name, then. What is her last name?"

"You don't expect to call her that and have her respond, do you?"

"Yes, I do. If she really does become a doctor, her patients can't be calling her Smoke Eyes. She'll scare people off with a name like that. They'll have to call her Dr. . . . whatever. Now what is it?"

Cody smirked at her. "Flynn."

"Katherine Flynn," Tessa murmured, wondering if Smoke Eyes would understand her own name if it was written out for her in the dirt. But if she copied it and memorized it, Tessa could tell her what it said later. One step at a time. She glanced up to find Cody bracing his elbows on the table edge and leaning forward.

"You wash and I'll dry."

"What?" She had been totally absorbed in her musings.

"The dishes."

"Oh!" Tessa jumped up, embarrassed that he'd caught her daydreaming. She found her apron and bent her head slightly forward as she tied it around her waist. Cody eyed her tiny waist, and suddenly he desperately wanted to place his hands around it and pull her against him. If she were any other woman he would have. But she was the town school-teacher and she'd made it clear that he'd better remember it.

"You didn't eat much," he commented, needing a distraction.

"Well, you ate enough for all of us," Tessa quipped.

"And you drank enough for all of us," Cody returned mildly, but Tessa felt reproved. "And as your doctor I advise you to go easy with the stuff. Otherwise you might end up the town drunk instead of the town school-teacher."

Tessa bristled. "You're not my doctor."

"Yes I am," he replied cheerfully. "I'm everyone's doctor in this town."

"Well, I hate to disappoint you, but I never

get sick and you'll never examine me," she said quite coolly, but the thought of his hands upon her skin made shivers run through her.

Cody wore a doubtful expression that said, "We'll see," and when she glowered at him his smile only broadened. She went to the washbasin and with a clean cloth began to wash the dishes.

"There's a towel in the pantry," she directed him. "And . . . oh," she added, "if you'd like an apron you can wear Mrs. Rawlins's there on the hook." She giggled, picturing him in it. Cody gave her a look of mock warning and went for the towel.

They stood side by side, Tessa washing, Cody drying. When she handed him the rinsed plate, she was careful to avoid contact with his long, reaching fingers. She hid a tiny smile at the incongruity of this big, rugged man helping her with the dishes. Yet somehow it made his masculinity that much more overwhelming.

"That's the last dish," she announced with evident relief in her voice. She nearly shoved the plate at Cody, so eager was she to have him gone. She started to haul the washbasin toward the back door.

"Here, let me get that," Cody offered, and took it from her before she'd moved a full step. He went out to throw the dirty dishwater far from the house, and Tessa took the broom from the lean-to and started to sweep the floor. He'd be gone in a minute she told herself, breathing relief at the thought. She didn't hear him come back in, and she took a backward step and nearly collided with him as he stood directly behind her.

"For heaven's sake, Cody—" she started to scold with exasperation, but stopped as his name fell unbidden from her lips. Tessa realized in that fleeting instant that she had been thinking of him as Cody and not Dr. Butler for some time now; only aloud did she use the formal Dr. Butler. Alarm flashed through her as he took the broom from her and put it aside, then took hold of her slight wrists and gently tugged her closer so that she stood mere inches from him. Her huge, almond-shaped eyes stared up at him untrustingly, but his lazy eyes smiled down into hers.

"Don't you think you've done enough work for one evening?" Cody drawled softly, his long, callused thumbs making little caressing circles on the sensitive undersides of her wrists. The soft breeze from the open window stirred the curtains and made the lamp flicker. Tessa shivered once. She swallowed nervously.

"What—what are you doing?"

Cody's handsome mouth slanted in an amused smile. "Nothing yet." He saw her eyes grow even wider. "But that's only because I recall you don't like the way I kiss. I intend to make you like it, Tessa," he promised in a dangerously silky voice.

"I'm not going to let you kiss me."

Cody chuckled. "We'll see about that." And

his hands slipped up her smooth arms and pulled her closer.

Tessa knew now was the time to scream for Mrs. Rawlins. But she didn't. She stood wide-eyed and rooted to the spot as Cody leaned slowly forward, lowering his dark head, and touched his lips to the side of her silken-skinned neck. A shuddering thrill flowed through her body. She felt his crisp hair brush her cheek; he smelled of wine and shaving soap and tobacco. Comforting smells.

Cody's mouth remained buried in the curve of her neck and his husky whisper was hot on her skin. "I like your hair like this, Tess. . . ." Cody's lips crept to her ear and he lightly nipped the soft lobe.

"Ohh—" Tessa moaned softly; her hand slipped through the thick, soft waves at the back of his head. "Stop, Cody . . . please . . ."

He chuckled low, ignoring her. His broad hands covered her slight shoulders now as he sprinkled little kisses up and down her neck, then touched the tip of his tongue to the outer rim of her delicate ear. "I won't stop till I'm sure you like it." And his breath drummed hot against her ear. Tessa quivered; her head fell back as Cody strung his kisses along her skin as if he were forming a necklace of fire jewels, and with each kiss a muttered, unintelligible word—words that made Tessa shiver with pleasure.

"Stop—" And her neck arched with the whispered, throaty plea. "I—I like it, Cody. But you must stop . . ."

He stopped all movement and lifted his head to look down at her. Tessa swallowed as his gaze intensely searched hers, trying to read what was in her eyes. She drew in a shaky breath and stepped away from him, almost backing into the cupboard behind her.

"I think I hear Mrs. Rawlins coming in."

Cody's lips quirked with amusement. He looked as if he didn't quite believe her. "Mmm. Funny, I don't hear anything of the kind. I think you're trying to pretend nothing has happened between us."

Tessa's slim, dark brows plunged together in a deep frown. "I admitted I like kissing you!" she snapped. "Isn't that enough?"

"Not really," Cody responded dryly. "If you like it, why do you fight it?"

"I said I like *it*, not you!" she spat. His burst of laughter infuriated her. She glared at him. "I am thoroughly convinced that you are the rudest man I've ever had the misfortune to meet!"

"Come, Tessa," Cody said more seriously now. "It's not me that's bothering you. Your eyes tell me you're hiding something. Why don't you tell me what's wrong?"

A sick panic gripped her. Tell him, you coward! Tell him you're married, that you belong to another man!

Tessa turned her dark eyes up to meet his. How could he have known that she was hiding something? Was she that easy to read? Or was he just that perceptive? Her eyes searched his lean face for some clue, but there was none. The flickering lamplight threw shadows on his strong features, and the cool breeze stirred his jet hair. He was just too attractive.

"There's another man," she blurted out.

Cody's eyes narrowed on her. He hadn't thought of the possibility of another man. He rubbed his jaw reflectively as he studied her, noting that she'd dropped her eyes again. A telltale blush colored her cheeks.

"Look at me."

Her eyes remained on the floor.

"I said look at me or I'll come over there and make you look at me."

Resenting his dictatorial manner, Tessa lifted her gaze.

"Who is this man?"

"He lives in Boston."

"I know lots of people in Boston."

Tessa's eyes widened and she nearly gulped. "You do?"

"His name."

"Michael Shea." Where that name had come from Tessa had no idea! But it was a stroke of genius because there could easily have been dozens of Michael Sheas in Boston! And she certainly did not want to give her husband's name. She held her breath, watching Cody. She hesitated before saying anything more. "He asked me to marry him," she lied.

"And?"

"He's coming to Kansas in the spring." That should give her plenty of time to concoct another fib!

For a long moment Cody's eyes contemplated her. Then he gave a noncommittal grunt. Tessa watched him stroll lazily across the room, his hands stuffed into his expensive trouser pockets. He stopped at the window and gripped the stick that held it open, then eased the bottom half of the window down. There was no more breeze now. The kitchen seemed quieter, closer.

Cody turned and glanced at Tessa standing stonelike by the chair, fingers entwined.

"So," he said, and nonchalantly hung his striped silk cravat around his neck. He did not bother to tie it. "I am to understand you and this Michael Shea are going to marry in the spring."

"Yes." Her fingers ached and slowly Tessa untangled them from each other and rested them on the back of the chair.

Cody reached for his jacket without taking his eyes from her. "And when every bachelor in this town comes knocking on your door, you're going to tell them the same thing?" He saw by the widening of her eyes that the idea of callers had not occurred to her before.

"That's right."

"Does that include Ned Winston?"

"Who?"

"Winston. The man you were flirting with in Grady's the other day."

Tessa stiffened. "I was not flirting!" She

saw the corner of his mouth lift in sardonic amusement. "If there was any flirting going on that day, it was with you and what's-her-name. . . ." Tessa made a vague hand motion.

"Angie," Cody said, his face expressionless, "Foster."

Tessa tipped her chin up haughtily. "Yes, Angie. Does Angie know about Lily?"

Cody laughed softly at her. "I find it intriguing that a bride-to-be is so interested in my . . . friends." Cody slung his jacket over his shoulder, hooking it with two fingers.

"You're a scoundrel with women aplenty and I don't intend to become another of your string of brokenhearted conquests."

Cody halted before her, his towering frame casting a shadow. Her heart tripped in her throat as he reached out a long, tanned forefinger and hooked it under her little chin, tilting her face up to his.

"And there's no danger of that since you're engaged to Michael," he murmured, his voice lightly mocking. Tessa twisted her chin away, tempted to smack his hand from her. But Cody was already at the doorway. "Good night, Tessa."

And he was gone. Who knew what disreputable place he was off to now, Tessa thought petulantly. Well, she was glad to be rid of him!

As she headed toward the stairs she thought all she wanted to do was to go to sleep and forget about Cody Butler. But sleep did not come easily. Tessa lay awake long after she heard Mrs. Rawlins turn in, and at last, after tossing and turning restlessly, she threw off the covers and padded barefoot over the cold floorboards, heading down to the kitchen for a cup of tea.

She sat at the table in her nightgown with just the lamp and the moonlight to keep her company. She cut herself a slash of rhubarb pie and finished it almost as quickly as Cody had earlier. And she didn't even like rhubarb pie! She glanced to the clock and was surprised to see that it was after three.

"Damn him!" she said after her last bite of pie.

She went to bed with an upset stomach but at last dropped off into blissful sleep . . . only to awake scratching. Oh, how she itched! Her fingernails scraped at her back and shoulders, her legs. She walked to stand before the mirror in the pearly predawn light. What she saw froze her. Her face and arms were covered with unsightly red blotches—hives! She remembered now why she didn't like rhubarb pie: every time she ate it she broke out like this!

Tessa tiptoed downstairs to summon Mrs. Rawlins. But Mrs. Rawlins claimed to have no experience with hives, and much to Tessa's horror, she sent Charlie next door for the doctor.

Chapter Six

✦ ✦ ✦ ✦ ✦

CODY ARRIVED, STANDING in the doorway of Mrs. Rawlins's bedroom with his black bag. Beard stubble shadowed his face and the white shirt he wore was the same he had on last night, only now it was half buttoned, as if he'd grabbed it and shrugged into it on his way out the door. Tessa sat miserably waiting for him on the edge of Mrs. Rawlins's bed. Even though she had drawn the pull-shades low against the blush of morning light, she wanted to hide her splotchy, swollen face from Cody.

He stood there in the doorway for a moment with a smile tugging at the corner of his mouth.

"What's the idea of dragging me out of bed on a Sunday morning?" he teased as he advanced toward the bed in a lazy stride. He grinned at the blush staining her cheeks red, even under her blotchy skin. "Is this the woman who claimed she never gets sick?"

"I'm not sick!"

"But I do aim to examine you." And his voice was low, and somehow threatening. He set his bag down on a nearby chair and opened it.

"You don't have to examine me!" Tessa protested, her heart thrusting against her ribs. "These are hives! Whenever I eat rhubarb pie this happens."

"Then why did you eat it?" he questioned dryly.

Tessa picked idly at a thread on the bedspread. How could she tell him that he'd had her in such a dither last night that she'd eaten it inadvertently?

"I like it."

Cody laughed. His eyes flickered over her puritanical-looking nightgown. "Unbutton the front of your gown."

"What?" Alarmed, she gripped the front of her nightgown almost up to her chin.

Cody regarded her with humor-filled eyes. "In order for me to examine you, I have to see what I'm examining. You might have the measles or cowpox."

Tessa eyed him distrustfully.

Patiently, Cody placed his hands on his hips as he gazed down at her. "Do you prefer Mrs. Rawlins present?"

"No!"

Cody looked at her in exasperation.

"I—I mean, no," Tessa said, more calmly. "I'm embarrassed enough as it is. I don't need an audience."

"Very well. Unbutton it." His mouth curled at one corner as Tessa's hands tightened on her gown.

Slowly she freed three buttons from their holes. She glanced up at him questioningly. "Enough?"

Cody was fast losing his patience. "For God's sake, Tessa, I have to see your back and shoulders! I usually examine the abdomen too, but I risk the danger of you going into convulsions if I try that!"

At last she complied, dropping her head forward to free the little buttons all the way down to the shallow valley between her breasts. Behind her she felt the mattress depress as Cody sat next to her. Tessa held her breath as she lowered her gown, showing him her bare back and shoulders. She thought she heard him draw in his own tense breath, but couldn't be sure. Surely her back must look hideous if he was making sounds like that!

His hands were moving expertly across her bare, warm skin. She nearly gasped as his fingers tested, gently skimmed, almost caressed her bare back and shoulders.

"Do they itch?" His voice sounded curiously hoarse.

"Dreadfully."

Without getting up, Cody leaned toward his bag on the chair and rummaged in it for some salve. His sturdy thigh pressed against Tessa's buttocks and she sat stone still, her heart leaping crazily in her chest.

Gently his palm smoothed the cooling cream over her skin and waves of pleasure overwhelmed Tessa. His touch was positively indecent . . . and positively wonderful. It seemed to caress her breasts and her nipples tightened.

Behind her Cody was forcing himself to regard her as a patient and not a woman. But,

God, she was beautiful. The hives on her back
barely marred her warm, golden skin. He'd
never touched skin so soft—softer even than
fine strands of corn-silk. His eyes ran down
her graceful spine and he clenched his jaw,
forcing his eyes up again.

"Move your braid," he ordered quietly, and
she swung it over her shoulder so it hung
down in front. Cody's eyes seemed glued to
the gossamer strands of hair at her nape and
he suddenly wanted to lean and press his
mouth to its hollow. He tightened his lips
with firm resolve and dabbed on the last bit of
ointment.

When his touch slipped away, Tessa felt
curiously disappointed. Abruptly Cody stood
up and turned away to hide the hardening of
his body from her.

"Urticaria," he muttered his diagnosis, pretending to busy himself with something in his
bag. "You can button up now. Here's the
salve." He dropped it on the bed to avoid
touching her again. "You can put it on the
other affected areas yourself."

"What did you say I have?" Tessa hastily
buttoned up her gown with fumbling fingers.

"Urticaria. Hives. You have hives."

"You're not telling me anything I didn't
already know," she said dryly.

Cody glanced over his shoulder at her.
"Careful, Tessa, you're at my mercy."

She resisted the childish urge to stick her
tongue out at him. Instead she asked him,

"Do you think these will be gone by tomorrow?"

His lips quirked with humor when he turned to face her. "Let's hope so for those poor children's sake."

Tessa laughed with him and the tension between them seemed to ease.

"Usually they don't last more than twenty-four hours," Cody said as he fastened the straps to his bag. "That salve will relieve the itching. Have Mrs. Rawlins help you apply it later." He turned to face her, one hand grasping his bag, the other resting loosely on his straight hip. "I'm sure you'll be fine."

"What do I owe you?"

"Now that I think of it," he said, rubbing his grizzled jaw as he regarded her, "you not only owe me for this visit but for the damage you did in my lab. Most folks pay me in produce or livestock. You have neither." His amused eyes flicked over her. "You owe me supper," Cody announced. "Next Saturday. You have to cook and you have to be there."

"What!" Tessa was outraged.

Cody turned to leave. "You heard me."

"But"—she swallowed when he looked back at her—"I'd rather owe you money."

"But I set the fee, and I say it's supper."

Tessa clenched her fists in frustration. "Why would you want to spend another evening with me?" He certainly wasn't getting any pleasure out of it!

"Let's just say it's a diversion."

"Find another diversion!" she retorted.

He only laughed. He stood at the foot of the bed and Tessa's glance went to his well-cut mouth, somehow beautifully defined in the shadow of his beard stubble.

"Supper," he said unwaveringly. "If you refuse I can always bring you to court for trespassing."

He had her there. But she tried once more. "I'd still rather pay with money."

"Supper or court."

Exasperated, Tessa cried, "Are you going to hold this thing over my head forever?"

"I'll forget all about it after supper Saturday."

"Oh, all right!" she snapped ungraciously. Besides, she could hide behind Mrs. Rawlins's skirts. She wouldn't put any devious behavior past Cody, but if Mrs. Rawlins served as chaperone, it would certainly minimize his advances.

Frowning, Tessa watched his broad shoulders pass through the doorway. Stubborn mule! She grabbed the tin of salve and applied a bit of it to a glaring red spot on her slender ankle. It occurred to her at that moment she hadn't even thanked him for stopping by.

The investigator settled back against the springy, red velvet seat in the second-class coach of the New York Central Railroad car. He stared down at the photo he held between his long fingers, captivated by the young woman's dark, luminous eyes. He'd been fortunate to obtain a passenger list in New York from the week she'd disappeared. In that week several single women had departed to various destinations, some alone, others with companions, but the investigator planned to follow each lead. Of course none listed were Tessa Amesbury but she could have used a different name—perhaps even worn a disguise.

She could be anywhere in the country. But she was a woman alone, and though she had taken money from Forsythe, more than enough for train fare anywhere, she would need more to live on. Before she married Forsythe she'd been a schoolteacher. Trouble was, which city? He'd searched for her in the northeast and now he was headed for Chicago.

Forsythe had promised him a bonus if he found the girl in less than six months. If he met the deadline, the investigator wouldn't have to work another day of his life. He smiled and tucked the photo back inside his pocket. He'd find her. There was no doubt in his mind he'd find her.

Silver-white frost glazed the ground that first week of October. In the early mornings Tessa hustled to school, her shawl gathered close about her shoulders, the heels of her shoes slicing footprints in the hard ground.

But by the time she reached the schoolhouse door the warm autumn sun had strengthened enough to melt those prints into mud.

Tessa had waited until after lunch each day to form her letters in the dirt for Smoke Eyes. Still, by Wednesday, there was no sign that Smoke Eyes had ventured close to the schoolhouse. During the schoolday Tessa kept a watchful eye out for her, sometimes glancing out the window during recitations or while walking from desk to desk.

Shortly after the noon recess, cries of "Lemme go, lemme go!" from outside rose above the low drone of the students' reciting voices. The classroom became utterly still. Teacher and scholars exchanged startled, confused glances. Only Sam Jordan was outside visiting the outhouse and it made no sense that he was yelling such a thing.

"Help! Enough!"

Tessa flew down the aisle and out the door, half the class right on her heels. She hoped she wasn't falling for another prank but somehow those desperate cries sounded real.

"Ouch!" The muffled voice came from behind the schoolhouse. Tessa dashed around the corner and the sight she saw brought her up short with a gasp. There was Sam all right, pinned to the ground beneath Smoke Eyes, who mercilessly pummeled him with her fists. Sam, one arm pushing at Smoke Eyes' face, struggled to be free.

"Stop!" he gasped, fighting for breath. "I said enough!"

Without a second thought Tessa hauled the girl off Sam and held her by the scruff of her dirty neck while Sam lay on the ground hugging his sides, trying to catch his breath.

"What is the meaning of this!" Tessa demanded crossly, shaking Smoke Eyes just a little.

Smoke Eyes scowled at the teacher. "*He* started it. I was mindin' my own business back here and he came along and picked a fight."

"Sam!" Tessa's angry eyes swerved to Sam, who still lay there. "Sam, is that true? Sam! Can you get up?"

The humiliated boy dragged himself to his knees, hung his sore head, and stayed like that a moment, sucking in air. His brother Josh looked even more ashamed than Sam.

"She stole my book that day, Teacher." Sam raised his head to narrow his eyes at the two females. "No one steals from Sam Jordan an' gits away with it!"

Tessa had to tighten her grip on Smoke Eyes to keep the girl from lunging at him again.

"Yeah, but I *did* get away with it!" Smoke Eyes taunted her foe, who stood at least a half-head taller than she was. "I gave you th' thrashin' of yer sorry life!"

"Stop it!" Tessa cried. "I've heard quite enough out of both of you. Sam, fighting in the schoolyard is the worst offense, as you know. There is no excuse for picking a fight." Her eyes went over his bruised, cut face. "It looks to me as if you've taken enough punishment, but if this ever happens again you'll be doubly punished. Now go wash up under the pump. Children, indoors!" As the children reluctantly turned to head inside, Tessa glanced back at Smoke Eyes. "Now, I want to talk with—" But the girl easily slipped from Tessa's grasp and she scampered off so fast Tessa hadn't even the chance to open her mouth and call out to her.

"Shee-it!" Sam swore in astonishment beside Tessa, marveling at Smoke Eyes' speed.

"Sam!" Tessa spun on him, shocked, yet controlling the urge to burst out laughing. "I said go wash up—and while you're at it, wash out your mouth too."

Sam hung his head and shuffled along behind the others, muttering something under his breath. Tessa's eyes moved out to the prairie; she wondered if she was wasting her time with Smoke Eyes. The girl had only made it worse for herself, fighting with Sam. It would be harder than ever to lure her into school now.

But Tessa's spine stiffened. No, she wouldn't give up. The child had every right to learn, just as the others. She glanced to the dirt where the children had scuffled, saw the letters of KATHERINE vaguely discernible there, and scratched over them, knowing the chances of Smoke Eyes coming back were bleak.

After school that day, Tessa stopped at the

general store to purchase a few items for Mrs. Rawlins. The store was a warm, welcome comfort after the crisp outside air and Tessa received a hearty greeting from both Eb and his son Mike.

"Anything we can do for you, Tessa?" Eb asked from behind his counter.

"I'm going to browse a moment," Tessa replied with a smile. "But I'll get back to you," she promised.

"Alrighty! Take your time!"

She breathed in all the good, rich scents as she strolled the length of the store. She admired the crockery and a dollhouse with miniature furniture, and a very beautiful, delicately carved music box behind a glass case. But her breath caught in her throat when her gaze fell on a stunning Japanese fan beside the music box; its delicate design of flowers was ivory and peach-colored against a background of night black, and a thin gilt line ran along its edge.

"Lovely, isn't it?"

Startled, Tessa glanced up to see a young woman standing there beside her; she had a sweet face with wide blue eyes and curly brown hair, and she was quite obviously expecting a child.

"It is lovely," Tessa breathed, with a trace of wistfulness in her words. She'd never owned anything nearly as lovely. "Expensive too, I'm afraid," she added ruefully. The other woman laughed, and looking at her, Tessa guessed her to be just about her own age, but there was something definitely girlish about her.

Tessa extended her slim hand toward the woman. "I'm Tessa Amesbury, the school-teacher."

"Oh, my!" the other exclaimed. "Here I am so enthralled with that fan I forget my manners! I know who you are, of course, and I've been meaning to get down to Mrs. Rawlins's house to meet you. I'm Mary Lyndon. My husband and I live about a half-mile from here out on our claim." She glanced shyly down at her round middle. "We haven't any school-age younguns yet. This will be our first."

"Congratulations! When is the baby due?"

"In February. Dr. Butler has been taking good care of me. Do you know him?"

Tessa felt a strange jolt at the mention of Cody's name. "Yes, I know him," she murmured, glancing aside now to the bolts of cloth on the counter. She did not want to discuss Cody.

"Well, he is simply wonderful," Mary said. "My husband says he feels completely safe with Cody—" She broke off, blushing. "I—I feel odd calling him that, but everyone does and he insists that we do. Anyway, Dr. Butler is most capable," she ended, still flushed.

Yes, Tessa thought dryly, capable indeed! She hadn't seen him all week and she was hoping he might forget his invitation to the widow's house on Saturday.

She watched Mary spread her hand across

some dark blue flannel, eyeing it wistfully. "I'm afraid I won't be making any new dresses before the baby is born. But I'm so tired of what I have!"

Tessa nodded to Eb's display of braid and ribbons. "Why don't you select some of that gilt braid and sew it around the neck and cuffs of an older dress? That way you'll feel like you have a new dress while saving the expense."

"What a wonderful idea!" Mary cried. "Listen," she said, laying a hand on Tessa's arm, "why don't you join us for a Saturday-night social sometime? I haven't danced lately, but it's fun just getting together with the town-folk."

"It sounds like fun," Tessa agreed, thinking she had no right to socialize at all. But what harm could there be in chatting with the local women? And it would be nice to get to know some of her students' parents. "Perhaps next week I'll be free."

"Fine, we'll stop by for you on our way."

"Thank you for thinking of me. And you take care of yourself."

Feeling lighthearted, Tessa bought some cornmeal and sugar and a tin of tea. She stopped outside with her bundle and started down the board sidewalk.

It was growing colder and the sun was a crimson smear in the purplish sky. Long shadows were forming in the dusty street and the chilly air nipped at Tessa's nose and fingertips. People hurried home to finish chores before supper and a few children lingered in doorways, waiting for their fathers. They called out to her, thrilled at seeing their teacher outside of school.

Tessa moved quickly on, her empty stomach tightening hungrily as she thought of her own supper waiting at home for her. She hadn't walked half the length of the boardwalk when she caught sight of Cody across the street in front of the post office talking to two men. Quickly Tessa ducked her head, hoping he hadn't seen her, and she hastened her step, but it was all in vain, for out of the corner of her eye she saw him crossing the street heading toward her.

"Hey, Tess."

Her step missed just a pace, but she sped up again, pretending not to hear him.

"Tessa Amesbury," he said, much louder now, so anyone passing by could hear. She spun around then, her eyes narrowing at him like a spitting cat.

"Don't call me that!" she hissed. "It's Miss Amesbury to you, Dr. Butler!"

He wore a knowing grin that sent her blood to the boiling point. "You're not going to start that again, are you?" he asked. "Not after what we shared Saturday night, and uh, Sunday morning."

Oh, my God! "Be quiet!" She whirled on him, nearly falling off the end of the boardwalk. She checked to see if anyone else heard him. When she saw they were alone, she glared at him.

"Ah," he said softly, approaching her. "I've

got your attention now." He smiled down at her teasingly. "How're the hives?" he asked, and peered closer at her in the shadows, pretending to search her flawless skin. He edged so close Tessa was forced to step sharply aside in order to avoid contact with him.

"Oh, stop that!" she insisted, exasperated. "You can see for yourself that they're gone! Now, what is it you want with me?" She could have bitten her lip as soon as she said it, but Cody let her words go without a choice remark.

"I have something of yours."

"What could you possibly have of mine?" She noticed then the white envelope he held loosely in his long, lean fingers.

"Your salary," he said. "And I apologize that it's late. You're to receive it the thirtieth of each month. This is for the two weeks you worked in September."

Tessa met his eyes in the semidarkness. "What are *you* doing with it?"

"As a representative of the school board, I volunteered to make sure it gets to you each month."

Tessa took it from his fingers. She didn't like the idea of him performing this particular duty. "I hope," she said, turning away from him, "that you get it to me on time from now on."

His wide hand caught her under the elbow, stopping her. "Why, you little minx! Someone sure could teach you some manners!"

Tessa's smile was deceptively sweet. "That someone certainly isn't you, though, is it, Dr. Butler? Now let me go."

She marched off, Cody's soft laughter following her. He stood and watched the slightly provocative swing of her graceful hips, and he felt the stirring of desire warm his blood.

Just for spite he called out after her, loud enough for the whole town to hear, "Don't forget—Saturday night! I'll be there six o'clock sharp!" He laughed outright when she did an about-face to glare at him. Unperturbed, Cody gave her a mock bow and laughed again when she swung off in a huff, leaving him to stare after her.

On her day off Tessa resented cooking for Cody and had to remind herself that she was simply paying a debt. As she prepared a giant chicken pie she thought how much fun it would be to include something awful in the pie—such as too much pepper or a field mouse. But poor Mrs. Rawlins would have to eat too, and Tessa couldn't play such a trick on her. As the day wore on and the two women baked companionably side by side in the kitchen Tessa found her Saturday had been pleasant and satisfying after all.

By suppertime it was dark and Tessa turned up the lamp wicks until the rooms blazed warmly. When she heard Cody's sharp rap at the front door, she tried to ignore the little catch she felt in her throat. Adjusting the pearl bar pin on her collar, she headed for the door.

But when she reached the door Mrs. Rawlins was already there, wrapping herself in her green woolen cloak.

Puzzled, Tessa frowned. "Why, Mrs. Rawlins, where are you going?" The door was open and she glanced out to the porch where she could vaguely make out a tall, dark figure.

"Why, Tessa, dear, you know it's Saturday. I'm going to the social—where else?" she said, surprised. She opened the door wider to allow Cody in.

"But—but . . ." Dumbfounded, Tessa stared up at Cody sweeping through the doorway, bringing the chilly air with him. A sudden gust of wind snatched the door from Mrs. Rawlins and it banged shut behind Cody. "I thought—I thought—" She broke off, feeling suddenly foolish as both Cody and Mrs. Rawlins turned waiting eyes upon her. Hugging her arms against the cold, she forced her eyes back to Mrs. Rawlins. "I thought you were going to stay here with me . . ." And Cody, she added silently.

"You don't think I'm going to miss a night of dancing, do you?" Mrs. Rawlins said lightly. She hooked two fingers over the edge of the curtain and peeked out into the night. "Here's Eb!" she announced happily, taking a step toward the door again.

Cody moved aside and opened the door. Eb met her on the threshold.

"Ready to go, Audrey?" He poked his white

head in and offered Mrs. Rawlins his arm, wrapped in plaid mackinaw. "Hello, Tessa, Cody."

"You two enjoy dinner," Mrs. Rawlins said. "And shut this door tightly so the wind won't come through."

And then they were gone.

Cody closed the door, then he hammered the panel with his palm, shutting out the cold. "There," he said, glancing over his shoulder at Tessa. "Shut tight."

Uneasily, she watched him turn and casually rest his back against the door. He was wearing a worn, heavy sheepskin jacket; and the smell of it combined with the fresh wind roused something deep and powerful within Tessa.

Cody folded his arms across his broad chest and lazily surveyed her. "You didn't tell me we were going to be alone." A hint of laughter lurked in his eyes.

Tessa glowered at him. "Don't you start. I had no idea until this very instant."

"Mmm." His eyes flicked over her slight frame clad in a high-necked cream-colored blouse and a long, unflattering brown woolen skirt that hid the tops of her practical, high-buttoned shoes. The only relief from all this drabness was the tiny gold-and-brown-striped buttons that ran all the way down her front; his eyes seemed to linger overmuch on them. His gaze lifted to her hair wound as tightly as ever on her graceful head. She watched all this, pleased at the disappointment she read on his face. But then his mouth twisted wryly.

"You look ready for the convent."

"I'm glad you approve."

He laughed, his white teeth flashing, his green eyes crinkling at the corners. "Ah, but Tessa," he murmured softly, "I am no priest."

Inexplicably something warm and sweet melted inside her, sluicing downward in a weakening rush. Blood scalded her cheeks as he kept his steady gaze upon her, and her skin seemed to tingle all over. To cover her embarrassment, she drew herself up sharply and brushed past his tall, rangy body, heading straight for the kitchen. She didn't glance back to see if he followed, but she knew that he had, feeling his stare on her back all the way down the hall.

The bright kitchen was warm from the cookstove and Tessa felt a little safer here. "Let's eat supper, shall we? The sooner I have this debt payed off the better I'll feel."

"Your enthusiasm for my company is overwhelming," Cody drawled.

"If you recall, you invited yourself," Tessa said snidely, and stepped to the stove where the pie sat. She grabbed a serving spoon and nodded to the hook on the wall. "You can hang your jacket there." As she reached for two towels to carry the hot tin with, she noticed the spread of Cody's wide shoulders shrugging out of that thick jacket. Fascinated, she watched him run a hand through his wind-mussed hair. When he turned he caught her staring and grinned that dazzling grin at her. Tessa started, burning herself on the tin after all, and she refrained from sucking on her fingers.

Lips set tight, Tessa whisked to the table with the pie, while Cody stood waiting by his chair, watching her. Why'd he have to be so impossibly handsome? Tessa wondered with a stab of annoyance as her brown eyes scanned his nonchalant stance. His shirt-sleeves were rolled up to his elbows and his collar was unbuttoned, revealing the tanned column of his throat. Tessa wrested her eyes away from that appealing sight and nodded to the chair.

"You can sit there," she said, and cut open the pie, the steam wafting up into her face; she spooned a huge chunk of it onto his plate. She all but slapped it down in front of him and Cody cocked his head at her, trying to get her to look at him.

"You wouldn't be trying to scald me now, Tessa, would you?"

She ignored him. "There're biscuits there and cranberry sauce so help yourself."

Amusement gleamed in his eyes as he watched her spoon some pie onto her own plate and seat herself across from him.

"How is teaching progressing?" Cody asked amiably, and popped a forkful of pie into his mouth.

Tessa thought of Smoke Eyes and sighed inwardly. "Between breaking up fistfights and rescuing students from Josh Jordan's pranks and pitching baseballs to both teams in order to prevent broken skulls, teaching is just fine," she answered, eyes sparkling with a touch of humor.

Cody laughed. "I'm surprised you lasted this long. The real test, though, is when the older boys come in."

"Oh? I didn't realize I was going to be examined."

Cody grunted. "Wait and see," he said, and Tessa didn't even want to think that there could be a tougher challenge than Smoke Eyes.

They ate their meal in companionable silence as the wind grew steadily outside the shelter of the warm house. At last, Cody wiped his mouth with his napkin, and leaning back lazily in his chair, he lifted his wineglass to his mouth and drank deeply. He looped one arm over the back of the chair, absently swirling the wine in little circles while his eyes considered Tessa across the table.

"Damn good pie, Tess."

She flushed with pleasure.

"Are you sure you made it?"

Her pleasure was short-lived. Her eyes blazed at him and Cody laughed softly. She didn't like the way he lounged in his chair, regarding her with that amused expression on his face. She wanted him to leave.

"Do you want some cake?" she asked, squeezing her fists tightly on her lap.

He cast her a wry, lopsided grin. "I ate half

that chicken pie. Believe me, it was enough."

The wind crooned outside the sturdy house. It sounded sad and lonely.

"I want to know more about Michael Shea."

Tessa's heart dived to the pit of her stomach. "What is there to know?"

He chuckled. "What's he do for a living? Why'd he let you come out here alone?"

I ran away from him because he beat me, Tessa thought with a strange, sick quivering as William's face blazed across her tormented mind. And if I told you, Cody, you'd send me back to him. And I can't ever go back to that!

"I refuse to discuss my personal life with you," she said evenly. "It's none of your business and I owe you no explanations. Now, if you'll excuse me, Dr. Butler, I have some schoolwork to attend to and I'd like to get to it while there is still time this evening." She stood, an obvious motion to dismiss him.

But Cody, in all his arrogance, did not move a muscle. Tessa saw his hard jaw tighten, and she shrank from the cold light in his dark green eyes.

"Your guest hasn't finished," he said with a sarcastic edge to his voice.

"Your hostess has," Tessa returned frigidly. "I have fulfilled my obligation to you, Dr. Butler. I have cooked dinner and shared the meal with you. I am not about to entertain you."

Their eyes clashed in a silent battle of wills. Cody's cold smile was a mere lift of his lip. "Fine," he said with no sign of softening in

his steely voice. He stood suddenly, his long
frame unfolding as he straightened, and he
leaned to put the wineglass down on the
table. "Before I leave I'll get the heater in there
working for you."

"I—" She began to protest but Cody wasn't
listening to her as he headed for the lean-to
where the coal was kept. Tessa rolled her eyes
at his back and left him to settle herself in the
chilly sitting room so as to look as busy as
possible when he came in.

She grabbed a book off a table and plopped
on the long sofa against one wall. She bent her
head over her work and tried to concentrate
while Cody built a fire in the stove. She heard
him strike a match and she peeked under the
skirt of her lashes to find him standing with
his back to her, hands planted on his hips as
he contemplated the fire. The soft lamplight
seemed to gloss his jet hair, which grew back
in soft waves to his nape where it curled up;
her fingers itched to touch it.

"There," he said finally, and she heard the
clatter of the stove lid as he set it back in place.
Oh, if only her heart would stop its wild
flailing! Surely he could hear it from here!
Cody turned to grin at her. "That should put
me in your good graces for a while at least."

Tessa smirked at him. "I wouldn't be too
confident if I were you."

He chuckled good-naturedly and she held
her breath when his shadow loomed before
her, covering the page she was pretending to
study. Then, much to her horror, he dropped

down on the sofa beside her, dark-clad legs sprawled out before him.

Tessa tensed, the small of her back pressing to the back of the sofa. "Just what do you think you're doing?"

Cody smiled lazily at her. "I'm warming up before you send me out into the cold."

As if agreeing with him, the wind rattled the glass windowpanes and now the hot stove was giving off heat, lending a dangerous, insidious coziness to the room. Tessa gripped her book; she felt as if every muscle in her body was locked with tension.

"And," Cody continued smoothly, leaning intimately toward her, "I'd like to see just what it takes to make you forget Michael. . . ." He reached out his hand and traced one long finger down the delicate length of her graceful jaw. Tessa drew back, trembling at the shivers of delight he aroused in her. He chuckled low, as if able to read her reaction to his touch.

No! She thought she said it but realized only her mind cried out while her body seemed to want to draw him near. His large hand cradled the side of her neck, gentle fingers slipping into the taut strands above her nape, loosening the pins. Wild, beating sensations expanded within her. Her wide brown eyes locked on his, smiling down at her, and her pulses beat too lightly, too quickly all over her weakening body.

Cody's free hand reached for the book she still held. But Tessa clung tightly to it, feeling if she relinquished it to him she'd somehow lose her hold on reality. It was a threshold she did not want to cross.

But Cody's strong fingers pried at hers and the book flew out of her hands, dropping heavily onto the floor.

"Leave it."

His commanding voice froze her; before she could react he captured her, pulling her close to his hard body, his mouth swooping down to seize hers. Tessa opened her mouth to object, but he took her protest away with his tongue. Everything dissolved within her as his driving, plunging tongue stroked hers rhythmically and explored her mouth with a hungry demand that made a fluid fire dance through Tessa's veins.

Please, please, she called on her drowned resolve, make him stop! Make *me* stop! But Tessa realized as her arm slipped around his neck and her fingers touched the curls at his collar that there was no stopping *this!*

Cody groaned into her mouth, leaning into her, ignoring the one palm she pressed to the hard swell of his chest, her last, tiny effort to keep him at bay. He'd already sensed her sweet surrender and the ache grew in him as her little tongue darted into his mouth, making the hot blood surge through his body.

Taking her face in his hands, his hard palms riding the smooth crest of her cheeks, Cody kissed her deeply, urging her backward bit by bit until she sank under the weight he eased upon her. Beneath him, Tessa panicked, and

she struggled, making helpless sounds into
his hot, open mouth, but his kiss was soothing
her, filling her with sweet, liquid surges and a
warm, throbbing excitement.

She felt the muscles in his shoulders shift
under her palms as he positioned his long
body so that one of his legs rested between
both of hers. And through her layers of underwear and woolen skirt, through the fabric
of his trousers, his masculine ridge pressed
insistently against the side of her thigh. Tessa
floundered beneath him, seeming to have lost
her breath, her hammering heart clogging her
throat. But he gave her no quarter.

"Tess . . ." Cody said hoarsely as he leaned
to nip her ear. His breath, hot and ragged,
pummeled her fleeing senses and she lay
wildly aware of his hard chest mercilessly
flattening her breasts, which tingled and
throbbed, feeling little protected under all her
clothes.

"Cody—this is wrong. You must stop—"
Breathlessly she pleaded in a voice that didn't
sound like hers at all. He made a gruff sound
and ground his hips against hers in answer,
and plucked her lower lip with his teeth,
releasing it with such tantalizing slowness
that swift currents washed through Tessa's
body with debilitating thoroughness. And all
the while his sturdy thigh pressed against the
most intimate, feminine part of her, bringing
there a fresh, surging warmth and a wanton
need. One of his hands still caressed the side
of her head while the other brushed her neck,

and his thumb stroked her jaw. He kissed her lilac-scented skin just inside the stiff collar of her high-necked blouse and little ripples shivered over her body. Somehow he'd managed to slip two fingers inside that collar and they skimmed across her silken shoulder . . . somehow her pearl bar pin was gone, and there was nothing fastening her blouse there under her chin.

"Cody, please . . ." Her voice was throaty, firing them both, and Cody touched his tongue to the pulse in the golden hollow of her throat. His hand wandered from her shoulder, which he squeezed reassuringly, to the front of her blouse where he found the buttons and Tessa felt them pop under his swift, expert fingers. Before she could draw a breath his open lips covered hers again, plying her mouth, and his fingers worked the ribbon of her chemise between her breasts until it fell open. He ran a palm up her bare ribs, bringing the lace-trimmed chemise with it, and Tessa fell still, her breath caught in her throat as he filled that palm with her warm breast. Her eyes flew open, meeting his, burning green, and then he leaned and kissed her slightly parted lips as he lifted her firm flesh, then pressed its resilient side so that her stiffened nipple stood straight. His thumb brushed it— just a whispering stroke—and Tessa's eyes shut slowly while her heart and senses beat like thunder.

Cody's warm lips slid to her neck, her shoulder, the swell of flesh he was kneading, and heat and tension built in Tessa to such an intensity that the anguish in her body was painfully sweet. He lowered his mouth and his tongue wet the point of her taut nipple, then stroked it once, twice, circling it, as a pleasured moan murmured up from Tessa's throat. His ardent breath warmed her skin as his mouth hovered for just a moment then took the hardened peak of her breast into his mouth where, between tongue and teeth, he gave it a soft, sweet tug, and she groaned, feeling everything tumble and slide inside her, creating a void deep as a well, yearning to be filled.

He tugged again with his teeth while her stomach tugged at her loins, and her fingers, without her knowing, twined in Cody's thick hair. Her voice, uttering his name, was strained and husky.

Cody leaned to taste her other breast while his hand fondled her abandoned one. Her breasts were gold-tinted like the rest of her, her taut nipples a dusky rose. They fit in his palms like warm, golden apples. The sight of them sent hot blood coursing through his loins, already heavy and full, and he growled low.

"I knew you'd be like this, Tess." His ragged whisper was hot on her skin. "I knew you were a passionate woman the first moment I set eyes on you. It's in your eyes, your mouth. Warm . . . made for a man's touch . . ." He stopped, looking up questioningly as her hands closed around his, pulling at them. He had no way of knowing that his voice and his words had the effect of a cold wind sweeping through her. Her deep brown eyes, looking deeper between her heavy lashes, despite the honey flecks in them, met his confused stare unwaveringly.

"Get off me, Cody," she ordered. "Now."

When he didn't move, but only lay upon her, she yanked at his wrists. But when he at last obliged, it was not in the way she would have him. Slowly he slid the length of his hard body up hers, and when his face was over hers, he placed a palm on each side of her head and looked deep, deep into her eyes. But they were cold.

"Tess." Not understanding, he leaned and brushed his lips across her unresponsive ones. He brought his dark head up and brushed the backs of his fingers gently over her cheek. She made no motion to even suggest he had touched her. "Don't expect me to apologize, because I am not sorry for what just happened between us. Maybe I just went a little too fast—"

"No, Cody."

Angry now, he moved himself away from her to the end of the sofa, riffling impatient fingers through his black, tousled hair.

"I'm off!" he barked. "Are you happy now?"

But Tessa was so shaken she couldn't trust herself to speak. How could she have let this happen? She forced herself to sit up, and as she buttoned her blouse her fingers shook uncontrollably. Only the wind and the sound of Cody's angry breathing broke the stillness in the room. She heard him swear with disgust and he brought his hand up to rub the back of his neck, then dropped it between his knees and barked again, "Say something!"

Tessa jumped at his tone, and tried desperately to keep the tears from her voice and eyes as she demanded, "What do you want from me, Cody? I told you"—and now tears sparkled like diamonds in her eyes—"for God's sake, that there's another man in my life!"

"That man," Cody snapped back, "is hundreds of miles away and more than likely won't ever make it out here! We belong together. Why do you deny it?"

"Oh!"

Frustrated and angry, Cody shot to his feet, his big fists clenched at his sides, his eyes spearing her to the sofa. "You're not married to him, dammit!"

Tessa's heart plummeted to her feet. My God, what kind of dangerous game was she playing?

Still, she gritted, "And how dare you suggest I sample every man in town because I'm not married to him!"

"Not every man. Just me."

Tessa's eyes widened on his. His solemn green gaze met hers and Tessa again felt the ache of tears surface in her throat. Even as her eyes filled, his intense gaze would not release hers. Oh, Cody, she thought, why are you doing this to me? Please don't complicate my life.

He stood there with legs braced apart, staring relentlessly down at her. "If there wasn't another man, would you?"

"What?" she croaked.

"Allow me to pursue you?"

His quiet words seemed to stab at her heart. He looked so vulnerable as he stood waiting for her answer. Oh, don't be ridiculous! she scolded herself. Cody Butler regarded her as just a new skirt in town for him to chase!

Tessa tipped her face up proudly and answered him steadily. "No." She saw his mouth tighten. "I'm not some cheap strumpet. I'm a schoolteacher." And she squared her slender shoulders as her eyes narrowed on him. "Get out of here, Cody! Go after some other woman like Angie Foster who would be glad to have you!"

Cody's jaw was rigid. "Maybe I will!" He sneered. "God knows, at least she doesn't mind admitting what she likes about a man!"

"I said get out!"

"I'm out!" he snapped, and stalked out of the room, taking long, angry strides until he was gone from view. But Tessa heard him storm down the hall and slam his way out the back door.

She saw her bar pin there on the carpet by the forgotten schoolbook and reached for it, but stopped and sank back on the sofa, cov-

ering her forehead with her hand as the tears
at last slid slowly from her eyes.

Chapter Seven

✦ ✦ ✦ ✦ ✦

TWO WEEKS PASSED and only once, from a distance, did Tessa set eyes on Cody. But even
for that instant—as she saw him talking with a
matronly woman outside the newspaper
building—she felt a strange quickening within
her at the sight of him. He had looked up and
seen her, acknowledged her with a nod of his
head, and walked on. And as she watched
those broad shoulders until they were gone
from view, she felt a curious sense of deser-
tion.

What was wrong with her? Surely, she had
been right to rebuff him. Then why did her
days seem so curiously lonely? Why did she
miss their quarrels, their bantering, yes, even
his outrageously indecent remarks? Worst of
all, why did images of Cody and that Saturday
night spring unbidden into her mind at all the
wrong times? The sweet shock of his long
fingers and mouth upon her was a memory
that soared through her too many times in a
day.

She buried herself in her work. Two of the

infamous older boys came into school one morning, and Tessa was surprised at their initial exemplary behavior. The elder, Sidney Chase, was almost seventeen, a tall, well-dressed boy with nice features and smooth brown hair. He was from the East and had an air of the city about him. The other, fourteen-year-old Drew Chapman, whose sisters had been in school from the start, was a short, stocky boy who showed a gift for writing stories. They were both well mannered and courteous, with no signs of belligerence.

Tessa still looked for Smoke Eyes every day, but there had been no trace of the child since her fight with Sam. And now, as Cody had predicted, the frozen ground had become too hard for her to carve letters into. She was beginning to lose hope that Smoke Eyes would ever come to school.

Because she was feeling poorly, Mary Lyndon had to cancel her plans to attend the social that first Saturday night after Tessa's supper with Cody. But she and her husband Timothy stopped by for Tessa promptly at seven o'clock the following Saturday evening.

"Why, don't you look wonderful!" Mary exclaimed, eyeing Tessa's dress of violet-blue wool. It was long-sleeved, the collar high-necked, and there was a pretty lace edging at her throat and wrists. Tiny round pearl buttons ran down the center of the dress, buttoning the bodice. She looked the perfect schoolteacher. She thanked Mary for her compliment and they all stepped out into the cold, clear night. Tessa glanced up and saw the black heavens filled with silver stars, so many of them that their points seemed to touch. She breathed deep of the frozen air, the cold going down deep into her lungs. And when she breathed out again her breath was smoky white.

As they walked toward the saloon Mary chatted gaily, clinging to her husband's arm so she wouldn't slip on the mucky road. Tim held the kerosene lantern up so Tessa could pick her way carefully over the iced-over puddles, hoping she would not splatter mud across her hem.

"I hope you enjoy yourself, Tessa," Mary was saying. "You wouldn't believe the transformation inside that saloon."

"No, you wouldn't," Timothy interjected, a bit dryly. He glanced down at his pretty wife. "But how would *you* know? Do you visit that saloon when I'm out in the fields working?"

Both women laughed.

Mary tapped him playfully on the arm. "Why, Tim, you're the one who tells me what it's like! The men go to drink liquor and play cards, but on Saturday evening the saloon is a place for the men to take their women and for all to have a good time."

Tessa couldn't help but notice that they were headed for the saloon Cody helped build. Already they could hear sounds of laughter and music spilling out into the night. Tessa had never set foot inside a saloon, of course, and a sense of exhilaration and excitement seized her now as they approached the false-fronted building.

When Tim opened the door, blazing light and laughter and music accosted them with a warm, vibrant gaiety. They stepped inside, shutting out the cold night behind them. It took a moment for Tessa's eyes to adjust to the bright light, and as they did she could see the room was packed with townfolk dancing, laughing, drinking, and eating. All the round wooden tables were pushed back against the walls, and chairs were scattered in clumps around the room for those who wished to sit and chat. The middle of the floor was cleared for dancing and was crowded with couples swinging and swirling to the music from the piano that was jammed into one corner of the saloon where a man furiously pounded the keys. Around the piano stood a man playing a jubilant fiddle and another plucking a banjo. People laughed and clapped their hands, and those sitting found it hard to keep their feet still.

There was a cidery smell to the saloon, mixed with wood scents and beer. Tessa's eyes strayed to the long, polished bar that held cakes and pies baked by the local women; there was tea and coffee and apple cider and beer to drink. The big saloon with its bright lights and warm woods was much cleaner than Tessa had expected, and she felt a strange dart of pride go through her as she remembered Cody's part in it. A library, she thought with some amusement, might not be as useful as this after all!

"Let's sit over here," Mary suggested, and they moved away from the door to one side of the room where a few vacant chairs were situated amid a group of women. Tessa recognized a few of them and they greeted the newcomers warmly.

"How good to see you, Mary, Tim, Miss Amesbury," welcomed Alice McGuire, little Jake's mother.

"Call me Tessa, please," she insisted with a smile as she and Mary removed their wraps and arranged them over the backs of their chairs. "I'm your children's teacher, not yours."

The women laughed with her, enchanted by the prim-looking teacher's sense of humor.

"Can I get you something to eat or drink?" Tim asked both Mary and Tessa as he helped his wife lower her cumbersome body to the chair.

"I'll take a cup of tea," Mary said. "I'm chilled through."

"Nothing for me, thank you," Tessa said, fascinated by the jovial atmosphere. She recognized Reverend Donaldson standing with a group of men, and there was Mike, Eb's son, and Mr. Mason, Will's father, and the barber whom she only knew as Harry, and there was Mrs. Rawlins with Eb! Tessa laughed and waved at the couple, who were helping themselves to some cake.

"Aren't they adorable?" Mary whispered to Tessa. "I think Eb is smitten!"

Tessa laughed. "I think so too!"

Tim came up with Mary's tea then and teased her that she was getting along fine without him, then moved on to talk with a group of men in one corner.

Martha Jordan leaned forward in her chair and lightly touched Tessa's forearm. Tessa had met her once briefly after church services one Sunday, and looking at her, Tessa knew where the woman's boys got their freckles. "Are my Sam and Josh settling down any?" she asked hopefully. At Tessa's hesitation all the women laughed again, including Martha.

"Honestly"—she sighed—"the two of them have kept me jumping since they were little mites. I think their father's too easy on them."

"Oh, you do, do you?" A man from above them all chortled. It was Ben Jordan, Martha's husband.

"Why, Ben, you've been eavesdropping on women talk!" his wife accused, turning to laugh up at him.

"Sure, that's the only way I get any information!" Ben chuckled gleefully as his eyes twinkled at Tessa. "An' my boys tell me this here new schoolteacher has got one heckuva good pitchin' arm!"

As Tessa turned a brilliant shade of pink Ben Jordan guffawed as if he, too, had just played a prank on her. Yet Tessa leaned toward him in a conspiratorial manner and said behind her hand, "If your boys think I have one good pitching arm, wait till they see me hit a ball! But I'm saving that surprise for spring!"

Their laughter nearly drowned out the dance music, which made the floorboards vibrate under their feet.

Ben moved on, still chuckling, and Tessa began to realize that both Sam and Josh had inherited their sense of mischief from their father.

It was then that Tessa noticed Ned Winston approaching her. She found herself blushing when she recalled Cody's accusation that she had been flirting with the young man. As Ned came closer it struck her again how youthful he looked and how soft his blue eyes were.

"Hello, Miss Amesbury. How nice to see you here," he greeted, almost shyly, glancing at the other women who watched the two with some interest.

"Hello, Mr. Winston, how are you?"

"Call me Ned, please." Belatedly, he added, "And how are you?"

Was he nervous talking to her? The way he kept shifting his weight from side to side made Tessa wonder. "I'm fine."

"Would you care to dance?"

Oh dear, dance? When was the last time she'd danced?

"Why, yes, I'd love to."

Once they were out on the dance floor Ned's blue eyes searched Tessa's. "Why haven't you stopped by the restaurant?" he inquired.

"Oh," she answered lightly, "teaching occupies most of my time."

"I'd like to show you some of my watercolors. Could you stop by some afternoon or on a Saturday?"

"You're an artist?"

A flicker of a smile touched Ned's lips. "You'll have to be the judge of that."

Tessa was suddenly intrigued. "I'd love to see your work. Yes; I will come by sometime to see it."

Ned's face lighted up as if she'd just awarded him a great honor. He was a very nice and gentle man, Tessa decided, and she didn't care what Cody Butler said about him.

If she thought her dance might be the end of her stint on the dance floor, Tessa was much mistaken. A curly haired man with merry black eyes named Jim McGafferty cut in, and after that it seemed as if Tessa danced with nearly every bachelor in town. There seemed to be many more bachelors than unmarried women in Harper City, and now there was one more single woman!

Angie Foster, fully aware of her seductive charms, worked her wiles on any man willing—and most seemed willing. Did Cody realize that his mistress—or whatever Angie was to him—went to such outrageous lengths to attract male attention?

As for Tessa, she hadn't had so much attention in all her life! Flushed and sparkling-eyed from dancing, she breathlessly begged her partner for respite and he graciously led her off the dance floor. They were intercepted, however, by Ned, who caught Tessa's wrists lightly.

"You must come meet my parents," he insisted, but just at the moment Tessa looked past Ned's shoulder, she saw Cody Butler come into the saloon.

Her heart lurched in her chest. She hadn't expected to see him tonight! Tall and broad-shouldered, he cut quite an awesome figure standing there in the crowded room. He wore a shirt of deep blue and over the shirt, a rough leather vest. He was freshly shaven and his hair was clipped a little shorter around his ears since the last time she'd seen him. He looked so flawlessly handsome that Tessa found it hard not to stare at him.

One of the townsmen greeted him and he flashed that fabulous smile, drawing the eyes of every woman in the room. Casually he slipped his hands inside his trouser pockets and made a quick study of the saloon. It was as if he was looking for someone—for her?

And at that precise moment he saw her. Across the crowded room his deep green eyes seemed to scorch a path to her and Tessa's breath went feather-light at the intensity in his gaze. All sound and motion seemed to fall away—all but the thud of blood in her ears. Now her senses flooded back to her with an acute awareness. The music seemed louder, the smell of beer keen in her nostrils, and Cody's eyes more penetrating as they suddenly dropped to Ned's hands locked on her delicate wrists. A dark scowl drew his eyebrows down.

As if sensing disapproval of the man behind him, Ned released her wrists. Cody started toward her. A flash of panic knifed through Tessa. Oh, she didn't want to confront him! But Ned was guiding her toward his parents now and Ben Jordan had reached out and grabbed Cody's arm, holding his attention with some words, and at last Tessa was able to let out a pent-up breath.

Tessa spoke politely with Grady and Hattie Winston for a few moments, then excused herself and moved toward the refreshment table to help herself to a mug of cider. The evening was changed now that Cody had come; her guard was up, and she desperately hoped he would leave her alone. But just thinking about the way he'd glowered at her when he first saw her with Ned made goose bumps spring up all over her skin.

"Hullo, Miss Amesbury!"

Tessa glanced up to see Hal Witherby, the wagon driver, and he looked surprised to see her here—as if he couldn't quite believe she hadn't fled town by now. She gave him a rather distracted smile as he hurried off to join old Abbott Robbins.

Suddenly the crowd stilled; a suspended air of anticipation hung over the saloon, and Tessa looked up to find their attention focused on the musicians by the west wall. She strained futilely to get a better look, but understood the silence when the haunting, plaintive notes of a harmonica whispered over her skin. She shivered, and something caught in her throat as the heart-tugging music keened mournfully in the hushed saloon.

Finally someone in front of Tessa moved aside and she stared fascinated at the man who played the instrument. She watched his mouth and hands move sensually over the instrument. He closed his eyes and breathed into it with such riveting tenderness that odd emotions tightened in her chest and she felt tears well in her eyes. Indeed, several other women wiped at their eyes and the men stood solemn and rock-jawed.

"Cody," she breathed, wanting to tell him how beautiful it was.

"He's something, isn't he?" a soft-spoken woman said beside her. It was Claire, Eb's daughter-in-law, and her huge gray eyes were misty too. She laughed a little and wiped an eye with the back of her hand. "I almost wished he wouldn't play."

Tessa smiled softly, understanding. "I had no idea he *could* play," she said, almost whispering, not wanting to miss a note.

"Oh, yes," Claire whispered back. "Cody is a very skilled musician."

Tessa blinked. "He is?"

"Yes, but he likes to play the harmonica best. He sings too."

"Sings?" Tessa echoed stupidly, her eyes dragging back to the man who held his audience spellbound. Admittedly he held a dread fascination for her too.

"Oh, Lord, can he sing." Claire laughed, noticing Tessa's wide-eyed stare. "But I'm not sure you're ready for that!"

Tessa flushed, pulling her eyes away from Cody and returning them to Claire with an effort. Then she laughed too. "I'm not sure I'm ready either!"

Without warning Cody broke into a lively, foot-stomping, hand-clapping tune in accompaniment with Charlie Pendleton on the fiddle. Tessa marveled at his sudden exuberance. This man was full of surprises.

But she was to learn that he possessed even more energy than she'd guessed. Cody, it seemed, was the topic of conversation as both Susan Miller and Beth Calvert joined Tessa and Claire at the refreshment table.

"Cody's the founder of Harper City," Claire told her. "Harper was his grandfather's name. He was very close to his mother's father."

"That's right," Susan Miller added. "He'd chosen this site and put down stakes here long before any of us came out. He returned to Kentucky to recruit us and a group of us came out together along with old Doc Rawlins. Cody had every intention of joining us later—he had other interests in other cities and a practice in Kentucky he had to tie up, but old Doc Rawlins died suddenly and Cody came out earlier than any of us expected. Folks from all over filtered in last summer and

I suppose we'll be bringing in more home-steaders come spring. Once the weather turns warm again, there'll be more building up this town. We'll make Harper City a city yet!"

The others nodded their agreement.

"What do you think of our town doctor, Tessa?" asked Beth.

Caught off guard, Tessa could only stutter, "I—I think he's nice." She didn't think he was nice at all, of course, but she couldn't tell these women that; they seemed totally enchanted with Dr. Cody Butler.

"Yes, he's nice all right, and Angie Foster thinks so too."

They all turned to look at the blonde, Tessa included. Angie was clinging to Cody's shirt-sleeve and gazing up at him in a most simpering way. Cody bent his dark head toward her to listen more closely to what she had to say. Tessa felt a tiny stab of jealousy, then turned her back on the two, telling herself she had no right to feel anything where that man was concerned!

"Well, he is a prime catch," Susan said, "with his money and looks and charm. . . ."

"Cody is rich?" It was out before she could stop it, and Tessa wanted to bite her lip—hard! But none of the women thought her interest in Cody was unusual.

Susan Miller chuckled. "Honey, he was *born* rich! One of the wealthiest families in the South. And Cody has invested his money wisely. The only reason he's in this little town is because it's raw, a challenge! That man's always looking for a challenge."

Why did it suddenly annoy Tessa that they were discussing Cody in such detail?

"I'm going to go back now and keep Mary company," she murmured. "Any of you coming?"

Claire followed her as she threaded her way through the crowd, back to where she'd been sitting. Twice she was stopped by young men asking her to dance but she begged off, feeling somewhat guilty for having abandoned Mary for so long.

But Mary was not alone. Tessa almost stopped short when she saw Cody sitting in *her* chair, leaning forward, elbows propped on his knees as he talked with Mary. His big, dark hands were cupped around a glass of whiskey, and as he raised it to his mouth and took a long swallow, his eyes met Tessa's over the rim. Tessa's heart somersaulted, then filled her throat with hard, thick thuds. Damn him, why did he provoke this response in her?

She saw his lips quirk in a little smile as he lowered the glass and straightened in his chair. His expression turned humorous when he saw the little upward nudge of her chin.

He was on his feet now, his tall body blocking out the others from Tessa's view. But, of course, she was not looking at the others. "Hello, Miss Amesbury," he drawled softly. "I didn't mean to steal your chair."

Her eyes flashed defiance at him. "I bet,"
she said under her breath, and he chuckled
appreciatively. His amused eyes went to her
tightly drawn-back hair, but she was flushed,
and damp tendrils of hair clung to her neck
and temples, contradicting her schoolmarm
appearance. "Do you mind," she asked, sar-
casm heavy in her sweet voice, "if I sit down?"

"Hell, no," and he grinned his most devastating grin at her as he gripped the back of
her chair and gestured for her to take a seat.

"Thank you," she said dryly, and settled
herself, hoping he'd take the hint and leave
now that there were no more vacant chairs.
But much to her dismay, Cody, in one swift
movement, crouched down beside her chair,
no farther than a foot away. She tried not to
glance down to where his trousers stretched
tight over his muscle-hard thigh, but she
couldn't resist. That masculine thigh, Tessa
thought, with both shame and exhilaration
racing through her veins, had touched her
intimately just two Saturdays ago. Remembering, she felt a surge of warmth and she cursed
herself for her weakness. She pulled her eyes
away and looked out to the dance floor,
wishing she could sprint from the room.

"Hey, Cody," someone called out, and
Tessa jumped, nearly spilling the cider out of
her mug, "here's a chair! I'm going to do me
some dancin' with Laura here."

Cody stood and Tessa's eyes followed the
length of him as he reached for the chair with
one hand and clapped it down beside her. He

swung a leg over it and dropped to the seat, his knees sprawled wide. Every nerve within Tessa seemed to clamor as she sat struggling with the urge to fidget.

"Tessa," Mary said gaily, "I wasn't sure if I was going to see you anymore this evening! You certainly are popular!"

It was something Cody had noticed too. He glanced now to her piquant face with its dark brows arched above her beautiful rich brown eyes, and found himself absurdly annoyed that she had been dancing with other men all evening. It was ridiculous to get himself worked up over that namby-pamby Winston, but he was. Maybe it had something to do with the way she had so vehemently fought off his own advances while she obviously welcomed Ned's attentions. Or maybe that wasn't it at all.

"Had your share of dancing, have you?"

Tessa brought her dark eyes back to Cody's face. His voice had been amiable enough, but she'd detected a sarcastic edge to it.

"Yes," she replied, keeping her gaze steady on his. She didn't have to answer to him! She watched that dark, censuring scowl pull his brows down yet he relaxed back, slouching slightly, tipping the chair so that just the two hind legs held his weight. Those green eyes surveyed her consideringly and in such a long, leisurely way that Tessa snapped under her breath, "Didn't your mother ever teach you how rude it is to stare!"

His laughter was drowned by the music,

but that deep, warm smile was left on his handsome face. Suddenly, decidedly, he dropped the chair on all fours again and leaned toward her, his long fingers circling her delicate wrist like a dark bracelet.

"Here's one man you haven't danced with," he murmured, setting down his glass on the floor beside him. He took her mug from her numbed fingers and put it down too, then urged her to her feet. As Tessa gave her wrist a halfhearted tug, Cody pulled her toward him. "I want to dance with you," he said forcefully.

"Well, I don't want to dance with you!" she returned with a sweet smile.

"Yeah, but what you want doesn't matter," and he laughed at her outraged indrawn breath as he ushered her to the dance floor. His hand, on the small of her back, seemed to burn through her clothing and into her blood, flowing warmly through her body.

His arm circled her slim waist and drew her close to his body, closer than any other man had dared all night. Tessa's eyes were angry-bright.

"Don't you know how to *ask* a lady to dance?"

Cody's mouth turned up in a mocking smile. "Sure. But if I asked you, you would've refused and I didn't want to cause a scene by dragging you out here by your hair. God knows," and his eyes flicked to her breasts, then up again, "I'd have to fight off at least a dozen men in a rescue attempt." Again, Tessa heard that sarcastic tinge in his voice. He pulled her against him and she felt a shock go through her, realizing he danced as smoothly and gracefully as he walked. She could feel the power of his body beneath his clothes. No other man this evening had managed to send her heart thrumming like this, and though she tried to fight the attraction she felt for him, there was no stopping those wild, beating things swimming through her. He smelled of leather and cleanness mixed with a hint of tobacco, and all these smells combined were Cody, only Cody.

"I didn't expect to see you here tonight," she managed at last. "I thought Lily's dance hall was more suited to your tastes." She tilted her face up to meet his eyes.

"Ah, there you go again, assuming the worst. What does it take to convince you that my interest in Lily is strictly clinical?"

"Perhaps you're right. Then again, *Angie* is here."

A trace of annoyance showed on his face. "I don't want to talk about Angie, dammit, and neither do you."

He felt her slender body tense and he had the sudden mad desire to drag her outside and kiss her until she melted in his embrace. His gaze lowered to her breasts and she colored. She remembered all too clearly how she had responded to his touch. When Cody raised his eyes again, Tessa caught the glint of amusement in them.

"You look the part tonight, Miss Amesbury." He dipped his head lower and his warm breath stirred the hair near her ear. "Who would guess that underneath that high collar and dull color the schoolteacher wears lace on her undergarments?"

Tessa gasped in shock and stumbled. When she regained her footing, she tried to break free, but Cody's arm was an unrelenting band around her narrow waist and he pulled her even closer against his long, muscular body. He nearly cut her breath off again; Tessa fought the slight sense of dizziness that made her knees go weak. She saw his sensuous mouth drawn in a sardonic smile, mocking her.

"You insufferable beast! Let me go!" She struggled again, but his powerful fingers gripped hers so tightly she feared he might crush her bones.

"The hell I will, lady." His voice was soft but there was no mistaking the steely determination in his words. Then he chuckled at the anger in her narrowed eyes. "We're going to finish this dance."

"You're hurting me," she managed, and immediately his hold loosened, and he muttered, "Sorry." His sudden gentleness made her blood tingle, and her body relaxed a bit, moving in time with his on the dance floor. When at last the song was over, Tessa allowed him to escort her to her seat, suppressing the desire to yank her elbow from his grip and run on ahead of him. Much to her relief, he left her with a little bow and headed for the bar.

For Tessa, the tone of the entire evening changed after that dance. The room seemed to take on an unreal quality, people's faces faded about her. She wiped the back of her hand across her damp brow, then pressed her palms to her burning cheeks and thought a breath of night air might do her some good. Not bothering with her coat, she leaned to tell Mary where she was headed and got up and left the saloon.

The cold night air was as bracing as a dash of ice water against her face, and Tessa leaned against the porch rail, dragging in great, clean gusts of it. The cold seared her lungs, reviving her. She dropped her head back to gaze up at the night sky; the stars had vanished, almost as if a giant puff of wind had extinguished them all, and racing clouds marbled the moon. The lantern light that hung from the porch above lent a kind of eerie glow to the scene. Behind her, a sudden burst of noise and laughter and music spilled out of the saloon as a small party of people tumbled out of the door and called their good-nights to one another. Their jovial voices faded as they descended the shallow wooden steps and started down the road.

But Tessa heard none of it. Her gaze lingered on the moon, heavy and full in the strange plum-colored sky, and everything but the sudden sense of reverence she felt for the night faded from her thoughts.

A deep, now familiar male voice from behind broke her reverie while seeming to embrace her. "You're going to catch pneumonia standing out here, Tess."

Did she shiver from the cold or from the caressing way he uttered her name . . . Tess?

He stood very close to her. She was acutely aware of his presence without turning to look at him—his tall body was shielding her against the northeast wind.

"It's a lovely night," she commented, looking out across the street at nothing but darkness, keeping her eyes away from him.

"That it is," he murmured.

"Is everyone always so friendly to newcomers here?"

"Most times."

"They've made me feel so welcome."

"No reason not to."

At last she glanced over at him. But he'd changed his stance and she was surprised to see, by the faint light of the lantern, his wide hand cupping a pipe as he lit it. He leaned against the post again and the fragrant tobacco smoke curled about her. She breathed deep, enjoying the rich, homey smell. He smoked his pipe in silence, contemplating her.

"Do you think we'll have a cold winter?" She knew her comments were trivial, but she couldn't seem to help herself.

She saw him shrug as he crossed his arms over his broad chest. "Can't always tell just because the fall has been cold."

They studied each other's shadowy faces for a moment. "Why did you come out here?" There! Finally she had asked what she was really wondering, and suddenly she wanted to recall the words.

Cody grinned at her, the pipe stem clenched between his strong white teeth. Softly he asked, "Still mad at me?"

Her heart seemed stuck in her throat as Cody's probing gaze filled her with some strange emotion. She hugged her arms to her thin body and tried to answer him, but he spoke again before she had the chance to reply.

"Not about what I said in there," he clarified with a terse nod toward the saloon door, "but about what happened on Mrs. Rawlins's sofa."

She hadn't expected him to ask that! Tessa's hands gripped the wooden railing so hard she feared she might snap it. She turned away from him again, offering her profile to him as her gaze fell to the road.

Cody reached out to touch her elbow, but when she flinched, he stuffed his hand into his trouser pocket. She was conscious of his green eyes drilling her, seeming to draw her close with their power, and suddenly Tessa wanted to hide from his intense, penetrating gaze. "Are you?" he asked gently, and she flinched again. She closed her eyes, fighting the sting of tears behind her lids.

"Please, Cody," she begged softly. "I don't want to talk about it."

Again he removed his hand from his pocket, and this time lifted it to slide under her chin, gently tipping her face up so he could see into her eyes. She tried to twist away—to hide from his dark, frowning eyes, but his long fingers tightened on her soft flesh. In contrast to his forceful fingers, his voice was silky, almost tender. "Don't be ashamed, little one. You're a desirable woman—even if you don't want to believe it. If you let me, I can convince you of that."

Mesmerized by the caress in his voice and in his eyes, Tessa replied in a voice that trembled despite her resolve to keep it even. "I don't need convincing."

His eyes seemed to glitter. So she did know. "And you don't want to be," he confirmed. "Desirable, that is."

Her eyes glittered back at him. "Not to you. To—to Michael."

Their voices had become breathy, hushed, intimate.

"Mmm." Cody let his fingers release her chin and he ran the backs of them up her delicate jawline. Tessa shivered again, but this time she knew it wasn't from the cold. He stood holding her with his eyes, letting his fingers trail over her cheek now. Tessa's stomach quaked. But she did not move. The sudden, terrifying notion came to her that she *wanted* him to kiss her—she wanted to feel his warm, compelling mouth cover hers, to have him pull her against his hard, warm body. But it was he, this time, who drew away. Disappointment flooded her.

She watched him lean back so he was half sitting on the railing, one foot on the porch and the other long leg dangling lazily as he stared back at her.

"Oh!" Tessa started as something cold nipped at her nose. She turned her face toward the black heavens and laughed as soft, fat snowflakes floated down lazily, dusting her eyelashes. She was astonished at the scene before her. It wasn't even November yet. "Why, it's—it's—"

"It's starting to snow," Cody finished laconically.

"Oh, yes!" she agreed, laughing again, delighted as the snow flew down faster and thicker now. "I love the first snow! There's something magical about it, don't you think, Cody?" She hugged her arms against her.

What he thought, in that moment, as her large eyes danced in delight, was that he'd like to take her home with him—now. There was something whimsical and girlish about her as she let the powder flakes kiss her upturned face. Watching her, Cody felt a tightening in his loins. He smiled when the tip of her tongue came out to catch a snowflake.

"What I think," he said, coming to his feet, "is that you better get inside. What are you doing out here without a coat on anyway?"

But she ignored him, pulling her elbow from his grasp. "Not yet. I don't want to go in until I start to shiver!" And then she shivered.

He laughed and his smoky breath felt like a warm mist in the cold night. She laughed with him as he urged her toward the door.

"Cody—Cody—"

Jesus. "What?" Didn't she know how she tempted him, looking up at him with those laughing eyes?

"Why didn't you tell me you played the harmonica?"

He smiled crookedly down at her. "It didn't come up in any of our conversations."

"You play beautifully." The laughter had gone out of her voice now. She saw his face sober, and now that they stood almost directly under the lantern, she saw the pleasure in his eyes.

"Thanks," he said roughly.

"How long have you played?"

"Since I was six."

"Six!"

He smiled his crooked grin. "My grandfather gave me a harmonica for my birthday. He seemed to know what made me tick."

"Claire says you play other instruments too."

"I like the harmonica best." He laughed suddenly. "My mother used to tease me and say I had gypsy blood running in my veins."

This time when her eyes met his, Cody could swear he caught a flirtatious sparkle in Miss Tessa Amesbury's night-dark eyes. "I wouldn't doubt it!" she tossed at him, and he chuckled and slid his arm around her shoulders, pulling her lightly against his hip as he reached to open the door. "Get in there, you little minx!"

And Tessa scooted ahead of him, her past,

and William Forsythe, a very distant memory in her mind.

Chapter Eight

✦ ✦ ✦ ✦

ON A CLOUDY, cold Saturday afternoon in November, Tessa was sitting close to the heater in the sitting room preparing lessons when she felt someone watching her. When she looked up, she saw Smoke Eyes' brown face peeking in from the porch. But the girl vanished as soon as Tessa returned her stare.

A secret smile curved Tessa's lips as she again bent her head over her work, waiting for the child to knock on the door. She'd be *damned* if she was going to chase her again!

It surprised her when the knock actually sounded. A strange sound since Smoke Eyes knocked with the butt of her palm on the window. Mercy! Hadn't anyone ever taught that child some manners?

Slightly annoyed now, Tessa put down her work and went to the front door. When she opened it, she was surprised to see Smoke Eyes standing there squinting up at her, freshly scrubbed and in new, clean buckskins. Under her fur cap her hair was pulled back in a thick, red braid, and now that her face was free of dirt and grime, her unusual coloring was clearly revealed. A sprinkling of freckles graced the bridge of her small nose and dusted her golden-brown cheeks; long, midnight-black eyelashes fringed her smoky eyes. The blood of both the Arapaho and Irish were stamped into her features.

Smoke Eyes must have caught the amusement on the teacher's face because she muttered defensively, "I been busy."

Tessa was barely able to keep the amusement out of her voice. "I can see that you have." She must have taken a month to scrub her skin so clean and make those new buckskins, Tessa thought. But when she saw Smoke Eyes jam her hands under her armpits to warm them, Tessa realized she'd forgotten her own manners. "Oh, I'm sorry, Smoke Eyes, won't you come in?" Tessa swung the door wide and reluctantly Smoke Eyes stepped inside. Her steely eyes skipped to the sitting room beyond.

The girl stood awkwardly, with her hands behind her back, looking like she was afraid to sit.

"How did you know I lived here, Smoke Eyes?"

The girl rubbed her nose. "I been watchin'. I din't want to go to the school no more, so I watched where else I could find you."

Tessa glanced to the girl's wind-reddened hands. "And how long have you been outside?"

Smoke Eyes avoided Tessa's knowing gaze and she shrugged. "A while, I guess."

"Would you like some tea? I know Mrs. Rawlins has the kettle on."

The girl shrugged and Tessa directed her to the kitchen where Mrs. Rawlins was preparing tea and cookies for herself and Tessa.

"Oh," the widow exclaimed when she saw Smoke Eyes, "we have company!"

The three sat at the table with their refreshments before them. While Tessa and Mrs. Rawlins sipped daintily at their tea Smoke Eyes was busy trying to cool hers enough to drink it. She leaned over the cup and blew so hard on it that the tea splashed over the rim and onto the saucer. When she blew again, drops splattered on Mrs. Rawlins's bodice. The older woman leaped back in surprise, but said nothing.

"Smoke Eyes," Tessa broke in gently, "why don't you eat some cookies while you're waiting for that to cool."

Smoke Eyes glanced up, shrugged, and grabbed a handful of butter cookies. She wolfed them down and reached for more.

"Cookies," she said through a mouthful of them, "I ain't had cookies since my ma—" She dropped her eyes and shoved another three into her mouth. Mrs. Rawlins ignored her tea; her eyes seemed glued on Smoke Eyes. The girl continued to munch her way happily through the entire plateful of cookies, and when she was done she looked around for more. But neither woman offered any more.

Smoke Eyes shrugged again and reached for her teacup, raised it to her lips with both hands circling the delicate china, and slurped the liquid down greedily. She set the cup down with a clatter and wiped the back of her hand across her dirty mouth. Then she belched.

Mrs. Rawlins pressed her fingertips to her own mouth and her startled blue eyes opened wide. Looking confused, she blinked owlishly at the child sitting in front of her as if she didn't quite believe what she had seen.

The old woman came wearily to her feet. "I think I'll go lay down for a while, Tessa. It's time for my nap."

"Of course, Mrs. Rawlins. I'll fix us a light supper so don't worry about that."

But Mrs. Rawlins just paled, and hurried from the room.

Now that the two of them were alone, Tessa tried to talk to Smoke Eyes. She leaned her elbows on the table and looked directly into the girl's eyes. "Your mother used to make cookies, Smoke Eyes?"

The girl's eyes went hard. "I don't wanna talk about Ma."

But Tessa persisted. "Did she teach you to eat them like that too?"

This time she quite obviously had struck a deep chord. Smoke Eyes' gaze flashed as it met Tessa's. She leaped to her feet, ready to charge out the back door, but this time Tessa was ready for her. Under the table she kicked the chair behind the girl so Smoke Eyes got her legs tangled and she sat down hard. Tessa was beside her in an instant, pinning the squirming child's arms to her sides, and for a moment she thought Smoke Eyes was going to spit in her face.

Tessa was shocked at her own actions but she was determined not to lose this child again. "Stop it!" she insisted as Smoke Eyes kicked at her legs. Her eyes blazed up at Tessa, but Tessa's were blazing too. She shook the child a little and by now the fur cap Smoke Eyes hadn't bothered to remove was rolling across the floor. "Don't you care about yourself, Smoke Eyes?"

"Let me go!"

"I won't!" and Tessa's voice trembled with fury. "I won't let you go until you promise me you'll sit and talk with me. You came here for a reason and I want to hear it."

Smoke Eyes' lips were a stubborn, thin white line. Her narrowed eyes were furious but Tessa felt some of the fight ease out of her thin shoulders. "Promise," she muttered. Still Tessa did not release her. The girl looked up at her disbelievingly. "I said I promise, din't I?" Smoke Eyes laughed shortly. "Hah! You don't trust me. Yer smart, Teacher."

"Please, Smoke Eyes. I want to talk with you."

Begrudgingly Smoke Eyes lowered her eyes.

Tessa backed slowly away. She eased herself back into her chair and Smoke Eyes raised her head. When Tessa was fairly certain that the girl wouldn't run, she let out a long, quiet breath. "Sam Jordan is very embarrassed because you thrashed him so soundly."

Smoke Eyes smirked. "He deserved it!"

"Smoke Eyes."

Their eyes met. And suddenly both pairs began to dance. Tessa wouldn't admit that Sam deserved what he had gotten, but both knew what the other was thinking. And both felt a smug pride that a girl had bested a boy.

"Boys brag too much," Smoke Eyes said simply, and Tessa didn't argue the point. "I got him good, din't I?" the girl said with obvious delight.

Tessa cleared her throat. "Still, it didn't help you, Smoke Eyes. And I have to tell you he is planning revenge."

"That sure don't surprise me. Mebbe he's gotta ambush in mind."

Tessa sobered. Ah, yes, the child would know all about that. "Sometimes you have to turn the other cheek, Smoke Eyes."

"Like my ma's people did?"

Tessa didn't know much about the Arapaho people. She only knew that most of them were living on reservations.

"I ain't ashamed of my people, Teacher."

"I don't want you to be, Smoke Eyes."

"But other folks want me to be. Lots of folks do, an' some ain't even sure why."

Tessa frowned. "They're wrong. And it wouldn't be that way at school if you just come in and give it a try."

"Ha! Jes give it a try ya say. Folks hate breeds. Hate 'em!" And her beautiful eyes narrowed. "But I wanna be a doctor, Teacher. I wanna save folks from dyin', from sufferin'. Doc Butler says I should. He's seen me fix up animals. He said if I go to school then he'd teach me lots 'bout doctorin'. He says when I git older, if I'm still interested, I mebbe kin be his"—she screwed her face as she struggled to say the words—"printis!"

Tessa smiled. "Do you mean apprentice?"

"That's it! Help him, ya know."

Tessa was still smiling as she thought of Cody with this little rapscallion in his lab. How on earth had *he* ever summoned up the patience to deal with her? "Cody said that, did he?" She hadn't realized she'd spoken aloud until Smoke Eyes grinned.

"You like him?"

The girl had caught her off guard, and her face flamed. "Like him! What does that have to do with anything?"

Smoke Eyes' smile was cunning. "Most wimmin do."

Flustered now, Tessa started to sweep cookie crumbs off the table and into the palm of her hand. "Well, I think he's just about the rudest man I ever met. *His* manners need work too."

"Ya, but you *do* like him."

Tessa dropped the crumbs onto the saucer. "We're talking about you, Smoke Eyes, not him," she said evenly. "Now you don't want to come to school yet you want to learn and study medicine. What is it you want from me?"

Tessa couldn't believe it when a pink stain colored the girl's cheeks. She dropped her eyes almost shyly and Tessa waited. "I—I kinda hoped you could teach me here—" and she made a sweeping motion with her hand. The ensuing silence seemed to embarrass her. Tessa knew the courage and sacrificing of pride that request had cost Smoke Eyes, and she knew she would have to tread carefully.

"I think," she said quietly, "it would be best if you came into school." At Smoke Eyes' rebellious look Tessa was quick to add, "Not that I would mind teaching you in what little free time I have, but I think, Smoke Eyes, it's time you learned to face everyone and blend with the others."

"But—"

"Hush for a moment and listen to me. However painful for you it might be, you *must* face folks sooner or later. Heavens, Smoke Eyes, you're going to be a physician! You can't hide from people!"

"I wanna help my mother's people."

"That's fine. But to study medicine you'll have to attend a university. And there'll be plenty of people there. And some won't believe a woman can be a doctor." She almost chuckled when Smoke Eyes puffed up her chest. "People, you'll learn, are both bad and good and most are in between. But you have a great deal of time to learn about life. Now you start by coming into school."

Smoke Eyes sat, mentally weighing Tessa's words.

"And one more thing. I'm going to start calling you Katherine."

The girl shot to her feet, hands clenched at her sides. "Fergit it! I ain't comin' in!"

"Don't be so stubborn! I have to call you that so you can fit in with the other children!"

"I don't wanna be like other children!"

Tessa sighed.

"Smoke Eyes is my name!"

"Katherine is your name too. It's the name your father gave you. Most people have two names. I'll use Katherine in the classroom and Smoke Eyes out of it. Does that sound reasonable enough to you?"

"No." But a hint of a smile came into her eyes. "But I guess I kin get used to it."

Tessa rose now too. "Come with me a moment," she said, and led Smoke Eyes back to the sitting room. Here she wrote "Katherine Flynn" on a piece of paper.

"That says your name. Katherine Flynn. Those are the letters you use to write your name. There are twenty-six letters we use to form words. I'll teach you them on Monday. But for now study that and try to form the letters." She handed Smoke Eyes the paper. "And," she said, leading her toward the front door, "if you'd like, I can buy your school materials at Eb's. You can pay me back later."

Smoke Eyes looked up at her gratefully. She hesitated on the front-porch threshold for a moment.

"Run along now, it's getting dark and your grandfather will be worrying about you," Tessa urged gently.

Smoke Eyes turned as if to dart away, but she stopped and looked up at Tessa. "I'm afeared, Teacher," she croaked.

Tessa's heart went out to the child. "I know, Smoke Eyes," she said softly, but before she could comfort the girl any further, she was gone.

You're not the only one who's afeard, Tessa thought somewhat wryly. For the last few of the "big boys" had all come in last week and she'd begun to realize what Cody had meant by "the real test." There was Lem Barnes, a fifteen-year-old boy who was Sidney Chase's shadow, and Stephen Fisher, a big blond boy who had no use for school except that his mother forced him to attend in the winters. Tessa secretly almost wished he'd stay at home. Getting him to study was harder than convincing Smoke Eyes to come to school. Stephen balked at every step.

There was Al Cobbs who was constantly trying to impress the girls, and Zach Fletcher. Zach was a dark, sullen boy, not quite sixteen, whose main purpose in the classroom, it seemed, was to test Tessa's patience, to see just how far he could push her. He smoked behind the schoolhouse during recess, slouched at his desk, and showed up anytime he pleased. But what bothered Tessa most was the way he looked at her. He was a few inches taller than Tessa and well built for a boy of sixteen. His hair and eyes were coal black, and his darkness lent him a kind of intensity lacking in most boys his age. When he looked at her, there was something in his eyes that told her he had acquired some experience with the opposite sex.

All the older boys were at an age where they were eager to sow wild oats and they were not about to take orders from a teacher who stood half a head shorter than them. But out of all the boys, it was Zach Fletcher who had Tessa feeling most uneasy. Between Zach and Smoke Eyes, Tessa was longing for Christmas vacation and a break from her duties.

On the first Monday morning that Smoke Eyes sidled into the classroom with the other children, she tried to look as inconspicuous as possible. But the children snickered when they saw her and the boys jostled her a little bit. Sam Jordan glowered and shook his fist at her.

"Class," Tessa announced when everyone had settled in their seats, "our new pupil is Katherine Flynn and I know you'll make her feel welcome. Hannah, slide over so Katherine can sit with you."

The little girl scooted as far as she could to the opposite side of the seat, not out of disgust, but out of fear.

Tessa discovered that first morning that

Smoke Eyes was a quick learner. She quickly mastered every letter in the alphabet and many of their sounds. When recess came, she did not want to join the other children outdoors but Tessa gently insisted. The boys teased her as much as they dared under Tessa's watchful eye, and when they tugged at her flaming braid, Smoke Eyes lashed out and chased them, scaring them off. No one dared start a fistfight.

That afternoon as the children studied their lessons Tessa walked from desk to desk, looking over shoulders and checking their work. When she came upon Zach Fletcher, he was sketching a picture of a clipper ship on his slate.

Tessa stiffened, clenching her fists in frustration. "What's this?" she hissed low, surprising him as she came from behind his desk to stand in front of it. Zach, who was slouched in his seat, ran his black eyes up her slim form to at last meet her eyes unwaveringly. His mouth gave a little smirk. "A clipper ship, Teacher."

"The name is Miss Amesbury, and you'd better remember it, Mr. Fletcher. Where is your grammar lesson? You are supposed to be diagramming sentences."

"That's boring." As if to prove it he let his eyes droop and he folded his arms across his chest.

Tessa grated her teeth and slowly counted to five. "Why, may I ask, are you even in school then, if you don't come to learn?"

His mouth lifted again in that ugly smirk and his challenging eyes came back up to her face. "You may ask," he drawled, "but if you don't know"—his eyes roved slowly to her breasts—"then I'd have to say yer mighty unconscious of yer charms, *Teacher*."

Tessa sucked in her breath, and he laughed softly, knowingly. Where on *earth* did this boy learn to talk like *that*? She wanted nothing more than to shake him and throw him outside, but her pride saved her from showing her temper.

Now Tessa returned his smirk. "That's not why you're here, Zach, and we both know it."

He tensed and sat up slowly, his eyes narrowed now. "You calling me a liar, Teacher?"

"Ah, I see I have your attention now." She spoke low so none of the others could hear her. Zach noticed this and he wanted to keep it that way. "If it's charms and women you're looking for, we both know there is plenty of that in town. You'll not find it here in the schoolhouse and your flippant mouth won't convince me otherwise."

Zach's eyes widened on her. No woman had ever spoken to him so frankly and he looked at this one now with a kind of wonder.

"Now, if it's clipper ships you're interested in, that's a different matter altogether. I have a book I can lend you on sailing and ships. Do you want it?"

His eyes lit up for a moment, but he quickly

doused their light. "I'm only up to the fourth reader. Probably too many words in that book I don't know."

"Oh, I don't think so. Besides, there are pictures in the book, and if you apply yourself you'll be reading much better."

He made his face go hard again but Tessa could see the interest in his eyes.

"I'll bring it tomorrow," she decided, "but I won't give it to you unless all your homework is done and those sentences properly diagrammed."

He grunted.

"That's not an answer, Zach."

He wanted to tell her she wasn't going to get an answer, but he wanted a look at that book in the worst way. "I guess you'll just have to wait till tomorrow, won't you, Teacher?"

She looked at him coldly. He cleared his throat.

"I mean, Miss Amesbury."

"Get going on those sentences."

She desperately hoped her ploy had worked, and she didn't even glance back to see if he was studying.

That afternoon as Tessa cut through town she almost bumped into Tim Lyndon, Mary's husband, coming out of Eb's store.

"Why, hello, Tim!"

"Hello, Tessa."

"Where's Mary today?"

An anxious shadow passed over Tim's features and Tessa suddenly felt apprehensive. "What is it, Tim?"

Tim passed a worried hand through his pale, thinning hair. Under the gas streetlamp his face looked drawn. "She's had some trouble—you know . . ." His voice dropped and he glanced away for a terrible moment. "She's having trouble with the baby. The Doc says to keep her in bed."

Tessa was shocked. The last time she'd seen her, Mary was the picture of health! "How is she feeling?"

Tim shrugged. "Oh, you know Mary— cheerful as ever. But she's in a bad way."

Tears burned the backs of Tessa's eyes. Mary wanted this baby so badly.

"Excuse me, please. I've got to get on now. She shouldn't be alone up there at the house, but I had to come to town for some provisions. I don't trust winter weather and I'd hate for us to get caught short if a storm does come up."

"If I can do anything to help you out, please let me know, Tim."

"Sure, Tessa, I will. And thanks." He slid his hat back onto his head and moved toward the wagon with a defeated slump to his shoulders. Tessa wanted to ask him more questions, but she knew it was too painful for him to talk about. Cody would be the one to ask, but she hadn't seen him in a couple of weeks. Wisely, she thought, she'd avoided the socials, much as she'd enjoyed her first. But men had come to call on her and she'd fended

them all off with the same lie she'd told Cody.
She was glad now that she'd thought of it. It
was a tiny white lie and it saved her from their
attentions. Only Ned Winston, out of all the
bachelors in town, seemed perfectly harmless
to Tessa. He'd shown her his artwork and she
delighted in it, especially his portraits of the
citizens of Harper City. He promised to do a
portrait of her in the near future.

Later that night Tim Lyndon's foreboding
came true. A storm, fierce and strong, began
while Tessa was sleeping. It woke her with its
howling winds, and snow, mixed with ice,
whipped against the windows. She shivered
and huddled beneath her blankets, wishing
she had a hot brick to warm her feet. She lay
in the darkness listening to the wind as the
snow mercilessly punished the house. Finally
she grabbed a spare pillow and pressed it to
her ear, shutting out the noise.

It snowed for two days. School was closed
and Tessa stayed indoors with Mrs. Rawlins,
watching the snow pile up outside. After the
first morning, they gave up looking out because the snow became so thick against the
windows they couldn't see through the glass.
They passed the time sewing and reading and
cooking and cleaning. Tessa also started to
compose a Christmas program for the children
to perform in a few weeks.

On the third morning the sun burst through
the frost on the windows, filling the house
with a warm glow. After a big breakfast Tessa

put on her coat and hat and headed toward town.

There was no wind now, and the world was a dazzling, brilliant white. Fat icicles hung from eaves and the ice was as clear as diamonds. Looking out at the softly rolling snow-covered wilderness, Tessa could see homes dotting the land and smoke from their chimneys curling up toward the deep blue sky.

She filled her lungs with the cold, pristine air and stepped away from the house. The snow was hard-packed under her thick-soled shoes and she took big strides, but before she had taken ten of them she thought she'd imagined the jingle of harness bells. Then she heard the sound again, this time louder, pretty little chiming of bells in the cold air. She turned her head and saw Cody's horse Major, his breath billowing white before him as he whickered softly. Major was pulling a sleek cutter and in that cutter was Cody Butler. Cody glided the sleigh up alongside Tessa and flashed his breathtaking smile.

"Cody!" Had he caught the delight in her voice? It surprised Tessa to find just how delighted she was to see him. She laughed to cover up her pleasure. "I thought you were Santa Claus!"

He laughed too. "Have you been good, little girl?"

She blushed, thinking of that time on the sofa. As if he had read her mind, Cody smiled devilishly at her. She quipped, "It's impossi-

ble to be good in the company of Cody
Butler."

His great laugh rang out on the brisk wind.
Even the cold air could not take her breath
away like Cody's grin could. He was hatless
and ruddy-cheeked and looking like he'd been
driving around for hours. He lifted the buffalo
robes beside him on the leather seat, making
room for her. "Climb in!"

Tessa hesitated; Major shook his harness
bells again and they rang clearly, merrily.
Suddenly she knew she couldn't resist. Cody
gave her a hand in and she had barely a
moment to tuck the robes around her when
the cutter sped off, its runners squeaking in
the snow. Since the cutter was made for two it
was a very close fit, and Cody's long limbs
took up more than his share of space. His
hard thigh pressed against hers. Tessa tried to
ignore the delicious thrill it brought, wondering if Cody felt it too.

"I've missed you," he murmured, and
Tessa caught her breath. Did he expect her to
say she missed him too? She couldn't! And
would never admit it to him if she had. But
she had.

"I guess you've been busy," she ventured,
hoping he wouldn't notice what she'd avoided
saying. But judging by the way the corner of
her mouth curled up, he'd noticed.

But Tessa had other questions to ask him.
"How's Mary?" she asked softly.

He glanced at her anxious face and his eyes
darkened with concern. "Not good," he mut-

tered. He glanced ahead again. "She might lose that baby."

"Oh, God!" Tessa felt as though someone had struck her.

Cody's lips tightened. "Oh God is right. He might be the only one who can help her at this point."

"Well, what's wrong exactly?"

"She's been bleeding, and her legs and ankles are swollen and seem to swell a little more each time I visit her." Cody rubbed his cheek with his gloved hand. "I guess she wouldn't mind me telling you all that. She'd tell you herself, no doubt. But, damn, I'm worried about her."

"I'd like to visit her," Tessa said hopefully.

"I'm going out there this afternoon," Cody said. "Want to ride along with me? I can swing by here after school."

Tessa didn't even hesitate. "Oh, yes," she breathed, thinking primarily of Mary, not of the ride alone with him.

Cody smiled down at her as he stopped the cutter in front of the schoolhouse. "She'll welcome a visitor, Tess."

Tessa tore her eyes away from his face and climbed out of the cutter. Cody's gaze sharpened on a lone figure standing by the schoolhouse. His eyes flicked to Tessa.

"Is that who I think it is?"

Tessa grinned. "Smoke Eyes."

Cody rubbed his jaw. The way he was looking at her made her skin prickle under all her wraps. But all he said was, "Well, I'll be

damned." Just then he had to duck his head
as a snowball whizzed by his ear. Smoke Eyes
stood grinning on the porch, arms folded over
her chest. Cody laughed and leaned over the
side of the cutter to scoop up a handful of
snow.

"You're not going to throw that at a child,
are you?" Tessa scolded, and shook her head
as he packed the snow into a ball between his
gloved hands. Exasperated, she headed for
the schoolhouse. She was halfway there when
Cody hurled his snowball and it hit her smack
between the shoulder blades, not hurting, but
hard enough to stun her. She whirled to find
Cody dashing off through the snow in his
cutter and she shook a fist as his laughter
enveloped her. "I'll get you for that, Cody
Butler!" But Smoke Eyes was laughing too.
"That was supposed to hit you, Smoke Eyes!"

"Aw, but he got you good, Teacher!"

As promised, at four o'clock Cody swung
by in his cutter. Tessa scooted the last child
out the door and hurried out. The buffalo lap
robe was warm and comforting and she
leaned back, preparing to enjoy the smooth
ride.

"So Zach's still around, is he?" Cody asked,
glancing down at Tessa. Her eyes seemed
enormous with her muffler covering half her
face. But he saw her eyes grow even larger at
the question.

"Why shouldn't he be?" she asked, her
voice muffled.

Cody glanced at Major's black mane. "He

dreams of going to sea. He's just the type who will up and do it."

"He's too young."

Cody looked back at her, his eyes smiling. "You sound like a mother. But younger boys than Zach have gone to sea."

"What holds him back?"

"Zach drifted out here last spring and he and his father staked out a claim. But Zach all but lives alone and works the claim by himself. His father is a drifter and a drunkard and he's gone months at a time. But what Zach's really waiting for is his mother, even though he'd rather die than admit it." At Tessa's questioning look Cody explained, "She left him with his father in New York when he was only six. But he remembers her. I think he knows once he's gone to sea, he'll be gone for a hell of a long time, maybe even years. And he's waiting to see her, to say good-bye."

The Lyndons' house had come into view. It looked tiny on the vast white prairie. Tessa thought of Zach living alone in such a house and wondered at the loneliness of it.

"Do you think his mother will come back?" she asked Cody quietly.

"No."

She let her breath out slowly and saw the mist it made in the cold air. "I can see why he's such a hard boy."

"But don't let him push you too far. He will push you as far as you let him. There may be a time when you need a man to help you with him."

"I can handle him." And her chin tilted up in typical stubborn fashion. Cody laughed.

"Mmm. I don't doubt it, minx." He halted the cutter at the Lyndons' door. "Now run inside while I bring Major to shelter out back. I'll be in in a moment."

Tim was surprised to see Tessa at the door, but he let her in with a wide sweep of his hand. "Gosh," he said, "Mary will be thrilled to have a visitor! Here, let me take your coat."

The Lyndons' front room was warm and cozy and Tessa waited there for Cody. He came in momentarily, stamping the snow from his feet, and he went in first to examine Mary. He came out sometime later and nodded for Tessa to go in.

Somewhat afraid of what she might find, Tessa cautiously opened Mary's bedroom door and peeped her head through the crack. "Mary?" she called out softly. She moved in a bit farther so Mary could make out her head and shoulders.

"Oh, Tessa!" she exclaimed. "Cody told me I had a visitor but that big tease wouldn't tell me who it was! I am so glad it's you!" Mary looked bright-eyed as ever, and her brown curls framed her sweet face as she lay back against plumped pillows, but there was no bloom in her cheeks and there were dark smudges under her blue eyes. She was cheerful, however, and that was a good sign.

"Hello, Mary. It's good to see you." Tessa crossed the room and pulled up a chair closer to the bed. "How have you been feeling?"

"Except for the fact that I'm utterly bored, I'm doing fine. I'm telling you—these men! They worry about nothing!"

But Tessa knew it was more than nothing and she suspected Mary knew it too.

"I brought you a newspaper," Tessa said, and handed it to her. "It's not today's but I didn't know I was coming here until I met Cody on the way to school. There's a good story in that one."

"Why, how thoughtful of you!" Mary exclaimed. "Mostly I've been knitting clothes for the baby and darning socks for Tim but I could use a diversion. Thank you, Tessa." She laughed. "Actually I shouldn't feel guilty lying abed and leaving the chores to Tim. Heaven knows, I'll be busy enough when the baby's born."

Tessa smiled. "That's for sure." But she couldn't help remembering Cody saying she might lose the baby. She uttered a fleeting prayer that both mother and baby would stay healthy.

The two chatted and laughed until it grew dark outside and the wind picked up. Cody's sudden rap on the door made them both jump.

"My goodness!" Tessa flushed guiltily, watching Cody come in and casually lean a shoulder against the doorframe. He crossed his arms over his broad chest and his eyes twinkled teasingly at Tessa. "I didn't realize it was so late!"

"Well, it is," Cody returned with a smile in

his voice. His eyes glanced from Tessa to Mary and back to Tessa again. "Ready to go?"

Tessa came to her feet. "I'll come again soon, Mary. Promise." She squeezed Mary's hand fondly.

"Me too, Mary," Cody said. "In a few days or so. Tim knows to come get me if you need me before that."

"I'll be fine," Mary said, sinking back onto the pillows, despite her effort to remain upright. "And thanks so much for stopping by."

Outside, in the cold darkness, Cody said, "You were good for her. She needed a visitor."

They coasted home through the crisp, star-laden night and said little. The wind was in their faces, making it difficult to talk. Cody turned his collar up and wore his hat low over his eyes. Tessa wanted to move closer to him for warmth. He was so big, so wide-shouldered that he blocked some of the chill wind.

When they finally glided up in front of Mrs. Rawlins's house where the lights were glowing warmly, Tessa felt half frozen. The instant the cutter stopped she pushed the lap robe aside and was clambering over the side of the cutter before Cody had the chance to assist her.

"Thank you for taking me, Cody," she managed from behind her numbed lips.

"My pleasure," he said, surprised how quickly she had escaped. He made a move to get out of the cutter, but her voice stopped him.

"Don't bother to walk me up," she said. "It's too cold." She half turned, careful to dig her heels in so as not to slip. " 'Bye, Cody."

"I'll be back."

Why couldn't he just say good-bye? And why did her heart seem to sail across her chest at his words? Then she realized she had misinterpreted his words. Yes, he'd be back— back to take her to Mary's. Maybe Cody just wanted to be friends now after all.

A week later they visited Mary again. Her spirits were good, and on the way home Cody told Tessa that her condition had stabilized. But on the ride home Tessa sensed a change of mood in Cody. As he drove, looking straight ahead, she could almost see the dark frown he wore on his face, and his big body was taut beside her. She tried in vain to engage him in conversation, but he only grunted once or twice. She asked him a question about Zach, but her words only seemed to drift off into the cold, windy night. When she finally saw Mrs. Rawlins's house ahead of them, she wondered if he'd heard one thing she said during the ride home. She didn't know whether to feel annoyed or worried. She asked him another question just to see if he was listening.

"Tessa, dammit! This is ridiculous!" Cody suddenly exploded, nearly toppling her off the seat.

She looked at him, astounded. "What?"

He halted the cutter abruptly. His compelling eyes, in the gloom, sought hers, seeming to probe her very depths. "Don't you know?" he demanded in a rough, angry voice. "How long do you expect me to continue exchanging pleasantries with you? Just the damned sight of you sets me—" He stopped, feeling her body tense beside him. He lowered his voice a notch, but he sounded hoarse. "I'm on fire, for God's sake. Do you think I'm made of iron—"

She jumped out of the cutter. But this time Cody sprang out quickly behind her, moving like a cat, and he was over the side of the cutter too, reaching out to spin her around by the shoulders. His breath came fast, fanning her face with its moist warmth, and Tessa's pulse thundered in her throat. Cody's hands dropped to her waist, pulling her close, and he pressed his hard body against hers while he rammed his tongue and thrust deep, between her open lips, searching her mouth almost violently. Her senses swam as the thrill rushed through her in a searing heat, running feverishly through her body. The taste of his kiss, the warmth of his tongue, ignited fiery tremors in Tessa's nerves. She held her palms flat against his jacket, wanting to push him away, but instead pressed harder, feeling the wild pounding of his solid heart beneath. Crushed against him like this, she could feel the vibrant life of him emanating from his entire being, so hot and fierce in this frigid night.

Cody groaned into her open mouth, then tore his lips from hers, muttering wild words against her cheek. He clasped her head in both hands, forcing her to look at him, and his eyes glittered as their breaths came raggedly, hurtfully.

"See what you do to me?" His voice was gruff, and as ragged as his breathing. Then he pulled her close again and kissed her mouth hard.

Tessa struggled to regain her senses even while her still-throbbing body was pressed tightly against his. When his arms finally loosened around her, she drew in a long, shuddering breath, and the bitter cold air funneled into her chest, helping her regain her senses. She took hold of his gloved hands and put them firmly away from her, then she backed up, keeping her wide, dark eyes glued to his.

"Don't do this, Cody," she begged low, shakily. "Don't ruin this. Don't ruin it for Mary."

He stood staring down at her, scowling slightly. The lantern light from the porch flickered, causing tiny shadows to dance across his handsome face. "Meaning you will not ride out there with me again if I pursue you?"

"That's right."

"You'd do that? Just to avoid me?"

It was her turn to be silent. Cody stared soberly at her. His jaw tensed. "Why don't we just leave Mary and your Michael Shea out of it? Neither of them has anything to do with *this!*" And he strode forward and caught her arms and pulled her against his hard, warm body again. But just as he lowered his head, he noticed the glitter of tears in her eyes. His heart lurched violently in his chest, and he didn't quite understand why. Frustrated, Cody dropped his arms to his sides, setting her away from him. Her large eyes hung on his, looking beautifully vulnerable even in the darkness. "Damn your eyes!" he cursed suddenly, harshly, and Tessa tensed. He clenched his big fists and gritted his teeth, locking the strange, almost hurtful welling in his throat. "Get in the house," he ordered roughly. And she flew.

Chapter Nine

✦✦✦✦

CHRISTMAS WAS FAST APPROACHING, and during the crisp, cold days of December, Tessa and the children were caught up in the flurry of preparations for their Christmas program. She asked Reverend Donaldson if she could use the church for the presentation.

"By all means!" the generous man agreed. And the children, in a whirl of excitement, began to create decorations for the church. Both Zach and Smoke Eyes thought all this activity was a bit beneath them and refused to participate in either the play or the singing, so Tessa put them in charge of decorations.

As busy as she was, Tessa still couldn't seem to put Cody from her mind. Why didn't the man just leave her alone? Hadn't any woman ever rejected him before? The man even invaded her dreams—she kept seeing those burning green eyes, those mocking, tempting lips, and kept remembering his long lean fingers on her flesh. Sometimes the images would startle her awake, and she'd hiss names at him in the dark.

On the night of the presentation Tessa ate a quick, light supper and dashed back to town in order to be at the church early. It was a cold, blustery night and the temperature was dropping rapidly. Tessa bent her head against the strong wind and struggled along the snow-packed route to the church. Its light and warmth were a welcome relief, and she stepped inside and removed her wraps by the coal heater. The church had been decorated earlier that afternoon and Tessa gazed about her admiring the streamers of green and red ribbons on the walls along with artwork of the various students. At the front of the church, before all the benches, stood the tiny papier-mâché Christmas tree Zach had created. Tessa smiled. With its school-made decorations, and again, the red and green ribbon, the tree seemed very lifelike.

"Oh, it's lovely," she breathed, her dark eyes shining.

"It surely is," came a friendly voice from behind, and she whirled to find the Reverend Donaldson smiling down at her. "Don't be alarmed—I didn't mean to startle you." He glanced about the empty church with a satisfied smile on his round, beaming face. "You've done quite a job with this school and these children, Miss Amesbury."

"Oh"—she blushed modestly—"the children are the ones who should be given credit. They've worked hard. And that reminds me . . ." She put her wraps aside, all business again. "I've got some last-minute things to do here myself."

His eyes twinkled. "I'll step out of your way. Tonight the church is yours, as I promised."

Before long, Mrs. Finegan, the organ player, made her entrance, and Christmas music soon filled the church. Parents began to arrive with their children, and as they seated themselves on the church benches, the children scurried up to the front of the church to take their places for the program. Tessa thought they were adorable—the boys in their suspenders and freshly pressed shirts and slicked-down hair, and the girls in their Sunday dresses and curls. There was much whispering and giggling as the church slowly filled, at last becoming so crowded that some of the men were forced to stand at the back of the church. Despite the frantic last-minute preparations, she noticed Cody's arrival. He was one of the last to enter the church, bringing in with him a gust of winter wind, so strong that it made the lantern lights flicker. He stood with widespread legs, his hands slipped into the back pockets of his trousers, his black hair tousled from the wind. When Tessa looked over at him, he smiled at her, a quick, easy smile that made her heart pound. She started to smile back, thought better of it, and looked sharply away, disturbed at the welter of emotions he stirred up simply with his presence.

The program was a success. The audience delighted in the children's recitations and performances. Tessa stood off on the side, giving silent instructions when necessary, trying her best to ignore the powerful presence of Cody Butler. Once she secretly peeked over at him, only to find his steady stare upon her; it was so unnerving that she kept her attention on the children from then on. She held her breath when seven-year-old Benjamin Worth took center stage to recite the lines he'd had such trouble memorizing, but he delivered them without a single flaw. When he finished, he glanced over at Tessa with large, dark eyes much like her own. He was a shy, darling child, and Tessa loved him dearly, wanting to hug him now.

The program ended with all the parents and townspeople joining in song with the children, and at last, Reverend Donaldson commending Tessa and the children for such a delightful show. At the end of the evening Tessa announced that she'd had a surprise visitor after school that day and he'd left something for all the boys and girls.

"Santa!" one of the children shouted, and everyone laughed.

"That's right," Tessa said, "and I'll need help passing these little packages out." As she and three others passed out the striped bags of candy from Eb's store there were audible gasps of delight and murmured thanks from grateful parents who could not afford such luxury this Christmas. The people put on their wraps and drifted out, tired now, but in good spirits. And it was then that Tessa noticed Cody was gone.

"He's been called out," Eb explained, coming up beside her. Tessa's startled eyes jumped up to his—wise, kind—and she wondered how he knew. But Eb only smiled. "Yep, that's right. A sick patient. But don't worry—Audrey has invited him and some others over Christmas Eve. You can wish him Merry Christmas then."

"But I—" She hadn't intended to wish Cody any such thing but how could she say so?

"C'mon now," Eb said, bending to pick up a ribbon that had fallen to the floor. "Let's get this all cleaned up. Sooner we do, the sooner we go home."

*   *   *

The day before Christmas Mrs. Rawlins and Tessa started baking as soon as the sun came up. They prepared baked goods for the company that would be coming and for the following day when they would be joining Claire and Mike for Christmas dinner at the Taylors' home. Mrs. Rawlins's kitchen was filled with rich, spicy aromas—pumpkin and molasses and cinnamon-sprinkled dried apples tucked neatly into pies. Throughout the day Tessa handed out cookies and sweets to carolers, many of whom were her students.

By midafternoon snow had begun to fall, and Tessa stood for a time at the parlor window, watching the large, soft flakes drift lazily to the ground. "Well, it's going to be a white Christmas," she murmured to herself, but Mrs. Rawlins came up behind her and watched the snow too.

"Isn't it lovely?" the older woman breathed, and Tessa was startled to see the usually twinkling blue eyes brimming with tears. Was she thinking of her two grown children whom she hadn't seen in three years? Tessa wanted, suddenly, to take the old woman's arm and tell her that she, too, was missing some sort of family—one that she never had. But Tessa was not given to bouts of self-pity, and she realized with a refreshing surge of emotion that Mrs. Rawlins had become her family. Impulsively she leaned forward and kissed the old woman's pink cheek. "I love you, Mrs. Rawlins."

Startled, Mrs. Rawlins blinked. And then she laughed, gaily, and returned the kiss and hug. "God knew what he was doing when he brought you to me!" she answered, her wonderful, suddenly renewed lighthearted spirit recharging them both. "Come, now, let's get dressed before the guests arrive!"

They went to their separate rooms and Tessa descended in her dark blue wool skirt and snowy white blouse with a blue ribbon bow at the throat, looking proper. Mrs. Rawlins, on the other hand, wore a scarlet-colored dress, and—shockingly—lip rouge of the same color. Where on earth had she obtained *that?* Tessa had to smile. And she could see absolutely no purpose for the tortoiseshell combs in Mrs. Rawlins's flyaway hair.

Just before twilight, their guests started to arrive. There was Eb, of course, and Mike and Claire with their little boy Ethan, and Susan and John Miller and Beth and Dan Calvert. Once they were settled in the parlor, the second bunch swarmed in and with them came Cody. As if there was no help for it, Tessa's eyes were drawn to his. They were warm and compelling and her heart skipped a beat as she quickly turned to busy herself with collecting wraps.

"Don't bother," Cody said, loud enough for everyone to hear, and for a minute, Tessa thought he had taken leave of his senses. "Get your coat, Tessa, we're going for a sleigh ride."

She drew back, not wanting to go anywhere

with him, especially in that cutter. But everyone else thought it a wonderful idea and went barreling out again, retying hoods and mufflers. Only Eb and Mrs. Rawlins and little Ethan stayed behind to pop corn. Tessa stood before Cody as he held her coat out for her, his deep green eyes twinkling devilishly as he gazed down at her. Of course she had no choice but to slip into the coat and wait for him to hand her her hood. He watched her, wearing that crooked grin of his that made her heart turn over. And all the time she was thinking how different he looked tonight in that dark greatcoat with the muffler hanging loose around his neck. She couldn't see what he was wearing underneath, but his trousers were black and well tailored. He turned to open the door, his great, broad shoulders filling her view, and she saw the snow melting in his hair, making it glisten.

"Be back later!" Cody called to Mrs. Rawlins, and she called something in return, something Tessa didn't hear as Cody's touch to her back, through her thick coat, sent tingles throughout her body.

Outside, in the deepening purple night, the soft, fluffy flakes of snow danced in the sharp cold, but there had been colder nights. Major tossed his head and his harness bells jingled softly, sweetly on the air. The other sleighs were swiftly flying in the direction of Main Street and Cody bundled Tessa into the cutter, then swung himself up easily, saying, "We'd better hurry if we want to catch up."

They were off with a jolt, speeding after the others, and Tessa hung on to her hood, even though it was tied on. "I can't believe you'd go this far!" she said, her voice rising over the wind. "If you are so god-awful bent on taking a sleigh ride, Cody Butler, why couldn't you have gone with someone else? Don't you ever give up?"

Cody grinned, slowing the cutter a little. "What's Christmas without a sleigh ride?" He laughed at her sour expression. "Besides, none of them know what's gone on between us."

"Nothing has gone on between us except your atrocious assumptions that I enjoy your pawings!"

He grinned sideways at her, unperturbed. "Assumptions?"

They passed the general store where a gas streetlamp showed the snowflakes in Cody's hair, making him look achingly appealing. Tessa turned her eyes to the street and waved at Mike and Claire, who passed them on the other side. She was all too aware of Cody's hard thigh pressed firmly against hers under the lap robe. He made no move to edge away; nor did she.

"Most definitely assumptions," she affirmed, but more quietly, and Cody's soft laughter contradicted her words.

"You put a damn good show together the other night," Cody said. "Sorry I missed the end of it."

"Oh, weren't they darling? I think Benjamin Worth stole the show."

"I think his teacher did," Cody said, and a wave of pleasure went through her at his words. He's just flirting with you! Tessa scolded herself, yet his flirting made her go all weak inside.

Dan Calvert called out across the street that they were heading back. Beth was cold and, indeed, a brisk wind swept through town, making Tessa gasp for breath.

"Want to head back too?" Cody asked, and she only nodded, hugging the robe tightly to her chest. He turned the cutter around, following the others. "Haven't you got your long johns on?" He laughed, feeling her stiffen beside him. He was remembering, as she was, just when he'd discovered exactly what kind of underwear she wore. "Maybe I can find out later, huh?"

Her look was more frosty than the night, but it was too dark for him to see. "Don't you start, Cody. Not tonight."

He chuckled softly. "You know, you work awful hard at appearing prim and snooty, and somehow it doesn't quite fit, Tess."

"What does *that* mean?"

"It *means* that I think you hide a great deal of what and who you really are."

Tessa felt a little sick. "That's ridiculous."

"Mmm. Maybe. But I bet I could prove it."

"I don't want to talk about me. Let's discuss something more interesting."

"I think you're the most interesting topic I can think of. Why *not* talk of you?"

"It's mighty vain, don't you think? Not to mention boring."

"Not at all," he answered mildly. "I have a feeling you haven't talked much of yourself at all, to anyone—ever."

The snow was thick now and powdery, swirling down from the black heavens, melting on their faces and shoulders. Tessa felt she was melting with it . . . and wanted to vanish just as quickly. But she was here, with him, and he was being persistent. "Not true," she said, and her voice sounded choked.

"It damn well *is* true. Tell me, what's your favorite color?"

"Oh, this is absurd!"

Cody calmly guided the sleigh. Up ahead they could see the candles glowing in Mrs. Rawlins's windows, their light falling softly yellow on the snow outside. "Looks inviting, doesn't it?" he said, nodding his head in that direction. "I won't let you out of this cutter or into that house if you don't tell me now what your favorite color is."

"Black!" she spat out.

Startling her, he threw back his head and laughed with real pleasure. The sound made her blood flush hotly through her. Still chuckling, Cody urged, "C'mon, you can do better than that. All I asked was your favorite color—not all your deep, dark secrets."

And God knew, she had plenty! Her mit-

tened hands toyed with the buffalo robe. "I—
I like blue," she admitted softly.

"Ah. Was that so hard?"

Yes, she thought, it was very hard. It was
true, she'd never much discussed herself with
anyone in her life. "I like green too." And she
was instantly sorry she'd said it because she'd
just named the color of his eyes. But he was
laughing, and she guessed he had not grasped
the connection.

"Well, this one is even tougher. When is
your birthday?"

"Cody, please."

"Don't beg me, Tess. I just might oblige
you."

The soft, serious tone of his voice sent
shivers through her. They had pulled up in
front of the house; just ahead of them Dan
Calvert was helping his wife out of their
sleigh. The candlelight fell softly on Cody's
rugged features and Tessa's eyes went over
them, as if committing them to memory. He
watched her eyes and saw something flicker
in them, something he could not read. Neither
realized how intently each was searching the
other's gaze until Dan's shout brought them
to their senses.

"Hey, you two! You planning on joining us
tonight or spending Christmas out in the
cold?"

"Bring me some of that brandy you brought
and I'll let you know," Cody called back
good-naturedly, easing his big body out of the

cutter. Dan laughed and he and Beth went inside as Cody reached for Tessa and helped her down. "I'll find out your birthday yet," he teased gently, and squeezed her hand.

Indoors it was warm and the house was filled with the smell of freshly popped corn. Laughter and chatter led them toward the parlor, where they all sat near the heater, some of them on the floor. Tessa took a seat near Susan Miller and Mrs. Rawlins pressed a hot toddy into her hand.

"Goodness, what rosy cheeks!" Mrs. Rawlins exclaimed.

"And a cherry nose," Cody teased her from across the room. They all laughed and Tessa was glad her cheeks were rosy because underneath they were flaming.

She darted a glance at him as he sprawled in a chair. Her eyes ran down his long, dark-clad legs, noting the firm muscles in his thighs. He was wearing a white shirt with a wine-colored cravat of the finest silk, and over these, a black brocade waistcoat. He looked dashing.

She took a sip of her toddy and over the rim of her cup her eyes met Cody's, and she knew, by the amusement gleaming in them, that he'd caught her staring. She also knew he was pleased by it.

She gave him a saucy glance, lifting her chin, and in the process tilted her cup so sharply that she took more of a swallow than she intended and the hot toddy burned her tongue. She almost spit it out, but to save face she swallowed it, feeling the fire in her throat, and then in her belly, where the brandy seemed to light her up with a warm glow. By now the amusement in Cody's eyes had changed to downright laughter and he wasn't bothering to hide it.

"Isn't that so, Tessa?"

Tessa started, shaken from her trance. "I'm sorry, Beth, what did you say?"

"You've gone out to see Mary, haven't you?"

Tessa looked quickly at Cody, but he was talking with John Miller now. Had he told everyone that he'd taken her out there? "Yes, how did you know?"

"Oh, Dan saw Tim yesterday. He says Mary is in fine spirits."

"Well, she is," Tessa agreed, "but I do miss her and I wish she could be here with us tonight."

The other women murmured their agreement and suddenly Beth cried out, "Why don't we all go out there tomorrow—early, before dinner, and visit with her? Just us women? I could ask my brother to drive us out and Dan can watch the children."

"That's a wonderful idea," Claire agreed. "It'll be such a surprise for her!" She glanced past the women to Cody.

"What do you think, Cody? Can Mary have visitors tomorrow?"

Cody was packing his pipe now and he looked up. "I think she'd like that. And it'll probably be the best medicine for her."

Tessa tried not to look at his clenched teeth

holding the stem of his pipe, but she couldn't help herself. Again he caught her staring and he cocked his eyebrow at her. Flustered, she looked away.

There was storytelling and nut cracking and pleasant eating and drinking and laughter until little Ethan's eyes began to droop and his blond head nodded on his little hand.

"It's time for us to go," Mike announced, shouldering his little boy and taking Claire's hand. "Santa won't come tonight if little boys stay up past their bedtime." They wished everyone a Merry Christmas, and Eb and Cody got up too, to see them out.

"Seems like the snow is piling up some," Dan mentioned, "the way it was coming down earlier."

"I don't care," Tessa said. "It can pile up to the eaves on Christmas, I love it so."

They all laughed.

"Incidentally, Tessa," Beth Calvert said, "the Christmas program was wonderful the other night." The others heartily agreed and Tessa murmured her thanks. "But," Beth added, and there was an impish twinkle in her eye, "Jim McGafferty says he wished he could've made it here tonight. He thinks you're something special, you know."

Tessa blushed up to her ears. How could Beth tease her so in front of all the men? She glanced to the doorway and saw Cody bracing a shoulder against the frame, his hands shoved deeply into his trouser pockets as he silently studied her. Why did he have to be standing there now? she wondered. And what had made her glance his way? Flustered, she jumped to her feet, asking if anyone would like another hot toddy.

"That would be great," Dan said, and Tessa was glad for the excuse to leave the room.

"I'll take one too," John Miller said.

From the doorway Cody lifted his cup, silently beckoning her. She went to him, asking with her eyes if he wanted another. But just then Cody passed his arm about her waist and drew her against him, lowering his head quickly to cover her mouth with his own. Tessa was so surprised she could not react. His mouth tasted of brandy and tobacco and he moved it warmly, possessively over hers. Crushed to his lean, hard length, Tessa melted, not knowing that she wound her arms around his strong neck, only succumbing to the weakness that washed over her. But as his kiss continued the others whistled and catcalled. Horrified, Tessa suddenly realized what a show Cody was putting on, and she struggled in his arms, pushing at his wide, strong shoulders.

"Cody!" she choked out, turning her head, finding little relief in the fact that he hadn't kissed her in the way he was accustomed— with his tongue. His eyes were laughing at her now as the blood rose hot and crimson from her neck to simmer brightly in her cheeks. What must they all think! But they seemed to have enjoyed Cody's public show of ardor.

"How dare you!" she hissed, but his mouth was curled in a roguish grin and she could read well by now the look in his eyes that bespoke no shame—only something else. Those devilishly dancing eyes now left her burning face to a point above them, and temporarily confused, Tessa followed his gaze. Above her hung a sprig of mistletoe.

"Don't be mad," he teased, "I couldn't resist."

Tessa felt torn between the desire to laugh with him or slap him. She did neither, just stood there staring up at him, looking into his lazy, caressing eyes. "I'll take that hot toddy now," he said.

She straightened her shoulders and nudged past him. "I think, Cody Butler, that you are hot enough!"

His burst of laughter followed her out of the room, and she could just imagine what the others were thinking. If only they knew the truth: that she was married to a man half-way across the country. She knew every person in that room would be shocked and appalled if they ever discovered the facts. But they wouldn't, she vowed, no one would!

She fixed the tray of hot toddies and carried them back to the parlor. By now most of the women were slightly tipsy and the men pleasantly mellow. The amiable flow of conversation continued long past midnight when John Miller made the announcement, "If we drink any more hot toddies, we won't be able to find our way home."

In the sudden flurry for wraps and the good-nights and Merry Christmases Tessa lost sight of Cody. They were gone, all of them, it seemed in one loud, happy moment.

"Well," Mrs. Rawlins said with a little clap of her hands, "that was fun! Shall we hang our stockings?"

Tessa laughed. "Oh, Mrs. Rawlins, I stopped doing that long ago."

Mrs. Rawlins pretended to be shocked. "What! Well then, it's time you started hanging it again!" She drew Tessa into the parlor and produced two stockings out of the scrap bag. "Come, now, let's hang them." And they did.

All the brandy she'd drunk put Tessa right to sleep and she did not wake until the sun blazed brilliantly into her cold room Christmas morning. She opened her eyes wide, shivered, and took a deep breath of coffee and baking bread. She jumped up, pushing the bedcovers back, and flew to the window, almost as if she were a child again, looking for signs of Santa. What a beautiful Christmas day! Sunshine sparkled on the snow and the sky was a clear, cornflower blue. The frost made delicate silvery patterns on the window. It was, judging by the brilliance of the sun, midmorning at least.

Teeth chattering, Tessa went to her dresser and pulled open her top drawer, rummaging through her clothing to find the few presents she had hidden from Mrs. Rawlins. She hugged them to her nightgown-clad chest and ran downstairs. Mrs. Rawlins was in the kitchen, which was warm from the heat of the stove.

"Merry Christmas!" Tessa cried from behind her, and planted a light kiss on the old woman's cheek. Startled, Mrs. Rawlins twirled around and laughed.

"My goodness! Merry Christmas to you too!" She glanced down at the gifts Tessa held out to her and her little mouth dropped open in a small "oh!" "Gracious, I didn't expect anything!"

"Be careful of this one," Tessa cautioned, touching the smallest gift, wrapped in green tissue paper.

There were gifts at the table for Tessa and she was surprised too. But she made Mrs. Rawlins open hers first. She cried out when she unwrapped two crystal bluebirds. "Oh, Tessa, they're just beautiful!" And she went to arrange them on the whatnot. "Perfect!" she said, clasping her hands with delight.

"They are lovely," Tessa agreed. "Now while you open this one, tell me why you let me sleep so late?"

Mrs. Rawlins laughed and began fiddling with her second gift. "Oh, I had to get those loaves of bread in and I plumb forgot about the time. I thought you might like to take a loaf to Mary this morning."

"Oh, my goodness! I almost forgot! They'll be coming to get me in just a short time!" Tessa jumped to her feet, but Mrs. Rawlins opened her two remaining presents—a blue

silk scarf and a lawn handkerchief edged with
snowy lace—and with glowing blue eyes she
thanked Tessa and waited for her to open
hers. Inside the first package was a beautiful
white hood made of rabbit's fur. Tessa gasped
when she saw it. She lifted it from the wrapping as if it was sacred, then brought it to her
cheek and rubbed the fur gently against her
skin.

"It's beautiful," she murmured.

"Well, try it on," Mrs. Rawlins urged.

Tessa put it gently over her hair and tied it
beneath her chin.

"You are beautiful, dear," Mrs. Rawlins
murmured.

"I can't thank you enough." Tessa beamed
and very gently removed the hood, vowing to
save it for special occasions. She laid it aside
and smoothed the fur once with her hand as if
to assure herself it was real and it was hers. In
the second package was a pair of mittens to
match the hood and in the third a book of
poems. She couldn't believe her good fortune.

"I think there's something in our stockings," Mrs. Rawlins said, eyes twinkling.
They went to the parlor and reached inside
their lumpy stockings to pull out oranges and
candy.

"Where did you get the oranges?" Tessa
demanded, laughing.

"Eb brought them. He was here early this
morning. He also brought something else for
us to share. Come—it's in the kitchen."

In one corner of the kitchen on the floor was

a large picnic basket with an open lid. Tessa peered in to see an orange kitten sleeping on a tiny folded blanket.

"Oh, he's adorable!" she cried, wanting to pick up the tiny creature. She crouched closer, the hem of her nightgown brushing the floor. "I didn't know Eb had kittens!"

"His cat had kittens a few weeks ago. And that one is a she, not a he. Her name is Ginger."

Tessa's eyes shone. "It's a perfect name, isn't it?"

"Yes, indeed. And there is nothing more this house needed than such a sweet little thing."

"I couldn't agree more," Tessa breathed.

"Now, come sit down here and eat and then you must hurry and dress before your friends come by. I suppose I'll see you at the church and we can go to the Taylors' house from there."

Tessa ate quickly and dressed in the red-and-green-plaid dress she had sewed for this day. She tied on her new white fur hood, and just as Claire and the others arrived, Mrs. Rawlins piled her arms high with baked goods, candy, and ginger tea for Mary.

Mary was so astonished by her visitors that Tim worried the excitement would be too much for her. But she hushed him and he was pacified by the selection of baked goods to choose from in the kitchen. He happily filled his belly while the women visited, and when it was time for them to leave, Mary, despite her illness, breathed happily, "This is the best Christmas ever." And, somehow, they all knew, it was a Christmas none of them would ever forget.

After church the group headed straight to Mike and Claire's for Christmas dinner. But there was no sign of Cody.

As Claire and Tessa set the table Claire mentioned his absence. "I wonder where he is. We'll have to eat dinner without him if he doesn't come soon."

He's probably with another woman, Tessa thought.

"If I know Cody," Eb piped up as he was passing by, "he's busy with a patient. There's no other excuse for that boy to miss a good home-cooked meal."

Except one, Tessa thought. And then she tried not to think of him kissing her under the mistletoe last night and how distinguished he'd looked in that black suit, of the feel of his broad shoulders under his hands. She tightened her lips, determined to chase the images away, but she had to admit there was something missing without Cody here today.

After the turkey dinner the happy group gathered around the Taylors' piano and sang Christmas carols. Later in the evening there was more dessert, and after the dishes were done it was close to eleven o'clock when Tessa and Mrs. Rawlins plowed home through the deep snow, feeling full and spirited.

As soon as Mrs. Rawlins fed little Ginger she went to bed, but Tessa was feeling strangely restless tonight. It was from all the excitement, she told herself as she stood before her dresser, taking the pins out of her hair. How wonderful the day had been, how filled with gaiety and laughter, how different it had been from Christmases past. Then why did an emptiness swell inside her? Why didn't she take off her clothes and hop into bed and go to sleep with images of how good her life had been since coming to Harper City?

But she didn't.

She lifted her hairbrush and began dragging it through her light brown hair. A sudden rapping on the door downstairs made her heart leap. She dropped her brush on the dresser top and pressed her hand to her thumping heart. Then before she knew it, Tessa was hastily rewinding her silken hair into its customary knot at the back of her head. She heard voices, and then, Mrs. Rawlins called up, "Tessa! We have company!"

"I'm coming!" she called back, trying to quell the tremor in her voice, wishing she had asked who it was. Of course, she knew who it was, and she didn't even try to analyze why her heart was hammering so fast and why her palms were so moist. She gave her hair a final pat and hurried down the stairs, trying to slow her steps, to make it appear as if she wasn't hurrying at all.

He stood in the parlor with his back to her, shrugging out of his jacket. His trousers fit the seat of his pants as snugly as Tessa's high collar hugged her neck. There was the smell of fresh winter wind in the parlor and Tessa breathed it in deeply.

Mrs. Rawlins stood before Cody in her flowered wrapper, holding something in her hand, and when she caught sight of Tessa she said, "Look, dear, Cody's here after all!"

Cody turned and looked over his shoulder at her and it seemed a long time before Tessa let out her breath. Then Cody turned all the way around and smiled over at her, and softly she smiled back. His throat ached at the sight of her. Watching those luminous brown eyes on his, Cody knew he never wanted a woman more. It was a damned startling thought that this slight little schoolteacher had him in such a state, and even more startling was that she was the only woman in town he wanted.

He glanced away from her and ran a hand through his wind-tousled hair and flashed a quick grin down at Mrs. Rawlins. "I wish I could've made it out sooner. It seems folks needed medical attention all day long. Pinky Murphy got himself a bullet in the leg and I had some trouble digging it out." He watched both women blanch. "His place is a good ways from town and I just got back."

So, he hasn't been with Angie, or any other woman, Tessa thought. And now he's come here . . .

"Is Mr. Murphy going to be all right?" Mrs. Rawlins asked politely.

"Yep," and Cody's eyes strayed toward Tessa again. She stood as still as a statue, listening to him and Mrs. Rawlins as if she were an intruder. He forced his gaze back to Mrs. Rawlins and grinned. "I almost didn't make it in time to wish you a Merry Christmas. But it isn't midnight yet. Merry Christmas, Mrs. Rawlins." And he leaned down and kissed her cheek. She returned the kiss heartily and squeezed his big hand.

"Cody brought me some heavenly perfume," Mrs. Rawlins said to Tessa. *"French perfume,"* she elaborated as if he'd brought her a pot of gold.

Tessa smiled, but her mind wasn't on the perfume; Cody was wearing a shirt of spruce green—the same color green in her dress— and she saw that the color matched his eyes.

Mrs. Rawlins could see that at the moment she didn't even exist—not to these two! "Well!" She broke the spell gaily. "I hope you two don't mind if I go to bed. I'm exhausted!" She turned and patted Cody's muscular forearm. "We missed you today, dear, but I'm glad you came here tonight. Thank you so much for the gift. Now if I don't go to bed, neither of you will see me for a week!"

They laughed and said good night. When they heard her close her bedroom door, they looked at each other in the dimly lit room. And Tessa knew she could have stood there and looked at him all night.

"You are quite late," Tessa finally spoke, and the words sounded as if they had come from a tomb.

Cody said nothing.

Tessa's heart beat so hard and so loud it felt like it would explode. There was thunder in her ears. Yet she forced her words to sound calm. "You missed a fine dinner at Mike and Claire's."

"I'm hungry now," he admitted soft, low. His voice and eyes said more.

Tessa felt a strong yearning deep inside her and she clasped her fingers together so tightly they ached. The tip of her tongue peeked out between her dry lips to moisten them. "We have some pie and coffee out in the kitchen. Want some?"

Cody raised his black brows suggestively at her. "You better believe I do."

Flustered, Tessa led the way to the kitchen, feeling his eyes on her back all the way down the hall. She put the coffeepot on the back of the stove while Cody made himself comfortable at the table.

"Look what Eb brought," Tessa said, going to the corner of the kitchen where Ginger curled in a sleeping ball in her basket. Cody came up close behind Tessa and looked in. Ginger opened one eye and looked up at them. Cody grinned.

"Hey," he said softly, and reached down a long finger to stroke the kitten's soft fur. He gently scratched around Ginger's ears and laughed when the kitten opened its pink mouth at him. Tessa watched, entranced, feeling strange quiverings within herself as Cody stroked the kitten. She did not understand the sudden, wild urge to grab his hand and clasp it to her, to feel his fingers stroke her in that same gentle way.

Needing to busy herself, she found the sugar bowl and set it upon the table. As she did so she came up short at the sight of three wrapped packages sitting there on the red-checkered tablecloth.

"Merry Christmas, Tess," Cody said softly. Her heart bumped against her chest as he said it, and she lifted her wide eyes to where he now stood behind the chair. Pleased at her surprise, Cody's eyes glowed at her. He stood waiting for her to move. But her eyes stayed wide on his and seemed to be asking him, "For me?" He nodded and still she couldn't move. Her eyes dropped once more to the presents. She hadn't expected this! Presents from Cody! She heard him pull out his chair and sit across from her. Her eyes strayed again to his waiting face, and at last he reached for one of the gifts with those long, lean fingers and handed it to her. She took it, her fingertips touching his. The contact brought that queer quivering inside her again. Quickly now, she untied the colored string and inside the package was a crystal bottle of amber-colored perfume.

"Oh," she cried, her eyes shining, "perfume!" She gently uncapped it and took a little sniff of the delicate scent. "Oh," she breathed, "it's lovely." It, too, was French perfume. Her eyes met Cody's. "Is it the same as Mrs. Rawlins's?"

"No. Hers is more . . . flowery."

Their eyes danced in impish merriment, thinking of Mrs. Rawlins's strong fancy for flowers. Tessa tipped the bottle then, wetting her finger, and she touched a dab of the perfume to the pulse point behind one ear-lobe. The sweet, delicate scent rose between them and lingered in the air, making Cody's head swim. She cast her eyes down as she let her finger trail down the column of her throat and Cody felt the pulse beat hard in his own throat. Damn, did she know what she was doing?

She let her lashes drop. "Mmm. Cody, it's wonderful . . ."

Watching her, he felt something clutch his throat. "Here, open this one." His voice sounded odd and strained. Tessa cast him a curious glance, then recapped the bottle and took the gift from him. She tore the paper away to reveal a small, delicately carved music box. Tentatively, she opened it and light, twinkling music drifted about them. His love of music made the gift an intimate, personal thing and Tessa read it in his eyes.

"Cody—" The music took his name and made it dance on the air. She closed the lid and he saw her slim fingers run over the intricate engravings on the wood as if caress-ing them.

"You got one more," he said hoarsely, pushing the last one toward her.

It was the beautiful Japanese fan she had so often admired in Eb's store. She simply stared at it as if it was still untouchable behind the glass case where Eb had kept it.

"Eb told me every time you went in the store you looked at that fan long and hard."

Her eyes raised to his.

"I thought you should have it," he explained softly, as if his gift giving needed explaining.

Tessa was deeply touched. No man had ever before given her presents. And these were all so lovely! But what did the gifts mean? "Why did you—" She realized, as soon as she started to speak, that she should have remained silent. But the ungracious words had already been spoken.

"Why did I do it? To bribe my way into your bed, of course," he answered her lightly, but his green eyes were hard and she flinched under his scrutiny. Was he hurt? My God, had those three thoughtless words cut him to the quick? She hadn't meant to hurt him, was surprised that she had the power *to* hurt him, and impulsively she reached to touch his hand. The gesture was a shock to them both, but she kept her hand on his.

"Cody, thank you. Everything is so beautiful. I've never had such lovely gifts. I . . ." Her eyes studied the flowers on the fan. "Thank you."

He gently squeezed her hand and rubbed his thumb over her knuckles. "These are not bribes, Tess. I wanted you to have them, that's all."

Her eyes went back to his, which were dark, sincere, probing. He shouldn't have had to explain!

"I know," she admitted softly, enjoying what his callused thumb was doing to the back of her hand. She pulled it free and turned her palms up in a small, apologetic gesture. "But I'm afraid I have nothing to give you."

A slow, wicked smile crept up one side of his mouth and his eyes looked satanical. She was blushing before he even said it. "Oh no? You could start with a kiss."

"Ha!" And she whipped around to the stove where the coffee was now bubbling furiously. "You got your kiss last night, Cody Butler."

"That?" he scoffed. "Hell, I've gotten less chaste kisses from my aunts!"

She reached for two coffee cups and filled them both. "I don't doubt it, you defiler of women! But I was not about to kiss you back in front of all our guests!"

"Would you now?"

Her hands trembled as she set the coffee cups on their saucers. "Don't even ask." She turned to bring the cups to the table and felt a quickening within her as she glanced at him. She saw the way he regarded her with his lazy, caressing look. He was leaning back in his chair, his hands locked behind his head, and the muscles in his shoulders and upper arms swelled against his shirtsleeves. She turned her eyes away and set the cups down on the table, quickly turning away again to rummage for two spoons in a drawer.

"Did you enjoy your Christmas away from . . . Michael?" he asked, his tone lightly mocking.

For an instant her hands stilled on the spoons. Then she whirled again to the table, avoiding his eyes, set the spoons down, and went for the pie. Smoothly sidestepping his question, she asked one of her own. "Did you miss your family?"

His lips twitched. "Sure, but I've missed Christmases before with them."

Tessa brought the pie to the table and started to slice it, remembering Christmases at the orphanage. Miss Crowell had always tried to make it special for the children. "The Christmas I was seven," she mused aloud, "Miss Crowell brought a lady to the orphanage who brought us all kinds of things—toys and clothing and food. She lived in a big house by the shore. It was wonderful. She sat me on her lap and told me a story. She was so kind and so pretty that I wanted to go home with her. She wanted a boy, though. She came back to visit several times after that Christmas, but in the end she took little Johnny MacKay home with her."

Cody frowned. "Orphanage?"

Tessa nodded and slipped a triangular piece of pie on a plate. But Cody didn't notice the pie.

"You lived in an orphanage?"

"Yes."

"Tess, why didn't you tell me?"

She glanced up, startled. She wasn't aware until this instant that she had been reminiscing aloud. Cody was leaning forward, his handsome face hard, and concern etched in his eyes. She forced herself to shrug lightly. "Don't look at me that way. It was a pleasant place. I had plenty to eat and a roof over my head and schooling. They took good care of me there."

But he was thinking of growing up in his own warm, close family and how that closeness was something she had never known. She was talking rapidly now of how she had enjoyed her childhood, yet all he could picture was Tessa as a child, a child nobody wanted. He tried to squelch the lurch of pity he felt for her, knowing she would not want this from him or anyone, but it was there just the same.

"Here's some cream," she said, setting it down in front of him. Funny, he hadn't even noticed she'd gone to get it. "Do you want some cheese with that pie?"

"Huh? Ah, no. Just pie will be good."

But when she finally sat across from him, Cody lost all interest in eating, and as if coming to a decision, he placed both broad palms on the table, one on either side of his plate, and he rose to his feet. "Come on, get your coat. I want to show you something."

Tessa drew back as he came around the table, looking at him in amazement. "Are you crazy? It's midnight!"

"I confess, Tess, I am crazy." He grinned down at her, slipping his hand beneath her elbow, bringing her to her feet. "But I thought you already knew that." He urged her out of the kitchen, snatching his jacket on the way, and told her once again to get her wrap.

"I refuse to go anywhere with you at this hour!" Tessa protested. But Cody was impatient and he lifted her coat from the peg by the front door and tossed it at her.

"Put it on. You have no choice in the matter. I'm bigger and stronger than you."

"But I bet I can scream louder."

"Sure. But Mrs. Rawlins won't pay any attention. I told you she trusts me completely. Now hurry up."

"Cody—" He flung the door open and the snapping-cold air snatched her breath away. "And grab a lantern too, so we can make out where we're headed."

"Where *are* we headed?" she asked dryly, buttoning her coat up tightly. When he looked back at her, she was wearing her white hood. He sucked in a swift breath between his teeth.

"Jesus," he muttered.

She had just time to grab the kerosene lantern before he reached for her, putting her hand in his warm, rough palm, and then he tugged her out the door.

Chapter Ten

✦✦✦✦✦

THEY DESCENDED OUT INTO THE SECRET, hushed white world where the black sky held only a few stars and a quarter moon that shed weak, silvery light upon the ground. They plowed through the crusted snow, which made a pleasant crunching sound as their feet stomped through its surface. Cody tugged her along, and Tessa tried to match his long, easy strides, but she was already out of breath.

"Cody," she panted, "where are we going?"

"To my house," he answered lightly, but she could hear the laughter in his words. She didn't know if he was telling the truth, but she stopped in her tracks, trying to dig her heels deep into the snow. But Cody tugged her hand and she came stumbling after him, falling against his tall, hard side. Her fingers clutched at his arm as she tried to steady herself, and in the darkness Cody's rich, baritone voice poured smooth as cream over her. "Don't tempt me, Tess."

Tessa jumped back as if he'd held a match to her skin. "You cannot force me to go with you!"

"Yes, I can," he answered cheerfully, much to her chagrin. "I can easily carry you. But I don't think you want me to do that. Or do you?"

"You're a brute and a bully!"

"Hell, I already know that." His big hand once again engulfed hers and they started to walk. "You've been reminding me constantly since you came to town."

"But why? Why are we going there?" Tessa asked, ignoring his teasing.

"I told you, I wanted to show you something."

She quieted, curious now. They crossed over one block and rounded a corner where a house loomed. Tessa recognized the area. Behind this house was Cody's laboratory. Her cheeks burned at the memory. But Cody did not break stride. In the front yard his shingle swayed in the wind.

Cody led her across the front yard and up the steps, letting go of her hand to fit the key in the lock. Impulsively, Tessa scooped a handful of snow off the porch railing, stood on tiptoe behind him, and swiftly dropped it down the back of his neck. It was just enough to give him an uncomfortable shock.

"Aah!" he yelled. "Holy—" But her laughter drowned out his swearing and she laughed even harder when he tried to reach behind to remove the snow. His attempt was futile since it had already melted and was slowly sliding down his back. He turned toward her and advanced slowly, mock scowling, his eyes locked dangerously on hers, ready for battle.

"Stop!" she pleaded, and laughed, pushing at his massive chest. "I owed you one, Cody!" She gave a little shriek as he scooped up his own handful of snow and held it threateningly within an inch of her nose. She gasped, pushing at his wrists, and managed to knock the snow to the porch floor. "I owed you for that snowball you threw at me!" She was still laughing, not in the least sorry.

But Cody was laughing too. "You're worse than those kids you teach! You brew more mischief than they do!"

She straightened, trying to look serious, but there was an irrepressible gleam of laughter in her eyes. "I beg your pardon! This"—she gestured with a sweep of her hand to the snow—"was not an act of mischief, but an act of revenge."

His eyes smiled down into hers and he lowered his head a little. Tessa knew he was going to kiss her. She darted away and danced lightly to the door, which she pushed open as if it was her own. Indoors the house was chilled since the fire had died down during Cody's absence.

Cody stood right behind her; she felt his body brush hers for a breath-stopping instant, and then he was gone.

She set the lantern on a nearby table and heard him say, "I'll get a fire started," and she took the chance to cast a curious look around her.

They were standing in the front room—definitely a masculine room with its leather armchairs and the oak desk and tall bookcases filled with leather-bound volumes. On the desk were books and journals and torn wrapping paper and cast-off red-striped ribbon.

Over the back of a chair hung a discarded shirt and a pair of dark trousers. It looked as if he had been reading his journals, unwrapping a gift, and undressing all at the same time. She pictured him doing this and had to smile.

Tessa felt suddenly nervous and shy, completely out of her element in this bachelor's domain. She heard the iron ringing of the stove lids as Cody built a fire in the heater, but she carefully avoided looking at him. Her eyes looked, instead, at the impressive certificates and diplomas hanging on the wall near his cluttered desk.

"Take your coat off, Tess."

She jumped at the sound of his voice and glanced toward him, but he was busy with the fire.

"Go ahead, it'll warm up in a minute."

She removed her coat and carefully placed it over the back of an armchair. She didn't know he was watching her now as he removed his own jacket and tossed it aside. Take that white hood off too, he thought, before I lose all control.

As she untied her hood and laid it over her coat, her eyes fell on a bootjack on the floor beside an oak chest. The cast-iron figure represented a buxom lady, her arms flung wantonly over her head, and legs spread wide to catch the boot heel.

Cody caught her studying it and grinned. "Someone with, er, rather questionable taste gave that to me." His grin broadened as he read the censure in her eyes, and he shrugged. "It serves its purpose."

He looked at ease standing with his hands planted loosely on his narrow hips, his feet braced slightly apart on the wide-planked floor. "Do you want something to eat?"

A slight scowl settled over her features. "No, Cody, I don't want anything to eat. I want you to show me why you brought me here and then I want to leave."

He flashed her an engaging smile. "First, let me show you my house." He picked up a lamp and gestured for her to follow him.

Tessa gritted her teeth and said evenly, "I don't want to see your house."

"What?" He made a face of mock disbelief. "You don't want to see the house of the renowned Cody Butler?"

Tessa bit the inside of her cheek to keep from laughing. "Don't you mean the *lair* of Cody Butler?" His face registered shock as if such a term couldn't possibly apply to him, and Tessa laughed, resigned. "Oh, hurry up and show me if you must."

"Please," he drawled as she came up beside him, "try to restrain yourself from exhibiting too much excitement."

There was something intensely personal about Cody showing her his home. It was almost as if he expected her to become a part of it too. Forbidden thought, thrilling thought, dangerous thought—but the thought was there just the same. As they walked together

down the shadowy hallway and Cody guided
her with his hand on the small of her back,
Tessa scarcely drew breath. At his casual, but
oh so intimate touch, tiny tingles ran up her
spine. Did he know of the strange, delicious
power he wielded over her?

He showed her his waiting room with its
long leather sofa and chairs and the operating
room with its white walls and long table. She
shivered and backed out quickly. Chuckling
now, he let her see the recovery room, and
Tessa realized every room in this house was
stamped with his indelible mark. Even the
kitchen with its cookstove and small table
pushed up by the window held an aura of
Cody's masculine vitality.

They stood at the threshold of his bedroom
now and Cody drew her inside without giving
her a chance to think about it. He set the lamp
on the dresser top and reached for a small
box, which he pressed into her hand. Inside
the box were four-inch-long figures of baseball
players carved from wood.

"My sister's son made those for me."

Tessa stared at the figures, noting the detail
in their whittled faces. She smiled as she
removed them from the box. "They're adorable."

"He did a good job, don't you think? He's
only eight years old."

"A talented boy," she murmured, and
handed him the box. But she kept her questioning eyes on his, bottle green in the lamplight. "So this is it? This is what you wanted to

show me? You brought me here in the middle of the night to show me these figures when you very well could have shown me any other time?"

How could he answer here the way he wanted? *No, I brought you here to seduce you, little one.*

But judging from her suspicious eyes and the accusation in her voice, he was convinced she'd already guessed. "I know what you're doing, Cody."

"What am I doing, Tessa?" He looked down at her with teasing green eyes.

"Actually, you've already done it. You've used an underhanded method to lure me into your home."

He wore an injured look. "Lure you? That's a harsh accusation, don't you think?"

"It's an accurate one," she returned coolly, and turned toward the front room to get her coat. But Cody's voice stopped her.

"While you're here, why don't you take a look at this?" He held out a photograph album to her. "You were asking questions about my family and they're all in there."

Tessa paused, glanced at him quickly, then reached for the album he held almost level with her breasts. "An album," she breathed, taking it in one slim hand as if it was something holy. He could see how a family album would be so special to Tessa.

Cody was surprised at how well his ruse worked; she sank to the edge of the bed, forgetting him, enraptured with what she held. As he watched her study the album, he felt a strange, unfamiliar heart tug of tenderness for her.

"That's my brother you're looking at," he said gruffly.

Tessa stared at the man in the photo; his hair was light and thick, his light-colored eyes were probably blue or gray. "He's so handsome!" she exclaimed, then glanced up at Cody in supplication. "Oh—so are you. I—I mean—" She broke off, blushing to the roots of her hair. "You're more handsome." The heat in her cheeks seemed to singe her eyelashes as Cody laughed easily.

"Thank you," he said with amusement in his voice.

Tessa bent her head again, willing her blush to fade. She pored over the album and from where he stood Cody told her what he could about the photos. His sister was a dark-haired stunning woman with three beautiful children. His home in Kentucky was an enormous brick house with five shuttered windows across the top story of the front and four below. Between the two sets of windows on the lower level was a front porch with tall, fluted columns and wide granite steps with wrought-iron hand railings. On the sprawling lawn before the mansion were several well-dressed people, posed in formal clothes. She recognized Cody, magnificently dressed, one hand slipped in his trousers pocket, the other holding a drink. He was laughing, and there was a woman beside him.

There was a photo of the horse farm, enclosed by a slatted white fence. And then one of an older man.

"Is this your grandfather?"

Cody came to the edge of the bed and bent very close to her, cocking his head to one side and peering at the photo. "Yep. That's him. John Harper."

But Tessa had lost all interest in John Harper; her eyes were on Cody's thick, black hair and her fingers tingled with the fierce longing to touch it. His hair seemed blacker than the blackest night. His jawline was hard, etched with arrogance. She saw a muscle tic in his lean cheek, and Tessa looked from it up to his gaze, which was now level with her own. She swallowed nervously.

"You have a lovely family," she ventured, and closed the album. "I . . ." The intensity in his stare was mesmerizing. Still bent close beside her, Cody lowered his dark head and angled it as his mouth came down over hers in a long, intoxicating kiss. His hand cupped the back of her head and he leaned one knee on the bed, his position allowing her to know the intimate feel of the inside of his hard thigh and his rigid manhood. Sweet, dizzying ripples of desire shuddered through her body as Cody groaned, his mouth opening hungrily over hers. The kiss deepened, his tongue plunged in a hot, searching, demanding rhythm while his fingers tangled in her hair.

"Ah, Tess, Tess . . ." He took her face in his hands, his long thumbs on her cheekbones, and the heat in his gaze sent a sizzling shock to her innermost core. He took her mouth with his again in swift, plucking little kisses that left her breathless. His tongue ran provocatively along the full length of her mouth, parted and plunged again, commanding her to follow his lead. He had her in a near-swoon as she eagerly returned his passionate kisses, her fingers caressing the back of his neck.

Oh, Cody, Cody, what are you doing to me?

His hard hips nudged hers again, and the power of his body urged her backward on the bed. They tumbled together, rolled, and Tessa found herself atop his sturdy chest, his body so hard and warm she wanted to melt into it. She braced herself by gripping his bulging biceps muscles, and laughed down into his face. "I'm a little disoriented after that ride."

He smiled back at her with desire-bright eyes, but his voice was deep and rough with passion. "Lady, that was nothing compared to the ride I have in mind."

There was no chance for panic to take hold; quick as a panther Cody flipped her onto her back and half straddled her body, his forearms braced on either side of her shoulders, his dark face just above hers. He dropped his head forward, his lips nuzzling a trail from her chin to her earlobe. Softly he breathed into her ear, his breath fanning her like dragon fire. Her heart leaped wildly at his urgent, ardent whisper. "Let me tonight, Tess. Let me take you . . ."

He touched his tongue lightly to the pulse point beneath her earlobe, groaning as he tasted the sweet scent she'd applied earlier. His lips eased their way back to her trembling mouth, and he ran his tongue briefly, lightly around its beautiful curves. In the deepest, tightest core of her belly Tessa felt something open up as Cody's warm mouth opened over hers, and his thrusting tongue drove hard and hungrily; each tongue thrust seemed to reach down and tug low in her belly, releasing swift, sweet currents of hot liquid that flowed through her body to pool between her thighs.

There was so much heat coming from him, their bodies seemed fused; Tessa felt the brand of his steel-muscled thighs against hers and the power of his hard length strained through the material of his trousers.

She moaned softly. She kissed him back with all the fire and intensity in her spirit, her hand plunged into the thick, soft hair at the back of his head, reveling in the way it curled between her fingers. It was her turn now to offer him this gift, and she let him know it had been worth the wait. It no longer mattered that he wasn't the man to whom she should offer herself—it ceased to matter that she was legally bound to another.

His hands moved down the front of her bodice; somehow he'd managed to be rid of her bar pin, and Tessa was dismayed to learn he'd unlooped every button down her front. Cody raised his head to gaze down at her with smoldering eyes. He lowered his hungry gaze and laughed softly at what he saw.

"Long johns!" He chuckled when she blushed. They were women's long johns, of course, white with a little bow fastening the collar. But it was the last thing Cody had expected as he remembered the lacy undergarments she'd worn before.

"They keep me warm," she confessed, her warm dark eyes clinging to his.

"Mmm." His nimble fingers were already making quick work of the tiny white buttons that ran down to her navel. "No need for them tonight, love. I'll keep you warm."

He was doing a wonderful job of that already; he leaned to drop a kiss upon her moist, parted mouth before opening the front of her underwear with both hands. He groaned when her golden breasts and shoulders spilled out of the material. Her nipples were pinched tight and straining toward him and Cody forced a tight clamp on the intense wave of desire that washed over him. He buried his face in her neck, telling himself to take his time with her, while consuming heat and fire in his blood pounded like demons through his loins.

"That day when you were covered with hives," he whispered against her satiny skin, "do you remember?" He slipped his hand inside her flannels and his palm slid smoothly up her abdomen, which she sucked in at his touch.

"I remember," Tessa gasped as his palm skimmed up her bare ribs. "I thought you found me unsightly."

"What I found"—he took her warm, aroused breast and cupped it—"was a woman more beautiful than I ever imagined." He squeezed her firm flesh gently with his fingers. Tessa's eyes drifted shut, his words as much an exquisite caress as his fingers. A soft sigh escaped her lips as Cody fondled her breast, watching her face. He did not touch the nipple, and the craving grew in a tight, warm spot in Tessa's belly. His palm contoured the underside of her breast while his thumb traced a light circle around her stiff nipple, still not touching it. Tessa made a sinuous move beneath him, aching for his mouth to caress those dusky peaks.

Cody lowered his head and touched his mouth to the swell of her breasts. His eyes watched her skin as the back of his knuckle grazed her hard nipple, then at last, slowly, almost reverently, he lowered his head again and took that aroused flesh into his mouth, wetting it with his tongue, stroking it, sucking it tenderly. Tessa writhed, her fingers losing themselves in his thick hair. She made an agonized sound in her throat as he continued to tug at her nipple, and in the pit of her belly the craving, the hot, deep need for him was almost unbearable.

Cody moved to her other breast and performed the same sweet torture upon it. He played with it, flicking his tongue across the nipple, then took it fully into his mouth and sucked it, making her gasp as fire seemed to shoot through her body. She heard his harsh breathing, felt it heat her bare skin and felt the pressure of his tumescent manhood against her thigh, rigid with need. Cody made a guttural sound and broke away suddenly, straightening, kneeling beside her. With his fiery eyes on hers, he tore at his shirt, jerking the buttons open to expose his bare, muscular chest, which heaved with each breath. He yanked impatiently at the shirttails, and when they came out of his pants, he was shrugging the shirt off his splendid, powerful shoulders, then flinging the shirt carelessly to the floor. He paused for a moment, kneeling over her, his knees slightly apart. Tessa's breath died in her throat. She gazed upon his manly beauty, dropping her eyes to measure the breadth of his big, sinewy shoulders, then moved over the muscles of his powerful chest lightly covered with curling black hair. Her gaze traveled to his hard, flat stomach; she saw, just below his navel, that dark line of hair disappearing under his waistband. Her eyes dropped even lower to where she knew that line of hair led and his snug trousers pulled taut over the ample swell of his manhood.

Slowly her eyes moved back up his magnificent form and found his eyes studying her with such an expression of want that they were deeper and darker and more luring than any forest. He slowly eased his bare chest to hers and his hoarse groan mingled with her soft sigh.

Cody cupped her jaw with one hand as his tongue slipped inside her mouth and stroked rhythmically against hers. His other hand reached for hers, and grasping it, he pulled it down quickly to press it firmly to the front of his pants, where that masculine bulge was straining against the warm fabric to be free. Tessa experienced a wild, surging thrill as he thrust his hips hard against her hand, but then he let her go, his own hand wandering, his long fingers brushing her bare stomach.

He found the buttons to her petticoats and set them free. Immediately, his warm hand slipped inside her undergarments and began to caress her silken skin, gliding over her slender hip, brushing across her thigh. Tingles prickled over her skin at the butterfly touch of his fingers; yet she stiffened, her palms pressing tight to the muscles in his back.

"Oh!" Cody's fingers traced patterns along the inside of her thigh, up, down, and up around her feminine warmth, arousing deep and powerful surges of sensation within her. He hushed her, whispering hot words into her ear, into her mouth, against her skin, so fiercely, so passionately, Tessa did not hear them, only felt them. His tongue seemed to fill her mouth, stroking vigorously, forcefully, erotically while his fingers moved feather-soft on her skin, just above the tangle of silken hairs, and Tessa felt quick little jumps like pulse beats under his magic fingers.

Cody's hand hovered and a million pulses now seemed to beat murderously fast within her, most wildly where he almost touched. And then he did, pressing his palm to that gentle swell that thrummed with life and desperate want. Cody pressed again, more firmly this time, and Tessa moaned, arching her hips against his hand, knowing just an instant of relief from the deep, deep yearning within.

Her eyes fluttered open and she breathed his name. "Cody." A hot surge of blood flared through his loins and just as he leaned to kiss her again a thunderous, insistent banging sounded at the front door, jolting them both out of their private world. They both stiffened, wondering if they had imagined it, but the hammering came again, more insistent this time, and even in the back bedroom, over the wind, they could hear the shout of the frantic man calling, "Doc! Doc!"

Cody's shoulders slumped and he relaxed his weight upon Tessa. "Damn!" he cursed, clearly frustrated and more than a little annoyed.

"Doc!"

"Cody!" Tessa managed, pushing at his sinewy shoulders, struggling under his heavy weight.

He muttered another curse, glancing at Tessa as if he had quite forgotten he was smothering the breath from her slight frame, and then he sat up quickly, running tired fingers through his thoroughly mussed hair.

"Doc!"

"Jesus," Cody swore, coming off the bed, "I'm coming!"

Tessa watched him walk out of the room, still bare-chested, moving with an easy confidence and masculine grace. Her eyes lingered hungrily on his back and shoulders as he left. She lay there waiting, hoping he would not ask the man in. From his appearance, it was quite clear what Cody had been doing, and if the man by chance caught a glimpse of her in Cody's bed . . . the horrifying thought made Tessa spring upright and she began fumbling with the buttons, finding that he'd undone every one of them on every article of clothing she wore, and she felt shame engulf her in hot waves. My God, how *could* she have let him! How . . .

But when he appeared in the doorway, looking tired, disheveled, and somehow endearing, she knew how it had all happened. His eyes flicked over her, sitting on the bed, trying to look prim and ladylike as she smoothed her hair back into its untidy bun.

Walking toward the bed, Cody said regretfully, "I have to go out. It's Ben Jordan. His boy Josh has had stomach pains since midday and they've gotten fierce, Ben says, in the last hour or so." He snatched his shirt from the floor and shrugged into it, keeping his sober green eyes on Tessa, whom he knew was regretting everything they had shared tonight.

Damn! Cody's jaw tightened as he buttoned his shirt. "I've got to collect my bag and head on out there."

Tessa's wide eyes searched his. "Will Josh be all right?"

"Can't say. It sounds like appendicitis. Ben's half crazy with fear." He saw Tessa's eyes look toward the front room, and he knew what she was thinking. "He's gone on ahead. I'll catch up to him." He was stuffing his shirttails into his pants, not noticing Tessa's vivid blush. "You stay here," he ordered.

"What?"

"I said stay here. I don't want you wandering off into the night by yourself. Stay here until I get back."

Tessa's delicate jaw tightened belligerently. "I will not!" She kept her eyes away from his trousers, where he was fumbling with the buttons. He glanced her way, seeing that she was struggling to her feet, and his warning look made her waver momentarily. "I can find my way home! I don't need you to lead me there like a child."

He looked around for his black bag, then remembered that he'd left it in the front room. "It's dangerous out there, Tessa. We have wolves here in Kansas."

"Don't try to scare me, Cody."

He was almost out of the room again. He looked back at her from the doorway and his expression made her heart kick in her chest. "Stay, Tess. If dawn comes before I get back, you can start home, but like I said, it's dangerous out there and I'll never forgive myself if something happened to you."

Were there really wolves out there? she wondered. He looked absolutely serious, but she didn't always know when Cody was teasing. There wasn't a trace of humor on his face now, though, and feeling defeated, Tessa opted to stay and she sat poised on the edge of the bed.

"I've got to go," he said, and turned his back on her.

"But what will I do when you're gone? What—"

"Read! Eat! I don't care! Just stay here till I get back!"

She resented his dictatorial manner and wanted to tell him so, but he was gone. She heard him stomping around the front room for an instant, then the front door slammed closed, and then there was silence in the house.

For a moment Tessa pouted. Read! Eat! Dear God, how could she even consider doing either of those when he'd left her in such a state! He'd coaxed her into his home, seduced her on his bed, had her nearly stripped beneath those expert, practiced hands, and had put his mouth to her flesh in ways that made her press her stomach hard now. Her knuckles dug into her belly, trying to rid it of that strange and wild hunger she felt when she merely thought of him.

The house was so empty without him here. He was a man of presence, was Cody Butler.

Tessa lay back on his bed. She pulled her feet up and stretched out on her side, lying there wondering at these feelings, these odd emotions that plagued her. Adulteress! No! her mind rebelled. She hadn't gone that far with him . . . but she knew she would have if not for that fateful interruption.

Oh, Cody! Why have you made me want you? she thought. Why do I still want you to take me into your arms even when I know how wrong it is?

The ache of tears surfaced thickly in Tessa's throat. Her eyes stung. She breathed in deeply—she could still smell his masculine scent on the bed. Her lashes drifted closed and hot tears slipped through, wetting them as she fell asleep.

When Cody returned, he saw Tessa's coat still hung over the back of the armchair. He raised his brows, a little surprised she'd stayed.

There was no evidence of her in the entry-way or in the kitchen, so stamping the snow from his boots and not bothering to take off his coat, Cody headed toward the bedroom.

Seeing her asleep on his bed brought him up short. This he hadn't expected. But she looked perfect lying there, asleep on her side, with one hand tucked under her chin, the other stretched across his pillow. Something gripped his throat as he watched her. He took two strides forward and stood at the edge of the bed, looking down at her.

She was once more buttoned up properly with the bar pin holding her collar snugly together under her chin. But Cody smiled to himself, knowing what she was hiding under those clothes. She was still as slim as a willow, but her graceful curves had ripened since she first came to Harper City. Mrs. Rawlins's cooking was very tempting, and out here it was easy to work up a hearty appetite.

Cody's eyes lingered on her hip, but he restrained the urge to run his hand over it as she slept. His gaze ran up her body to her face; a striking, intelligent face with those slim, dark eyebrows, a graceful nose, and wide, full mouth that hinted at the passionate creature she was.

A slight scowl drew Cody's brows down. Never had a woman excited, intrigued, frustrated, and infuriated him more than Miss Tessa Amesbury. She was different, refreshing. Nothing like the fast women he'd enjoyed since adolescence. She was like no other woman he'd ever known—shy, bold, yet utterly, naturally feminine—and she somehow made him forget all about those others and crave only her. It was her sweet body and kisses he yearned for—and yes, her soul too—selfishly, he wanted all of her, and wanted no other man to touch her. But he knew she was promised to another man. . . .

His frown deepened and Cody reached out

and brushed the backs of his fingers across her cheek. Tessa stirred and snuggled deeper into the mattress. Cody stirred too, and he fought the hardening of his body.

"Tess."

Spurred awake by his voice, Tessa opened her eyes slowly and stretched lazily, staring up at him. He was standing over her, his hands shoved into his back pockets, his heavy jacket open, his jet hair mussed, and his cheeks ruddy under his beard stubble. She smiled up at him, and gently he smiled back. Tessa's coffee-brown eyes suddenly widened, startled now as the last vestiges of sleep drifted away and reality came back to her with a jolt. She came up on her elbows, then quickly swung her legs over the side of the bed.

"Take me home now, Cody," she said, her voice still husky from sleep. Her eyes jumped to the clock on the dresser. "My God, it's four-thirty!" she exclaimed. She'd slept all this time—at his house! She raised her eyes to his and her gaze immediately softened, seeing how tired he looked. Her voice softened too. "How's Josh?" she asked.

"I took out his appendix. He's feeling poorly right now as anyone would, but he should be all right. I'll check him again in a few hours on my way out to Pinky Murphy's." Cody passed a weary hand over his eyes and sank to the edge of the bed beside her, controlling the urge to fall backward and let sleep take over.

"You must be tired," Tessa said, also controlling an urge—the urge to reach over and lay a hand upon his forearm—to smooth the tousled hair from his weary brow. "Bring me home now, Cody, and you can come straight back here and sleep."

"I'm tired," he admitted. "But I want to talk with you before I bring you back."

Their eyes met—hers wide and searching, questioning, and his deep and probing. Emotion welled in her throat.

"Cody—no. Take me home."

But his eyes continued to probe hers. "Not the way you're feeling. I can see guilt written all over your face, Tessa, and I'll be damned if I'm going to let you go home feeling guilty. Or mad at me."

She drew in a slow, shaky breath. "Cody, I've told you—"

"I know what you've told me, and I also know what you're body tells me—"

Tessa jumped to her feet, but Cody's hand shot out and gripped her wrist, pulling her back down between his legs, and her backside plunked down on his hard thigh. "Settle down, you little hothead!"

Tessa squirmed and wriggled, trying to break free of his tight hold. "I don't want to sit on your lap," she said through gritted teeth, trying to pry his steely fingers from her wrist.

"We'll be back on that bed again if you don't stop all that wriggling."

She stilled immediately. She'd learned what little provocation it took to arouse him.

She wouldn't look at him, instead lowering her gaze to the strong masculine hand that held hers, the long fingers he'd twined with her slim ones. His thumb idly rubbed the back of her hand as he spoke low. "When are you going to stop lying to yourself? When are you going to stop telling yourself that you don't like me? That you and I could be good together?"

Her elegant brows merged in an angry frown. "Good at what, Cody? An illicit affair?" In an almost tired gesture she pressed her fingertips to the center of her forehead. "I suppose I can't fault you for wanting that. God knows you're used to that from women. But aren't you getting enough from Angie?"

My God, had she actually said that?

"It's been a long time since I've had a woman, Tess."

She glanced to his eyes and arched her lovely brows at him. "Oh? How long? A day or two?"

With grim humor he returned her stare. Balancing her easily on his knee, he rubbed the back of his neck as if to ease the tension there, and he sighed. "Last night," he said, "Mrs. Rawlins asked me to bring a woman with me if I wished. I could have brought Angie if I wanted to."

"You should have," Tessa returned blandly. "I'm sure she would have proved much more entertaining than I was and much less frustrating for you."

"Dammit, Tess!" For a moment Tessa

thought he would drop her right to the floor, but she kept her balance. "I never touched her. And compared to you she's a very boring, shallow woman at that!"

His admission opened up a dam of emotions within her and the sudden flood made tears fill her eyes. She looked sharply away from him to keep them from spilling over.

"You wouldn't be kissing me the way you do if you were in love with Michael Shea," he coaxed, noting the trembling of her mouth.

Their locked hands seemed to blur before her eyes. Tessa blinked her tears back rapidly, but her lashes were wet. "You're damned persistent, Cody!"

"Damn right I am," he said huskily, and as he lowered his head, his breath stirred her hair. But Tessa whirled on him, her eyes a curious blend of fire and water. "Don't you *dare* kiss me now, Cody Butler! I am promised to another man! Can't you understand that?"

"I guess I could if he were living here in Harper City."

"So I should be unfaithful just because he doesn't live a mile away?"

The blue in Cody's eyes seemed to deepen. "It's not that and we both know it. You're not in love with Michael Shea and you don't want to be married to him."

"I am in love with him!" she cried fiercely, suddenly afraid.

Cody snorted. "You're scared to talk about it too. Why, Tessa?"

She almost shot out of his lap again but his

arms tightened around her waist. She glared at him. "I want to go home."

"Sure you do. But I told you you're not going anywhere until we have this thing out."

"There's nothing to have out! Hasn't a woman ever denied you before?"

The silence in the room was shattering. When Tessa saw the perplexed frown on his rugged features, she almost smiled. Cody rubbed his stubbled jaw, as if he were trying to think of one such woman.

Tessa did smile now. "It doesn't surprise me," she said dryly.

A slow boyish smile stole across his handsome features. "Well, there was one when I was fourteen . . ."

In a tender gesture Tessa smiled and laid her palm on Cody's stubbled cheek. "This woman is denying you, Cody."

She felt the muscle jump under her palm. His eyes seemed to harden and then they grew warm again. He took her palm from his face, turned it over, and kissed it. She let him, watching the dark curls at the back of his head. "If he doesn't come out in the spring," he murmured, his words tickling her sensitive flesh, "I'm comin' after you, Tess." She shuddered when he raised his burning green gaze to hers. "You just try to deny me then, woman." But he said it gently.

They stood together and Tessa suddenly felt oddly bereft, oddly abandoned by him, and she wished somehow it could all be different.

He held out his callused palm to her and she put her hand into his welcome warmth. "Come," Cody said, "let's get you home now."

And they both left the room, still feeling as though this matter lay unresolved.

Chapter Eleven

+ + + +

THE DETECTIVE STARED DISMALLY out the hotel window at the driving ice and snow. Damnable blizzard! He'd be trapped here in Colorado for two weeks now and he'd be trapped until the trains got through.

He sighed and thought of the girl—by God, he'd even dreamed of her! He'd traveled to San Francisco and Santa Fe and San Antonio. Tessa Amesbury was in none of those cities. There were only two remaining cities on his list. St. Louis and Harper City, Kansas. Harper City was his next destination, though he doubted she'd choose to hide herself in a small town rather than a city like St. Louis.

If only it would stop snowing!

* * *

If he doesn't come out in the spring,
I'm comin' after you, Tess.

The words had her tossing and turning for nights. She dreamed of his burning green gaze, of his devastating smile, of his hungry, seductive mouth upon her flesh. Damn you, Cody! She'd wake up shivering in the cold bedroom, her teeth chattering in the dark, with that steady fire growing and burning within.

"I'll tell you," Mrs. Rawlins said cheerfully one icy January morning, "I can't see you with a better boy than Cody. I love you both as if you were my own."

Why didn't Tessa have the courage to correct her? She wanted to tell the dear old woman that she'd misconstrued what existed between her and Cody, but instead she'd kept quiet, flushing guiltily.

She'd even considered an annulment from William, as she'd considered it in the past. But that would only help bring William to her, and he was so clever she knew he'd contrive a way to get her back to Boston. And into his home.

Tessa shivered just thinking about William. He was truly evil. She couldn't believe she had ever agreed to marry him. But she knew she had had to marry him. If not for her own happiness, for the sake of the orphanage and those in it. Wealthy widower William Forsythe had lent the orphanage money to add a new and desperately needed wing for their overcrowded building. When they were unable to make the payments, Forsythe suggested that if Tessa agreed to marry him he would regard the loan as paid in full. Though Tessa recoiled at the thought of this cold man as her husband, she could not bear to watch the orphanage—her home and family—fold.

When he took her home that night and started beating her—no! She would not think of it! It was over! There would be no annulment because there was no need for an annulment. She was not going to become Cody's mistress come spring or any other time, no matter how persuasive the man was.

Yet . . . did he really think she was beautiful? Sometimes Tessa would stand before the mirror and study her face as if she'd never seen it before. No one had ever called her beautiful except Mrs. Rawlins and that wasn't quite the same. And he must have meant it— he *must* have—or he wouldn't have looked at her that way. . . .

January was bleak, empty, and unbearably cold. Trudging back and forth to school in the bitter weather was, to Tessa, comparable to a prison sentence. On her way home one blustery afternoon she saw Cody standing with a group of men by the hitching rail across the street. She stopped, her eyes on him; he seemed to stand alone in the cold blue light of winter dusk, taller and broader than any man there. In that instant his eyes found hers and

Tessa felt an ache in her stomach—like the feeling of coasting swiftly downhill and sharply up again. He stepped across the street and Tessa watched him come toward her in those long, purposeful strides, closer, closer. Her stomach trembled when he stopped in front of her, blocking out the cold, sharp wind. He was hatless and his hair fluttered wildly, and she hated herself for wanting to smooth it. He lifted a hand to touch her, then shoved it back into his jacket pocket and clenched it.

"Tess."

"Hello, Cody."

Their breath, frosty white clouds in the purple air, mingled, seemed to kiss, and drifted lazily away. In the frigid twilight, a mutual molten fire seemed to explode through their veins at the sight of the other.

Does she feel the fire like I do?

Does he tremble inside as I do?

They both cleared their throats. But Cody spoke first. "Can I ride you home, Tess?"

"No!" She answered much too quickly, much too nervously.

His eyes were unsmiling on hers. "It's not much further."

"No . . . thank you. I—I like walking . . . Cody, how is Mary?"

"She's about the same. The baby's still moving." The silence seemed oppressive. "She misses you, Tessa."

"I'd like to buy her some things at Eb's.

Could you bring them to her the next time you visit her?"

"Why don't you come along and hand them to her yourself?"

"You know why." Her voice was husky. She watched his broad shoulders lift a little under his jacket then relax as he let out a long breath. "Sure," he said, "I'll do it."

And the smile that broke across her minxlike features made him catch his breath sharply. But she was off, the heels of her shoes kicking up little clumps of snow as she trotted toward Eb's store. Watching her, he felt something clutch tight in his vitals . . . and didn't know if he could wait until spring.

Tessa not only felt incredible tension when she was near Cody, but she was tense in the schoolroom as well. Of course there was the ongoing feud between Sam Jordan and Smoke Eyes, which at times seemed almost ludicrous.

"I'm gonna *git* you!" Sam would hiss at any opportune moment.

After a couple of months of listening to this idle threat Smoke Eyes had taken to laughing at him. "Hah!" she jeered. "Yer jes yeller! Ya ain't got yer little brother to back ya up now either!"

"You jinxed Josh! Ya put some stinkin' Injun hex on him an' he got fierce stomach pains! Ya witched him!"

This was enough to make Smoke Eyes double up her fists and bring her freckled nose within an inch of Sam's face. "Yah, mebbe I did, an' if ya don't git outta my way I'll be witchin' you too!"

Sam paled. Smoke Eyes laughed jeeringly at his blatant fright.

"I'm still gonna git you!" Sam promised, only weakly now.

"Yah, when?"

"For pity's sake!" Tessa broke in, coming upon the two by the side of the schoolhouse. "I can't even think straight with the two of you constantly bickering. Enough! Or I'll sit you beside each other in the classroom."

This threat was enough to make Sam stay clear of Smoke Eyes for a week.

But not only Sam disliked Smoke Eyes: many of the girls did too. They found her offensive and unruly and everything their own mothers were raising them not to be. There were days when Tessa felt it was hopeless trying to teach the girl social graces, but just as she was ready to give up, Smoke Eyes would say or do something that would strengthen Tessa's resolve to guide her.

"My ma was real p'ticular 'bout manners," Smoke Eyes informed Tessa one afternoon as the children put on their wraps to go out for recess. Smoke Eyes was staying indoors to study for a spelling test. "Pa, now, he din't care. He said what's it matter? No one 'round to see us eat. But Ma, she was real p'ticular."

Tessa studied the bent auburn head. She glanced to the few older girls huddled around the heating stove, then back to Smoke Eyes.

"And you share you father's view on manners?"

Smoke eyes shrugged. "Sometimes." She scratched a few letters onto her slate. "Pa din't think I needin' schoolin'." She raised her beautiful gray eyes. "Ma thought I should have it. Ya think it'd be different, wouldn't ya?" She glanced to the slate, then back up again. "She had eyes like yours, Teacher."

The admission moved Tessa in a deep way.

"She'd be proud of you now, then, wouldn't she, Smoke Eyes?"

Smoke Eyes lifted her gaze once more and Tessa saw the mist of tears in them. But the child tightened her jaw and gripped her slate pencil. "I guess she would."

Out of all the children only Zach seemed to admire Smoke Eyes. He was intrigued by her buckskins and fiery temper. Unfortunately sometimes he and Smoke Eyes joined forces against Tessa. Once Tessa found the both of them smoking Zach's cigarettes behind the schoolhouse. She was so furious she made them smoke them all until they turned green and pledged they'd never bring another cigarette to school.

There was friction, too, between Zach and Sidney Chase. Sid seemed to think himself a touch above every other boy in that classroom—whether it was due to his age or his smart appearance Tessa didn't know—but there was an animosity between the two boys

that seemed to grow every day. And late one
afternoon that animosity exploded.

She was gathering up her books and papers
at the end of the day when she heard little
Amy Peterson crying frantically as she flew
fast as she could up the icy steps. "Miss
Amesbury! Miss Amesbury! Fight!"

Tessa ran to the doorway and nearly slid the
entire precarious way down the steps, not
caring in the least about her dignity. Not Sam
and Smoke Eyes again! But it was Zach and
Sid slugging it out in the snow. A group of
children had gathered about, shouting their
encouragement until they saw the teacher and
scampered off.

"Stop!" she cried, cringing at the thuds of
the boys' solid fists upon flesh. "Stop, boys!"
She looked helplessly about, not daring to
step into the fray and risk a fractured jaw.

She turned and ran quickly back up the
slippery steps to the entryway, where she
grabbed hold of the water pail on the bench by
the door. She lugged it back outside, the icy
water sloshing over the sides, and at last
made it back to the scene of the battle, which
had turned savage. She lifted the bucket high
and flung the water up at the boys' faces. The
frigid shock of it stunned them in the raw air
and they both stopped, gasping for breath.

"I said stop!" Tessa yelled, her hands
planted furiously on her slender hips, the
water bucket dangling free from one hand.

Out of their torn and bloody faces the two

peered at her, and from what Tessa could see, Sid had gotten the worst of it. They suddenly looked more wary of this fuming, hotheaded teacher than they did of each other.

"Get inside—both of you! Children!" she snapped, wheeling around to find the few stragglers who possessed the daring to remain despite their teacher's wrath. "Get home with you—now!" She caught sight of Smoke Eyes standing some distance back, but then the girl quickly turned and dashed off. Tessa turned her glare back to the two boys, who hadn't moved a step toward the schoolhouse. "I said get inside," she said through her teeth, and they moved ahead of her. On the way Zach bent down to scoop up a handful of snow to hold over a swollen eye. Sid seemed to be having trouble walking.

Inside, Sid just about collapsed into a seat while Zach perched a hip on one of the desks, regarding Tessa coolly through a half-closed eye. Tessa was seething as she faced them.

"There is no excuse for this—none! I will not tolerate fisticuffs among the younger children and I certainly will not tolerate it from you! This is not a barroom and I will not have you subjecting these grounds to barroomlike brawls!" Looking at their battered faces, Tessa felt her insides churn. "There is no excuse for this," she repeated, more quietly.

" 'Cept one," Zach broke in laconically.

At his words Tessa thought she could use a splash of that icy water she'd flung at them earlier; heat swam through her blood and made her eyes burn as Zach got up to saunter out.

"Mr. Fletcher!" she hissed in her most effective schoolmarm voice. "If you leave this classroom now I promise you you'll never come back."

Zach turned and flicked his cool gaze over her. He did not return to the desk, instead leaning against the back wall of the schoolhouse and folding his arms across his chest. His black eyes glittered back at her.

"Would you mind explaining what you meant by that 'except one'?"

Zach glanced to Sid. "Ask him."

Sid lifted his head to look at her. Tessa waited.

"Aw, Miss Amesbury, he was just causing trouble, like he usually does."

Zach straightened and Sid seemed to see him out of the corner of his eye. His next words seemed to tumble out of him between gasping breaths. "All right, I was just talking to that little breed and he jumped me—from behind, I'll tell you—and for no good reason!"

"I bet Smoke Eyes wouldn't think it was fer no reason," Zach said coldly.

Sid spun in his seat to face his enemy, and he held tight to his aching ribs. "Smoke Eyes!" He sneered. His narrowed glance went to Tessa. "Did you hear what he called her, Miss Amesbury? Smoke Eyes."

"It's her name, Sid." Tessa said it quietly,

beginning to understand exactly what had gone on here.

"She's an ugly little dirty breed and my pa says there's only one thing a squaw is good for!"

Tessa blanched. A sick emotion snaked through her.

Zach swore. "An' is that what you was tryin' to prove when ya grabbed her?"

"Aw, I didn't grab her. I just roughed her up a little, that's all."

Tessa actually stepped toward him. But she stopped when she saw his eyes widen. "Just . . . roughed . . . her . . ." She couldn't even finish she was so outraged. She had the most incredible urge to grab his ear and pull it until he had an idea what grabbing was all about. "If you ever lay a hand on that child—*ever*— Mr. Chase, you will be immediately expelled. And if you ever call Smoke Eyes a dirty little breed or any such derogatory name you will be expelled. Is that absolutely clear?"

"Yes'm."

"I have a good mind to take this up with the school board and keep you out of school for a while. Until I make up my mind about it you may go home and tell your parents exactly what I've told you. You realize, of course, that if you don't graduate you don't attend college in the East come fall."

Sid seemed to whiten before her eyes. It was of the utmost importance to Sid and his family that he attend college in the fall.

"Now get on home and tend to yourself."

With great effort Sidney raised himself from his seat and sidled past Zach, who made a move to follow him.

"Stay here a moment, Zach."

When Sid was gone, Tessa gestured for Zach to take a seat, but again, he only leaned against the edge of a desk. She looked directly into his black eyes.

"I want to thank you," she said.

Zach smiled grimly, then winced, pressing a thumb to his split lip, which oozed blood. "Fer fightin', Miss Amesbury?"

"I'd never thought I'd say it, but yes. Of course, you didn't have to carry it so far . . . and of course, you know I'm really thanking you for protecting Smoke Eyes."

Zach looked uncomfortable. "She ain't got no one to look after her."

"*Hasn't* got anyone to look after her," Tessa couldn't help but correct him gently.

His laugh sounded like a bark. "You never miss a chance, do ya, Miss Amesbury?"

She smiled back at him. "Never." She wanted to tell him to go home and have his mother tend to his cuts but knew there would be no one there for him. "Stop by Dr. Butler's on your way home, Zach. He'll fix you up."

"Aw, I'm all right."

"Yes, but I think Dr. Butler would enjoy some company," she said with a hint of laughter in her eyes. Zach's answering smile was little more than a painful lift of his lip.

"I guess I'll stop in and say hello."

Say hello to him for me too, Tessa silently requested, watching Zach make his way out.

"Oh, and Miss Amesbury," he said, turning, "thanks fer not kicking me out."

Now *that* from Zach Fletcher was enough cause for a celebration!

Under the cold red sun Tessa walked home, feeling spent and tired, and more worried than ever about Smoke Eyes. Had Sid really "grabbed" her? And could this get even more out of hand? Oh, what a dismal month!

By the time Tessa turned up the lighted walk to home her footsteps were lagging. Even the smell of hot, rich beef stew couldn't rouse her weary spirits when she opened the door. She sat at the table, picking idly at the chunks of beef and carrots and potatoes swimming in the thick brown gravy. Halfway through the meal Mrs. Rawlins stirred her with the words, "I have some grand news for you tonight, Tessa."

Tessa lifted her brown eyes to Mrs. Rawlins's blue ones. "Hmm?"

"Eb and I are going to get married come February!" She said it in a light, breathless rush, almost girlishly.

Tessa's spoon dangled, forgotten in midair. She blinked her eyes, slowly absorbing the words as Mrs. Rawlins sat waiting for the younger woman's reaction. "Married? You and Eb?" And it suddenly dawned on Tessa that her reaction was not quite what dear Mrs. Rawlins expected. "Oh, my goodness, Mrs. Rawlins! Why—why, that's wonderful!" She jumped up and flew around the table, hugging and kissing the old woman, truly happy for her. Laughing, Tessa demanded, "What brought this on?"

"Well, let me catch my breath!" Mrs. Rawlins laughed, blushing with pleasure. She made Tessa sit down again and her blue eyes twinkled as she said, "Eb and I are not getting younger, you know. So I told him, either we can continue the rest of our days unmarried and pining for each other, or married and . . . fulfilled. He saw the logic in that especially when I told him I'd refused to keep him company *unless* he married me!"

Tessa laughed, her eyes dancing. "*You* proposed to *him?*"

Mrs. Rawlins laughed gaily and made a trivial hand gesture. "At my age you çan't wait for the man to propose! Heavens, men are so slow on the draw! But that doesn't stop them from getting randy! Why, Eb—"

"Please! Mrs. Rawlins—" Tears of laughter were in Tessa's eyes now, yet she was blushing to her hairline. If what Mrs. Rawlins meant by "randy" was what she and Cody were doing on Cody's bed, she didn't want to hear any more details. Besides, it was a shock that old folks had the same yearnings younger people had. "I get the idea."

But another thought had suddenly occurred to Mrs. Rawlins. A little frown flitted across her brow. "You won't be afraid here alone, will you, dear?"

Oh! Tessa hadn't thought of that! But of

course she would be alone. She felt Mrs. Rawlins's eyes scrutinizing her and she forced a smile to her lips. "You don't want to leave this big house all for me, Mrs. Rawlins. You could take on some more boarders and I'll go live at the hotel."

Mrs. Rawlins looked horrified. "Oh, I wouldn't hear of it! This is your home as much as it is mine! And who, in heaven's name, would be coming out to board at a place in the dead of winter? You must stay!" Her eyes softened on Tessa. "Unless, that is, you don't want to live here alone."

"That's not it. . . ." Tessa said vaguely.

"There's no need to be afraid. I'll leave Ginger here with you, of course, so you can keep each other company. And I'll ask Cody to check on you from time to time. He won't mind."

Her eyes widened. That was all she needed to hear! Leaving her with Cody was like leaving her with a vulture! "Oh, heavens, no! I'll be fine, Mrs. Rawlins, really. I'll miss you, that's all."

The following day during the noon hour a hand-written note was delivered to Tessa at her desk. Tessa smiled when she read the note:

Tess—

Early this morning Mary had her baby. She and the boy are both fine. I'm going to visit her this evening. Come with me.

Cody

Tessa folded the note and tucked it into her satchel. This, she promised herself, would be the last ride she ever took with Cody. Yet, strangely enough, as the day wore on, she found herself looking forward to it.

Cody was excruciatingly polite to her during the ride to and from the Lyndons. Even when they had passed baby Jeremiah between them, he avoided contact with her—almost as if she had leprosy, Tessa thought to herself.

The next time she saw Cody was on Mrs. Rawlins's wedding day. They'd both been invited to Mike and Claire's after the ceremony, but Cody kept his distance from her all evening. He didn't even offer to escort her home. Mike and Claire let her off at the empty house and Tessa found herself wondering if Cody had lost all interest in her. Had he gone home to another woman? The thought should have eased her mind. Oddly, it depressed her.

By mid-February there were so many students absent with coughs and other illnesses that Tessa was teaching only half the class. One gusty morning as she was building a fire in the heater before any pupils arrived, Smoke Eyes came up behind her.

"My goodness," Tessa exclaimed, "it's early, Smoke Eyes! Why are you here at this hour?"

"My grandfather is sick," Smoke Eyes answered solemnly. "He seems awful sick, Miss Amesbury. His throat is real sore an' I gotta take care of him."

"Has Cody—Dr. Butler examined him yet?"

"I'm on my way up to his house now."

"Oh, Smoke Eyes, it's freezing out! Can't you find someone to give you a ride?"

Smoke Eyes held her mittened palms up. "No. But you know I'm a fast runner, Miss Amesbury." And Tessa couldn't help from grinning.

"Run along then, and I'm sure I'll see you by the end of the week. And take care of yourself too, Smoke Eyes. I don't want you getting sick."

That same evening when Tessa trudged up the stairs to her home, a note attached to the door caught her eye. Reaching for it, Tessa recognized Cody's handwriting. She opened the note quickly and read:

Tess:

>*Young James Calvert has died of diphtheria. Stay in the house. Don't come out until I put another note on your door. It will be a few days at least. I'll come by to check on you before then. There are several cases of the disease in town and I'm concerned about you since you're constantly exposed to the children. When I knock on the door, don't open it. Just let me know how you are through the window.*
>
>*Swab your throat with iodine, eat plenty of soup, and if your throat gets sore, keep hot towels on it and let me know by hanging a strip of red cloth on the doorknob. Stay in.*

>> *Cody*

Tessa closed her eyes a moment, letting her mind absorb the horrifying facts. James Calvert, dead. Beth and Dan's son. A quiet, handsome boy who never gave her a moment of trouble. He was only nine years old. My God, Tessa swallowed thickly, I cannot believe it.

And then another shocking, startling thought: Smoke Eyes' grandfather was sick. Did he have diphtheria? Would Smoke Eyes become sick too?

Tessa pulled the door open and quickly stepped inside. Ginger greeted her with a soft meow. Tessa scooped her up and rubbed her cheek against the orange fur, mainly for her own comfort. How many of her students had it? Would Cody get it? Oh, dear God, please, not Cody.

The claim shanty was cold where the wind seeped through chinks in the walls and under the door. Despite the warmth emanating from the cookstove in the kitchen, the shanty didn't seem to heat up.

Hannah and Bessie Brown lay together on their bed in the front room, burning with fever. Cody peered down their throats and did not like what he saw. Large dirty gray patches grew thick and were slowly turning yellow. The girls choked, fighting for breath. Cody looked up at Ellen Brown, their mother.

"Get more beef broth, Ellen," Cody ordered. "The more liquid we force down their throats, the better. Keep the water boiling out there. The air has to stay moist."

The frightened woman moved quickly to do the doctor's bidding. As Cody leaned and felt Hannah's pulse, their father, Ron, dropped onto a worn chair, rubbing his hands wearily over his anguished face. Cody stood and went over to him.

Ron looked up at the doctor with hollow brown eyes. "I done everything I could, Cody, to keep those little girls healthy. Soon as we found out what's goin' on, Ellen an' I, well, we took care of them, swabbin' their throats just like you said. But that didn't do no good, did it? My little girls is goin' to die, ain't they?"

"Don't give up, Ron. Some live through it." The children thrashed wildly on the bed behind him. He turned to them but Ron's despairing voice stopped him.

"Don't lie to me, man. I'm goin' to lose my babies, an' I know it."

Cody tightened his lips. He realized Ron was distraught, but still he said flatly, "No one's ever called me a liar, Ron. And if you give up now, you may as well get the hell out of here until I'm done doing everything I can to save those girls."

Ron blinked. "Hell, I'm sorry. What should I do?"

"Get some more hot compresses ready. And pray to God the membrane doesn't extend to the larynx or windpipe." That's what happened to James Calvert and others, and in those cases the patient almost always choked to death. At least ten children had died in the past four days, but he'd been able to save a few too. He was exhausted; this was the fifth house he'd called on today and now Cody rubbed a weary hand over his red-rimmed eyes. But a choking sound behind him made him spin around. Little Hannah was coughing and spitting, writhing in agony on the bed as her lungs gasped for air. Ellen came running in with the broth, her face panic-stricken.

But Cody had already sprung into action. "Ellen, take Bessie into the kitchen—quick!" Ellen snatched the feverish child and ran into the kitchen with her.

"Doc—what're you gonna do?" Fear and doubt were stamped on Ron's face as he watched Cody with a sharp instrument in one hand lean toward the little girl whose slight body arched in a desperate attempt to find breath. But Cody didn't have time for answers. Quickly, efficiently, he made an incision in the child's throat and opened her windpipe. Placing a sterile handkerchief over the incision, he put his own lips to the opening and sucked the lethal secretions from the larynx until Hannah could breathe again.

"Sweet Jesus . . ." Ron sank to the bed, his stunned eyes riveted to the man who was giving life to his child. "Sweet, sweet God."

Ron's eyes were glued to those long, skilled fingers as they now sewed the incision, capably, calmly. Tears coursed down the father's face as he watched his little Hannah, now sedated.

When it was over, Cody stood, his face tight, his eyes bloodshot with exhaustion, and all he said was, "Do you have any whiskey in the house? I'd like to clean out my own throat."

Shakily, Ron came to his feet. He reached and clutched Cody's hand. "My God, man, if I didn't see it with my own eyes I'd've never believed it. You saved her. An' at the risk of your own life."

"She's not completely out of danger yet," Cody said grimly. "And you have another one in there"—he nodded toward the kitchen—"that needs looking after. Just do what I tell you and things might turn out right. Now I need some clean water to wash my hands. And I sure as hell could use that whiskey now."

Ron nearly stumbled over his own feet in his haste to please Cody. In his eyes this man was nothing short of godlike.

Cody accepted the full bottle of rotgut whiskey and swigged it all the way back to town. He held the bottle up in the snapping cold air and grinned. "Well, Major," he said to his horse, "this isn't such a bad ending to such a bad day after all, is it?" But Major only whickered softly and Cody laughed, leaning back in the cutter. He wanted nothing more than to fall into bed and sleep for three days straight, but he made it a point to check on Tessa at least once a day, usually before he went home. She couldn't know the relief he felt when he saw no sign of a red strip of cloth tied to the doorknob. Diphtheria was a great scourge of children, and sometimes took the old, but Tessa's contact with her students had been close enough to seriously endanger her.

When the cutter pulled up before her house, Cody leaped out and took the steps two at a time, despite the hazard of slipping, despite his exhaustion. He knocked on the door, and when she didn't come he leaned against the house for a moment and closed his bleary eyes. He could easily sleep right here in this house. He smiled to himself at his own private joke, then slowly straightened and rapped again. But she was at the window. For a moment he simply stared at her. She looked visionary, there, through the pane of frosty glass, the soft glow of lamplight from behind illuminating her. She raised a slim golden hand to clear the window of her warm breath that clung there and fogged his image. Cody resisted the urge to raise his own hand and press it to the glass, to get as close to her as he could. He thought it ironic that they stood face-to-face with just the glass between them—nothing and no one else; not Mrs. Rawlins, and not Michael Shea—yet they stood trapped and staring as if they'd been caught in the very act.

"Cody?" Her deep brown almond eyes reached fathoms into his. "Cody, are you all right?" Tessa called. She didn't think he looked all right. He stood there red-eyed and unshaven, a whiskey bottle clutched in one hand, looking as though he would like to fall asleep standing up. And no wonder. He had been keeping this town alive for days. He'd gone to house after house, treating the sick, risking his own life to keep others from dying. He'd traveled out to the claims as well as all through town. And he'd done it all by himself. He'd report to her each day who had been stricken, and who had survived. The disease had taken Smoke Eyes' grandfather. As soon as she heard that, Tessa had wanted Smoke Eyes brought to her, but Cody refused. He placed her with a safe family, but Tessa could imagine how miserable the girl must be there. And what if Cody caught the deadly disease? What if he died? She suddenly banged on the window with her hand. "Cody! I want to help you! Tomorrow, stop by and pick me up!"

That seemed to sober him slightly. "No! Dammit, Tess, don't you get any ideas!"

"I won't get sick! I never get sick. But you will. You're exhausted! You can't keep on like this! I can help you, Cody!"

He tried to ignore her. "Now that I see you're feeling fine I'm going to head home. I'll stop by tomorrow night." He turned his broad back on her.

"Cody—don't you ignore me!"

But he'd gone down the steps. Angrily, Tessa left the window and stomped to the

front door, yanking it open, feeling the wonderful, cold fresh air surge into her lungs—the
fresh air she hadn't felt for days.

"Cody Butler!"

He spun around. His dark brows were
pulled low into a frown. "Damn you, Tess!
Shut the goddamn door! I just came from a
thoroughly infected house—shut that door!"

"I just want to know—"

"Shut the door!" he shouted, and she did.
The bang sounded somewhat muffled in the
snowy night, but for damn sure she had
slammed it with all her might. Cody shook his
head and laughed. There she was again, banging on the window. "What!" he hollered, not
moving from the bottom step.

"Did you find Zach?"

Cody frowned again. Zach hadn't been
home for a week, and there was no trace of
him anywhere. It was Cody's guess that the
boy had gone trapping or perhaps antelope
hunting to get out of town for a while, but
Tessa wouldn't be satisfied with that answer—
not until the boy came back, if he did at all.

"No, not yet! Tess, I haven't been up there
for a couple of days. He'll be fine, I'm telling
you!" But he could see by the troubled look on
her face that she didn't believe him.

"I'll check again tomorrow—first thing!" he
promised, but she'd let the curtain drop back
into its place and he saw her silhouette move
quietly away.

By the end of the week the diphtheria had

run its course and there were no new cases reported. The disease seemed to have left the town limp, sapped of all energy. The lost ones were buried and the living tried to go on. For days Tessa saw no trace of Cody and she grew worried that he had taken ill, but Susan Miller stopped her in town on Saturday and told her that Cody had traveled to a town thirty miles east to tend those injured in a terrible fire.

"It was awful—in a saloon crowded with townfolk, they say. I understand some have died, but Cody is doing his best to save those still alive."

His dedication seemed more than human, Tessa thought as she walked toward the folks who were housing Smoke Eyes. Yet Cody continued to plunge himself into other people's tragedies, trying to use his knowledge and skill and healing hands to ease their pain. How must it be for him to witness the horror, the fear, the agony and death of those poor suffering souls?

Oh, Cody, Cody, she thought. I wish I were there to help you.

She went up the front steps to Jeb Jones's place and knocked on the front door. His wife, Sarah, answered. The two had two small boys under five years of age and had been kind enough to take in Smoke Eyes. But Sarah looked weary and Tessa knew it was time for Smoke Eyes to get settled elsewhere.

Sarah showed Tessa to the bedroom Smoke Eyes shared with the two little boys.

"Has she been behaving herself?" Tessa
asked in a low voice before she stepped into
the room.

"She has," Sarah answered, "but she's not
real talkative. Fact, I don't think I heard her
say yes or no the whole time she's been here.
Just kind of sits there all day, poor mite. She's
been helping with the chores, though."

Tessa smiled at Sarah. "Thank you," she
said and Sarah left for the kitchen as Tessa
walked into the room. She closed the door
behind her. Smoke Eyes was sitting cross-
legged on the bed, staring out the window.

"Smoke Eyes?"

The girl turned and stared at her. For a
moment her gray eyes went hard, then she
looked out the window again. Her voice
soundly oddly mature when she spoke. "I
knew you'd come, Miss Amesbury. I knew
you would."

Tessa perched on the edge of the bed, not
too close to the girl. "I would've come sooner
if I could have."

"I know."

"These people have been good to you?"

"Yes."

A lump seemed to grow in Tessa's throat as
she watched the pitiful child beside her. She
saw her little jaw work back and forth while
Smoke Eyes gritted her teeth, as if trying to
clamp back the emotion welling within her.
She turned to Tessa and fixed her with brimming eyes filled with a kind of indignant
ferocity and desperation and a terrible aching

sadness. Her ragged voice tore at Tessa's insides. "I ain't got no one now, Miss Amesbury, *no one!*"

She flung herself into Tessa's arms, her little body trembling with all the pent-up anguish within her, and Tessa held her tight, tight, letting the girl sob brokenly against her, letting herself cry into the child's hair. "Please don't cry so, Smoke Eyes," she begged softly, her voice just as broken as the girl's. "You do have someone. You have me."

Smoke Eyes lifted her head, her gray eyes wet and anguished and searching. "Can I come live with you, Miss Amesbury? Can I?"

Tessa's heart lurched. "I've found a family who wants you desperately, Smoke Eyes. No! Don't pull away! She's my best friend. She has a baby boy and she wants a daughter and can never have one. I told her about you. She wants you, Smoke Eyes. And you can have a family!"

"You don't want me!"

"I can't raise you by myself. It'd be best for you to have a family."

"I *had* a family. They're all gone now. I don't want another one. I want you, Miss Amesbury! Please. Yer the only person who unnerstan's me. 'Cept the doc."

The child's plea tore at Tessa's heart. She knew what it was like to be alone. But a family was what Smoke Eyes really needed and Mary would welcome her with open arms. "Can't you just try it at Mary's and see how you like it, Smoke Eyes?"

"No."

"I thought you had more courage than that, Smoke Eyes."

The girl stuck her lip out. She began to cry again, the tears rolling off her brown, freckled cheeks, a curious mixture of stubbornness and vulnerability. "If I behave fer you, will ya take me in?"

"That's not the point, Smoke Eyes," Tessa said gently, smoothing her tangled auburn braid. She watched the girl swipe a sleeve across her eyes. "Please give Mary a chance. You know I wouldn't just send you to someone I didn't trust and like. I've told her all about you—"

"I jes bet ya tol' her all about me."

Tessa squeezed her arm. "Give it a chance, Smoke Eyes. If you truly don't like it at Mary's, I'll see what I can work out for you. But you must really try—no pranks." New tears welled up in those slate eyes. Tessa reached a hand to the wet cheek and brushed the tears tenderly away from it. "And I meant what I said, Smoke Eyes. You'll have me— always."

"Always?"

"As long as I live."

Smoke Eyes' lip trembled. "Will she call me Smoke Eyes, Miss Amesbury?"

Tessa felt the tears sting her eyelids. "Yes." And she held out her arms again and Smoke Eyes came against her and wept softly.

Chapter Twelve

+ + + + +

THE MARCH WINDS HOWLED, driving the snow and ice away but battering the house until it seemed to wail from abuse. Tonight, swathed in her flannel nightie and wrapper, Tessa curled up on the sofa and read the book of poems Mrs. Rawlins had given her for Christmas. As she read, she gently stroked Ginger, who was asleep beside her; the half-grown kitten purred contentedly.

By midnight Tessa's eyes were closing sleepily and the book fell open upon her lap. She let her head drop back and the sounds of outdoors pummeled at the fringes of sleep.

An abrupt knock at the front door shattered her drowsy state. Startled, she sat up. The muffled pounding came again and her bare feet touched the carpet. She hurried to the door, pulling her wrapper closer about her slender body and shuddering when her feet touched the icy floor in the entranceway.

She knew who it was even before she opened it. Cody stood there in his well-worn coat, looking indomitable in the punishing wind and snow as it blew all around him and whipped at his hair. Yet that gust of frigid wind made Tessa gasp for breath, and she clutched her wrapper at the throat, shivering uncontrollably in the drafty hallway.

Cody stepped in and closed the door behind him. His eyes went thoroughly over Tessa, from her unbound hair to her bare toes, and slowly up again, as if they were able to penetrate her wrapper, and see her nipples tightly shriveled under the material. She told herself that their reaction was from the cold and not from his intense gaze, but she knew she was only fooling herself.

It was the first time Cody'd seen her with her hair down; and it fell straight and long, past her shoulders, down her back: a silken, honey-streaked sheet. His throat ached at the sight of her; it looked almost as if she had been waiting for him.

Without words he held out his arms and took her into them, drawing her close, pulling her against his tall, rugged body. One hand cradled the back of her head, and his fingers buried themselves in her silky hair. He just held her, pressing her head to his hard shoulder, and Tessa closed her eyes and slipped her arms about his middle, holding him too. Beneath her cheek she felt his heartbeat, strong and sure. She shivered and snuggled tighter into him, and the heat of his hard body made her heart beat faster.

"You're like a vision, Tess," he breathed against her hair. "A goddamn vision after these last few weeks."

Tessa leaned back in the circle of his arms and looked up at him with her warm, dark velvet eyes. "Was it very bad, Cody?" she asked softly. "The fire?"

She felt his arms tense around her, and his facial muscles tightened. His eyes looked hard and bleak. And even though he looked down at her for a long time, Tessa knew he was still seeing that town and those faces, and not her. Almost painfully he pulled her close again, squeezing her slim body once, and she felt him swallow hard. Words were not necessary.

Together they walked to the warm sitting room, and Ginger lifted her head from her paws to look at them.

"You look so tired," Tessa said, sympathetically, her eyes running over his drawn face, the weariness and strain about his eyes. "When did you get back to town?"

"Not even a half hour ago. I took care of Major, then came here." He saw the unspoken question in her eyes and he answered her with a look of his own: Don't send me home. He kept his eyes on her as he shrugged out of his jacket, and knew when she reached for it, that it seemed right to her too, that he'd come to her, almost as if he'd come home.

He handed her his jacket and his eyes dipped to find the outline of her breasts under her wrapper. Too tired to stop himself from the direction his eyes were taking, Cody let his gaze wander down to her slim ankles; in the past they'd been invariably covered by her high-buttoned shoes, but now only the hem of her nightgown brushed them, and he saw that they were slender, graceful, offering a hint of what her legs must look like.

Watching the direction of his gaze, Tessa's knees went watery and her stomach trembled. "I'll hang this for you," she said shakily, and

cherished the feel of the heavy sheepskin coat
in her fingers. She pressed the jacket to her
thinly clad breasts, partly to shield them from
his penetrating stare, but its weight against
her was almost as intimate as his skin against
her; she raised her eyes to his again and felt a
quickening, a liquid longing.

"Sit there, Cody," she invited softly, "and
I'll fix you a tray. I hope some cold meat and
bread is sufficient." But she didn't wait for his
answer, she was so eager to get out of his
sight, and she didn't know if he'd answered
anyway, as tired as he was.

All the way down the hall she fought the
desire to press his jacket to her cheek. It
smelled like him. Warm and masculine. And
as she hung it on the peg Tessa let her fingers
trail over it, thinking of his broad shoulders
filling it.

She found the chicken and bread and bottle
of wine and put it all on a tray and brought it
into the sitting room, but Cody was not in the
sitting room. Only his worn leather boots
stood by the front door.

"Cody?" Puzzled, Tessa glanced about,
then noticed dim lamplight coming from Mrs.
Rawlins's room off the parlor. With the tray in
her hands she moved toward the room and
saw Cody collapsed on his back, sprawled out
on Mrs. Rawlins's wide, comfortable-looking
bed.

Oh dear, Tessa thought, eyeing the kerosene lamp turned down low on the dresser
top. She stood frozen in the doorway, her

hands gripping the edges of the tray, and pondered him silently. By his closed eyes and the slow rise and fall of his broad chest, breathing easily, she could see that he was sleeping.

Oh, no, she couldn't let him stay here! But he looked so exhausted she didn't have the heart to wake him. And who would know? What harm was there in letting him sleep in Mrs. Rawlins's bed—for just a few hours? She could read in the sitting room and wait for him to wake up.

Tessa tiptoed into the sitting room and placed the tray quietly on the bedside table, then turned around to look at him. His eyes were still closed and his shirt was unbuttoned; one arm was flung over his dark head while the other curled across his bare stomach. She stared at him hungrily, taking her fill of this man at her leisure as she'd wanted to for so long now. While he slept, her eyes savored the look of his hard, muscular chest, and she yearned to run her hands through its curling hairs. Her gaze lowered and halted on his pants, which were pulled snugly in little wrinkles across his groin. Finally, she looked away, fighting her own private longings. She pulled the belt to her wrapper more tightly around her slim middle and crept to the trunk at the foot of the bed, opened it, and rummaged through it, finding a heavy quilt. She went back to the side of the bed, her cheeks burning at the sight of his naked, masculine chest, and she looked sharply away while tossing the quilt haphazardly across his body. She considered pulling the quilt up to cover his chest, but afraid of her overwhelming need to touch him, she left it as it was. Just as she started to back away his husky, murmuring voice stopped her.

"You sure know what a man wants, Tess." Now that his eyes were half open Tessa could see that they were a soft, smoky green in the dimly lit room, and she could read the meaning in them clearly. He lounged there lazily, holding her with his eyes, his long fingers idly scratching the surface of his wide, strong chest.

Tessa wanted to back up a cautious step but she stood frozen. "You need your sleep," and her voice was husky too. "I—I didn't mean to disturb you. You can cover yourself with that quilt." But just as she turned to flee, Cody reached out, and her heart stopped in her throat as his warm, callused hands closed over her slight wrists, and he pulled her close to the side of the bed once more as he reclined upon the pillows. Tessa's pulse thundered.

"I've never seen you with your hair down," and his tone softened, was almost silky. "You've got beautiful hair, Tess."

Her stomach cartwheeled. Ignoring his hands on her wrists and trying her damnedest to ignore his compliment, Tessa pressed her lips firmly together and dropped her eyes, refusing to meet his. She tried to make her voice crisp and efficient, but even she could hear the slight tremor in it when she said,

"You better catch all the sleep you can be-tween now and dawn, Cody, because I plan to waken you and have you out of here before the first light. I don't want the entire town to know where you spent the night." Now she glanced up at him, and immediately knew she had made a mistake. His mouth went crooked on her in that devilish, lazy smile of his and her traitorous body weakened.

"With your hair falling down like that and you in your nightgown"—his eyes went over her—"how do you expect me to be indiffer-ent?"

Tessa tried to back away again, but it was a futile attempt. She glanced down at those strong, imprisoning hands and Cody's low, rough voice rippled over her. "You know I want you, Tess. And you know how badly. What do you want me to do? Beg?"

But it was she who was begging now, with her dark, turbulent eyes—pleading for mercy. Her mouth trembled. "Cody, please—"

But he had only to give her a quick tug and she was down on the bed, almost on top of him, her surprised hands upon his hard shoulders, her thighs pressed to the iron strength of his, the quilt somehow gone. And there was something about the way he lay there so lazy and amiable, his green eyes smiling into hers as if he'd just bested her in a contest, that made the tension ebb away from Tessa's body. She smiled back at him.

"How can you even have the energy for this?"

His soft, lazy smile made things beat wildly inside her. "I've missed you, Tess. I feel like I've been gone from you for a year. And seeing you like this . . ." He lowered his head and put his lips to her graceful throat and uttered something she could not hear. Goose bumps shivered over her skin as his lips moved sensuously, and through her thin wrapper Tessa could feel that his body had already grown hard for her.

Cody touched his tongue to the hollow behind her ear and his velvet whisper rode lightly, phantomlike over her skin. "I've waited so long for you. . . ."

Her pulses beat so fiercely Tessa thought she might faint from their sound. His practiced hands untied the belt at her waist, and just as Tessa became aware of his fingers upon her shoulders, she felt the wrapper float away from her body. She was allowed no protest as Cody pulled her closer and felt her firm breasts crushed to his pounding chest. He made a low sound deep in his throat, knowing her breasts were bare under her nightgown, and the feel of her nipples straining at the thin material sent a flash of fire ripping through his loins. He ran a hand over her firm, rounded buttocks, up the curve of her graceful back, to slide sensuously into her silken hair, and they both moved so that their lips met, their tongues touched and stroked, warm, wet, and mingling.

"Ah . . . God . . . Tess . . ." Cody's words sounded torn from him and then his tongue thrust deep into her mouth as his big hands pulled her hips to his.

His kiss triggered a flood of sizzling little explosions within her as Tessa kissed him back, her palm on his lean, stubbled cheek, her other hand lost in the wealth of thick curls at the back of Cody's head. Cody groaned and rolled her beneath him, kissing her with a kind of hungry desperation. He took her face in his hands, and he kissed her eyelids, her nose, her soft, lush mouth. When he lifted his head to search her gaze, the green flame in his eyes seemed to burn with fever.

"Cody." Tessa traced a forefinger lightly along his bottom lip, hard and full with wanting. She watched the trail of her lazy finger and seemed to lose her thought.

But Cody forced her to look at him. "What? Don't? If you want me to stop, I will here and now." He spoke in a low, almost gruff voice. The thundering of his heart felt like it might crash through the walls of his powerful chest. His blazing green eyes seemed to singe her face as he looked down into it. "But you don't want me to stop, do you, Tessa?" His ragged voice caused her skin to tingle. His voice, his eyes, his hard body drove all protests from her lips. He smoothed her hair back from her temples, dropping little persuasive kisses on her mouth, and the tip of her nose, her cheeks and lashes. His eyes, looking into hers again, were anguished. "If we start this tonight, nothing and no one is going to come between us—understand, Tess? Tell me now." He waited, braced on one elbow, his compelling eyes on hers. The lamp guttered in the utterly silent bedroom. Tessa's dark, honey-flecked eyes went over Cody's face, tight with restrained passion.

He doesn't know who I really am, she thought with a twinge of guilt and surge of tenderness for him. *He doesn't know what I come from, why I'm here.*

But he's not asking, Tessa. He doesn't care. Take this moment, this one golden hour, and let him love you as you want him to love you. You might never know this again in your life.

At last, she raised her eyes to his again and reached up to brush the backs of her fingers against his hard jaw. "Whatever happened to spring, Cody?"

His chuckle was low, seductive as he leaned to capture her mouth with his. "Ah, don't you know, darling," and he ran his damp tongue along the bottom lip of her generous mouth, "spring came when the clock struck twelve." He jammed his mouth over hers and plunged his tongue inside, kissing her with such ferocious passion and heart-rending tenderness that Tessa felt she had dissolved into him. She arched her hips against his hard length and ran her slender fingers up his tautly muscled arms, over the hard biceps, up to his big, sinewy shoulders, which were shrugging off his shirt. She helped pull the shirt off those muscular shoulders and Cody flung it behind him, never removing his lips and tongue from hers. And now Tessa ran her hands up his

broad, powerful back, up, up, to delve again
into his thick, soft hair, then down to explore
the rippling muscles under her fingertips.
Cody groaned inside her open mouth and the
sound seemed to rumble all the way down to
Tessa's core, her secret center, where everything surged and throbbed in feverish longing
for him.

He whispered something against her mouth
as one by one he unbuttoned the tiny buttons
all the way down to her waist. Tessa felt his
fingers skim her bare skin as he slowly, sensuously, slipped her nightgown off one
golden shoulder, and for a pleasured moment
her eyes drifted shut. But they came open
again at the sound of his husky whisper.
"Like silk, Tess . . . your skin's like silk." He
dropped his dark head lower, tasting her
flesh, touching his tongue to the swell of one
breast, ignoring the drawn-up nipple. Tessa
stirred beneath him, her breath caught in her
throat. He pushed the gown from her other
shoulder and her breasts were bared to his
gaze. Her heart swelled and her blood beat
and she waited for him to touch them. Cody
bent his head to kiss her smooth shoulder,
and then his lips touched the shallow valley
between her breasts. He made a hoarse sound
in his throat, torturing himself as well as her
for making them wait. His tongue wet her
skin and trailed tantalizingly closer to a nipple
as the heels of his hands pressed the outside
curves of both breasts, lifting the nipples
toward his seeking mouth. Tessa made a

movement beneath him and a soft, murmuring sound. Cody lightly brushed his lips across a rigid nipple. Tessa tensed, clutching his hair, waiting. But he teased some more. He cupped and caressed and kneaded her firm, bare breasts, watching them with worshiping eyes, still ignoring the taut rose-dusk nipples that quivered with painful expectation. Then, at last, he leaned to touch his lips to one, and kissed the tight flesh with his lips only; his hand, covering the other breast, took the nipple and rolled it, then squeezed it gently between his fingers. Tessa drew in a short, swift breath and held it tensely, then released it with his name upon her lips.

"Oh, Cody . . ."

He sensed the impatience in her, watched her dark eyes become heavy-lidded. He pushed her gown up to her hips, and his hands moved slowly over her silken thighs, making her gasp. Boldly his palm slid up to caress her bare hip; lazily his warm, rough hands moved over her slim waist and belly, and the nightgown bunched in little folds over his wrists as he lifted it. Up his fingers stole, reaching for her breasts, and his palms skimmed her desperately aching nipples; her breathing became light, shallow, rapid. But again Cody ignored those tempting swells of golden flesh and, in one deliciously sensual move, ran his hands up her smooth upper arms to take off her nightgown. Suddenly shy, Tessa jerked her arms down to her sides, to hide her body, to protect herself from

Cody's exquisite touch, afraid now to go one step further.

"Don't, Tess," Cody whispered hoarsely, "don't be afraid. I'll be gentle with you, love. . . ."

The wild wind roared outside the house, but here, inside, Cody's soothing words seemed to wrap her in a sheltering cocoon. She let him raise her arms again and glide his hands over her smooth skin, freeing her limbs from the garment. Obligingly, Tessa lifted her head, her eyes now closed, as Cody slipped it back, and the flannel nightie was gone and she lay totally unclothed beneath him. The nightgown fell from his fingers to the floor, forgotten. She heard him draw in a sharp, ragged breath as his eyes roamed over her in a slow, indulgent journey. They traveled over her round breasts, down her slim waist, to her belly, and he smiled when he saw her hand covering the dark triangle between her slender thighs. Her legs were long and shapely, her ankles graceful, her feet slim and narrow. Cody lifted her hand and dropped low to place a kiss there on her feminine secret. Tessa gasped as a dart of fire shafted through her. "Cody!"

Easing back up, he smiled into her eyes. "No secrets tonight, love." His dark green, aroused eyes made her heart leap with a force that hurt her chest. He looked like he wanted to lunge at her but he gently lowered his warm, half-clad body; and it seemed no other woman had ever fit so perfectly to his hard male form. She was soft and warm and golden all over and he used every ounce of control he possessed to slow his surging passion. Taking her head in his hands, he began to kiss her again, slowly, meltingly, long, and leisurely until the flame grew steady, became ravenous, torrid, urgent.

He tore his mouth from hers with a groan and strung his feverish kisses down her throat to her breasts, where he whispered ardently against her skin, "You're all golden-colored, Tess. Like honey . . ." His tongue slid along the lower curve of a breast. "And I need to taste you. . . ." His full lips captured her ripe, rosy nipple, tugged at it, as his wet tongue danced around it, upon it, and sucked it greedily. Tessa writhed beneath him, pleasured sounds escaping her throat, her fingers lost in his night-black hair as she held his head to her breasts. He moved to her other breast and tugged at its rigid tip, sending shafts of hot, rippling desire down her body. Her fingers glided over the rigid muscles in his shoulders and arms, bunching and flexing under his skin. He was up again, his hungry mouth open over hers, his tongue plunging and probing inside her mouth, reaching deeper, and the yearning in Tessa swelled, the pulsing in her most intimate parts clamored for relief.

She arched against his rigid arousal, feeling his hard length through his pants. Still kissing her, his hand went to the front of his trousers, fumbled there, and in an instant the trousers were gone, kicked off the end of the bed. When he pressed the full length of his naked body to hers, Tessa knew the shock of his full arousal. It was so hot! Tessa wanted to look, to touch him, but dared not—yet!

Cody's tongue was once more tracing light patterns over her flesh; his lips found a nipple and he suckled it between his tongue and teeth, then slowly released it as Tessa gasped, the sweet pleasure-pain flowing in wet currents down her feverish body.

She felt drugged under the blanket of his kisses. Cody's hand slid to the gentle juncture between her legs where it was hot and moist from his loving, craving his touch. Tessa's breath caught and held in her throat as his fingers gently probed, paused, then eased into her silken folds. His long middle finger moved, stroking her silken flesh, and Tessa moaned, her fingers gripping Cody's shoulders with an ecstasy unlike anything she'd ever known. Her eyes slid closed, her lips parted as he plied her. His hot, open mouth covered hers, and his tongue slipped in, imitating the rhythm of his expert finger while Tessa moved sinuously under him. His fingers teased, caressed, and generated a fire inside her yearning body; she felt the stoking up of banked heat, the mounting hot awareness, and flames suddenly leaping, licking higher and higher, reaching a blazing intensity and spreading, beating, throbbing, then, like lava, pouring thick, and melting down. She arched, hovering in that timeless place, clinging to

Cody's shoulders, crying out his name, as wave upon wave of intense ecstasy gripped her within until the final sweet shudder sailed through her and she lay drenched, drowning in that fire-lake that made even her arms and legs feel immersed in languor.

Her eyes came open to the green flame of his.

"Oh, Cody, I—" But his mouth hushed her, his tongue tracing the outline of her softly swollen lips. Cody scarcely dared to draw breath for fear it would explode with the demands of his swollen, raging body. His lips brushed her cheek and he ordered hoarsely, "Touch me, Tess . . . like you did last time."

Tessa's mind flickered back to that time, but now she was afraid.

"Come on, Tess," he urged, an ache in his voice. His lips dampened hers as he waited. Tessa touched his ribs shyly, and then slowly, tentatively slid her palm down his hard, flat abdomen, fingers touching the line of hair that tapered to his groin. Cody waited, still as stone. Tessa squeezed her eyes tight and daringly reached for him, opening her damp palm and taking him into it, her fingers closing around his flesh, long and hard, and incredibly hot. Cody stiffened and sucked in a hard breath between his teeth. He caught her wrist with his steely fingers and forced her to hold him, just hold him, so she would not make that fatal move that would tease his body to its ultimate bounds.

The moment seemed frozen. And then

Cody released her wrist only to grasp her hand firmly, to tighten her fingers around his tumescence and show her how to stroke him. And then he let go of her altogether, letting her explore him.

A sweeping tenderness flooded Tessa as she stroked him, up and down, learning the feel of him, his long length, the surprise of his silken skin. She reached lower to cup him where it was warm and slightly damp, the skin even silkier. But then Cody made a harsh, guttural sound in his throat and thrust his hips hard against her hand. Quickly he swung his body over her so his hardness and fullness rested upon her, between her thighs, and Tessa lifted her hips ever so subtly in invitation—an invitation Cody did not need. Gazing down at her, he braced away, his forearms on either side of her head, lost in her eyes, soft and brown as a doe's. "God, Tess, you're lovely." He leaned to lightly brush his mouth over hers.

"So are you," she whispered against his lips, and they both smiled as he brought his aroused body close again and started to enter her, very gently. Tessa stiffened as his hot flesh pressed and he whispered, "Easy, love," then slid his full length into her, groaning as her sleek flesh welcomed him, surrounded him in warm silken folds. He stayed that way—his pounding chest pressed to her breasts, his harsh breath abrading her skin, letting her get used to the feel of him. Tessa stirred beneath him, little knowing what tremendous restraint he used as he stayed buried in her like this.

And then Cody began to move, raising himself up on quivering arms as he thrust rhythmically against her, and Tessa answered him with a matching rhythm as the yearning spread through her like wildfire. Slowly his length eased in and out of her, his hot hardness stroking her with such drawn-out ecstasy that Tessa thought she might die from the pleasure of it. She arched her throat, her graceful back, and moaned softly as Cody thrust deeper, filling her as she offered her all to him. His eyes watched hers as his body increased its tempo and his head came down; he plunged his tongue into her mouth, savagely exploring its inner silkenness, and then he pulled away with that same tortured breathing, his chest and ribs heaving.

Deep within Tessa the fiery pulsations started, the incandescent heat mounting in her loins, that feverish, consuming, gripping heat that felt like tiny suns bursting in her darkest depths, exploding puffs of white-hot fire, sizzling high, up, as she cried out his name again—and once more—as she slowly simmered into a liquid ecstasy that pleasured every nerve of her gratified body.

Still dazed, Tessa moved her fingers lightly along the hard, rippling muscles in Cody's back, soothing the long, raised lines that her nails had made when he'd taken her to her highest, blinding peak. Her caressing fingertips absorbed the faint sheen of perspiration on his skin as she lifted to him, drawing him into her, still fully aroused by the pull and drive of his magnificent body.

And Cody, propelled by his savage hunger, lunged against her, every muscle in him tensing as he held the motion, and he cried out hoarsely as he climaxed in shuddering release, with all the energy and power his body had always promised.

Chapter Thirteen

✦✦✦✦

HE LAY UPON her and still in her as their ragged breathing slowed, became even. Spent, sated, their bodies lay entangled as Cody rested with his jaw to her temple and Tessa's fingers stroked the back of his neck. She heard him swallow, and—had he tensed?—curiously, startlingly, too abruptly, he rolled away, leaving her with the stark shock of abandonment. The closeness, the comfort of his body and his intimacy was instantly snatched away. Something was wrong—desperately wrong—and a hot, sick sensation swam through Tessa as she watched Cody, his hands locked behind his head, his biceps muscles bulging as he stared silently up at the ceiling. Hadn't she suited him? She knew, after making love with him, after that initial wondrous feeling, that now she should not feel so empty.

Tessa lay there in confusion, not understanding, and tentatively she opened her mouth to utter his name, but she hesitated when she caught his formidable frown. His head, on the pillow, was turned toward her and his darkening eyes chilled her through. "You're not a virgin," he stated harshly, coldly. "I mean, you weren't before I took you."

His eyes and his words stabbed into her like cold, vicious blades, and Tessa's insides seemed to drop out of her. Her fingernails bit into her moist palms yet she kept her expression carefully blank and her eyes stayed passively on his, hard and hurting. "No. I was not."

Cody swore and Tessa flinched.

"And all this time you've been holding out on me!" Tessa cringed. His words were so crudely put! "Well, I'll be a stupid son-of-a-bitch!" Cody sat up abruptly, his big fists clenched, the sheets tangling about his waist. His eyes, in his hard face, looked black in the dim light, and they glittered queerly, with an odd expression of anger and hurt. He swore again, savagely, through his teeth, and saw the fear in her own eyes as she lay there, daring not to move. "You're giving it out anyway when I held off in a state of near eruption for how many goddamn months! And how many others in town have had a piece of you? Have you been doing this with every man who suits your fancy back in your precious Boston too?" He flung the words at her with the rage that was building in him, not aware that he was slicing off precious pieces of her heart, her soul. His fist came down hard on the mattress, making the springs sing in outrage at this unjust punishment. "*Damn!* And what took you so long to get into bed with me? Just what was it about me that didn't suit your tastes?" he exploded, his masculine pride deeply wounded.

Outside, the cold wind howled. Tessa lay stiffly on her back, her arms crossed over her breasts. She forced herself to lie so, looking completely unaffected. For a moment she thought he might hit her. But her fear had made her brave. She glanced over him—his heaving chest and shoulders, the tight lips, his narrowed eyes. Her voice, when she spoke, came huskily, hiding other emotions. "By the looks of you, you're in a state of 'near eruption' now." She allowed a slight, depreciating smile to touch her beautiful lips. "Does it really make such a difference to a man whether or not the woman he takes is a virgin? The fact that I wasn't did not stop you from—" But she couldn't finish. The way he was looking at her—so hurt! She felt a death grip on her heart.

"From what?" Cody barked. "From spilling myself into you? Well, let me tell you, it's damn near impossible for a man to hold back with a woman like you under him—or I should say a woman who moves like you. But then"—he sneered—"you should already know that, Miss Amesbury!"

Tessa withdrew even further inside herself. Her dark eyes were veiled. But she managed to say, "So you're piqued because I was not a virgin. What difference should that make to a man as experienced as you?"

Ordinarily, it wouldn't have made a difference at all, Cody admitted to himself. Why did it drive him mad with rage and jealousy that with this woman others had come before him? There was no reason for the fury he felt, no reason for the overwhelming urge to kill every one of her past lovers. "So," he said in a harsh voice, "how many men have you had?"

Tessa could not bear to meet his accusing, venomous eyes, the hard hurt in his face. She twisted away from him, closing her eyes to arrest the salt sting of tears in them. Real pain assailed her as she drew the sheets up to her shoulder and shut him out of her vision. But Cody read only aloofness in her action. How could he have been so wrong about this woman? Gritting his teeth, he was over her in a vicious movement, gripping her arms, making her meet his furious green eyes. "I said how many?"

Tessa stared past him, her face a beautiful mask.

Cody shook her. "Answer me!"

Bravely Tessa brought her gaze back to his. "Why?" she demanded. "Because your masculine pride is at stake?" And now her eyes narrowed, anger surfacing in them. "I owe you nothing, Cody Butler!"

"Owe me!" Cody's voice shook dangerously with a violent emotion. "We're not talking about owing here!" He drew in a long breath, calming himself. His long, steely fingers relaxed their grip on her soft upper arms, but he did not release her altogether. And his eyes were icy cold. "One thing I have a right to know, Tessa. Are you a loose woman?"

"No!" she spat.

Staring down into the mysterious depths of her nearly black eyes, Cody clenched his teeth, his jaw hardening. Her eyes were so dark he couldn't make out the pupils in them.

"Yeah, well, one or twenty—what's the difference?" He sneered.

"Hypocrite!"

"Me?" Cody scowled. "What the hell are you talking about? *I'm* not the hypocrite here! I don't walk around pretending I'm something I'm not!"

"You are a hypocrite! You can have as many women as you want and expect the next woman you take not to say anything about it! You're accusing me of something you're equally guilty of, Cody! But it's different for a woman, isn't it?"

Taken aback, Cody stared at her. He had nothing to say about that. Dammit, it *was* different for a man and a woman! And no one he'd ever known had felt otherwise. But *this* woman—

"I hate you!" Tessa choked off childishly,

hating his frown, his disappointment, his expectations of her, and not really hating Cody the man. "Go away! Leave me in peace."

"The hell I will! You want to dismiss me like a schoolboy when you're done with me?" He'd emphasized the word "schoolboy" and Tessa cringed. She tried to edge farther away from him. "Is that what you do with all your lovers? Well, I'm not a schoolboy, Miss Amesbury, and I expect some goddamn answers!" And he fired off another merciless question. "Have you taken that fiancé of yours to your bed?"

Tessa bit her full lip that even now Cody wanted to kiss. He saw that lip tremble, and her eyes dropped as she said, "Yes."

"Why, you little liar."

Startled, Tessa's eyes flew up to meet his, then quickly her gaze darted away again. With one wide hand Cody grasped her face, his fingers hurting her soft skin. Tessa tried to jerk it free, but he held her fast, forcing her to look at him. The way Cody was searching her face for some kind of answers made tears fill her eyes with a shimmering sadness. But Cody was looking further than her tears and he saw in her eyes something he'd never seen before, and he knew, somehow, that she had lied about all this.

Tessa tightened her jaw and lifted her chin belligerently. Her eyes turned brittle. "Go to hell, Cody." She'd made her voice purposely hard, and wanted to wince at her own caustic words.

But Cody was no longer fooled. Her pretense at hardness was no longer convincing. All traces of anger were gone now from his face and eyes as he hung over her.

The sad, keening wind seemed to fill the room. The sound released a stark despair in Tessa, and as memories flooded back to her she felt the emotion rising within her, an awful ache that swelled to the surface and threatened to burst. Should she tell him? She wanted to, so badly. But what she would tell him was only half of it all, and she wasn't sure which half was worse. When she told William he'd started hitting her. But somehow she knew Cody wouldn't.

She glanced at him again. She had hurt him so unjustly, lying here with him, sharing his intimacy, sharing more with him than she ever had with any other person. And he was waiting, his eyes softening, though his face was still hard. She had the feeling he'd wait all night if he had to.

Tessa swallowed; her mouth opened as if to speak, then she closed it again. Though her eyes were wet, her mouth and throat were hurtfully dry.

"Tell me, Tess," Cody urged softly. He was leaning over her, his hand now sliding into her hair, gently massaging the side of her head. Tessa closed her eyes briefly. Oh, that name! The name he had for her.

Her eyes came open. "When I was fifteen I was raped."

And now Cody's eyes shut, understanding. Her voice sounded hollow and she dropped the words like poison pellets from her mouth. "Do you know how long ago that was? At times it seems like yesterday."

In the horrible silence Cody opened his eyes again. They looked anguished with the pain he felt for her. "Oh, Tess," he breathed, and moved to gather her close.

But Tessa pulled away, rolling to the far side of the bed, burying her face in the crook of her arm, her back to him, "I don't want pity, Cody. Not from you, not from anyone. I just . . . well . . . maybe I do owe you an explanation." She drew in a long, shaky breath and thought about that day, each fragment coming back to her with a heightened clarity. "In the orphanage I was taught that if I was good, then life would be good to me. The girls were told we would be sure to find a kind, wonderful man who could make us happy. I believed it. I . . . I thought I *had* been good up till then. . . ." Tessa flung herself around now, one arm tucked snugly beneath the pillow under her head, the other arm drawn across her waist. She met Cody's frowning eyes, then glanced up at the ceiling and saw, in her mind, that day.

"I'd gone to the market in the city—only the older girls were allowed this privilege—and we were to go only with another girl. But my friend was sick that day and I went alone. On

the way back I had to cross a deserted lot. I
didn't know until I was halfway across that a
man had been following me. He was a sailor
from the docks. He was dirty and"—she swallowed—"I didn't have the chance to run, you
see, he just grabbed me and threw me down
in that old dead grass and my basket of
produce fell and everything spilled—the to-
matoes and potatoes and squash—and I was
so young, that made me maddest of all. I
was on my knees, frantically scooping up the
vegetables, thinking of how mad Cook would
be. . . ."

"Don't, Tess," Cody said quietly, fiercely,
with the ache thick in his own gruff voice.
Tessa felt his thumb brush at a tear on her
cheek, but he did not move, honoring her
request for distance.

But Tessa had to tell him, had to purge
herself. "He was clawing at me from behind,
and as I struggled, he got mad and rough, and
finally he pulled me down under him and
started tearing at my clothes. I fought him
then. But, God, he had a knife and he told me
if I didn't stop struggling, he would slit my
throat and leave me—"

"Tess!" Cody didn't want to hear anymore,
didn't want to hear her hurt. Jesus Christ, just
watching her tormented face made his own
chest fill with anguish and an impotent rage
that someone could do this to his sweet Tess,
even before he'd known her.

But Tessa didn't hear Cody. She spoke
desolately, almost as if she'd reentered the

body of that fifteen-year-old girl. "He kept pressing and pinching—and he seemed to like it when I fought despite his threats. He called me a little firebrand, and yes—I was made for this—" She made a gesture of disdain at the rumpled sheets, at their unclad bodies. "And that he'd done me a favor and helped me realize what I was made for." And now her tormented eyes turned to Cody's. "Just like you said once—that time on the sofa. Remember, Cody?"

Cody felt a stab of remorse. He cursed himself for having contributed to her private hell. Her agony clawed at him and settled like acid in his belly. "I'm sorry for that, Tess." His voice sounded oddly thick.

Tessa reached a hand toward him and ran her forefinger down his bare side. With her eyes on his, she whispered, "I know. You couldn't possibly have known." She let her hand trail to the sheets between them, but now Cody caught it and he leaned to pull her into his arms now whether she wanted him to or not. He settled her close against his hard, muscular frame and pressed her head to his chest. Tessa snuggled tightly against him, her arm flung across his muscular middle, welcoming his warmth, his strength, the sure, strong beat of his heart under the hard muscles of his chest. Cody kept a soothing hand in her hair, rubbing the silken strands between his fingers; he could envision it all as she carried him back with her.

"I think he would have done it again but it

was almost dusk and he knew that the night watchman would be in the area shortly. He wouldn't let me move until he had fastened his pants—he made me watch him do that. And when he finished he put the point of the knife to my throat again and warned me not to tell anyone. That he'd come back and find me and kill me if I did. He told me he knew I came from the orphanage and he'd be watching me. For the longest time I felt he was. But I wasn't about to tell anyone anyway—I was so ashamed.

"At last he left. I remember just lying there for a while, not believing it happened. I was sick and scared. I sat up and vomited in the lot. Everything hurt. But I remembered they were waiting for the vegetables and fruit at the orphanage. I stood up and straightened my clothing and smoothed my hair and cleaned my skin with my own spit and a strip of my petticoat. I picked up my basket and started back and nobody ever knew." Until William, she thought, and shuddered.

The thud of Cody's heart beneath her cheek brought Tessa slowly back to the present. His hand had fallen still in her hair and now it dropped to her bare shoulder and he caressed her satiny skin with a callused thumb. Her arm circled his ribs and Tessa pressed close to him, needing him. She felt the vibration of his deep voice as it rumbled up from his broad chest.

"You're ashamed of it still, aren't you, Tess? You think that somehow it's your fault. Just like you think being beautiful is a fault. That's why you hide those wonderful eyes of yours."

She lifted her head to look up at him and was startled to find his own eyes misted with tears. Oh, this man! She let out a pent-up breath and water flooded her eyes and over-flowed them. She touched her lips to his neck as hot tears spilled out between her closed lids. "Oh, Cody," she breathed, the name trembling from her lips, and she touched them again to his warm skin. She pulled her head away and lay on her side to face him, and found his eyes on her wet lashes, spiked like stars. "He went *inside* of me, Cody. Can you imagine what it's like to have someone violate your spirit through your body? That man robbed a part of me that I will never have back. He stole a part of me—and I couldn't prevent him from doing it. I'm ashamed—yes! I'm ashamed of not being strong enough to fight him off, of not be-ing able to prevent it. I'm ashamed of not being able to kill a man like that."

Cody's grip on her neck was almost painful. "God damn him, Tess. God damn him for making you carry this with you for so long."

It seemed it was Cody who needed soothing now. Tessa unclenched his big fist and linked her slender fingers through his long, lean ones, clasping his hand tightly to her chest.

"It's true that for a long time I felt dead inside. But I came to realize that he hadn't killed me, and I was glad for that. I didn't want to die. So I buried it and started to live again. I had to bury it or I would have gone insane."

Cody rubbed the back of her hand with his thumb and said quietly, "But you haven't buried it completely. You're afraid to call attention to yourself—" She started to pull away but Cody held her tight in his arms, refusing to free her. "It's in the plain way you dress—the severe hairstyle you wear." And his eyes went to that hair, now loose and flowing freely about her naked shoulders, a golden strand caught in his fingers, and he thought how this enticing, natural picture of her captured the real Tessa precisely. She was a free spirit—it was reflected in her huge, cocoa-colored eyes, staring up at him now. "But you don't want to be that way—you cover it by being prim and proper. You're a beautiful woman." He pushed a loose strand of hair behind her ear, then let his hand trail to her throat. Tessa closed her eyes and tears slipped through her lashes, wetting his skin. Why couldn't William have been like Cody? she thought. Why couldn't he have understood? But he had been outraged. But now Cody, more tender and understanding than she ever thought he could be, had only guessed a part of it. Because she was hiding the rest of it from him. A real pain gripped her heart at her unwilling deceit. It wasn't fair—as kind as he'd been—to continue lying to him. But if she told him . . . God, if she told him, he'd never believe any of what she'd just confessed. And he'd hate her. And somehow she couldn't bear the thought of Cody hating her.

As if reading her thoughts, Cody's deep, rough voice broke into her turbulent thoughts. "What about that fiancé of yours? What are you going to tell him when the time comes?" Cody looked at her intently. He wanted her to say that Michael Shea meant nothing to her because she wanted him.

Tessa gulped. "I don't know . . ." she answered vaguely. "I don't want to talk about him." Because Michael Shea was, of course, William Forsythe in her mind. And she had just committed adultery against him. And she was making Cody inadvertently sound like a fool every time he mentioned Michael Shea.

Cody's wide palm cupped her chin and he lifted her face to look at him. Her eyes hungrily roamed over his handsome face, and lingered on his black hair, which tousled over his forehead, rumpled from their lovemaking.

"Good." He grinned. "Because I don't want to talk about him either." But inwardly he was not satisfied with her answer. He lay back now, one hand cupping the back of his curly head. His green eyes darkened as they probed hers. "What is it, Tess?"

God, *could* the man read her mind? She rested her hand upon his bare, muscular stomach. "I've never done this with any other man. You are the only one."

She felt his stomach muscles move against

her hand as Cody let out a tense breath of selfish exultation. He was her first man.

He was over her in an instant, taking her face in his hands, his eyes poring over her features. He buried his own face in her neck, his lips touching her skin. "Tess," he said, and a sweetness washed over her. "Oh, God, Tess, I'm sorry—sorry that any of this happened to you." His thumbs caressed her cheeks, his concerned eyes held hers. "But I'm not sorry about tonight, because it's right. You see that, don't you?" His dark, sincere face was so close to hers she wanted to touch it, but kept her palm on his strong neck and watched his eyes gaze down at her earnestly, intensely. "This is natural between a man and a woman; there is nothing sordid about it, and it has nothing to do with the outrageous violation of you that man committed. You understand that, don't you, Tess?" Did she? "No tears," he begged softly, watching the water gather again in her large eyes, making them strangely beautiful in this faint light.

The tears balanced on the rims of her eyes; if she blinked even slightly they'd fall, and just as Cody thought it she did blink, and the water glistened like dewdrops on her silky lashes. Tessa brought her hand up to his cheek then slipped her forefinger under his lower lip, sliding it across the hollow. "Tess," she whispered. "No one's ever called me Tess before." She touched his temples. "I love it when you do."

His thoughtful eyes returned her stare; it seemed a very long time before he whispered with an aching tenderness in his voice and eyes, "Kiss me, Tess."

Her breath caught. She glanced to his hard, handsome lips then back up to his eyes, understanding what they conveyed to her. She was free to refuse him, yet he wanted her to know he still desired her after what she'd told him. Some men wouldn't have.

Yet he wanted her to make the first move.

Slowly, with her damp eyes still open on his, she lifted her mouth, slid her arms around his neck, and clung. Slowly he lowered his head to meet her lips. His mouth covered hers and lingered upon it for a long, leisurely time, searching, asking permission. Cody moved his head in little circles, nudging her full lips open. Her little tongue touched his provocatively, and Cody drew it into his own mouth, danced around it, then invaded her mouth, probing with his masterful tongue, pleasuring her. His kiss intoxicated, drugged, seduced her. When Cody eased away, his lips but an inch from hers, Tessa murmured, "I thought *I* was supposed to kiss *you*."

He laughed against her mouth, then raised his head to gaze down at her with burning green eyes. "Be my guest, darlin'."

At his words, Tessa's vitals leaped with longing. With her slim fingers splayed along his hard jaw, she took his mouth and kissed it thoroughly with all the burgeoning emotion within her. With the tip of her tongue she touched his upper lip, looking for admittance. Cody groaned and grasped the sides of her head, opening his mouth wide over hers to thrust his tongue inside her sweet, untaught mouth. She kissed him back, of course, but made a small sound of protest at his usurpation of her right to be in control. Even as she wriggled under his weight Cody would have none of it, and she knew why when she felt the heat of his arousal against her bare thigh.

He tore his lips from hers and blazed a trail to her ear, where his whisper was hot and tormented, "I want you again, Tess. Do you want me?"

Tessa kissed his hair and breathed into it, "Yes, Cody, yes." Tonight he was hers. Tonight the past was wiped out, because there was no past, just here and now.

Cody ran the back of his forefinger over her cheek, along her jawline and down, down to the center of her chest, around each trembling, aroused breast, until she caught his wrist and brought his palm against one to cup it. She closed her eyes in bliss as his hands, one on each breast, smoothed over them, contoured their firm curves, tantalizing her with the motions. His mouth and tongue followed, bathing, suckling, dancing upon each peaked crest. Tessa made soft sounds in her throat, her fingers clutching his curls, as Cody groaned, whispering wet, hot words upon her skin. He lay between her parted legs, and every time he tugged a nipple with his teeth she felt the heat shaft downward to that feminine part of her only he had claimed, and the firm pressure of his hard middle was gratifyingly welcome there.

Cody slid lower, and his hands slid too, gliding over her slim curves and hollows and shallow hills, and he was kissing her everywhere, his lips and tongue pressing love words across her smooth skin, leaving tiny brands in their wake. But suddenly Tessa realized where his explorations were taking him. She tried to wriggle beneath him but there was incredible force in his weight holding her down.

"Cody, no—" Tessa pushed feebly at his head, but he agilely dodged her battling hands. He lifted his head to fix her with incredibly intense, incredibly ardent green eyes.

"Trust me, Tess," he rasped, his voice sounding as if it hurt him to speak. He dipped his head to run his tongue along the valley where Tessa's slender thigh joined her body, and she shuddered, the pleasure almost unbearable. She made a strangled, wordless entreaty; but Cody soothed her. "Shh. You'll like it. Promise." He said the husky words against her, just before his hot mouth possessed her.

Oh! The ecstasy!

His tongue danced upon her and within her, driving deep, lifting her high and away, prompting the sweet swell of sensation that blossomed and slowly opened under the stroking flame, then gripped her in flowering rhapsody, the delicious force of it engulfing her in pulsating spasms that swam outward to her limbs. Tessa writhed one final shuddering moment, then collapsed beneath him and lay limp, satiated.

She was hardly aware of his hands tugging her languorous body down the bed; he met her halfway to cover her with his own body, needing release for his own fierce need. And when he came into her, Tessa arched her hips, ready and wanting him. He was all hard flesh and muscle and hot throbbing power. His thrust and ebb was fierce, then incredibly tender, then wonderfully fierce again. He went rigid as she brought him to the brink, her name but a hoarse utterance on his lips, and Tessa knew the sweet thrill of her feminine power as Cody's body gave a convulsive jump and filled her with his powerful eruption. His weight fell upon her breasts, and Tessa clutched him close, knowing vast fulfillment for having given the same to Cody.

For a while they slept. Tessa awoke shivering, her naked limbs half under, half over the covers. She snuggled closer to the warmth beside her—Cody. She glanced past the wide expanse of his chest to the window and saw that it was still dark, but the darkness was turning to gray and she knew it was just before dawn. Sometime in the night, the storm had ceased. The lamp still burned low on the dresser top and she knew soon she would have to get out of this warm bed and snuff it, but first she brought her gaze back to the man who lay sleeping beside her.

She smiled, studying his relaxed face. His black brows and lashes were so thick, his nose strong and proud, his mouth, even in sleep, was firm, resolute. His beard was a darkening shadow and Tessa brought her hand up to run the backs of her fingers across his bristly cheek.

She moved her hand higher to touch his soft hair and smiled again at the way it tumbled over his forehead. She had learned so much with this man tonight. Her smile faded; she should not have learned much with this man tonight. It was wrong—but no! She didn't have to think of that yet. It had been too good to end so soon. The splendor, the magic was still with them.

Her lips brushed his temple. She kissed his neck and made a soft murmur, breathing in of him. He didn't stir. Tessa lightly pressed her palm to his furred chest, feeling the strong thud of his heart beneath. She closed her eyes and pressed her mouth to the firm pectoral muscle, easing back to watch him, to see if he'd waken. But Cody was sleeping the sleep of the dead. She kissed the opposite pectoral muscle, warm and firm under her lips. She was having a great deal of fun, kissing him at her leisure. But it disturbed her that he had become so dear to her.

Tessa pushed herself away. No, no, she mustn't have feelings for him too. But she did, oh, God, she did. She suddenly knew an emptiness so great that she leaped from the bed to save herself from experiencing it any more intensely. She scooted naked across the cold floor to the dresser, blew out the lamp, then dove back into the warm bed beside Cody who now stirred and, in his sleep, reached for her, curling an arm about her waist and pulling her close. Tessa was content to nestle against him, struggling with unwanted thoughts which, for now, must be kept at bay . . .

. . . She must have slept. Her eyes came open slowly and blinked once, finding Cody's warm, lazy eyes smiling down into hers. "Good morning, love."

Startled, Tessa jumped up, sitting straight-shouldered, the quilt falling to her hips. Cody's eyes flickered to her bare breasts, and he reached out to fondle one, but she pushed his hand away and grabbed the quilt to her chest. He lay still with a slow, seductive smile on his face, his eyes making her insides jump about queerly, and he gave one leisurely, sensuous stretch like a lazy tiger roused from sleep, but Tessa had the idea he'd been awake and watching her for some time. Her eyes narrowed suspiciously on him.

"How long have you been awake?" she demanded, clutching the quilt tightly to her bosom.

Cody laughed, his eyes crinkling at the corners, the flash of his teeth as white and sparkling as the snow outside. "Long enough," he drawled. "Long enough to know things about your body I bet you don't even know." And his eyes traveled suggestively to her peach-colored shoulders, then lazily back up to meet her eyes, dark and wide.

"I know everything I need to know about my body," she returned flippantly.

"Mmmm." His hand found a breast under the quilt and he caressed it, watching her eyes flicker, hearing her breath quicken as she weakened. "Not everything, I bet," he whispered.

Tessa fought the yearning, tried to fight the pleasure rippling over her. She closed her eyes as Cody's long fingers lifted her flesh, cupped the bottom of her breast, gently squeezed the rigid nipple. She caught his wrist and pressed his palm hard to her thickening breast, gasping with delight. She opened her luminous eyes to find his boring relentlessly into hers, and the room was filled with a rosy-pink glow from the light outside. "Cody," she said softly, "it's dawn."

He caressed her cheek gently with the back of his hand. "So it is, love."

"But you have to go."

"I want you once more before I go."

Tessa could see by the way his body lifted the quilt that he did indeed want her—very much. But it was already too late—he should have left at least an hour ago. Once more she glanced at the window and now, with the first light of day creeping about them, misgivings and guilt and self-castigations washed over

Tessa with the force of a swollen river water bursting its banks.

But as if he'd sensed her guilt, Cody slid his hand up her smooth arm and tugged at her. She looked at him, all rumpled and disheveled on the sheets, and he cast her an endearing, lopsided grin. "Come on over here and hug me at least." He pulled at her. But Tessa didn't need persuading; she did as he wished, tightly burrowing her face into his warm belly. But then she was up again, worry written in her dark eyes as he lay there like a lump, looking as if he'd like to spend all day in bed. "You've got to go," she said, pushing at his hard shoulders; but each word tore at Tessa. Already she was feeling the poignant pain of separation even though Cody hadn't moved a muscle. "Cody, you've got to go now—don't you see?"

She said it softly, tenderly, but the way he kept his sober eyes on Tessa's made her heart hurt. "I see," he said quietly. "I was just trying to prolong my stay." He smiled at her, but the smile wasn't in his eyes. And then he rolled away from her and onto his feet as lithe and fluid as a panther. He stood flexing and stretching his muscles, then ran lean fingers through his tousled hair. Tessa watched him hungrily, devouring his naked magnificence with her eyes. She was tempted to call him back to bed and have him stay with her all day.

Cody reached for his pants and slid into them, and then he found his shirt and shrugged it on, leaving it unbuttoned as his eyes found hers. He came to the edge of the bed and leaned over her with his arms on either side of her shoulders as she reclined back on the pillows. His voice was rough and hoarse, his eyes concerned, as he said, "I don't want to leave you, Tess, because I know you'll think too much about this, and I can see you're having regrets about it now."

She wanted to close her eyes against his face, but she kept them there upon him. And only one word of truth came from her dry throat. "Yes."

"Dammit, Tess!" Cody swore, pushing himself away from her, straightening to his full height and placing his hands loosely on his lean hips. He knit his black brows in an exasperating frown. "What we just shared was more than a casual mating! There was more to it than that, goddammit! Don't you go bringing that fiancé of yours into this bedroom and into our lovemaking, because he has no place in it!"

Tessa closed her eyes, swallowing her pain and his. She opened them and her eyes beseeched him. "Cody, please—don't ruin last night by talking about him."

"You don't care about that man, do you, Tess?"

Pinpricks of alarm scooted over her skin. It was uncanny the way this man could delve into her soul. Cody came down on the bed again, to sit beside her, taking her shoulders in his big hands. "Face it, Tess, it's a long way from Boston to Kansas and I'm not sure the man is willing to make the trip."

"What are you saying, Cody? You want to continue seeing me? Like this? You want to have a cheap affair?"

Cody's lips tightened. What did she want from him? She was the one with the fiancé. He ran a knuckle down a shivery path between her breasts while Tessa couldn't ignore the quickening in her body at his casual touch. "You call this cheap, my lady?" And his voice was thick.

But she closed her slim fingers around his strong wrist. Her rich brown eyes probed his. "Is this all I'm worth, Cody?"

He cursed, and she shrank back from him. "What do you want from me, Tessa? An offer of marriage?" At his words he saw the blood drain from her face and he laughed shortly, harshly. "I can see the idea of it appeals less to you than it does to me." But suddenly he grew tender again and lowered his head to brush his lips across hers. "I'd treat you right, Tess." He could sense her weakening as his mouth lingered upon hers. His fingers fanned under her chin, along her delicate jawline. "And no one would have to know"—his tongue flicked the corner of her mouth—"if that's the way you want it. . . ."

But with enormous control, Tessa stiffened and put his warm hands away from her. Her eyes darkened as she glowered at him. "I don't want an affair. I don't want marriage."

She drew in a deep, bracing breath because what she would say next was hardest of all. "I don't want you, Cody." At the hurt look on his face Tessa had the most overwhelming urge to kiss him and soothe his wounded pride. But all this was harder for her than it was for him. He'd get over it—with a different woman. But Tessa knew she wouldn't get over this night—ever.

Cody snorted with disgust and disbelief and he came to his feet again to resume dressing. "When you get lonely, don't come to me."

"Cody, don't be angry—"

"Angry?" He laughed shortly, the sound like an assault on her ears. He stuffed his shirttails into his pants, and with a quick jerk, fastened his waistband over his lean middle. "You flatter yourself, little lady. Mad's got nothing to do with this. Need is what we're talking about here."

Tessa pressed her fingers to her closed eyelids. She was *not* going to cry! When her eyes came back to his, they were dark, furious, stormy. "I told you, Cody Butler! I told you to keep away from me!" She watched him, so strapping big, seemingly unaware of the absolute power of his sexuality. He was buckling his belt now, glaring back at her. "I said yes to you once, and we had each other the way you wanted. Isn't that enough?"

Cody's eyes impaled her on the bed. "The way you wanted it too. Not just me, Tessa. I made certain of that, remember?" He waited for her to nod, and when she did, his jaw went rigid. "And no, it's not enough."

"Cody—"

"Christ." He muttered a curse and was at the side of the bed again, leaning over her, his riveting eyes holding her prisoner on the bed. His mouth swooped down and covered hers and he kissed her hungrily, almost hurtfully. "There is no keeping away from you, don't you know that, Tess?" His gruff voice shivered over her. But he pushed himself away from her and she watched him walk barefoot to the doorway where he lingered a moment, with one palm braced high on the frame. Then he turned to look her over. "It's not over between us, Tess. I won't let it be." He stood with a thumb hooked on the waistband of his trousers. "You say your man there is coming out in the spring. Hell, it's almost that now. I'll keep away from you until the first of May, but by God, on the second you'll be in my bed again, and we'll be making up for lost time." She nearly gasped at his boldness. "And if by chance he does come out, he's going to have a fight on his hands." He turned his broad back on her. "Now catch some sleep. By God, you're going to need to be rested by the time I get my hands on you again."

And with that, he was gone.

Chapter Fourteen

✦ ✦ ✦ ✦ ✦

HARPER CITY EXPERIENCED a warm spell the following week; it appeared spring would be early this year. Snow melted into slush and only patches of it remained on the muddy ground. Water dripped from the eaves and the wind blew soft and mild. In the schoolhouse Tessa opened the windows wide to let in the sweet air and sunshine.

She was grateful for the work and worries at school, for these kept her mind off Cody—at least during the day. Her nights were a different story.

Most of the children had come back to school now, but there were those who would never come back—those the diphtheria had taken. And Zach's seat was still vacant. Had he really gone hunting or trapping like Cody believed? Had his father come back to take him somewhere else? Or had he at last gone to sea? Tessa hoped he would've said goodbye if that was the case. But then, Zach had been unpredictable at best. She worried constantly about him and knew she would not relax until she'd received some word of his whereabouts.

Ned Winston had asked permission from Tessa to paint a portrait of her in her natural element—at the schoolhouse with the children. During the warm noon recesses, the sight of Ned at his easel became a common one. Tessa often forgot his presence and would join the children in their play, hitting the baseball farther than most of the older boys. It not only delighted the children but Ned as well, and he found himself becoming quite enchanted with the lively young woman who was so different from anyone he'd ever known.

During one of the springlike afternoons, an odd premonition came over Tessa; she felt as though someone was watching her. She glanced toward South Street and saw a stranger standing there, shading his eyes to look at her. She could only see that he was probably middle-aged with gray side-whiskers, and that he was stout, but she did not know him. A shiver ran over her skin, but when the man turned and walked off, she shrugged inwardly, telling herself he was most likely a curious newcomer perhaps looking for directions.

The warm weather seemed to breathe new life into the town, and the boom began anew. New buildings were springing up; it seemed wood skeleton frames appeared out of the ground overnight, not only on Main Street but along side streets as well. The rasping of saws and the ringing of hammers on wood soon sounded familiar to the townfolk. It was a chorus that brought to Tessa's mind the first day she had arrived in town . . . and had met a man who'd changed her life. And that was precisely why she avoided walking through town now.

But one day after school she met Mrs. Rawlins at Grady's Restaurant for a cup of tea. Coming out, she caught sight of Cody on the skeleton roof of the building across the street, adjacent to the restaurant. Tessa's heart stuck in her throat as his eyes met hers. As he started down the ladder, Tessa bade Ned and Mrs. Rawlins a hasty good-bye. She planned to be clear out of sight by the time Cody had descended.

But halfway down the boardwalk a strong hand clenched her arm, causing her to gasp, and she was hauled back between buildings and found herself looking up into Cody's furious sun- and wind-burned face.

"What the hell are you doing with *him?*" he said through his teeth.

Tears of pain smarted Tessa's eyes, and she could only think of shaking free. "Cody, let go—"

Only then did he realize he was hurting her and his fingers released her arm, but he still stood close, glowering down at her.

Rubbing her arm, Tessa glowered back up at him. "How dare you manhandle me as if—"

"Never mind that," he cut her off impatiently. "I asked you a question."

Indignant now, Tessa flashed her dark eyes back at him. "And I don't have to answer you!" She gave him a haughty lift of her chin and started to move past him—his presence was almost her undoing—but Cody grabbed her arm again, and his voice was husky, low, when he said her name. "Tess."

She shuddered.

"You got me half crazy, woman." He leaned close and put his lips to her neck, murmuring against her skin. "Do you know what these nights have been like without you?"

"Shh!" She pressed her fingers to his chest, but his shirt was open and touching his bare skin was like an aphrodisiac. She closed her eyes as his lips nuzzled her ear. "You mustn't, Cody. Someone will see us." Oh, yes! She knew what the nights were like without him. Almost unbearable. She longed to be in his arms again, to feel his hard male body against her. She'd punished herself, remembering the bliss, the rapture, the tenderness and passion of this man. And then the guilt would wash over her like a hot, sick wave.

His lips brushed hers now. "Oh, Cody, Cody." She pressed her lips to his; his hard thighs touched hers. "We mustn't . . ."

"Ahem."

Tessa froze as a female voice interrupted them. There stood Angie Foster, her blue eyes narrowed hatefully on them.

"Is this how the schoolteacher spends her afternoons?" she purred.

Tessa wanted to die. But Cody was unperturbed; he still held Tessa in his arms. "Do you mind?" he barked.

Angie's lips thinned and after one final glare she picked up her skirts and flounced

off. Cody chuckled, but when he turned back
to the woman in his arms, she was glaring at
him too.

"Now look what you've done!" she accused.

A hint of laughter showed in Cody's eyes.
"It's time she got the hint anyway."

Tessa wriggled out of Cody's arms, putting
a safe distance between them. "This is no
laughing matter, Cody! That woman is angry
enough to smear my name all over town! My
job will be—"

"Calm down, will you? She caught us kissing, not—"

Tessa held up her hands and closed her
eyes. "Please, don't say it." She opened her
eyes again and they were filled with guilt.
"We both know she could have caught us at
that just as easily."

Cody's mouth pulled down. "Out here? In
the street? Tessa, give me more credit than
that!"

"Stop joking!" she cried. "You promised
me you would leave me alone until May!"

"I'm finding that a hard promise to keep."

Me too, she thought, and closed her eyes
again. She felt him move closer, and wanted
to stop him. He wore new denims and the
faint starchy smell of the cloth mingled with
his sweat and the hint of worn leather.

"I've got to go," she choked out, but he
stopped her.

"Tess, I've got something for you—from
Zach."

Her eyes widened. He nodded once as he reached into his back pocket and pulled out a folded piece of paper. His large brown hand reached across the space between them and pressed the paper into her palm. Tessa stared at it a moment and felt a thickening in her throat. "He's gone, isn't he?"

In the silence she stared at Cody's dusty leather boots.

"Why don't you read the note?"

She glanced up to his eyes. "When did he leave?"

Cody's lips tightened. "Few weeks back." He watched a frown flit across her brow.

"Did you read it?"

"No. He wrote me one too."

She clenched the note tight in her palm. "Damn his parents, Cody."

At her words something tightened in his chest and his voice came low, gruff with emotion. "I know."

A wagon turned in the street, stirring up a cloud of dust that settled around them. Tessa coughed and waved the dust away. "Thank you for delivering it, Cody."

He nodded, but as she turned away from him he stopped her once again. "Are you going to the social tomorrow, Tess?"

"No!" She heard the panic in her own voice and tried to calm it. "I mean, no. I have plenty of work to do."

Cody's mouth tightened. "Don't be afraid of me, Tess."

She wanted so badly to touch him; her

nerves seemed to clamor for his attention. With her eyes on his face, she said softly, "I'm not afraid of you, Cody. I'm only afraid of what happens to me when we're together."

At her admission Cody caught his breath sharply. Something flared in his deep green eyes in the instant before he reached for her, but she slipped away like a will-o'-the-wisp. He let her go, but stood there for a long time, watching her walk away. Then he sighed and ran a hand through his wavy black hair, telling himself he'd damn well win her back.

Purposefully Tessa headed homeward. She opened Zach's note and bent her head, reading it as she walked.

Miss Amesbury:

> *I knew you'd be worried about me. Seems like you and the Doc kind of kept an eye out for me. Anyway, I'm gone to sea just like I always said I would. You said I could keep that book you gave me so I did. Thanks for it.*
>
> *I want you to know you're the best woman I ever knew. Maybe I'll come back and see you. Take care of Smoke Eyes. Make sure Sid don't git her.*

> *Zach*

A swell of emotion filled Tessa's chest. Oh, Zach. Her time with him had been too brief. She could have taught him so much more. She thought of his black eyes in his purposfully hard face and felt another pang. Godspeed, Zach, she wished him silently. Godspeed.

Her vision blurred with the sting of tears as she folded the note. And at that precise moment she bumped smack into the stranger who'd been watching her a few days back.

"Oh!" Startled, Tessa stumbled against him, and in the instant his hand steadied her elbow the stranger's eyes looked hard at her. "Excuse me," she mumbled, embarrassed.

The side-whiskered man lifted his hat and smiled, concealing his elation at having found her at last. "My fault, ma'am."

Tessa dropped her eyes from his hard stare and mumbled another "excuse me." She hurried past him, unable to shake the strange uneasiness snaking through her. Surely she did not know him! Why did he make her feel so uneasy?

Jubilation gleamed in the investigator's eyes. He'd found her! And he'd met his deadline after all. He smiled to himself and patted his pocket where her photo was concealed. Next destination: Boston, to report his findings to Mr. William Forsythe.

Tessa sat sewing by the open bedroom window, listening to the soft spring rain falling upon the new, wet earth. It was the Saturday-night-social hour and from town the sounds of music and laughter drifted to her on the gentle spring wind.

Two weeks had passed since she'd talked

with Cody. He'd kept his promise and kept his distance. But time was running out and Tessa had the distinct feeling that Cody was secretly planning his strategy, like a cat waiting to pounce on an unsuspecting mouse. And she would have to be prepared, once again, to keep Cody at bay.

With a surge of guilt she recalled the afternoon she'd spent with Ned Winston. The last few Saturday and Sunday afternoons she'd posed for him in his small studio above the restaurant. Mild-mannered Ned was perfectly harmless . . . or so she thought. Until this afternoon when he'd asked her to marry him.

Dismay was her first reaction. "Oh!" Then a kind of ludicrous panic gripped her. "Oh, no!"

Ned feared the worst. "I didn't mean to offend you, Tessa. And I realize we haven't known each other all that long, but"—he hesitated, his soft blue eyes gazing earnestly into hers—"you are the most wonderful, most unspoiled woman I've ever known!"

Unspoiled! Hah! If he only knew, she thought with some pity for the man who knelt at her feet. She'd been twice "spoiled," and here was a man, gentle and kind as he was, who would never understand this about her. But looking down at him as he took her slender fingers in his, she knew she would have to tread carefully here so he wouldn't be hurt when she rejected his offer.

"Tessa," he said, and kissed her fingers, and Tessa wondered that she felt none of the shivery stirrings she did when Cody kissed her, "I've fallen in love with you."

Emotionlessly she stared down at the dark blond roots of his hair.

"I know you're promised to a man in Boston, but I don't really think he's coming out, and he shouldn't have let you come out here alone anyway." Again he lifted his head and his blue eyes were faintly pleading. "You don't have to answer me right away. I'm willing to wait."

Staring back at him from her little stool, Tessa fought the hysterical laughter bubbling within her. This, she thought, is utterly ridiculous! Why didn't I come out here under the guise of a widow? I could have used the excuse of mourning to stave off these men. But now her whole life had become a deception. And she was caught in the tricky task of juggling both Cody and Ned.

It was then, as Ned waited for her to speak, that Tessa realized she could use Ned's proposal to her advantage, as a ploy to stave off Cody. Dreadful guilt surged through her, but in the end it would soften the blow for Ned too.

"Please, Ned, stand up," she begged softly, and when he did, she stood too. "I'm flattered that you ask for my hand, Ned, truly I am, but it's so sudden—"

"I know," he agreed, "and that's why I said you don't have to answer me now."

Tessa dropped her gaze, feeling that desperate guilt again. "I—I do need some time to think about it." She was startled when he grasped her hands once more and squeezed them. "But I'm not promising anything. There is still my . . . betrothal to—to Michael I must consider. And other things . . ."

"Of course! I understand!" His eyes shone at her and Tessa hated herself for giving him false hope. But it bought her time, time she desperately needed.

Now, as she sewed by the window, she pressed her lips firmly together and made faster stitches. Cody's face seemed to take form on the material she gripped between her hands.

"Ow!" She'd stabbed her forefinger and stared dumbly at the ruby droplet forming on her fingertip. Tears of pain sprang to her eyes. She leaped to her feet and sucked the blood away. But that pain was nothing compared to the pain in her heart when she thought of Cody.

The music from town seemed to swell and swirl around her and it was always the harmonica she heard most clearly. Piercing, poignant, melancholy music. She gripped the stick that held the window open, whipped it from the ledge, and slammed the window down, shutting out the music, the spring night, the visions of Cody.

She went to the dresser to comb out her hair before retiring, but there her eyes fell upon the music box Cody had given her for Christmas. Tentatively she reached for it, and her fingers lightly ran over the delicately carved box. She hadn't opened it since Christmas night. Because she remembered. She remembered what the music had done to both of them, capturing them in its seductively sweet spell. But now Tessa's fingers touched the lid. And gently, slowly, she lifted the lid. Light, tinkling notes escaped and danced like dainty fairies on a summer breeze. The music seemed to wrap around her heart and cradle it, and Tessa closed her eyes. Goose bumps dotted her skin. Cody, she thought, I don't want to hurt you. Forgive me for my lies. She knew nothing could come of the night they'd shared, yet she missed him so much she ached.

When she opened her eyes again, they reflected her torment. Maybe, she thought, maybe it was time for her to file for an annulment. It would certainly make her life somewhat less complicated. Still, she would not become Cody's plaything. Never that! Yet she would be free!

The familiar, lively sparkle returned to her brown eyes. "And next Saturday," she told her reflection, "I shall wear my new dress to the social. I've been cooped up like an old bird long enough!"

Wearing her new deep pink dress with the ivory buttons, Tessa entered the saloon with Eb and Audrey. As always, the room was filled to capacity, and the floorboards shook with the stamping of the dancers' feet.

Mary was the first to greet her, and she swept Tessa away from the older folks to join her in one corner. "Tessa, my goodness, it's been so long! You look lovely!" Her eyes ran appreciatively over the softly swept back hair, the deep rose of Tessa's dress, which complemented her warm, golden skin. She leaned close to whisper, "Cody's not here yet." And when Tessa stiffened, she laughed lightly. "Oh, I'll keep your secret, but it's plain to see you two are sweet on each other!"

Tessa opened her mouth to protest, but Mary tapped her lightly on the arm. "Don't deny it! And why should you? He's mad for you!"

"Mary—"

Mary laughed again. "Tessa, for heaven's sake! I consider you my best friend. You're not going to try to hide such a thing from me, are you?"

Tessa gave in, laughing back at Mary's dancing blue eyes. She squeezed her hand. "Please don't say anything to anyone."

"Oh, don't worry. But it's hard to keep a secret everyone can see for themselves! Mmm! You smell wonderful! Did Cody give you that perfume?"

Tessa's eyes widened at Mary's perceptiveness. But Mary only laughed and drew her closer to their circle of friends. It was almost sinful to wear the perfume he'd given her, but she was a woman, after all, and it made her feel feminine and wicked. When she'd touched it to her skin, it felt like the touch of his mouth upon her. Running it down the path between her breasts had been a truly arousing sensation.

"How is Smoke Eyes faring with you?" Tessa asked, seating herself beside Mary. She laughed ruefully. "Or perhaps I should ask how *you* are faring with Smoke Eyes."

Mary laughed back. "Oh, she's a handful, just as you promised." Her eyes glowed. "But I love the child. She's trying so hard. In fact she's minding Jeremiah tonight."

"Why, that's wonderful. It sounds like she's already a part of the family."

"She was part of the family from the first day you brought her to us."

In no time Tessa was on the dance floor, whirling from the arms of one man to another. When she was dancing with Jim McGafferty, she heard Cody's deep voice. "Mac, may I cut in?" And her heart took flight.

In his arms Tessa drank in the sight of him; he wore black trousers and a white shirt, the sleeves rolled up to his elbows, the collar open at the throat to reveal his strong, tanned neck. Hungrily her eyes went over his deeply tanned face to at last meet the caress of his warm, green eyes.

Cody took his fill of her too—the softly swept-back hair, streaked in places by the sun, and the dress, the deepest rose pink, which matched the tint in her cheeks. "You look beautiful," he told her.

Tessa flushed her pleasure. But if they didn't stop staring at each other in this posi-

tively indecent way, then surely the others
would guess what Mary already knew. "What
are you building in town," she asked him
with a winsome curve to her beautiful lips,
"another saloon?"

He threw back his head, startling her with
his laughter. "Ah, you always think the worst
of me, Tessa." His eyes smiled down into
hers. "And for that you'll just have to wait
and see." His blue-green eyes probed hers so
deeply that Tessa let her lashes fall. "And
speaking of waiting," he continued huskily,
"I think I've waited long enough for you."

She tried to still the wild, fierce pounding of
her heart, but every nerve in her body seemed
to reach for him, yearning. For a mindless
instant she was tempted to throw all her
misgivings to the wind and charge headlong
into a passionate affair with him, but Cody's
low words and the power of his eyes drew her
back to reality.

"He's not coming out and we both know it.
And I want you, now more than ever."

"Don't!" Her wide, honey-flecked eyes
shimmered up at him. She felt a sharp pang
when she realized this man would never be
hers, could never be hers. She felt his arms
tense around her waist, and she made an
effort to soften her voice. "Not here, not now.
Please, Cody, let's not talk about this
tonight." She saw his jaws clamp tight and
she knew she was not going to get out of this
easily. He had her trapped here in the
crowded room so she couldn't run from him.

"Then when, dammit? My patience has worn mighty thin!"

Now Tessa's eyes flashed up at him. "*Your* patience! I've tolerated just about all I can from you, Cody Butler, what with all your pawings and demands and—" She glanced around the room, her cheeks flaring with anger—yes she was going to say it! "And your *insatiable* sexual appetite!" She heard his indrawn hiss of breath between his teeth, but intrepidly went on, venting her own frustrations. "I'm sick and tired of fending you off, Cody Butler! And I'm not going to tolerate your persistent demands one more instant!"

Cody's lips thinned. "Tolerate? I would hardly call what we did in that—"

"Don't you dare say it, Cody." Her voice was cold. Their eyes locked in a silent battle of wills. Cody let out a tense breath between his teeth.

"What have you ever offered me, Cody, except life as your harlot?" She said it softly, but the words cut him deeply. He wanted to shake her and would have, by God, if they were alone. Tessa fought back rising tears; what *did* she want him to offer? God, she was so confused! And knew, shamefully, that she was weak enough to offer every bit of herself, and rejoice in the offering.

She saw the muscle bunch in his hard jaw. "I thought we already discussed what I have to offer." But his voice had softened now too. "I told you I'd be good to you and we could be discreet."

"Yes! Until you tire of me! Then what?"

He gritted his teeth. Women! "What do you want from me, Tessa?"

"Nothing! Let's just get this dance over with so you can escort me off the dance floor." He did shake her then, just enough to startle her. That martyred look she wore was just about all he could bear—as if she truly did find his presence repulsive. "At least you could pretend to enjoy it."

The lump she dreaded all night had surfaced and was bobbing in Tessa's throat. Yes, she would have to hurt him after all; there was no way around it if she intended to keep her life intact. She lifted her fine jaw and her eyes turned brittle. "You are not the only man in my life."

He snorted. "A fact which you've constantly reminded me of since you hit town."

"I don't mean Michael Shea." Her words were very even and she saw his eyes narrow on her. "Ned Winston has asked me to marry him."

She wanted to close her eyes against the thunder in his voice. *"What!"* His steely fingers gripped her hand so tightly she thought he might snap her bones. Yet she forced herself to keep her aloof stare on him.

"I believe you heard me, Dr. Butler."

He pulled her so closely against his hard body that Tessa lost her breath in a gasp. "Don't you dare call me Dr. Butler after what we've shared," he warned through tight lips, and Tessa was hardly able to endure the icy blast of his green gaze. Cody, she reminded herself, was not a man to toy with.

He was still scowling down at her, his heavy brows drawn low. "And what did you tell Mr. Winston?"

Tessa raised her chin and forced her eyes to stay on his. "I haven't told him anything yet."

"You like to keep men dangling, do you?"

Now her own lips tightened. The thick-headed lout! She wouldn't be in this mess if it wasn't for him and his damned desires! Oh, but a little voice nagged at the back of her mind, they were *your* desires too. Never mind that! Arrogant Cody Butler needed to be taken down a notch or two!

"Ned," she returned coolly, "has more of a chance as a husband than you do as a lover."

Cody's insolent eyes raked coldly, crudely, over her. "Is that right?" he bit out icily. "I'd never thought it of you, Tessa, but it sounds as if you are offering your . . . ah . . . charms as booty, a prize of war, so to speak." He ignored the stiffening of her spine and his mouth turned hard as he continued coldly, "If that's your game, how about if I offer my hand in marriage too?" His eyes mocked her.

Tessa struggled to loosen Cody's hold on her, but he would not relent. And he continued dancing with her as smoothly as if they were lightly discussing the weather. Her emotions were a churning sick knot in her stomach. "Are you asking me to marry you?" she gritted out while giving him her most dazzling smile—provided for onlookers.

"Sure," he said lightly, too lightly, and a muscle tensed in his hard jaw, "and then when I've had my fill of you, I'll politely withdraw my offer. Would that satisfy your requirements?"

Tessa froze. She would have slapped him had she the opportunity. "Why, you ba—"

His brow shot up, pretending surprise. "Now if the town schoolteacher starts swearing, I'll know I really am a defiler of women! What would Ned say? And Michael Shea? Now there's a man who's been truly wronged." His fury and jealousy made him ruthless and Cody didn't fully understand why he persevered with the subject. But there was one thing he did understand; every time he mentioned Michael Shea, Tessa dropped her eyes. "Look at me," he hissed. When she wouldn't, his arms tightened hurtfully around her waist. Without thinking, Tessa let her eyes meet his and Cody drew in a sharp breath at what he saw. *Guilt.* The guilt of betrayal. But the guilt was not felt for her betrothed. It went deeper than that. And suddenly Cody knew. His next words dropped on Tessa like a ton of lead. "You're married to him, aren't you?"

He felt her answer in the way her body slumped against his. He saw his answer in the deep brown eyes that had always been honest with him. Dread and pain and fury exploded within him, and it was worse than any rage he'd ever experienced before.

Fear swelled to a crescendo within her. Open your mouth, Tessa, she cried inside herself. Deny it! Say something, do something—anything—to obliterate that awful look on his face. But she couldn't. She was struck dumb.

The music had stopped and Tessa fell against Cody. She saw the fine white line that had sprung up around his taut mouth and he let loose a string of vicious expletives that set fire to the tips of her ears. His name from her lips sounded like a death rattle. "Cody—"

But like a steel shackle his hand clamped over her upper arm, and he steered her ruthlessly toward the saloon door. Out into the black night he shoved her, slamming the door behind him. They were alone. Soft rain came steadily down, leaving dew on their faces, silvering their hair.

Cody released her roughly, and Tessa stumbled against the porch railing, banging her hip. The sharp pain almost made her cry out, but she bit down hard on her lip.

"Don't look so tragic, my sweet. I don't plan to beat you—against my better judgment." He laughed shortly, harshly. "Damn, but you're a remarkable actress, *Miss* Amesbury. Tell me, what's your real name?"

He was breathing heavily, almost as if it hurt him to draw breath. His face was dark and fierce. His eyes, glittering queerly in the porchlight, condemned her. She'd never make him understand!

Tessa clung to the railing, blinking the mist from her lashes as her anguished voice pleaded with him. "It *is* my real name—"

His harsh laugh sounded like a bark. "So that's why you were not a virgin! All that fabrication was mighty impressive, Miss Amesbury. Raped, were you? I'm even stupider than I gave myself credit for!"

Tessa blanched, her huge eyes like dark moon shadows in the night. She shook her head in helpless denial, stricken that he did not believe even *that*. "No, Cody, it was true!" she whispered, but it seemed as if he didn't hear her. She pressed her palms to her damp, burning cheeks and begged him to listen to her. "Please, Cody, let me explain—"

"Explain!" he snarled, making her wince. "There *is* no explaining this! You left your husband in Boston and traveled out here under the guise of a schoolteacher, isn't that true?"

"Yes. I mean no, not all—God, if you'd just let me explain!" Tessa's voice broke and the tears gushed from her eyes now, hot and fast.

His features seemed to be carved of granite; his stare was icy with rage, as was his voice. "I will not assist in making a cuckold of a man. By God, if you were my wife I'd kill you."

His words swept through her like a cruel, chill wind. He wasn't even going to listen to her! She wanted to fling herself against his chest and make him listen! "Damn you, Cody—"

"You stay the hell out of my sight, lady."

His voice was an icy menace. "You're a liar and a cheater and this town has every right to run you out on the next rail."

Oh, God, would they? "Cody—" He'd turned his back abruptly on her and was down the saloon steps, already out in the road. "The hell with you!" she called out weakly after him, but he didn't hear her and she wondered, half hysterically, when her language had gotten so bad.

She gripped the railing, watching Cody's tall form until it was out of sight. Then she sagged against the porch post and stared back with drenched eyes up at the black sky. "I'm sorry, Cody," she whispered, "I'm sorry . . ."

At his desk Cody sealed the letter he'd written to Dr. Roger Norton in Kentucky. He'd mail it today, by God, and his replacement would be here within a couple of weeks. It was damn well time to get out of town.

He tore a hand through his hair and rubbed the back of his neck, massaging the knot of tension there. Then he reached for the half-empty whiskey bottle on his desk, tipped it up to his mouth, and drank long and deep. He slammed the bottle down again and wiped the back of his hand across his lips.

The sun streaming in through the opened drapes hurt his bloodshot eyes. He narrowed them and his lips thinned as he envisioned Tessa. "Let me explain!" she'd begged him, and a cold rage filled him. There was nothing *to* explain. She was married, and that was the final truth. The thought was like a sharp kick in the gut and Cody took another long pull from the whiskey bottle.

"Damn!" he growled. How could he have bought all her lies? And why the hell couldn't he get drunk after all the whiskey he'd swallowed in the last two days?

How long would it be before he could forget her? Would he ever be able to blot out the memory of her silken skin, her fathomless dark eyes, the way she'd cried when she'd told him about being raped? What a consummate actress! he thought with disgust. *No, Cody, it was true. . . .* His long fingers gripped the neck of the whiskey bottle so tightly that surely the glass would shatter and break into a thousand shards.

Someone pounded on the front door. Cody swore. But the pounding continued and he knew if he didn't answer it immediately then the door would come crashing into his front hall.

Angrily he crossed the room in long, quick strides and flung open the door, swearing, "*What,* dammit?"

The tall blond man staring back at him from the porch frowned reproachfully at him. "Well, that's a helluva greeting for a brother you haven't seen in a year!" He turned to his companion and said, "Maybe we ought to take the next train home, eh, Seth?"

But Cody was laughing now, his teeth sparkling white in his unshaven face, and he pounded his brother on the back in affection-ate greeting. "Goddamn, you sly son-of-a-bitch! Why in hell didn't you let me know you were coming out?" Cody demanded, hauling his brother aside. "Hey, Seth—" he greeted his childhood friend with a hearty bear hug and another pound on the back. He hugged his brother again and stepped back, looking him over. "Jesus, but you look good, Bryce."

Bryce's light blue eyes went over Cody's unshaven face, noting the tension lines, the bloodshot eyes, and he rubbed his jaw wryly. "Wish I could say the same for you. Up all night?"

Cody rubbed his own grizzled jaw and muttered, "Could say that." But his brother's arrival was the perfect antidote to Tessa—at least for a while. He glanced at Seth—big, burly, curly haired Seth—and again at Bryce. "So what brings you two to Harper City? How long you staying? Goddamn, it's good to see you!"

Bryce's keen eyes took in more than Cody would have wanted him to. "I'm getting mar-ried in September. I wanted to celebrate my final days of bachelorhood with my brother."

Cody grinned. "You've come to the right place." He was glad for the diversion. "We'll head on over to Lily's; she'll take good care of us." Maybe one of Lily's girls was just what he needed to drive Tessa out of his mind, out of his blood.

"You might want to shave first," Bryce suggested dryly.

"Still bossing me around, eh?" Cody grinned, heading for the kitchen where he kept his shaving gear. His glance hit the letter on his desk. "Before we hit Lily's," he said, "I've got to mail a letter." Maybe, he thought grimly, he'd leave this town for good.

Bryce waited outside the post office for Cody, hands in his trousers pockets, whistling a ditty between his teeth. He was feeling lighthearted and jaunty and missing his Caroline more than he could have imagined.

The sweet April day was a balm of moist air and warm sun in the late afternoon. Bryce let his eyes scan the town his brother had financed. Ah, but Cody was an ambitious man! He was also a wise investor. And he'd done a damn fine job with this town too. Bryce glanced to the general store across the street where Seth had gone to purchase a pouch of tobacco. When he turned to glance back inside the post office window, a slim young woman wearing a broad-brimmed straw hat rounded the corner and barreled right into him.

"Oh!" Tessa exclaimed, grasping wildly at her armload of books, but they spilled ignominiously to the boardwalk. Both she and Bryce crouched down simultaneously to pick them up. "I'm sorry!" she apologized, hanging on to her hat with one hand.

"No problem. Apology accepted." Bryce smiled amicably, scooping up a couple of books in one broad hand. He tried to hide his amusement as the woman, on her knees, pressed the crown of her hat to her head while stacking books and papers.

"I—I can get these myself. Sorry," she said again, and, curiously, her voice trembled. She'd been daydreaming again, thinking of Cody, trying not to, and now, miserably, she was remembering that he used to tease her about tripping over her own feet. She kept her head bent, too embarrassed to face this stranger, and gathered her books up only to drop them again. "Damn!" she breathed, hardly aloud, but Bryce heard it and chuckled.

Their eyes met over the spilled books and Tessa blinked. She recognized him immediately. "Why, you're Cody's brother!" she exclaimed, without thinking.

Bryce was equally startled. How in hell did she know that? Unless Cody had showed her his family photographs . . . and there would be no reason for that unless Cody . . .

"Ah," he said at last, and they both stood. "And you are?"

"Miss Amesbury," cut in a cold, derisive voice from above and slightly behind. Tessa froze. How long had Cody been standing there? "Miss Tessa Amesbury, Bryce. She's our town schoolteacher."

Tessa turned her gaze up to Cody's cold green eyes. She saw the muscle tense in his strong jaw and wondered why he'd kept the "Mrs." part of her identity a secret.

Unknowingly Bryce broke the thick wall of tension between them. He took Tessa's slim golden hand and, bending over it, brushed his lips against her skin. Even then, Cody felt a searing pang of possessiveness for her, and he despised himself for it.

"Not this lovely lady!" Bryce exclaimed as he straightened. Tessa noticed that he was almost the size of Cody—just a couple inches shorter, and not as broad at the shoulders. His lean, tanned face was just as handsome as it was in his photographs . . . light blue eyes, as warm as a tropical sun, and thick, blond hair waving back off his forehead. But it was Cody's presence at her shoulder that made Tessa's skin tingle; and it was he she wanted to put her arms around. "Do you remember our teacher, Cody? Miss Dougless?" Bryce's amused eyes flicked to Cody who stood stone-faced, purposely not looking at Tessa. Ah, Bryce thought, there is something between them. He was not sure what, but it was definitely *something*. And it surprised him, it did, because the schoolmarm was not Cody's type. Although, looking closer, Bryce could see that her dark eyes, under the brim of that hat, could bewitch even the most respectable of men and her wide, full mouth promised passion.

"I remember," Cody returned curtly, looking out now toward the general store. "Has Seth come out yet?"

He can't even bear to look at me, Tessa thought miserably. Does he hate me so much? She wished Bryce would stop talking so she could flee.

"No. Anyway," Bryce continued, looking back into Tessa's dark eyes, "Miss Dougless was a woman who didn't know how to smile. I swear she sucked a lemon just to keep her mouth pinched. Cody and I used to make wagers on which of us could crack her reserve, but it was to no avail. Hell, the pranks we—"

Annoyed, now, Cody broke in impatiently, "Dammit, Bryce, let's get Seth and hurry the hell up to Lily's."

Bryce saw Tessa stiffen and the hurt on her face. Damn, the insensitive bastard! He wanted her to know where he was headed all right. Whatever was between them was no light matter! Bryce had never seen Cody try to make a woman jealous before. But he was sure as hell rubbing Miss Amesbury's nose in his business now!

He didn't even say good-bye to her. He started across the street in long strides, hands buried deep in his pockets, scowling blackly.

Bryce winked at Tessa. "Nice meeting you. You've got all your books collected?"

"Oh, oh, yes. Thank you. Nice meeting you too, Bryce," But her troubled eyes were on Cody. Bryce hurried off, catching up to his brother.

"You were damned rude to that woman!"

Cody tightened his lips. "Keep out of it, Bryce."

And Bryce held his words—for now.

Lily's Dance Hall was, by eleven o'clock that night, flooded with smoke, glaring with bright lights, and vibrating with the pounding, vulgar piano music and boisterous calls of the men. Cody and Bryce sat drinking at a table pushed against the back wall while Seth danced with every woman in the saloon.

"Are you coming home for the derby?" Bryce asked. "Pa's racing Royal Blue and Lancelot this year."

"I'd like to," Cody admitted, "but I'm going west for a while, Bryce." He leaned back in his chair and tossed off another shot of whiskey. A muscle jumped in his cheek and for the moment Bryce did not press him.

"You gonna make it for my wedding?"

Cody grinned even though his temples throbbed with the heat and the noise and all the whiskey he'd drunk. "Hell, I wouldn't miss that for a straight year of wenching! I'm surprised Caroline waited for you all this time."

Bryce laughed into his mug. "What about you? You're not that much younger than me, brother. When the hell are you gonna settle down?"

Cody sobered. "You know I'm not the marrying type, Bryce." He reached for the bottle and poured them both another drink.

"Oh?" Bryce said casually, lifting his drink. "Does that schoolteacher know that? What's her name . . . Miss Amesbury?"

Cody's eyes narrowed dangerously on his brother. "Damned perceptive of you, Bryce."

Bryce shrugged, not intimidated by his brother's fierce scowl. "Perceptive, hell. You two looked like you were caught naked in front of the whole town." He laughed when Cody slammed his drink down on the table-top, causing the liquor to spill. "I give the woman her due. She's the only woman, ex-cept Ma, who has ever captured your heart. Believe me, I know, it's like a sickness."

"The only thing that is like a sickness is that we're sitting in a roomful of willing women and all we can talk about is capturing my goddamn heart."

Bryce laughed then as Ruby, one of Lily's prettiest girls, plunked her backside down on Cody's knee and looped her arms possessively around his neck. She leaned her half-bared bosom into his strong chest and pouted pret-tily. "Lily sent me over to see if there is anything I can do for you. She's worried about you. She says you haven't danced all evening. Are you pleased with the entertainment, Dr. Butler?" she purred, her red lips pursing as she traced a forefinger down his hard jawline. Cody's lips quirked and pretty Ruby glanced at them.

Cody looked toward Lily, who stood smil-ing at him from the bar, and he raised his drink to her in a silent salute. Then he re-turned his attention to the blonde on his lap. "The entertainment pleases me fine," he said, letting his eyes rove over her creamy skin, down to the front of her gown where her breasts swelled temptingly. And he felt . . . nothing. He found her skin too fair . . . it was not the warm golden tint of Tessa's. Ruby was blatant and practiced and . . . she was not

Tessa. His fingers gripped his glass, but Bryce noticed and Cody heard him chuckle. He smiled a tight smile at Ruby. "But my brother and I have much to discuss. Our pleasure will come later."

Ruby glanced at Bryce, who smiled at her. She sighed and reluctantly disengaged her arms from around Cody's neck, then stood. Both men watched her slink away.

"I think, brother," Bryce said slowly, "that this whiskey is the only pleasure we're gonna be getting tonight."

Cody laughed. "Ah, but it's liniment for the soul."

Bryce groaned. "The doctor speaks."

Cody laughed again. "Seth's taking enough pleasure for the three of us." They glanced to their friend, who was trying to dance with three women at once while drinking from a whiskey glass with one hand. Cody turned thoughtful green eyes on Bryce. "Why is it that none of these women look good to me, Bryce?"

"Ah, God, man, don't you know?" He laughed and clapped a hand on Cody's hard shoulder. "You're in love with her, man! Don't glower at me! I speak from experience. Look at me! Out on the town! For crissake, I can't get Caroline's face out of my mind. I can't wait to get back to her. Recognize the signs in yourself, Cody. Drunkenness, sleepless nights, misery, gnawing jealousy! Hell, it's love."

It was a stark, sobering thought. Love? By

God, yes, he loved her. And suddenly the picture of Tessa half hidden under her straw hat that afternoon flashed through Cody's mind. And other pictures followed: the first day she'd arrived in town wearing the same straw hat, that day he'd caught her in his lab and he wanted to throttle her, running after Smoke Eyes out on the prairie, holding Mary's baby, her beautiful mouth after he'd kissed it, that look in her walnut-brown eyes when she'd told him she had been raped. She *couldn't* have feigned that.

Cody gritted his teeth so hard that a muscle bulged in his jaw. He was in love with another man's wife.

Bryce's hand gripped his shoulder. "Welcome to the ranks, man."

Cody looked over at him with bleak eyes. "I can't say I'm glad to be a part of them."

Chapter Fifteen

✦✦✦✦

IN THE SUNNY spring days new young grass sprang up over the rolling green prairie, stretching out to the clear blue sky. The children brought Tessa bouquets of wildflowers picked on their way to school. The older boys were back in the fields now, plowing and planting. And one day soon, Tessa learned, Cody would be leaving Harper City.

After a short visit with Eb and Mrs. Rawlins one afternoon, Tessa came out of the general store and found old Abbott Robbins and Hal Witherby standing on the boardwalk in front of the store chewing and spitting tobacco and discussing "the Doc's" bad temper of late. Tessa froze when she heard Cody's name, and she stood peering into Eb's front window, trying to appear as if she was admiring a pair of shoes and not eavesdropping on the men.

"Yessir, Cody's been broodin' and snappin' for near two weeks now," Abbott drawled, as if confused by Cody's behavior. "He's been in a devil of a temper. It ain't like Cody, it ain't. I heard tell he scared the stomach pains right out of Jem McGee. An' Clara says he answers his door like a grizzly. Mebbe it's good he's leavin' town for a while."

"Well," said Hal, shooting a brown stream of tobacco from the side of his mouth, "I heard tell he likes to wander a bit. Gits restless, the way I used to when I was young. Think he'll come back?"

Abbott shrugged. "Who knows? I sure hope he does. Town won't be the same without Cody. I know he's found a pretty good doc to come in an' take care of us while he's gone. You know Doc Norton?"

"Naw. Where's Cody goin'?"

"Out west somewhere. Colorado, I heard."

"Well, I'll be jiggered."

Tessa forced herself to move on, but the

pain of his leaving was stark and keen within her. *She* should be the one to leave. But she had nowhere to go. She should go to his house, explain to him why she'd married William, why she'd run from him, but Cody wanted no explanations, she reminded herself miserably. She'd tried to explain once, and the fact that she was married was all he cared to hear.

Damn him, she thought angrily, and full of hurt. He'd found comfort in Lily's arms. But he had that right, and *she* had no right to resent it. Abbott had spoken the truth: the town wouldn't be the same without Cody.

The next day, at dismissal time, Tessa was helping little Hannah Brown with her sunbonnet when a shadow fell in the doorway. At first, when her heart kicked, Tessa thought it might be Cody; but when she glanced up she saw Bryce.

"Run along, Hannah," she said gently, and when the child was gone, Tessa's eyes met Bryce's light blue ones. Her throat grew tight. "Is he gone?"

"Rode out this morning." Bryce saw her swallow, and the glint of tears in her beautiful brown eyes. He also saw the soft honey lights in those eyes, and the warmth and depth of them. Unconsciously his eyes ran down her slim form, over her breasts, and back up to her passionate mouth, and he knew then that she had a special, different beauty. He saw how easily his brother could have fallen in love with her.

"And when do you leave?" she asked him quietly, turning away now to wash the blackboard.

"Tomorrow on the nine-twenty." He watched her for a moment, swiping at the blackboard, and thought how gracefully she moved—like a dancer. In the lovely, sweeping line of her backbone he could see the spunk and spirit and inherent sensuality she must have shown Cody. And Bryce found himself wondering again what had happened between the two of them.

He spun his hat between his hands, knowing he was about to step in where he had no business stepping in. "What have you done to my brother, lass?" He saw her back stiffen and for a moment she stopped all movement. Then, slowly, she began to wash the board again.

"What do you mean?" she murmured, careful not to look at him.

Bryce stepped into the room and leaned against the back wall. "He's besotted with you. And Cody's never been besotted with a woman before."

At last Tessa turned to favor him with a glance. "Oh, I doubt that, Mr. Butler. Why, he finds plenty of comfort in Lily's arms, I'm sure. Heavens, you should know that. You were with him."

Bryce's blue eyes flicked over her. Cody would probably kill him if he knew what he was going to tell her. "Nothing happened at Lily's, ma'am."

Tessa's mouth fell slightly open and her heart skipped a beat. But then she quickly dropped her eyes from Bryce's and wrung the wet cloth over the water pail. "You're his brother. You're only defending him."

"Hell, I'm not defending him. I think we both know that Cody wanted you to believe he was with Lily, and if I was defending him I'd let you go on believing that. But I'll tell you all he did was drink at Lily's. He's been drunk and crazy for you these past weeks, and no fun at all."

Their eyes met and they smiled at each other.

"In a devil of a temper," she murmured, thinking of what Abbott had said about him.

"Damn right." Bryce took out a cigarette from his pocket and lit it. And as Tessa watched him she thought, Cody hasn't told him. He hasn't told his own brother that I'm married. That I hurt him. And she wondered at his loyalty, especially when he'd been so angry with her.

"And damn right I'm his brother and I care about him," Bryce went on, taking a drag on his cigarette. "Cody is infatuated with you. Why, at Lily's, he turned women away!" Bryce continued, "I can see you're the only woman for him."

"You don't even know me," Tessa protested.

"I know enough. I know Cody's crazy for you, and I'm not sure he knows how crazy. And I don't know what happened between you, but it's time one of you did something about it."

A shadow crossed Tessa's features. "We—we had an argument. He won't listen to me."

Bryce studied her closely from where he stood. "Another man?"

Startled, Tessa's eyes jumped to his. These Butler men had incredible perception! "Not—not in the sense you're thinking. I don't even like this other man—"

Bryce laughed. "Good! He's jealous. That's a good sign, Miss Amesbury. Cody's competitive as hell, and if anything, the thought of another man in your life is enough to drive him back here."

Tessa shook her head. Her throat ached. "No, you don't understand."

But Bryce wasn't listening. He was reaching inside his jacket pocket, and he took from it a folded piece of paper. "He made me vow I wouldn't give his address in Colorado to anyone, but here's mine in Kentucky. If he's muleheaded enough to stay away for too long, contact me. I know for sure he'll be home in September. And don't give up and turn to that other man. Cody and you are right for each other."

"But—" She had no choice but to take the paper from Bryce, the way he was waving it in her face. What was the point in explaining?

Bryce grinned, and Tessa thought he was almost as handsome as Cody. "Next time I see you you better be on Cody's arm." He saw the ghost of a smile cross her lips, a flicker of pain in her eyes. Cody, he thought, for crissake, you idiot! Don't wait too long.

"Does Cody know he has such a match-maker for a brother?" Tessa teased lightly.

"Nope." Bryce grinned again. "And there'll be hell to pay if he ever finds out."

"Don't worry, he won't." But not for the reason you're thinking, Bryce. There was no chance she'd be seeing Bryce again—ever. And she began to think again that she should be the one to leave Harper City, not Cody. When school closed in June, Tessa knew she would hand in her resignation. She could move on—somewhere—and Cody could return to the city he'd been building. One of them had to leave; they couldn't continue to painstakingly avoid each other. And, after all, Harper City needed Cody more than it would ever need her.

Despite the ache she felt at the thought of leaving her new home, she knew it was the answer. Still, there wasn't one night that April and May when she didn't think of him. She wondered who he held in his arms, and if he would ever come back. She yearned to dismiss him from her mind, the memory of his touch from her body, but signs of Cody lingered. The new doctor was situated in his room at the hotel—temporarily. He had the keys to Cody's house in case of an emergency. And Tessa resented the man. She was sure he was very nice and capable, but if he hadn't come to relieve Cody, Cody would not have been able to leave.

I'm surely losing my mind, Tessa thought
one morning on the way to school. And Bryce
was wrong about Cody. He was not besotted,
not infatuated with her. He was proud and
stubborn and had been made to look a fool—
so he thought. And if he'd stopped his blus-
tering for a moment, she could have told him
that her marriage to William had not been
consummated. Small comfort, perhaps, but
Cody should know he was the only man she'd
ever taken to her bed.

"I *must* put him out of my mind," she'd
hissed under her breath as she walked past
the new building he'd put up before he left.
Hal Witherby and a few other men were
unloading crates from his wagon and she
hushed herself as Hal glanced up from his
work.

"Mornin', ma'am." He straightened and
squinted against the sun at her.

"Hello, Mr. Witherby." She glanced to the
new building where the men were bringing
the crates. They went inside and came out
empty-handed, then unloaded some more
crates. "What are all these crates for, Mr.
Witherby?"

Hal scratched his head. Of all people *she*
should know. "Why, fer the new library,
miss! Cody's been waitin' for this shipment of
books from the East fer over a month now.
Too bad he ain't here to see 'em come in."

Tessa stood aghast. Tears flooded her eyes
quickly, but she had to hide them from Hal.
He'd done it for her. She knew he had. She'd

mentioned that library last fall and he had remembered.

"Ma'am?" Hal wondered why she had fallen so quiet.

Tessa blinked hard, grateful for the wide brim of her straw hat. "When will the library open, Mr. Witherby?"

Hal shrugged. "I thought it might be up to Cody. Don't know now. Ain't up to me."

"Has anyone heard from Dr. Butler?" Tessa asked briskly, trying to cover the hope in her voice.

"Not a one," Hal returned.

And all over again she was thinking, *Damn* him! She wanted to cast him from her mind as he so obviously had cast her from his!

She tried, in her own way, to set things right before her departure. When she told Ned she was not going to marry him—that she liked him only as a friend—Ned accepted it in his own dreamy way, informing her that he had planned to go abroad to study art. It had been much easier than Tessa had anticipated.

But when Smoke Eyes came in with a slingshot one May morning, and used it at recess, Tessa took her aside and gave the girl the worst scolding she'd ever received. She was afraid for the girl—afraid she might lose her good home if Mary became exasperated with her pranks. And worse than ever Tessa wanted Smoke Eyes in a secure, safe home when she left town.

"Does Mary know you have that slingshot?" she demanded, pinning Smoke Eyes' shoulders back against the schoolhouse. And without waiting for an answer, she ranted on, "Do you like living with Mary and Tim? Do you?"

Smoke Eyes bit her lip. Her eyes narrowed up at Tessa's. "I din't do nuthin' wrong."

"Mary's responsible for you, do you realize that? If you hurt another child with that—stupid toy—then Mary will have to take responsibility for your behavior!"

"You tellin' me I do somethin' like playin' with this and I can't live with Mary no more?"

At last Tessa released her grip on the girl's thin shoulders. Her own shoulders sagged. "Smoke Eyes, you're thirteen years old. You're turning into a young woman—"

Smoke Eyes scowled. "Don't have to remind me of that. Mary's doin' it all the time."

"Then *why* are you playing with this—this—"

"Boys' toy?" Smoke Eyes sneered.

"Yes!"

For a moment they stared each other down. Smoke Eyes' jaw tightened. "Don't try to change me now, Miss Amesbury. I like usin' it and I will."

"I don't think you like it as much as you pretend. Oh, don't puff up your chest that way." Now Tessa leaned back against the schoolhouse, beside the girl. She ran a weary hand over her eyes. "Mary says you're behaving wonderfully. You use your manners, and stay clean, and help with the baby. She says you study hard. You're growing up, Smoke Eyes, and sometimes it can be a frightening feeling."

Smoke Eyes snorted.

"Stop pretending with me! I know you better than anyone in this town!" Tessa exclaimed. And, she thought to herself, I told you once I'd never leave you. Someday soon I'll have to tell you I am. Another betrayal.

Smoke Eyes had grown quiet. The two of them stood there while the noise of the other children in the schoolyard drifted around them. "It's true," Smoke Eyes muttered at last. "I—I started that—that awful mess wimmin start."

Tessa lifted her head from the wall behind her. Their eyes met. "Menses."

Smoke Eyes blushed and lowered her gaze. "That's it. It's dreadful embarrassin.' "

"I guess you've told Mary."

Smoke Eyes nodded tersely. But Tessa was smiling.

"It's natural, Smoke Eyes."

"I hate it."

Tessa laughed. "I did too."

Smoke Eyes looked at her. "You mean you like it now?"

Tessa laughed again. "No! It's just something you get accustomed to." And I thanked God that it came a week after Cody left my bed, she added silently.

"Hmmph! It ain't fair!"

"Not in the least."

And then they were both chuckling.

"How is everything else going for you, Smoke Eyes?"

Smoke Eyes shrugged. "I miss my grandfather. Sometimes I go up there—to our old house. But Mary an' Tim are nice as ever. And Mary bakes cookies. An' she's showin' me lots of things—how to keep house an' all. I'm learnin' lots about babies. An' that'll help with doctorin'."

"It certainly will."

"She's real good to me. An' Tim's addin' on a new bedroom fer me. I 'preciate what they're doin' fer me." She rubbed her nose. "So, what's wrong with you, Miss Amesbury?"

Tessa blinked. "What do you mean?"

Smoke Eyes folded her arms over her chest. "Well, you got all that outta me. I ain't goin' back inside till you tell me what's makin' you so sad."

They measured each other.

Smoke Eyes sighed. "Why don't you jes admit it?"

"Admit what?"

"You know. How bad yer missin' him."

It was Tessa's turn to look away. Her eyes scanned the horizon where the sky met the green earth. "I miss him so bad I can't even talk about it."

Smoke Eyes studied her teacher, her friend, silently. "I love him too, Miss Amesbury."

Tessa's startled, tear-filled eyes collided with Smoke Eyes'. "No," she began to deny, "I don't—"

But the child had taken her hand and she

squeezed it. "Hush, Miss Amesbury. I unnerstan' exactly."

The last Saturday in May was glorious, blindingly bright, and clear. Late that afternoon as Tessa scrubbed her laundry in the backyard the sun burned hot on her neck and arms. She was wearing one of her old cotton dresses, the long sleeves pushed up past her elbows, her honey-colored braid falling over one shoulder as she toiled diligently, head bent.

She was suddenly cast in shadow. She stared at the boots planted before her, not recognizing them. But she did recognize the voice she heard from above.

"Hello, *Miss Amesbury*."

Paralyzed by fear, Tessa grew still as stone. *William*. Her heart stopped for one agonizing instant before it began to pound wildly in her breast. The wooden washboard fell from her still fingers to the ground. As the panic and fear clawed coldly at her insides, she bravely ran her eyes up his tall form to meet his ice-blue eyes. "William." Her mouth formed the word but no sound came out. She was washed white—pure, bloodless white.

And William smiled his cruel-lipped smile down at her. "How appropriate. You're on your knees."

The panic surged within her. His eyes narrowed on her, his lips thinned. "Get up."

But she couldn't move. The blood was

pounding thickly in her temples and she started to shiver despite the heat of the day.

William suddenly reached down and shoved his hand into her hair, twisting it as he cruelly jerked her to her feet. At her cry of pain, his hand tightened and he pulled her face in close. His blue eyes blazed hatefully down at her.

"Do you know how much money you've cost me, you bitch?" His hand tightened again and Tessa moaned, sure he would tear the hair right from her scalp. "You're a slut, a thief, and the only reason I had a detective trace you at all was so I could take my revenge on you!" And he thrust her away from him as if he couldn't stand the sight of her. In pain, Tessa held her head, trying not to cringe from him, trying to collect her senses and drive her fear away. But when he took a menacing step toward her, she did shrink from him and he laughed coldly. "I'm going to take you home, *Miss Amesbury*, and before I do I'm going to let this town know you are really Mrs. Forsythe, liar and deserter."

"Oh, God, but I'm not!" she protested.

"What?" The icy word snapped out of his rigid form.

Tessa rubbed her scalp, backing away from him. "I said I'm not. I'm not your wife! Our marriage was never consummated."

The harsh planes in Forsythe's face seemed to sharpen as his teeth gleamed back at Tessa in a wolfish grin. "Are you begging for it?" When she shuddered he laughed. "I could take you into that house and bed you now. I could rape you over and over again and no one in this town would lift a finger to help you because it is my legal right to treat you as I wish." His cold eyes seemed to savor her terrified features. "That's a word you're familiar with, isn't it, Tessa? Rape." Slowly he edged toward her and Tessa's blood ran cold.

"Don't you dare move one step further," she warned, wondering at her own sudden flood of courage. But he only sneered at her.

"Oh? Are you threatening me?" He had her back up against the wall of the house, and his long, talonlike fingers closed about her slender upper arms.

"You'd be wise not to force me to do anything against my will, for I have something of yours, William—or, rather, your first wife's."

William's fingers seemed to bite into her bone. "What does *she* have to do with any of this?"

"I have her journal. Your maid gave it to me the morning after you beat me and left for God knows where. She told me you did the same to your first wife and there was some suspicion over your wife's 'accidental' death."

William's grip loosened. His crafty eyes studied her closely. "The maid took that journal? Do you know how I hunted for that—I—" His eyes suddenly narrowed again. "What did she write?"

Tessa stared coldly back at him. "You know as well as I do. That you tried to poison her.

That you beat her so unmercifully sometimes she would have to stay in the house for days. That she was afraid for her life. And that she was wealthy in her own right and you'd inherit that wealth if she were to die. There was enough evidence in there to put you in prison for the rest of your miserable life." Tessa winced when his fingers tightened on her arms again, surely bruising them.

"I want that journal. Now."

Tessa's heart thundered savagely. If she gave him the journal, he would surely abuse her again. It was the only weapon she had against him. "I left it with a friend." Please, *please* don't let him search the house.

William's eyes blazed down at her in icy anger. But as Tessa unflinchingly returned his stare he began to think it might be wise to try an approach other than force. He needed to get his hands on that journal. He had no reason to believe she wouldn't have left it with a friend. But he had to persuade her to give it to him so he could destroy it.

He released her. Purposely he moved away from her and made himself look relaxed, though hate and rage were writhing in his belly like a coiled snake ready to strike. His eyes grew hooded, and looking at him, Tessa could tell that he believed her. And oddly, in that silent moment, Tessa thought how handsome he could have been with those blue eyes and salt-and-pepper hair, the lean, carved features. But a harshness and cruelty were etched into those features, and his blue eyes held no trace of warmth, humor, or compassion.

"My first wife," he said in a falsely soft, tender voice, "had a most unfortunate accident. She fell and struck her head on the corner of a table and bled to death." William paused, and his nostrils flared slightly as he drew in a deep, controlling breath. "You are correct. She did have a substantial amount of money. But the woman was insane. I wasn't trying to kill her. She was a simple, silly, and selfish woman who imagined all these nightmarish events."

The transformation of William from cruel and ugly to warm and charming caught Tessa off guard. She thought she saw a softening in his eyes, but when he reached a hand toward her in gentle appeal, she remembered the strength in those lean hands, and their brutality. She swallowed. "I might believe you, William, if I didn't suffer under your savage fists myself."

Again, that strange flicker of emotion in his eyes. Surely she had imagined it! This man hadn't a kind nerve in his body! But his voice, when he spoke again, was soft and coaxing.

"Come now, Tessa, I was only enraged as any man would be on his wedding night to learn that his bride was not a virgin—"

"I *told* you why—"

"Yes, yes, I know. And I reacted a bit hastily—I'll grant you that. But," and he let his eyes go over her with a certain wistful longing, "you can understand how I felt when

I learned another man had gone before me."
He held up his hands when she began to
protest again. "I know it wasn't of your own
doing. I know that now, but *then* . . . understand, my dear, that I had dreamed of you for
months. You were the sweetest, most desirable woman I'd ever seen." He smiled smugly
inside when he saw her brown eyes widen.
Ah, his charms were working on her! he
thought. Women! Fools! All of them! "And
now"—he lowered his voice and moved a
shade closer—"now I can only dream of having you back as my wife. Of taking you back
to Boston and treating you the way you should
have been treated from the start. Come with
me, Tessa. We could have a good and decent
life together. Never mind our beginning. I've
been miserable without you these months.
Please come home with me."

Tessa leaned her head back against the
house and closed her eyes. God, *God!* What
was he doing? She'd never seen this side of
him, and it almost frightened her as much as
his black side. She could almost *forget* his
black side with his soft words and appealing
eyes. She swallowed, fighting tears. She was
so weary of fighting and hiding and denying,
so weary of her fears. Maybe he *had* been
enraged that night. Maybe his first wife had
been mad. And maybe . . . maybe it was time
to go home. Cody was gone, and she would
be leaving in June anyway.

Tessa's eyes came slowly open and she saw
the cold, calculated glint in William's eyes as

he read her uncertain features. She shuddered. And she silently cursed herself for wavering even for a minute—even silently. Her jawline tightened; she hugged her arms over her breasts and answered him coldly.

"No," she said, "I will not come back to Boston with you. I can't understand why any man would beat a woman the way you beat me. And you did it once. I'm sure you'll do it again."

William felt an anger beyond belief. He'd gone through all *that* and she'd denied him in the end anyway. Bitch! But he quickly and carefully hid his fury from her. "Very well," he said crisply, "I can see that all you need is some more time. I want you to come home with me, I want you to be my wife. But I don't want an unwilling wife. I intend to stay here and convince you that we could be happy together. I'm staying at the hotel in town. I'll be back in the morning. Perhaps we could breakfast together."

Good heavens, where had all this charm come from? For a moment they measured each other in the lengthening shadows, but Tessa could see—for all that he tried to hide it—the black rage in his eyes.

With a pounding heart and clenched fists, Tessa watched him walk away, tall, lean, and correct. She didn't realize, until he was gone from view, that she had been holding her breath, and when she let it out in a tense burst, she sagged against the wall of the house. "Oh, my God," she breathed. What was she going to do? She had to get out of here for one thing. William would come back for that journal—tonight—when it was dark. He would want to make certain she didn't have it in the house and he would return under the cover of darkness. Because that was the way William did things.

Heart thundering, Tessa flew upstairs to her bedroom, unlocked her trunk at the foot of her bed, and yanked out her carpetbag where she'd kept the journal all these months. Fingers trembling, she stuffed it into the bodice of her dress, slammed the trunk shut, and ran back down the stairs and outside.

In the western sky the setting sun balanced on the horizon like a golden ball. Soon, Tessa thought, it would be night, and she had no place to run, no place to hide. But she moved swiftly away from the house, glancing over her shoulder to make certain she wasn't being followed.

If she ran to Mary or even to Eb and Audrey or to Ned, and tried to explain this mess, all would probably be won over by William and agree with him that she was legally bound to him. Her rightful place was beside her husband. No one would see what a monster he really was. It would not be easy for them to understand why she left William in the first place.

Scared and lonely and feeling more bereft than ever, Tessa found herself standing in front of Cody's white house. His shingle, swaying on the post, creaked back and forth in the gentle wind. Without him, the property looked as forlorn as she felt.

She knew he was gone and everything was locked but she ran up the front steps to the porch and tried the front door. She would have peered in the front windows but the shades were drawn low. Wearily Tessa slumped against the door. *What was she going to do?* God, she was afraid. More afraid than when she'd fled Boston. Because now he'd found her. He'd find her wherever she ran to. In her frantic mind she saw William's cruel-lipped smile and chilling eyes, and she knew, in due time, he'd kill her too.

"No!" The word tore from her throat and she was off the front steps like a hunted rabbit, flying toward the back of the house to Cody's lab. She ran to the door and forced her shoulder against it only to find she needn't use force at all when the unlocked door burst open and she tumbled into the room. Stunned, the breath knocked out of her as she lay there, Tessa rested only a second before she sprang up. On her knees she slammed the door shut. And as she knelt there drawing in air, her palms flat against the door, she saw the padlock resting on a nearby table. She reached for it and locked herself in the room.

She sat there for a long moment, her back against the door, feeling the thud of her heart in her chest where the journal pressed against her. She opened the bodice and slid the book out, then placed it beside her on the floor. She would stay here tonight where it was safe.

William would never think of looking for her *here*. But what would she do about tomorrow and Sunday night? Monday she had to teach school. Oh, I'll worry about that tomorrow! she scolded herself.

Outside, through the high window, Tessa could see the sky darkening—it was deep mauve now, with a touch of dusky rose. On trembling legs she stood and crossed the room to light the lantern there on a low table. She hoped by lighting it that none of Cody's mysterious potions would explode. Although, she thought, with a miserable laugh, it might be preferable to end it all now that way.

"Stop it!" she hissed to herself. She went to the door again and sat in front of it on the floor, leaning back. Now that the lantern light, low as the wick was, fended off night shadows, Tessa felt comforted. I'll think of something, she reassured herself, some plan to get me out of this mess. She closed her eyes and pressed her knuckles against the lids. If only Cody were here. He would know what to do.

Tessa's eyes slowly opened. Her chest ached and her throat tightened when his image leaped into her mind. She couldn't stop herself from feeling the pain every time she thought of him—and that was too, too often.

She glanced around the lab—over the bottles and flasks and microscopes—and she remembered that time she'd snuck in here and he'd come upon her and scared the wits from her. A smile flitted across Tessa's lips as memories swirled around her.

That time she'd tripped out on the prairie as she was chasing Smoke Eyes . . . he'd kissed her that day and it had been like nothing she'd ever experienced before . . . or since. And that day she'd been covered with hives . . . she closed her eyes and let herself remember what he'd said. *What I found was a woman more beautiful than I ever imagined.*

He was such a compelling man! She thought of his slow, lazy smile, his dark, intense eyes, and his long fingers and male mouth upon her flesh . . . the night she'd lain with him, the hurt she'd caused him when he'd learned she was married.

And her heart wrenched with pain.

"Oh, Cody—Cody!" she cried aloud. "I love you! I love you, Cody. . . ." Salty hot tears flooded her eyes and throat at the astounding admission. But then Tessa straightened her back against the door and whispered fiercely, "I do love him!" with an intensity that was almost frightening. From the start *I've loved him,* she thought incredibly, and all this time *I've had to fight and bury it.* But now, in her revelation, she knew a soaring sense of freedom.

Wearily she let her head lean back against the door. Her long silken lashes fluttered closed and hot tears slipped unheeded from beneath them. Quietly her shoulders shook as she wept in the bittersweet knowledge that she could never tell Cody she loved him.

Chapter Sixteen

✦ ✦ ✦ ✦

THE DOOR RATTLED against her head and startled Tessa awake. She blinked, her bleary eyes focusing on the low-burning lantern, then she jolted upright. Damn! That lantern light must have guided William right to the lab! Panic throbbed in her throat when the door rattled again threateningly as the man on the other side tried to force the lock. Tessa flung her slim body against the door and pressed her weight against it, knowing she'd lose the battle in the end because William was much stronger than she. But then she heard a curse.

"Dammit! Who the hell is in there?"

Cody! My God, it was Cody! Joy and relief flooded through her; with quaking fingers she unlocked the door and whipped it open. In the fleeting glance that passed between them Tessa saw the confusion on his face, but without thinking she flung her arms around his strong neck and clung tight. She felt him stiffen in shock but she pressed her body tightly against his. "Cody," she murmured against his skin, and she breathed in the scent of trail dust, sweat, and leather. It felt so good to be against him like this as he pulled her close to the comfort of his hard, familiar body; and with her ear now pressed to his massive, rock-hard chest Tessa felt the hammering of his heart against her cheek. Cody closed his eyes and rested his chin on top of her head, feeling his throat tighten as love for her surged through him. But he quickly smothered these emotions.

Both remembered why he'd left in the first place and they stepped cautiously away from each other, though Cody still held her hands in his. He looked travel-weary and was deeply tanned by the hot western sun, looking more handsome than ever. Tessa's heart throbbed with pain and love. His mouth twisted wryly as he took in her disheveled appearance— her faded calico dress with the bodice half-unbuttoned and her unpinned hair tumbling down her back.

"Well, I didn't expect that kind of greeting, but I'll admit I'm glad to see you too, Tess. But what in hell is going on here? I rode in and saw the light in the window. What are you doing in here?"

Tessa swallowed, her eyes wide on his. "Cody, he's here."

Cody's black brows came down low in a frown. *"Who's* here?" His puzzled eyes flicked around the lab, and seeing no one, he looked again to Tessa.

She drew in a deep, slow breath and kept her eyes on Cody's. "My—my husband."

Immediately he let go of her hands, as if she'd suddenly grown thorns. Tessa saw his lips tighten grimly just before he turned his broad back on her. "Then it's him you should be with tonight—not me."

Desperately Tessa clutched Cody's arm. "Please, Cody. *Please*, listen to me now!" Her fingers dug into the hard muscle in his forearm when he stared down at her stonily, impaling her with his eyes.

"Why should I listen to you when all you've done is lie since you've come to town?"

Because I love you! she wanted to cry out, but of course, could not. "Because," she said, the ache in her throat making her voice husky, "you never gave me a chance to explain why I *did* lie to you. You must understand I never meant to hurt you. Believe that, Cody! Just hear why I married William. If you must, you can send me back to him when I've finished telling you, but please listen to me!" Somehow, Tessa knew, she'd escape if it came to *that!*

Cody lowered his brows again. "Who the hell is William? I thought this man's name was Michael Shea."

"Oh," she said lightly, "I just made that name up."

Incredulous, Cody stared down at her, one of his thick black brows cocked higher than the other. He was amazed that she could dismiss the lie so easily. But Tessa was beyond feeling guilty for *that*: there were more important things to feel guilty about!

She shrugged lamely. "Well, I had to make something up, don't you see?"

Cody's lips tightened again and Tessa thought he hid a smile. But as they stared at each other he quickly sobered and it was then that Tessa noticed the tension lines etched into his handsome face. Oh, God, had she done that to him?

Annoyed with himself for letting her eyes beguile him, Cody grunted. "I'll listen under one condition. That if I don't like what you tell me, I can personally hand you back to this William and see you off on the train Monday morning."

Tessa's mouth fell open. He wouldn't! She saw his jaw muscles tense and realized he would! She gave the tiniest of nods.

"Come on," Cody said, letting her pass before him, "let's go inside."

She was already over the threshold when she remembered the journal. She ran back into the lab and scooped it up as Cody grabbed the lantern and held it up so they could see as they made their way around front. In the black, star-filled night there blew a soft wind, and behind her Tessa felt Cody's big body shielding her from lurking shadows and strange rustlings in the grasses. She was feeling surprisingly dauntless with Cody near; though at this point he'd probably throw her to the wolves if he had a chance!

Indoors Cody dropped his worn leather saddlebags on the floor, then lit a few lamps. "Sit there," he ordered gruffly, nodding his head to the leather armchair by his desk, and he headed straight for the kitchen to make a pot of coffee. Tessa watched him, her eyes hungrily going over his broad back and wide shoulders, down to his waist, where half of his shirttail had come out of his denims, and her gaze lingered on his hard buttocks, then slowly traveled down his long legs to the heels of his leather boots. Slowly, longingly, her gaze moved up again. His new denims were already starting to fade and they hugged his body as tightly as Tessa wanted to hug it. Oh, she loved him. She smiled slightly, basking in this newfound knowledge. And then she clenched her fists. He wasn't hers. He would never be hers.

Cody shifted his weight to one hip and from behind Tessa watched, with a sudden quickening, the rakish slant of his backside. Cody shoved his hands into his back pockets and silently studied the coffeepot on the stove. His forearms were as brown as an Indian's; his hair, thick and curling at the nape of his neck, gleamed blue black in the brightly lit kitchen.

He was so contemplative! What was he thinking as he stood there? Did he hate her? Tessa glanced away from him; watching him was too painful.

But Cody was thinking how very much he loved her. It had been more than a shock to see her come tumbling out of the door tonight and into his arms. For weeks he'd been trying to drive her from his mind; as he'd lain on his lonely bed at night the vision of her face and graceful, sensuous body tormented him, aroused him, burned in him like an indelible brand. By working long, exhausting hours, he'd avoided sleep as long as he could, but the memory of her interfered with his work too. Why did she haunt him so? That he'd left town and continued to brood over her was insufferable! Yet the thought of a future without her was even more insufferable.

But she was married.

The aroma of perking coffee permeated the kitchen and Cody lifted the pot from the stove and poured two cups of the rich brew. As he came through the doorway his eyes fell on Tessa sitting in his oversized armchair, nervously entwining her fingers as she studied his medical-school diploma. She looked a mess—a desirable mess with her hair undone and falling down her graceful back, and her bodice unbuttoned almost to her breasts.

Her eyes met his. "You studied in Scotland?"

Cody's lips tightened as he set the coffee cups upon the table. "Yes. University of Edinburgh."

An awkward tension filled the room. Tessa had noticed his grimly set lips and she worried. He *had* to believe her! He was certainly powerful enough to send her home with William.

Cody seated himself across from her and leaned forward, taking the coffee cup into his broad hands. The steam wavered up into his face and he stared into the brown liquid.

He didn't even look at her when he asked, "How long has he been here?"

He sensed her stiffen at the reminder of William and his jaw flexed. She was damned scared for sure.

"Since this afternoon—late."

"And how long have you been here?" This time he met her gaze and his green eyes seemed to delve into her heart.

Under his hard stare Tessa started to stammer, but she managed, "Since ten minutes after he left me."

Cody raised his mug to his lips and gulped, not caring that the coffee scalded his throat. The pain felt good. Frowning, he raised his eyes to hers again. With a sarcastic inclination of his dark head he said, "Begin."

But how could she, the way he was pinning her with his relentless stare, as if measuring her for the truth? How could she make him understand? Tessa drew in a shaky breath; her fingers trembled in her lap. And—astonishingly—she felt tears burn her eyelids. "I— please don't look at me that way." Her voice almost broke but Cody kept his merciless stare upon her. "I promised you the truth."

"I'm waiting, Tessa."

She bristled at his dictatorial tone. Yet her throat hurt when she attempted to speak again. "I—I'm not *really* his wife—"

Cody was half out of his chair, ready to toss her out, when she pleaded, with tears trembling on her lashes, "Cody, please! When I say that, I mean our marriage was never

consummated. That's the truth! That night—
that night you and I made love—" She choked
off, seeing his face go hard. She was making a
miserable mess out of all this! But she had to
go on, making him believe. "That night was
all truth, Cody—all except the part I left out
about William. But I only wanted to be with
you—I've never had another man—"

"Goddammit!" he bit out harshly, making
Tessa jump. "Start from the beginning!"

His sharp, impatient words cut through her
rising hysteria. Tessa leveled her gaze on him
and drew in a deep breath. When she let it
out, her words followed fluently. "After I was
raped—" Again Cody moved, only now it was
to lean his hip against the arm of the chair. His
booted feet were planted apart on the floor,
and his body tensed, as if poised to spring at
a quick, wrong touch. Tessa felt her heart
pound hard as she continued, her hollow
voice seeming to echo in the silent room. "I—
I decided to stay on and teach at the orphanage. It was a way to stay safe, to avoid men, to
keep any man from finding out what had
happened to me. Girls my age left and married. But I stayed and thought it would be my
permanent home—and I was happy with that.
But then William came into my life." She
could not stop the shudder that rippled
through her body, and for a second she closed
her eyes. When she opened them, she was
staring at Cody's tight face. His jaw was
working and his eyes stared back. "I didn't
know it at the time, but the orphanage was in

financial straits. A couple of years before it added on a new wing—it had become so overcrowded—and the orphanage couldn't make its payments to its lender of money— William. But he made a deal with them. If I married him, then he would meet the orphanage payments in full. I—I was horrified, and refused. But when William authorized diminished rations for the children, I knew he'd starve them for sure. And I knew the children would end up on the streets. So . . . I agreed to marry him. But only after he payed the orphanage's debts in full. By then it would be too late for him to go back on his word when he learned I wasn't a virgin."

Tessa stopped and drew in another shuddering breath. Cody watched her jawline tighten and her eyes become brittle. Her fists were clenched so hard in her lap that the small white knuckles bulged. "On our wedding night—just as we were retiring, I told him I'd been raped. That there would be no virgin blood on the sheets. I . . . I tried to explain that it wasn't my fault . . . that I didn't even know the man who violated me . . . but he wouldn't listen." She lifted her sorrowful eyes to Cody. "He wasn't like you, Cody. God . . . I thought he'd kill me. He hit me—and accused me of horrid things—sleeping with other men—and all the while he kept hitting me—in my face—"

"Tess!" Cody stood now, his own fists clenched at his sides, his face going white under his dark tan.

But Tessa threw her head back, defiantly, almost impudently, and glared at him through her tears. "What? Don't tell you the sordid details? I thought you wanted an explanation, Cody. I'm giving you that and I have to make you understand what it was like. What it feels like to have a man backhand you across the mouth—making you wonder what it was you'd done to deserve the pain. Oh—" He'd seized her by her upper arms and gripped her hard, his tormented eyes pleading with her, staring down into her tragic face.

"I understand," he said gruffly. "Please, Christ, don't go on."

Tessa stared back, the tears slipping unheeded down her cheeks. She shook her arms free and watched him straighten, towering over her with a black scowl on his face. "Well, he left me that night," she went on coolly while Cody swore and turned his back on her, "and went to a wench at the local tavern. We never consummated our marriage. I don't know how, but I fell asleep. And when I woke up, the maid told me that William had gone away on business and would not return for two months. When the maid saw my bruised and swollen face, she tended to me and empathized with me because she, too, had suffered her share of abuse under William's anger. She also told me that William had treated his first wife like this—that there's been suspicion about his first wife's allegedly accidental death. The maid had possession of the wife's journal and there are passages written in it stating that she is afraid for her life.

"I was desperate to get out of Boston—as far away from William as possible. I searched the newspapers and saw the advertisement for a schoolteacher and knew it was my answer. The maid insisted I take the journal, and I did. And I left. Only I did not know that William had hired a private investigator to find me. And now William's back." She bit down hard on a knuckle, remembering that afternoon. She was hardly aware that Cody had stopped his pacing, but knew that a monumental silence had dropped between them.

At last Cody swiveled around and watched her face carefully. "Is that all?"

The way he'd said it—so casually—made Tessa flinch. "What?"

"Is that all?" he repeated, harshly now, and his hand tore through his jet hair as his eyes hardened on her. "Is there something you've neglected to tell me? Perhaps you have a child or two somewhere? What other secrets of your past are you hiding?"

An agonizing pain swelled in Tessa's chest, seeming to crush the breath from her. He didn't believe her! She shot to her feet and was halfway across the room before Cody grabbed her and yanked her back so abruptly that she slammed into his hard body. And then she began to fight. Weeping with pain and frustration and humiliation, she fought wildly, pounding on his chest and shoulders like a mad thing. "Damn you, *damn* you, Cody! Damn you for everything!" The anguish came thick in her throat, through her tears. "I won't go back to him; you can't make me go back to him!"

Cody ducked his head aside as she swiped viciously at his face. She sobbed once as he caught her wrists and drew her tightly against him, cradling her trembling form to his chest. And he held her fiercely to him as she wept brokenly, her tears soaking his shirt. Cody swallowed and he felt his own eyes burn. "I believe you, Tess. But the truth hurts almost as bad as the lie. It hurts because I couldn't save you from it all, love."

Tessa caught her breath in a sob; she kept her face pressed to his shoulder, needing him more than ever. Cody caught her up into his arms and Tessa clung to him as he walked her to the sofa. As he lowered her to the sofa she kept her face hidden from him, ashamed of her tears. But Cody went down on one knee before her. He reached and took her hands away from her face and his eyes searched hers. He held one of her hands, tracing his thumb over her knuckles while he let her other hand drift free. "Don't hide your face from me, darlin'—ever." He ran the back of a knuckle over the smooth crest of her damp cheek. "Do you know how glad I am that you came to me instead of someone else?" Now she was returning his stare, the flecks in her deep, soft brown eyes looking like gold, and all he wanted to do was pick her up again and carry her to his bed and tenderly make love to her. But instead he made himself speak practically. "I don't need proof that this monster who calls himself your husband tried to or actually *did* kill his first wife. But the sheriff will. Is that book you brought in here the woman's journal?"

Tessa nodded.

"Good. We'll go to him with it first thing in the morning. And I assume you'll be wanting an annulment?"

"Yes." Her voice trembled.

For a long moment they simply stared into each other's eyes. Cody was still on one knee before her and she relished the warmth of his callused hand. She was afraid what he might see in her own gaze, but she could not remove it from his Kentucky-green eyes that had haunted her since she'd first set her own upon them.

With her free hand, Tessa reached up to place her palm against Cody's lean, hard cheek. "And you . . . why did you come back, Cody?" Against her hand she felt a muscle jump in his jaw as he clenched it.

His voice was hoarse. "I think you know."

"Tell me."

At last he straightened and threw himself down on the sofa beside her. With legs sprawled in front of him, he slumped low in his seat and began wearily rubbing a hand over his eyes. He spoke with his eyes shut, his fingertips resting on the bridge of his nose. "Because I couldn't stay away from you—

wrong as I knew it was. Dammit, woman," he swore, now piercing her with his relentless stare, "I had to come back—even if it was just temporarily. I needed some answers, even if they were all the wrong ones."

Tears bathed her eyes. "Cody . . . I . . ." She dropped her eyes to his leg, firm and warm against hers, and—she couldn't resist—she rested her palm there on his hard thigh, feeling the muscle tense as she again lifted her long-lashed gaze to his. "I missed you so *much.*"

In an instant he captured her in his arms and pulled her close, his mouth coming down on hers in a long, achingly deep kiss. Cody groaned, plunging his tongue inside her mouth, stroking, seeking, tasting the hot sweetness of her love. Tessa clung to his broad shoulders, making soft, whimpering sounds in her throat. Would it never end? Please, don't let it ever end. The intensity of her feelings for him made her limp and she gripped him close, feeling the sinewy muscles in his shoulders ripple under her hands. Words of love fought to escape, were blotted against his seeking tongue, and Tessa kissed him back with all the hunger in her soul.

"God," Cody groaned again. He ran his tongue once over her full, moist mouth and they both shuddered with exquisite desire. "I've got to have you again, Tess." His voice sounded hoarse, tortured. "You're in my blood, woman, worse than any fever I've had to battle—pounding like a demon—" He gripped her face between his hands, his tormented eyes blazing green heat into hers. "Can you understand that? Do you feel the same?"

He put his lips to her arched throat and she cried against his soft hair. "Yes," she whispered, "I know—I understand." Her lashes fluttered, half closed as his mouth grazed hers. Inside she wept and rejoiced, knowing, still, that she could not let him take her as his mistress. She loved him too much for that.

With every iota of willpower Tessa could muster, she forced herself to ease away from him. Not understanding, Cody frowned, his face close enough for her to see the blue flecks in his eyes darken. Those frowning eyes asked her a question she did not want to answer.

"I'm leaving," she told him.

"What do you mean 'leaving'?"

"I mean I'm leaving town," Tessa replied solemnly.

"You can't do that."

"I must. I can't go on like this; I can't be your mistress. The town schoolteacher just does not do that. I've already made plans, Cody. I'm leaving as soon as school lets out for the summer."

His scowl deepened. "What the hell are you talking about? You're free now. You can do anything you damn well please."

"Free? To do what? Lower my personal code of ethics? I still have morals, Cody." She laughed wryly. "Much as I'd like to abandon them when it comes to you."

But Cody was not laughing. "You're not leaving town."

Tessa stiffened. "You can't change my mind."

Cody grunted. "We'll see about that." He came easily to his feet and went to the trunk against one wall, opening the lid to extract a quilt. He came back to the sofa and tossed the quilt at her, then stood watching her with his hands on his hips.

"You're sleeping here tonight." At her wary look Cody smiled crookedly. "I won't touch you—*if* that's what you wish."

"How ungentlemanly of you to even hint otherwise." He knew very well that that was *not* what she wished, and his short laugh told her so. Her fingers tightened in the folds of the quilt. "What if the townfolk learn I've slept here? It certainly doesn't seem right."

Cody stared at her in disbelief. "You're worried about your reputation at a time like this?"

Tessa sniffed at him, her nose elevating a degree. "I guess not, since I'll be leaving town anyway."

Cody gave her a warning look as he gathered the coffee cups in one broad hand. "Get under that quilt." Without looking back, he headed for the kitchen, where Tessa heard him washing out the cups. When he blew out the lantern, she knew he was ready for bed too.

Reluctantly she slid her shoes off, dropping them to the floor with a thud. She raised her eyes to find Cody standing with a shoulder propped against the doorway, his arms folded across his chest. He smiled at her when she lifted her nose at him once more. She realized he was just going to stand there until she finished removing her stockings so she peeled them off, feeling strange under his scrutiny. For heaven's sake, Tessa thought, exasperated with herself, they're only my bare toes! He's certainly seen more of me than them! But when he strode lazily across the room to cover her with a quilt, Tessa snatched it away from him and scowled crossly. "I can do it myself! I'm not a child—or one of your patients!"

Cody's mouth twisted wryly. "Maybe I ought to send you back to William," he muttered with disgust, but when she paled he knew it was no joking matter. The son-of-a-bitch.

Quietly Tessa lay down, pulled the quilt up to her chin, and closed her eyes. Within seconds she was asleep. Cody stood over her and studied her lovely face; her lashes were still damp, like wet charcoal smudges upon her cheeks. He felt a pang of love and tenderness grip him. How he'd like to get his hands around Forsythe's neck for what he had done to her.

But damn the little wench for wanting to leave him now! How bleak his life would be without her. He couldn't let her go; he *wouldn't* let her go . . . yet how could he force her to stay?

What an impossible woman! Cody let out a

tired laugh, knowing she wouldn't like it if he slept here with her. But he threw himself down in a chair close by and dragged it up to the edge of the sofa. Stretching his long legs out before him and lacing his lean fingers over his belly, Cody let his eyelids drop as he continued watching her. His gaze warmed on her sleeping face. Yes, he'd stay here with her all night and protect her with his life.

Predawn light colored the room with soft blue-gray shadows when Cody nudged Tessa awake. Exhausted, Tessa burrowed under the quilt.

"C'mon, lazybones."

Cody's deep morning voice startled her and even more startling was the flood of love she felt through her heart at hearing his voice first thing. She wanted—oh, so badly!—to fling her arms around his neck and hug him, to bring him down with her to the sofa. But she buried her desires and slowly opened her eyes to find Cody standing over her—bare-chested, with a towel hanging around his neck.

Tessa drew in a swift breath. Try as she might, she could not avert her eyes. She let her gaze linger on that broad expanse of chest, the crisp, curling mat of black hair upon it, the hard muscles that shifted as he brought his hands up to tug at the towel. His hair was damp and curly from his morning face washing, and when Tessa continued to stare, Cody grinned at her.

"Darlin', you can't imagine what your morning image is doing to my male impulses. If you don't get up off that sofa quickly, I'm afraid we'll never make it out of this house."

Blushing, Tessa bolted upright, her gold-highlighted hair spilling down her back. She swung her feet to the floor and caught Cody's appreciative glance to her bare ankles.

"Cody."

He glanced up to her eyes.

"What if William's gone? What if—"

"Shh. Stop worrying. Get your face washed and your hair combed and we'll head on over to Sheriff Cooper's. And don't forget that journal."

As the sun came up in an explosion of reds and oranges Tessa and Cody walked across town to the jailhouse, just a block away from Lily's Dance Hall. Sheriff Cooper listened to Tessa's story, looked over the journal, and wasted no time in sending his deputy to the hotel where William was staying.

Within a half hour Deputy Banks was leading a manacled William to the jail. It was too early for spectators, and Tessa breathed relief at that, but the look in William's icy eyes made her shudder against Cody's side. When Cody put his arm around her and drew her close, William sneered at them.

"Is this the 'friend' you left the journal with? You little slut!"

Tessa felt Cody tense beside her. Cody directed a look at Deputy Banks to remove William's manacles. The deputy did so and

William laughed shortly; but that was the only sound he made as Cody reached for the front of his shirt and hauled him up closer.

"You son-of-a-bitch," Cody said. He drew his arm back, then let it fly with a tremendous punch to William's face. Blood spewed from his nose as he went down, nearly unconscious, moaning in the dust at their feet.

Tessa stood horrified, hearing the sheriff's voice buzz around her ears.

"I wouldn't let any other man get away with that, Cody. But I would say he deserved that. What say you take this pretty lady home now. We'll keep him locked up properlike till the Boston authorities come fer him."

Numbed, Tessa let Cody lead her away from the others. As they walked she heard the splash of water against William's face as they tried to revive him.

"I—I think you broke his nose," she murmured, and her voice sounded like it had floated from her body.

Cody's fingers tightened under her elbow. "He deserved it—and a broken jaw too."

She didn't argue with him, just let him lead her back to his house where he insisted on making breakfast for her. She thought the way he flipped the pancakes from the griddle to the plates was endearing. "God, I love you, Cody," she whispered; she started when he turned to look over his shoulder at her. Had he heard? But all he said, with a grin, was, "I hope you're hungry, Tess."

She wasn't, but she couldn't tell him that.

Not after all the fuss he'd gone through preparing her breakfast. "Starved." She smiled at him. But as soon as he turned his back again she closed her eyes and massaged her temples. Her fingers shook and she felt clammy cold inside . . . when she should have felt elated! What was wrong with her? Why wasn't she celebrating? Tessa swallowed miserably. Soon, she thought, as tears welled in her eyes, soon I will have to leave him. And I don't want to.

She felt his touch—warm, callused fingers closing over hers, bringing them down to her lap. She opened her long-lashed gaze and found herself staring into his eyes, earnest and probing.

"What is it, Tess?"

Tessa stared into his grass-green eyes for what seemed an eternity before she drew in a slow, shaky breath. "I can't stay here and have breakfast with you, Cody. It only makes things harder for us. It's best we don't see each other at all until it's time for me to go." She felt his body tense and the pang she felt was like the stab of a knife through her heart. A knife that came out too, too slowly. Shakily she came to her feet. For a moment she thought she might collapse against him. She held his eyes with her own. "Thank you, Cody. For everything."

His jaw tightened; his voice came hoarse and hard. "Don't you dare thank me, Tessa. For anything. Ever."

Her teeth clamped tight on her bottom lip so it would not tremble. " 'Bye, Cody."

But even as she flew from the room, even as she felt the hot brand of his stare on her back, he never once said a good-bye of his own.

Chapter Seventeen

✦ ✦ ✦ ✦ ✦

It was a mild June evening and Tessa, fresh from her bath, stood by her bedroom window in her nightgown and wrapper, fluff-drying her hair with her fingers. The rose-scented breeze reminded her that summer was truly here at last . . . and in a week it would be time for her to leave.

She thought she'd travel farther west, but she didn't really know where. She was free now; William was gone and she'd hired a Boston attorney to file papers for an annulment. And Cody . . . a feeling of despair swept through her. She wondered if she would ever be able to forget him, if, when she left, his image would fade from her mind and heart. Would the memory of what they'd shared continue to haunt her? And would she ever be able to listen to music without remembering the way he played the harmonica?

Tessa shivered now as the piano music from town drifted on the summer night. Sadly she smiled. Saturday-night social. Cody would be there, probably dancing with some pretty woman.

Suddenly the piercing notes of a harmonica surged over the piano music and made goose bumps spring up on Tessa's arms. She rubbed them, trying to rub away the emotion that welled up in her throat, but it was no use. It was music that spoke of Cody's soul. Why it sounded so close it could have come from the front porch!

Tessa clutched her wrapper at the neck and leaned out the window; the forlorn, poignant music spiraled up and gripped her heart. Her blood raced frantically. Why, it *was* coming from the front porch! Cody was down there!

Her heart rapped an urgent rhythm in her chest. Barefoot, she swept downstairs and stood in the front doorway, waiting for him to finish. She saw his shadowy form through the screen, sitting on the swing, an ankle draped over a knee as he played that instrument with his sensual mouth. The music was so tender and trembling with such sorrow that an ache swelled in Tessa's throat.

When Cody stopped playing, he looked up, arresting her with a piercing stare Tessa could feel more than see in the night shadows.

Cody's throat tightened as he let his eyes drink her in; she stood in the doorway like a dream, the porchlight outlining the curves of her slender body through the thin wrapper she wore. Her hair stirred in the soft wind, and it fell loose, slipping down her back, the way he liked it.

And then she spoke. "Are you serenading me, Cody?" Her voice was breathy, hushed, intimate.

Without taking his eyes from her, Cody came slowly to his feet, his movement one long unfolding of his big body, and he slipped the harmonica into his pocket. A leap of longing sprang to life inside Tessa as Cody stood, his eyes moving over her face. Even in the dim light Tessa could see his mouth curl in a soft, slow smile. And his voice was soft too. "You bet your books I am, Miss Amesbury." The music from town gently embraced them. "Come here."

The screen door bumped softly behind her. She glided toward him, carrying herself with that natural air of seduction that never failed to stir him. She stopped before him and stared up into his intense face. Cody slid his arms around her and tucked her close against him; he closed his eyes and breathed in the lilac scent of her hair. They began to dance slowly, tenderly, in the dark, the age-old choreography of lovers. Tessa moved with him in time to the piano's seductive, haunting love song. The whisper of their clothing, the scraping of his boot heels, his warm breath against her hair aroused her in a sweet and powerful way. Cody's rock-hard thighs shifted intimately between Tessa's, and she knew a longing so intense she clung even tighter to him. Pressing her cheek hard against his shirt buttons, she heard his rampaging heart and its thunder matched her own. She turned her lips to the solid muscles of his chest and kept her kiss against him as tears seeped from her eyes to his skin.

Cody lowered his dark head and moved his mouth warmly, tenderly, upon hers. His wide hand came up under her chin, and cupping it, he lifted her wet face so her wide, weeping eyes met his. The fire in him burned its way to her soul. "I love you, Tess." The words sounded hoarse, tormented, and holding her face between his hands, he leaned toward her trembling lips, his tongue warm and stroking. Even as they danced he kissed her, long and slow and deep, until Tessa felt that their spirits and hearts were dancing as well as their bodies. "Love you," he whispered raggedly against her hair.

"I know," she whispered, tipping her head back as his kisses rained down her throat. But at her words Cody lifted his dark head and stared down at her with disbelief.

"You know? Dammit, I've never told a woman that before! I think it's a damned revelation that a skinny little schoolteacher with a funny Boston accent can make me admit it too! And all you can say is 'I know,' as if you had it coming." Her fingers against his lips shushed him and Tessa was torn between laughter and tenderness.

"I know," she said, "because I love you too,
Cody. With an intensity stronger than anything I've ever known."

She saw him swallow. "Hurts like hell,
doesn't it?" he whispered gruffly. And when
he saw the glint of tears in her eyes, he pulled
her in close again, pressing her nose to his
hard shoulder. His wide hand splayed low on
the small of her back and he gently rubbed her
spine, hearing her breathe against his chest.

"I love you, Cody." She didn't care that she
shouldn't, only knowing the truth of her own
heart. Once more she kissed his neck, then
pulled away to his mouth, which met hers
hungrily, eagerly, voluptuously. Tessa's blood
raced; her heart was a deafening storm in her
ears. She felt Cody's hands move low to
cradle her hips, and he thrust his hardness
against her. "Oh," she moaned when everything surged within. His tongue danced inside
her open mouth, savoring her lovely sounds.
She clung tightly to the breadth of his shoulders and his voice rumbled low in her ear.

"So where does that leave us now, darlin'?"

She didn't know, she didn't care, even as he
led her to the door, an arm around her waist
as he guided her inside. Together they stepped over the threshold and closed the screen
door. Tessa watched Cody hook it with his
long, tanned finger, and she felt love and
yearning stir within her.

They moved toward the staircase and kissed
halfway up, laughing when Ginger dashed
past them as if to beat them to the bedroom.

"She better not be in that bed." Cody grinned down at Tessa as they continued to walk toward the bedroom.

"She sleeps at the foot of it every night," Tessa said, lacing her fingers with Cody's. "And she's very jealous."

"Hmm," Cody grunted. "She's gonna have some fierce competition."

"Oh?"

They were in the bedroom now, where the light was turned low, and Ginger was nowhere to be seen. Cody turned Tessa toward him, his hands curved over her slender shoulders, and he brushed his lips over hers. Tessa sighed. Cody glanced toward the quilted bed. "You don't know how long I've dreamed of you in this bed . . . all alone . . . waiting for me. . . ." He kissed her as her nimble fingers ran down the buttons of his shirt, opening it, spreading it wide with her palms running over his muscled chest. He pulled in a sharp breath at her delicious caress.

"And you don't know how long I've been dying to touch you." And she ran her fingertips along his bare, taut skin, then her palms over his rippling back muscles. She could feel his shudder of desire like a wind current pass through her as well. She kissed his sinewy shoulder as Cody loosened the sash to her wrapper.

"There's no other woman that can satisfy me the way you do. . . ." His thumbs skimmed her hard nipples—just once—before he slid the wrapper over her shoulders and watched it drop to the floor. His adoring eyes drifted down to the outline of her breasts, tantalizing him through the thin cotton of her nightgown. He dragged in tortured breaths of air, wanting her now, wanting to forget the preliminaries, yet wanting to savor every second she was in his arms.

"I've only done it with you once," she purred as he caressed her thickened breasts through her nightgown.

His warm green eyes smiled down into hers. "I mean to change that, lady."

What was happening to her? She felt languorous and lazy and wanton. He made her feel wanton. And she liked it. She wanted nothing more than to fall back on that bed with him and have him stay forever. She didn't even care that she was leaving . . . that nothing could come of this except momentary fulfillment. She wanted him worse than she wanted life. He was right—it hurt like hell.

But now—now! Think of now, Tessa, and not later.

He guided her hand to the front of his trousers, and her palm pressed him where he was hard and long and the heat of his urgency was bulging to be free. Through the warm fabric of his trousers Tessa fondled him, cupping his fullness in her hand. Cody nudged his firm thigh between her legs and pressed upward, thrusting once, and then he was undulating rhythmically against her, and she answered him with her own rhythm. His

mouth covered hers and opened, his tongue
filling her mouth with a deep, lustful satisfaction.

"Ah, honey."

His kiss drugged her so effectively she
didn't remember raising her arms for him to
remove her nightgown, but she stood naked
before him, proud and beautiful. With worshiping hands Cody cupped her trembling,
aroused breasts, capturing her nipples between his middle finger and forefinger; he
gently squeezed the rosy flesh and Tessa
moaned softly. Her fingers drifted lovingly to
the waistband of his trousers, fumbled with
his belt buckle, and Cody made a hoarse
sound as he half dragged, half carried her to
the bed. There he kissed her down onto the
pillows. Chest heaving, he stood over her and
their gazes locked, simply becoming drunk on
the sight of the other.

Cody's shirt skidded from his magnificent,
bronzed shoulders and Tessa let her eyes
roam yearningly over his broad chest with its
mat of dark curling hair. And when he unfas-
tened his trousers, his hot, dark eyes sent a
wave of unbearable longing through her.

She reached for him and he was down
beside her in less than an instant. The demand
of his tongue was relentless and, breathless,
Tessa gasped, "I love you, Cody."

Her words fired his blood, and he became
lost in her, tasting her, touching her, adoring
her, until he became lost again and didn't
even know when she had come over him and

her hair cloaked his body like a gossamer mantle. She placed careful, lingering kisses upon his smooth skin; her hands and mouth worked enchanting magic on him till Cody's heart hurt with its wild pounding and he burned with ardent desire. She satiated his senses with the gift of her love. When he felt her moist mouth taking him, he drew in a swift, sharp breath and grabbed her by the sides of her head, lifting it so his burning eyes could look deep, deep into hers. "Where'd you learn how to do *that?*" His voice was ragged.

Tessa's eyes shone up at him, soft with love. "You've loved me this way. I only wanted to love you the same. Am I doing it properly?"

Cody's laugh sounded hoarse, almost tortured. "Honey, there's nothing proper about it." His hand was buried in her hair at the back of her head, and he urged her up to meet his kiss. The thrust of his tongue made her move sinuously against him until, in a fluid movement, he turned her beneath him, and he was bracing away, on his elbows, looking down at her with eyes filled with love.

He came into her, and he began to move with long, slow strokes. "Love you, Tess," he whispered, his mouth grazing hers. And his strokes became harder, deeper, filling her with a rich ecstasy.

They loved each other with infinite tenderness and a kind of wild desperation.

"Please," she sobbed.

And Cody drove hard against her, uttering hot, ardent words into her mouth. "This," he rasped, the love in his eyes saturating her soul, "is forever."

The only sound in the room now was the sifting of the soft summer breeze through the screen; it dried the sweet sheen of perspiration on the naked, lovingly entwined bodies. Cody nestled Tessa close to his side with one arm, his other hand cupping the back of his head. Lazily his hand wandered over her bare ribs, her back, her buttocks, creating shivers of pleasure over her body.

"Marry me, Tess."

The husky words seemed to catch in Tessa's chest. Emotion and love flooded through her. Her eyes glowed as slowly, grinning, she came up on her elbow and leaned over him, her hair tickling his bare chest and stomach. Cody sucked in his breath sharply. "Don't we have this backward?" she murmured, tracing a path through his chest hairs with a forefinger. She laid her palm flat above his navel and felt his breath quicken. "Aren't you supposed to ask for my hand first, and then we make love?"

Cody grinned back at her and ran the back of his knuckles over her flushed cheek. "This relationship of ours has been unorthodox right from the start. Why try to change it now? Or later?"

"Provided I marry you," she teased, savoring her female right to do just that.

Cody's eyebrows shot up in surprise. "You mean you're willing to become just my mistress after all?"

Tessa reached and pulled his armpit hair.

"Ow!"

She giggled. "You deserved that. And besides, I don't remember mentioning that I'd filed for an annulment."

He gripped her arm. "You little tease. Did you?"

Tessa smiled. "I should let you wait after that last comment."

"I've waited long enough, you little minx. Now, yes or no."

Tessa's eyes sparkled with delight and pure love. "What if I say no?"

"I'd say you've learned too well how to become a coquettish female. And if you hold out on me too long, then I may as well go elsewhere with my proposal . . . like down the street to Angie Foster's." He said it just to tease her, but was surprised when she laughed outright and pressed her warm body the length of his.

"You'd have to go pretty far with that proposal, Cody Butler. If you'd stuck around town, you'd have learned by now that Angie has married Jim McGafferty and they've moved to California."

Cody's mouth curled in a teasing smile. "Well, I'll be. And here I thought I'd broken her heart."

Tessa's lashes dropped just a fraction of an inch as she thought, No, you broke mine, Cody.

His curled forefinger came under her chin and lifted it so her eyes gazed into his. "You broke mine too, sweetheart," he admitted huskily.

Tessa leaned to press her lips to his. The imprint of his mouth stayed with her as she raised her head again to look down into his green eyes. "Will you always be able to read my mind so, love?"

"Always," he promised. "And I guess that means you'll marry me, huh?"

"Under one condition."

"For crissake, what do I have to do to get a yes out of you?"

She laughed and kissed him again. "Will you promise to serenade me even after we marry?"

His slow, roguish smile made her heart turn over on itself. "Every damn day for the rest of my life."

Her heart skipped with love and joy. Impatient now, Cody reached for her and pulled her naked body beneath him. He leaned over her, his elbows braced on either side of her head, and the caress of his eyes created a warm glow within Tessa. "I want you to say it, woman."

Tessa reached up and touched his dear face. "Yes," she breathed. "Yes, yes, yes." She smiled up at him, deciding to tease him some more. "And do you know why?"

"I'm not sure I want to know why, but what the hell, tell me anyway."

"Because you're a heavenly kisser."

His grin was slow and seductive, and his eyes danced wickedly. "Well, come here, darlin', I got plenty more where that came from."

THIS SUPER-SELLER FROM
PAGEANT BOOKS WILL
CAPTURE YOUR
HEART!

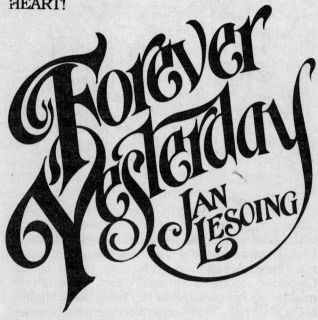

Forever Yesterday

Jan Lesoing

Annie Ellis is a lady's maid in her mistress's clothing,
but the outfit is a wedding gown! Coerced into a
marriage meant for her mistress, Annie leaves
Chicago for the sandhills of Nebraska with her new
husband. Their hardworking days and sensuous
nights soon evolve into grand passion—but can
Annie shield the dangerous truth of her identity? Or will her new husband forsake her to shield
his wounded heart?

ISBN: 0-517-00623-5   Price: $3.95

AVAILABLE AT BOOKSTORES NOW!

About the Author

Maureen Reynolds left her Massachusetts home at seventeen to see the world, beginning with a trip to England and Ireland. Then, in true romantic fashion, she married, had three sons, and continued her love of reading and writing, mostly while her children slept. Now Maureen uses her imagination to charm readers of romantic fiction, creating worlds as she'd like them to be—brave, passionate, and full of promise. Look for Maureen's next book, *Wild Nights, Silver Dreams*, forthcoming from Pageant Books.